LIGHTYEARS
TRILOGY

Books by Troy D. Wymer

Lightyears Trilogy
Treasures From Afar

LIGHTYEARS
TRILOGY

TROY D. WYMER

WYMERNOVELS
atheneum of the mind

WymerNovels, the "Atheneum of the Mind" tag line, and books logo are trademarks ™ by Troy D. Wymer

Published by WymerNovels

www.WymerNovels.com

ISBN: 978-1-54392-459-6
eBook ISBN: 978-1-54392-460-2

First Edition: 2018

Printed in the United States

PREFACE

Growing up, I was inspired by many science fiction films and books. I was 15 years old and my creative writing started to flow onto paper. I hand wrote *Lightyears* a little at a time, starting August 1984. Soon after, I purchased a typewriter. In February 1986, I finalized *Lightyears*. For *Lightyears,* I didn't really have a structured outline. I just wrote as it came to me, pantser-style. I wanted it to be on a galactic scale, but it ended up being much larger than that. The novel included two galaxies and even mentioned a third one, as well as time travel. When I finished *Lightyears,* I immediately knew that I wanted to write a sequel to it. In fact, the original manuscript also said "To Be Continued…"

In December 1987, I started writing my second book, *Lightyears II: Intragalactic Terrorism.* I used the term intra—meaning within—because the terrorist problem was only within one of the two galaxies in the *Lightyears* universe. With *Lightyears II: Intragalactic Terrorism,* I was able to tie up some loose ends and was very satisfied with the outcome of the novella. There is a dedication at the beginning of *Lightyears II: Intragalactic Terrorism* for my late cousin Heidi, who I sought advice from during the writing process. I finished *Lightyears II: Intragalactic Terrorism* in August 1988.

It could have easily stopped there and become the *Lightyears Duology,* but in August 1989, I decided to write a short story that took place after the other two books. *Lightyears III: Ominous Intervention* (formerly *Bi-Galactic Peace*) was a short story that I completed just a month later in September 1989. I did not dedicate enough time for the writing process and was not happy with the short story. I felt that I should include the third story in the final work because it was, after all, a part of the *Lightyears* universe. For this to happen, the revision for *Lightyears III: Ominous Intervention* was basically a total rewrite, using only some of the original framework, making it a novelette.

The original typewritten manuscripts needed to be scanned. Using OCR technology, the text was converted and edited, which was a lengthy and tedious process. The *Lightyears Trilogy* is the result of compiling the three stories into one published book. It took me two years, but in 2018, I completed the revisions to my original manuscripts, which have enriched the stories to a whole new level.

—Troy D. Wymer,
January 14, 2018

LIGHTYEARS TRILOGY
CONTENTS

LIGHTYEARS

LIGHTYEARS
CONTENTS

PART ONE
THE BLUEMAR REIGN

PROLOGUE
PREVIOUS INCIDENTS

SPACE AND TIME are infinite. The universe is infinite. There are many galaxies in the universe, each galaxy containing many star systems, and many star systems containing planets. There is past time, present time, and future time.

In a time of the past—lightyears beyond the farthest hope of freedom—there was the BlueMar Empire...

The following is an excerpt from a commander's notes on an LRA robot built by the BlueMar Empire on the now destroyed spaceship of *BlueMar Empire One*:

> *I built KEN-102—a Labor Robotic Automata—on* BlueMar Empire One, *before it was destroyed. I built him as my personal labor robot and incorporated some experimental cognitive intelligence into him. As time went on, he worked throughout the BlueMar Empire and not just for me. At one point, he was assigned to Olossky Cantin, an electronic scientist that we*

outsourced for a short time. Olossky later found out some vital information about the BlueMar Empire planning to conquer the remainder of the BlueMar Galaxy and—in the future—the Regulominuss Galaxy as well with our recent secret discovery of a wormhole. After learning this, Olossky fled from the BlueMar Empire. KEN-102 was last seen with him. I should have never let my robot be assigned to outside help!

—Notes from Rigid'n Morrwhell,
Commander of the BlueMar Empire
(From the city of Uree-Stanonn on the planet of Iasesheenia)

CHAPTER ONE
THE CONTROLLER INCIDENT

A BOY NAMED Baas and his brother, Roedie, lived on a sand planet in the BlueMar Galaxy called Kaskoon. Not many people or other life forms lived on Kaskoon, as it was fairly desolate. The planet had only two settlements. The largest of the two was the city of Astossky. There were many buildings in Astossky, including towers made of mirrored glass and titanium. There were stores, companies, intoxication joints, restaurants, and homes in the large city. The other was the town of Kanthas. The town was a small place that consisted of the Kanthas Archive Historical Building, a residential store, an old factory, and a few other buildings and houses. The old factory once manufactured space vehicles. The buildings reflected the sun's light on their shiny surfaces.

Just outside of Kanthas, Baas and Roedie—at the ages of sixteen and seventeen—lived with their father, Olossky Cantin. They lived in a Nemnalon-style house. They owned many robots that could be found everywhere inside the house and out. The inside of the house was clean and organized, but it was not the finest house on Kaskoon. The outside of the house was hot, with the sun beating down on the dusty desert sands.

The wind gusts were whirling sand particles around in eddies next to the house and a shed that was nearby. The sand particles landed on rippled waves of sand. To the right of the house, there was a sand hill that broke the eddies from whirling to the backside of the house. Behind the house, there were kilometers of endless dunes of sand and rock. They seemed to stretch for an eternity.

Above the house, white cumulus clouds sat against a sky of brilliant blue. The blue color of the sky came to be what it was from ozone filtering out ultraviolet rays in the planet's stratosphere.

The house itself was made of rock that had been melted, formed, and cooled. The style was developed by Monroe Nemnalon, thus the name. There were little sparkling crystals in the walls. The house had a metal door to the left corner of it, which opened using either the control panel keypad or by inserting an electronic key. On top of the house's flat roof, there was an antenna that received digital tele-vid signals from the city of Astossky.

The shed that was on the left side of the house was also a Nemnalon-style. It also had a flat roof and a metal door with a control panel.

In the hot sun, KEN-102—a robot with silver plating on his body—was fixing the control panel on the shed when a second robot came from around the side of the house to offer him some help. The second robot had gray colored metal plating. His features looked similar to that of KEN-102. His name was GRA-135.

Inside the house, Baas, Roedie, and Olossky sat in the living room eating dinner. Baas and Roedie sat in two chairs to the left of the outside entrance with a table between their chairs. Olossky sat next to a small table facing the same direction as the door. The walls of the living room were an off-white. There were pictures of intriguing characters on two of the walls. Baas, Roedie, and Olossky were enjoying their meal quietly when their waiter robot came into the living room from the kitchen to clear a few empty dishes. The robot had a chrome-plated body. One of his legs had been damaged.

"How is your dinner?" EX-87 asked.

They were enjoying their meal of fried kahsaahs, a very popular type of meat on the desert planet Kaskoon.

"It's great. Thanks for asking," Olossky said.

With a couple dishes in his hands, the waiter robot returned to the kitchen and stacked the dishes into the dish cleaner. A red robot sat in the right corner of the living room. His name was EF-7. He was an energy storage robot. He looked very old and worn.

"EX-87 has been a great waiter robot," Roedie said to Olossky, brushing his blond hair from his eyes.

"Yes, he has. Tomorrow, I want you two to clean all the robots and fix EX-87's damaged leg. I'll have a surprise for you two when you've finished," Olossky said, setting his drink on the small table next to his chair.

Sunlight came through the window above Olossky and lightened the living room. It brightened the greenery of plants in the corner. The plants, which sat to the right of Olossky, had strange shapes and fragrances. They needed a lot of water, since it was a very dry planet.

People of Kaskoon needed to drill wells using ultrasonic drills to tap their water. Most wells were drilled directly below the kitchens of people's homes.

When they were finished eating their meal of fried kahsaahs, EX-87 and their domestic robot, TX-2000—who had been in the kitchen— picked up the dishes. Baas and Roedie stood up from their seats and stretched. They went up a few metal stairs to their rooms.

On Kaskoon, dinner was served late and most people retired for the evening after dinner.

On the way to his bedroom, located to the back of the kitchen, Olossky said to EX-87, "I'll have the boys fix that leg in the morning. Goodnight."

"Goodnight, Olossky," EX-87 said.

KEN-102 and GRA-135 came into the house and locked the electronic door, retiring from their work for the day.

Lying on his bed, Roedie said, "Goodnight, Dad, Baas, TX-2000, EX-87, EF-7, KEN-102, GRA-135, TELAX-90." It was just Roedie's routine he did each night.

Then Olossky and Baas shouted, "Goodnight, Roedie!"

They all fell to sleep, except for the robots who turned their functions down for the night. It was a dark, hot night outside. The stars were glistening with a bright brilliance that slightly colored the sands of Kaskoon with a blue tint. Those same stars brightened Kaskoon's single satellite, Kasmarr, with a dark blue contrast.

In the early desert morning, the two boys—dressed in beige robes— gathered the robots and lined them all up in a row by the shed. After they finished lining them up, Baas and Roedie looked at each other.

"I'll fix and clean EX-87 and clean EF-7 and TX-2000. You can clean the other three, Roedie," Baas said, his brown hair shining in the morning sun.

Hey, wait a minute. Where could he be? Roedie thought.

"Speaking of a third robot…KEN-102 and GRA-135 are here, but where's TELAX-90?" Roedie asked, referring to their other labor robot.

There was a puzzled look on Baas's face. "Hang on. I'll check in the house."

He walked through the dusty sand to the door of the house and punched in a five digit code that opened the door without using an electronic key. The door slid aside and Baas stepped into the living room. He peered into his room and his brother's room. The robot was not there. He went into the kitchen. The robot was not there. Olossky's bedroom door was shut and Baas did not want to bother him, so he went back outside. He passed Roedie and looked in the back of the house. The robot was nowhere to be found. Baas came back around the side of the house and stood in front of Roedie and the five robots.

"I can't find him. The last time I saw him, he was with GRA-135 at the Controller," Baas said.

Roedie thought of what could have happened to the robot.

"Oh, no…He could have been struck by lightning at the Controller." Roedie's gaze followed the dunes to where they met the blue sky.

"That Controller collects enough energy through lightning in the atmosphere that if he was near it when it was charging, he could be blown to pieces," Baas said.

Baas followed Roedie's gaze with his own eyes. They both peered out across the dunes of sand and rock.

Olossky came out of the house. He looked at the two boys and the five robots standing in a row by the shed. His brown hair shifted as a gust of wind came from the south. It made his white robe ripple with a sudden looseness.

"What is the problem, boys?" Olossky saw the troublesome look on each boy's face.

"We can't find TELAX-90. What if lightning got him or Sandkeens? The last time I saw him, he was at the Controller, yesterday morning, with GRA-135," Baas said.

Olossky turned and looked at GRA-135. "Do you know where TELAX-90 is?" he asked.

"He told me to come back to the house with KEN-102. He said he would finish switching the Controller to its charge mode," the robot explained.

Olossky looked toward the Controller that was so many kilometers away. "You boys clean the robots and fix EX-87's leg. When you're finished, take two laser rifles with you, take the Airglider, and look for

TELAX-90 at the Controller. Also, take KEN-102 with you," Olossky said.

The two boys went to work on the robots, cleaning them with some tools they had gotten from the shed earlier. Olossky turned around and went back into the house.

When Baas finished cleaning EF-7 and TX-2000, he went into the shed and brought out a black and blue labeled bottle of a liquid-type metal. He filled the hole in EX-87's chrome leg. The liquid hardened within a few seconds.

When they were finished with the robots, Roedie went into the house and grabbed two laser rifles from Olossky's bedroom closet. He passed his dad in the living room on the way out.

"Be careful," Olossky said.

"We will," Roedie said as he opened the door and went outside into the hot sun.

Baas already had KEN-102 in the Airglider. Baas and Roedie hopped into the Airglider simultaneously. Baas was in the driver's seat. He started the Airglider up and it slowly rose from the sand with a hiss. He locked it into automatic and it took off, leaving sand particles whirl in the wind. Baas turned the Airglider from where it was in front of the house toward the back of the house, passing the shed. He increased the acceleration. The Airglider flew parallel to the sandy ground at a very high rate of speed. It would not take long to reach the Controller.

The Airglider was a craft designed for very high velocity. Its anti-gravitational capability made it a convenient method of transportation. On Kaskoon, the vehicles tended to pick up sand particles in their engine parts.

In the sand hills of Kaskoon, all was quiet except the sand particles blowing around from the winds. Roedie remembered when he had visited the Kanthas Archive Historical Building with Sanalia, a girl he had dated in Kanthas. He remembered what they had seen and learned there about the Tarr Kingdom. There were so many things about the kingdom in the Kanthas Archive Historical Building.

After migrating from Kelsar I, the new colonists settled in colonies on Kaskoon. Out of all the colonies, one came to rule all the others. It became a kingdom, located in the southern hemisphere of the planet. Great leaders ruled the kingdom. These were Phatom Tarr, Kelis Torb, Webler Dicott, Ci'is Moro'oe, Ricot Lomana, and Vela Dor'bist. The Tarr Kingdom had its place on Kaskoon. It was a beautiful place. There were sand hills leading up to temples that sat there. Buildings were hidden behind immense outcrops for armadas to stage their forces and prepare to go out and conquer the other dying colonies. Shrines were built to resemble the old leaders. A beautiful landscape of sand and rock surrounded the kingdom. A trail extended downward from the temples that stood on the hills of sand and rock. The trail was made of hardened rock, which was crumbling and showing signs of its age. Golden colored sand sat on each side of the trail.

Although the kingdom was powerful, their focus was not on space travel. Most of the spaceships they had migrated to Kaskoon in were destroyed and lost in the sands. The initial focus of their technology was creating biological creatures and then later it shifted to missile development.

Intelligent, but dangerous creatures known as Sandkeens were created at a lab in the kingdom. It was the most terrifying experiment the Tarr Kingdom's scientists had ever developed. The creatures killed most of the scientists. When the scientists created the Sandkeens, they named the first Sandkeen Angleo. Angleo escaped his captors and fled from the Tarr Kingdom with some high tech equipment. He lived in caves that were below the surface of Kaskoon. He always kept a whip with him that he created from their equipment. It had energy flowing within it. Whatever it struck, electrical bursts of energy flew from it.

As time went on, the rest of the Sandkeens escaped their captors and found the caves that Angleo lived in. They became known as the Caverns of the Sandkeens. When Angleo died, the other Sandkeens produced more of the whips that Angleo had developed. Soon, every Sandkeen carried one of the whips, which were known as Angleo's Death Cords.

The Sandkeens mysteriously reproduced. The scientists had only developed five Sandkeens and there were hundreds of them on the planet approximately 458 years later.

The Tarr Kingdom lasted a great many years until Nyton Radell of the BlueMar Government seized control over it in the year 230655 SA (Space Age). The BlueMar Government was spreading through the galaxy rapidly, spreading its evil intentions. The BlueMar Empire continued to rule throughout the known parts of the galaxy many years after the fall of the Tarr Kingdom, but they did not control every facet of people's daily lives.

A small figure came over a sand hill in the distance. It moved closer and closer. It was the Airglider. When Baas stopped the Airglider on top of a hill, they saw a large, black metal object mounted in the sand in the distance. It was the Controller. It had a long, rectangle-shaped base with different height metal rectangles on each side of it. There was a flat piece of metal on top of the base. A long metal beam was sticking up from the flat section with four electron collectors on it. It would collect energy from the static lightning that frequently occurred on Kaskoon. The Controller supplied power to both Kanthas and Astossky and had been designed and developed by Olossky Cantin who was an electronic scientist.

When the Airglider reached the Controller, neither Baas, Roedie, nor KEN-102 could see any sign of TELAX-90. Baas turned off the Airglider and it lowered to the ground. Baas and Roedie stepped out with their laser rifles in their hands and started looking around for any sign of the robot. KEN-102 waited in the back of the Airglider while they searched for the robot.

Baas looked ahead of the Airglider and Roedie looked around a stratum outcrop that was located to the left of the Airglider. Rocks were scattered about the beige sand and around the outcrop. The missing robot was not there.

"There's no sign of him here. Let's check the other side of that hill," Baas said, pointing to the hill on the right with his laser rifle.

Roedie walked through the dusty sand to Baas's side, his sand boots kicking up dust particles.

"*Man,* it's hot as a pirate's bitch out here," he said.

"Spare me with the details, bro," Baas said, the sun's light shining off from the perspiration speckles on his face.

They returned to the Airglider and KEN-102 said, "My sensors are picking up some type of object on the other side of the hill. It seems to be—" KEN-102 was cut short from the roaring engines of the Airglider. They did not hear his warning as the Airglider flew over the sand hill. "—Sandkeens," he finished.

Holy cosmos! Baas thought.

He stopped the Airglider and it hovered a half meter above the sandy ground. Roedie pointed his laser rifle at one of the five Sandkeens that stood there.

"Shoot the damn thing. Shoot it!" Baas cried.

Roedie just sat staring at the creature in shock. The Sandkeen took a whip from a hook at his waist and snapped it toward Roedie's arm. Blue sparks of energy flew from his arm in all different directions. Baas took his own laser rifle, shot the one Sandkeen that whipped Roedie's arm, and flew the Airglider over another sand hill as quickly as he could.

Some distance away, Baas stopped and said, "Why didn't you shoot him? He could have killed you."

"I don't know." Roedie was still in shock, startled from the creature's looks.

"Are you all right?"

"He hit my arm. It's bleeding and charred."

"Those whips have a lot of electrical energy flowing through them. We'll have to take you to the Med-Center in Astossky," Baas said. "But first we need to get you home."

He put the Airglider on automatic and took an alternate course home.

The Airglider came from the direction behind the house. Baas stopped it by the shed, where Olossky was waiting for their arrival.

"Did you find TELAX-90?" Olossky asked.

"No. I have no idea where he is or what happened to him. But we ran into some Sandkeens and one of them whipped Roedie's arm with an Angleo's Death Cord. They have electrical energy in their whips," Baas said, turning off the Airglider in front of Olossky.

"Let me see your arm, Roedie," Olossky said. He walked over to the side of the Airglider and looked at the wounded arm. "We'd better get you to the Med-Center right now."

Olossky ran over to the house door and punched five digits on the panel. The door opened. He went into the house while Baas flew the Airglider around to the front of the house. Inside, Olossky told the robots that they would not be home for a while. Olossky went back outside, turned around toward the panel, and punched in a code to lock the door. He turned and hurried toward the Airglider.

"You'd better bring your rifle, Dad, in case we run into more Sandkeens," Roedie said, sitting in the front of the Airglider with Baas.

"Your two rifles will do fine, boys," Olossky said, looking toward the back seat where KEN-102 sat.

Baas moved over when Olossky got into the front seat of the Airglider. He flew the Airglider toward Kanthas. At the edge of the small town, he turned the Airglider perpendicular on the dusty sand road and headed toward Astossky. On the way to Astossky, they passed the Northern Sand Ridge, which was the northern magnetic pole. It looked like a small, sandy ridge. It made electronic compass LEDs flash wildly when it was passed.

The temperatures at the Northern Sand Ridge and the Southern Sand Ridge were approximately the same as the rest of the planet, very hot.

When they arrived in the city, there were different people and other types of life forms on the streets, going about their business. Olossky turned the Airglider into the Med-Center's parking lot as he listened to several spaceships take off in the distance.

They stepped out of the Airglider and went inside the building. Inside, there was a secretary in an office on their left. Her name was printed on a pin that was fastened to her blue uniform, Lu Bluestar.

"Yes?" she asked.

"A Sandkeen whipped my son with an Angleo's Death Cord. I don't know how bad it's damaged, but his arm's bleeding and burned pretty badly," Olossky said, looking toward Roedie.

The secretary punched a few keys on a computer and came around from behind the office wall.

"Right this way," she said.

She led them through a corridor to an office on their right. There was a man sitting behind a desk in the office. He had black hair with some gray here and there. He was the doctor of the Med-Center, Dr. Mills Deal. The doctor called a nurse on the com after the secretary had told him what the problem was. The doctor had an interest in victims of the Sandkeens, but he was too busy to inspect Roedie that day. He had piles of papers on his desk.

The nurse's name was Tylo Biakk. After arriving at the doctor's office and hearing the problem, she led them down the corridor to another room. When they stepped inside, she looked at Roedie's arm. She held a device of flashing LEDs over his arm.

After observing the device, Tylo thought, *Oh, no...I'll have to have the medical robots take care of this one. I've never seen an arm so damaged by a Sandkeen before.*

She turned off the device and put it on a tray next to him.

"I'm going to have to let our medical robots work on his arm," she said.

"Why?" Olossky asked.

"Because of the extent of damage to his arm, they are better suited to repair it than I am. It's right down the corridor," she said.

She led them to a waiting room down on the left of the corridor. She gestured Baas and Olossky into the room. The room had several chairs and a large window in it. On the other side of the window there were two medical robots. The nurse led Roedie up the corridor and into the room. Inside, the two med-robots, DX-20 and his assistant SX-94, were waiting for a patient.

After the nurse explained to the med-robots what the problem was, she left the room and went to some other part of the building. The two med-robots started their work on Roedie's arm.

Roedie's stomach was in a knot from his fear. He had been nauseated ever since they left Kanthas.

Why me? Out of all the people and other beings in this galaxy, why did I have to get whipped by a Sandkeen? Why me? Roedie's mind was racing.

DX-20 started working on Roedie's arm while his assistant, SX-94, handed him medical tools with his long, metal arms.

In the waiting room, Olossky and Baas were watching through the observation window. Olossky was worried about Roedie. Were they going to have to amputate his arm?

In the medical room, the robots stopped working on Roedie's arm, looking at each other. Roedie noticed that they had stopped. He looked up at them.

"Well?"

The robots slowly turned toward Roedie. "Well, Roedie, we're all finished," DX-20 said.

"That's *it?*" Roedie asked.

"Yes, that is it," DX-20 said.

A sigh of relief fell over Roedie as he stood up from the medical chair.

"Watch yourself from now on, Roedie," the electronic voice of SX-94 said. "Those Sandkeens can be rough. Give that a little while to heal. We have given you a pain reliever as well."

"I'll be more careful. Thanks," he said as he left the room. He met his father and his brother in the corridor.

"Is everything all right?" Olossky asked.

"Perfect," Roedie said, looking down at his healing arm.

They walked to the office where Lu Bluestar gave Olossky some papers to sign. Olossky signed them, paid them their credits, and went out the front door followed by Baas and Roedie.

When they stepped into the Airglider where KEN-102 was waiting for them, Olossky said, "Now, for that surprise that I promised you two the other day."

"What is that, Dad?" Roedie asked.

"I'm taking you two to eat at the Sand Star restaurant for dinner."

"Good. I'm hungry," Baas said.

Olossky flew to another street in the large city and they saw the Sand Star restaurant on a corner.

This is great, Roedie thought as they flew into the restaurant's parking lot.

They stepped out of the Airglider and went inside. KEN-102 stayed in the Airglider. Olossky, Baas, and Roedie went through a doorway after the electronic door swiftly slid aside and they walked to a seat and made themselves comfortable.

There were green plants next to their table. The plants were beautiful setting against a white wall. Two different types of spices sat on the table in gold colored shakers. One was called Kasaa and the other was called Kinabah. The restaurant was air-conditioned and was a lot cooler than the heat outside.

A waiter came to their table after waiting on a creature from the Thisis System at another table. The waiter was dressed in a tan silk suit that resembled the desert sand. He handed a menu to each of them and went to wait on someone else.

"Kahsaahs sound good," Baas said, looking at the menu.

"We had those at home yesterday," Roedie said.

"How about some Kytusk with Thubeese sauce?" Olossky suggested.

"That sounds good," Roedie said.

"Okay," Baas said. "And some Sevela to go with it."

After the waiter came, took their orders, and served their meals, Roedie started talking about their incident at the Controller.

When they were finished eating, Baas and Roedie thanked their father for the surprise. Olossky paid for the meals and they went back to…a damaged house.

CHAPTER TWO
THE MINING ASTEROID

A SMALL SHUTTLE departed from a vast ship that was slowly drifting in space. The vast ship's engines were temporarily shut down. Lights for docking bays and hull repair were glowing in the darkness of space. Light, emitting from the distant stars, brightened a portion of the hull. The starlight revealed the name on the large ship. It was the *BlueMar Empire Two.*

The shuttle that departed from the ship was slowly proceeding toward a mass of asteroids in the distance of space. It was the Zyvenous Asteroid Mass, located in the Ipsinittorr Star System. The destination was a mining asteroid called Zyvor that had lights on its surface.

Inside the shuttle, the aide for the emperor of the BlueMar Galaxy, sat on a black leather seat. He was a bald man named Con. Two guards sat across the aisle from Con. They were dressed in light gray uniforms and had laser rifles slung over their shoulders. Con, himself, was dressed in a black, silk jumpsuit.

Con looked out an observation window. They were getting ever closer to Zyvor…a lot closer since the last time he had checked out the window. He was sent to the mining asteroid to recruit four enforcement agent investigators. Emperor Quarrel Duelco wanted the recruits to travel to the BlueMar Empire's main realm on the planet Andron and talk business with him. The mining asteroid was a great source to hire enforcement agent investigators, since many of them worked there as an additional source of income. Enforcement agent investigators were freelance professionals that excelled at finding individuals of interest for a specific fee.

The asteroid was a BlueMar Government mining operation. An extremely heavy element called Lysithium Star Crystal was mined there. It was atomic number 220.

Con looked down at the floor of the shuttle, elbows on knees, hands on forehead. It had been a long day and he was tired. He shut his eyes, letting everything he worried about slip away. Slowly, he fell asleep. He was startled when he felt the ship shift its course and looked out the observation window. Brown colored asteroids partially covered with frozen water and methane on their surfaces drifted just meters away from the shuttle. Con backed away from the window and looked toward the pilot at the other end of the aisle.

Suddenly, the lights on Zyvor's surface brightened the inside of the shuttle, emitting through the observation window. Con saw the docking bay come into view. The shuttle flew into the asteroid docking bay through a parallelogram-shaped opening. Flashing lights were equally spaced around the opening. The shuttle proceeded into the asteroid. Con could see metal walls on the sides of the docking bay. He also saw miners and other people busy accomplishing their tasks. The miners climbed up and down metal ladders that were located next to the docking bay wall. Their boots could be heard echoing throughout the docking bay. The ladder wells led to higher and lower levels of the asteroid.

As the shuttle came in, an electronic field across the docking bay entrance was enabled from some unseen person to prevent the air inside the asteroid from escaping into space more than it already did around the shuttle. Slowly, the shuttle came to a halt. Con and his guards stood up and headed toward the shuttle door.

So, I can finally see the BlueMar Empire's Lysithium Star Crystal mining operation, Con thought.

The shuttle door opened. Con and his two guards stepped out onto the metal floor.

The head of the mining operation walked toward the fixed shuttle. He had been in his office, filing an old piece of jewelry, when he had to rush to the docking bay to welcome Con. He wore a dark green uniform and cap. The cap covered dark, black hair. When he reached the shuttle, he held out his hand to greet Con.

"Greetings, Con," he said.

"Greetings," Con replied. "You must be Crees Flytaniir...I believe you know why I'm here."

"Yes. We received a message over the com pertaining to you seeking enforcement agent investigators."

"Four of them," Con said.

"We have a lot of enforcement agent investigators working for us here. As you may know, many of them work here mining as supplemental income. I'll have one of my men talk to you about their names and details. He'll find them for you. But, would you like a tour through the mines first?" Crees asked.

"Yes. Thank you," Con said.

"Right this way, then," Crees said, leading him toward the docking bay wall. "We'll all have to put on these helmets first."

He handed two helmets to Con's guards and one to Con, taking them from a rack on the white, angled wall.

"What are these for?" Con asked.

"They're to protect your lungs from the air. We'll put on uniforms when we get to the bottom of the shaft. You don't have to put on your helmets until you get down there," Crees said.

He walked over to the ladder well and started climbing down the metal ladder. Con and his two guards followed him.

For a moment, while climbing down the ladder, Con was facing a white circular tube, until he saw the ceiling of the lower level. They stepped off from the ladder and stood on another metal floor. They were in a small room that had an electronic door at one end of it.

Crees walked over to a metal wall and grabbed four black uniforms from a hook, laying them on a metal bench that was located next to the wall.

"Guards, you are required to leave your laser rifles here," Crees said.

"Why?" one of the two guards asked.

"Because if a laser was to go off in the mines below us, the laser beam would reflect off from the walls of the tunnels and cause an explosion that would blow this asteroid into space dust. It's been done before. Have you ever heard of the Kynimaw Asteroid Belt in the Dolmreen Star System?" Crees looked at the two guards.

"Yes. That was where that asteroid exploded," Xeron Ttions said. He was the taller of the two guards.

"Lysithium Star Crystal was mined there. And do you know what made the asteroid explode?" Crees asked, looking at the other guard.

"A laser," Tryl Vess said, looking down at his rifle.

"That's right," Crees said. "Here. Slip on these uniforms over your clothes."

They each took a black uniform from the bench. The guards put down their rifles on the metal bench. They had a hard time getting into the tight uniforms. When they all had their uniforms on, Crees handed each one of them a pair of gloves.

After they had put on the gloves, Con asked, "Do you want us to put on the helmets now?"

"No. Look inside the helmet first."

They did so.

"See that first switch on the right, inside there? Switch the setting to ten."

They did so.

"Now you can put them on."

They each put on a helmet. When Con put on his helmet, he noticed red LEDs around the tinted, transparent plastic as he looked through the visor. He also noticed a light blue bar at the top of the plastic visor indicating the helmet's power charge level. He saw green LEDs to the right where he had turned the switch earlier. The LEDs brightened the inside of his helmet. He noticed two more switches next to the first one. And to his left, there was a voice communicator. He was amazed at the helmet technology, as were his two guards.

"When we get into the speed-lift, the air pressure will decrease slightly. Don't remove your helmet or safety garments. The helmets filter the air that you breathe and mix the oxygen in the rectangle-shaped mini tanks on the back of the suits," Crees said through the communicator in his helmet.

"Shall we go now?" Con asked through his voice communicator.

"Right this way," Crees said, walking to the electronic door at the end of the small room.

He pressed a lit button on a panel next to the door and the door opened. They stepped into the speed-lift and the electronic door closed behind them.

"We'll be going down to sub-level five. There is little work being done down there," Crees said through his communicator.

He pushed another lit button that had the number sub-five labeled on it. There were eleven lit buttons on the speed-lift's wall panel. The speed-lift was lit with only dim illuminators. The door opened to reveal a dark corridor with rough rock walls and ceiling. The floor was made of metal, like the rest of the finished floors in the asteroid.

Illuminators were lit at the far end of the corridor. They stepped out of the speed-lift and into the dim corridor. The door closed behind them. Con turned as the door closed and noticed a red lit button on the panel next to the door.

"This isn't the main corridor of this level. There are other corridors leading off from this one. They are the ones that are being mined," Crees said.

They proceeded through the corridor. Crees stopped where a smooth ledge was located on the side of the corridor. The ledge was used as an element staging area. A few small rocks sat on the ledge.

"Slide one of those rocks into the palm of your hand, Con," Crees said, pointing to the ledge.

Con walked over to the ledge and cupped his hand below the ledge, sliding a rock into his palm. The rock dropped from the ledge into his palm. Con fell to the metal floor, dropping the rock. It sent vibrations through them when it hit the floor. Con looked up at Crees.

"You've got to be joking. Those rocks are heavier than hell. This asteroid must weigh…" Con was awestruck.

Crees held out a hand and helped Con to his feet.

"Lysithium Star Crystal is very heavy," Crees said.

"If Lysithium Star Crystal weighs that much, then how can people use it in laser artillery and weaponry?" Con asked.

"The Lysithium Star Crystal has to be much finer than that rock that you…dropped," Crees said. "It can also be used in jewelry in very minute amounts."

He led them around a corner and into another corridor where two miners were drilling with electronic tools. They passed the miners and disappeared around another corner of the corridor. It was much lighter there. An anti-gravitation vehicle was on the floor of the wide corridor next to the rough, brown rock wall. Workers could be seen mining and working along the wide corridor further down the line. The wide corridor had illuminators in three parallel rows on the ceiling.

"We can use this Airglider to see the rest of this level," Crees said.

They got into the Airglider and Crees turned it on. It slowly rose from the metal floor with a hiss that echoed through the corridor. They started moving toward the group of workers. Miners were working atop tall mining scaffolding that reached the rock ceiling. The ceiling was five times as high as it was in the corridors they had been through earlier. Metal stairways led down from different entrances at the higher levels. Workers went up and down the stairs with clipboards in their gloved-hands. The Airglider slowly flew by the workers.

"The shipment of Lysithium Star Crystal that we mine from this level will be transported to Monomos, a small planet in the Rrijial Star System," Crees said.

"What did you say the atomic number of this element is?" Con asked.

"It's element number two hundred and twenty," Crees said.

"How many elements have been discovered?"

"You really aren't up on your science, are you? There are currently two hundred and twenty-four known elements," Crees said. "Lysithium Star Crystal's name is given to it because it looks like a star crystal."

"Is there anything else done to the Lysithium Star Crystal process before it is used in laser weapons?" Con asked.

"Yes. It is dipped into a substance that covers the crystal-like surface and hardens on it. It gives it a higher electrical conductivity," Crees said.

Con said nothing, revealing a dumbfounded expression.

The floor slanted upward from that point forward, the corridor's width became narrow, and the ceiling dropped back to its normal height.

"We will be passing the liquid dipping operation in a moment," Crees said.

The Airglider flew majestically up the narrow corridor. They passed large pools of liquid that were not being used at the time.

"Those are the dipping tanks right there," Crees said, pointing to the pools of liquid. "That's about it for the fifth sub-level."

He slowed the Airglider to a stop near a speed-lift door and turned it off. It slowly settled to the floor.

"I'll have one of my men talk to you about the enforcement agent investigators when we arrive at the main level," Crees said, stepping out of the Airglider.

Con and the two guards followed Crees to the speed-lift door. After stepping into the speed-lift, the door hissed shut and it started upward. When they were in a small room identical to the one they had come down to earlier, they removed their helmets, uniforms, and gloves.

"That was some tour," Con said.

"Thanks…I think," Crees said.

"Who is this man that I will be talking to about the enforcement agent investigators?" Con asked.

"His name is Nikk Eneb Oszon. I'll take you to him now. I'll have your rifles that are in the other room brought to your shuttle pilot," Crees said.

They went up the ladder well and came out into a corridor with illuminators along the ceiling's edge. He led them to a room where a gray haired man was standing in front of a computer.

"Nikk, this is Con. And these two are his guards. He is Emperor Quarrel Duelco's aide. He needs to know some information. Con, I have some other business to take care of. It was nice meeting you," Crees said before walking out the electronic door.

"So, you're Quarrel Duelco's aide?" Nikk smiled.

"Yes. And I would like you to locate four enforcement agent investigators here on Zyvor for me," Con said.

"Okay, I'll check the computer to see who's available," Nikk said, checking the computer that was in front of him.

"They'll need to travel to Andron," Con said.

"Let me see. Ah…no, there are no enforcement agent investigators working for us at the present time. I can check to see if there are any scheduled to work for us soon," Nikk said, lying about the enforcement agent investigators not mining on that asteroid at the present time.

"You've got to be joking. Emperor Quarrel Duelco checked on our computer and it stated that there are currently several here on Zyvor," Con said.

"Well, apparently, there must be a mistake," Nikk said, looking at the computer. "Just a moment. I'll go check the computer in the information room."

Nikk came around from behind the computer and went out the door.

Not here! *Don't tell me they're not here, asteroid scum! I didn't stay up without sleep just to find out there are no enforcement agent investigators here,* Con thought, outraged.

He walked over to the computer and glared at it. It had several enforcement agent investigators listed on its screen, including several currently employed there.

You piece of shit! I'll get you, personally! Con thought.

At that moment, the door opened and Nikk stepped into the room.

"No, there's no enforce—" Nikk broke off.

Con looked up from the computer. Rage was written all over his face.

"Why did you lie to me?" Con asked.

He came from around the computer, his hands wide open at his sides. Nikk backed up a step as Con came toward him. The electronic door slid to the inside of the wall and he backed out into the corridor. He started to flee down the corridor and ran straight into Crees. They both fell to the metal floor. Con and his guards came to a halt where the two men were on the floor.

"What's going on here?" Crees asked, getting up from the floor along with Nikk.

"I asked him to look for the enforcement agent investigators that I'm here to locate. He said there are none listed in the computer and he left to check another computer. But when he left, I checked the same computer and there are several enforcement agent investigators listed here," Con explained, looking from Nikk to Crees.

"Is that true?" Crees asked Nikk.

"Well…yes, it is," Nikk said, fear in his eyes.

"Why?" Crees asked.

Nikk looked down to the floor and did not speak. He looked up at Crees.

"I see," Crees said. He waved to two of his own guards that were at a corridor intersection behind them. They came to his side. "Bring Nikk to my office. And I want one of you to guard him until I get there."

"Yes, sir," the guards said as they grabbed Nikk. They dragged him down the corridor.

"I am truly sorry about this. How embarrassing. I'll personally find four enforcement agent investigators for you," Crees said. "But I have to check something out first. Would you like to wait for me in the lounge?"

"That would be fine," Con said, thinking *Emperor Quarrel Duelco will hear about this incident!*

"Right this way."

Nikk sat in Crees's office chair, looking at the guard that stood by the door. It was a small office with white walls. The desk sat in the middle of the room.

"What did you do, Nikk?" the guard asked.

Nikk did not say anything. He looked down, away from the guard. His eyes came across a sharp, metal file setting beside some jewelry on the desk.

A sharp file!

He looked toward the guard. The guard's attention was on something else since trying to have a conversation with Nikk was impossible. Nikk slowly reached his hand toward the file, all the while looking at the guard. His attention was still on something else! Nikk felt his fingers touch the handle of the file, then his thumb. He slowly slid it off from the desk.

If he sees me, I'm dead, Nikk thought.

With the file in his grasp, he slowly retreated his hand to his side. Ah, the file was out of the guard's sight!

"I'm getting tired. You don't mind if I stretch, do you?" Nikk asked.

"No. Go right ahead," the guard said.

Nikk stood up from the chair. His hand holding the sharp file was slightly behind his back. When the guard was not looking, Nikk threw the sharp file across the room and it slid into the side of the guard's skull. A narrow spurt of blood speckled the white wall. With a quick roll of the eyes, the guard fell to the floor. Nikk headed toward the door at the same moment that it opened to reveal Crees peering in at him.

"Are you going somewhere?" Crees asked.

Nikk let out a sigh.

"I checked your name on the computer. You're from the resistance, working on the inside, trying to destroy the BlueMar Government from within," Crees said.

"It's hardly a government. It's a sick and twisted empire!" Nikk sneered.

In the docking bay, Crees introduced Con to the four enforcement agent investigators who agreed to take the job. "This is Santu, Zantar, Zaggon, and Salasting," he said. "They will be accompanying you to Andron."

Crees Flytaniir said his farewells to Con. Nikk Eneb Oszon—in shackles—was now a prisoner for the BlueMar Empire. He stepped into the shuttle, followed by Con and his guards. The enforcement agent investigators went to their own ships and prepared to board the *BlueMar Empire Two*.

Chapter Three
The Tarr Kingdom

The large spherical sun with its bright orange glow sat on the horizon, just above the sand dunes of Kaskoon. Reddish colored clouds sat in the foreground against the orange backdrop. The beautiful sight was blended into the horizon along with a lavender sky. Seemingly endless sand hills that formed countless different shapes from the blowing winds extended into the distance. Each evening on Kaskoon, a silver glow emitted as the sun reflected from the tall glass buildings in Astossky. The glare could be seen as far as Kanthas.

The buildings of Kanthas were not tall, like the ones in Astossky. What few buildings Kanthas did have, they were still beautiful at sundown, their tan surfaces glowing bright. The beige sand that surrounded the town contrasted their glow.

The bright orange horizon of the sun called Kaskar settled behind kilometers and kilometers of sand and rock hills, directly behind the Cantins' house. Far in the background, Baas could barely see the black Controller setting against the horizon. His mother, Leress Cantin, always told him to be careful of the Sandkeens who would strike without notice. Although they went through an experience with a Sandkeen attack, he still liked to explore and investigate things. He thought of how he always wanted to explore the landscape of Kaskoon when he was a small boy. Baas and his brother, Roedie, had never been off-planet. He wanted to travel through space and go to different worlds.

His mother, Leress, died from the Tabaannaann Plague. She had been a medical student at the Academy of Sciences in Astossky when the plague was set free from a canister leak. Baas missed his mother a lot. After she died, their family went into a state of depression. Olossky lost his job as an electronic scientist after refusing to return to work with his last assignment. The Cantins had to sell all their robots they had owned at the time in order to survive. They had to sell Karrii-207, a robot they had owned for a long time. Baas could not even remember when they had purchased Karrii-207. But he could not forget the time Karrii-207 had been sold. They had since acquired more robots, including KEN-102.

Roedie was off attending an electronics course at the Academy of Sciences and was going to be gone for a week. Baas didn't understand how he could take classes in the same facility where their mother had died. Olossky was in the house watching some show on the tele-vid, so Baas just stood outside looking at the horizon fade into night. He had time to think. He thought about the time he and his grandpa, Serenitol Cantin, had walked to the Controller and put it on its charge mode. They had some good times. At least they were getting paid by the city of Astossky to operate the Controller that Olossky designed, which gave electrical power to Astossky and Kanthas. His grandpa had moved to another planet looking for a job that Kaskoon could not offer him. Doing so, his grandpa found a job *and* a woman on a planet that was a rich provider for both.

For a moment, Baas felt all alone in a world of nostalgia and sorrow until KEN-102 asked, "Is something wrong?"

Baas turned around with a tear rolling down his cheek. "No...I'm all right," he said.

"I know how you must feel. Sometimes I feel the same way with my artificial senses."

"Thanks for asking, though, KEN-102," Baas said.

The robot turned around and went back to finishing the repairs to the house and shed. The Sandkeens had caused damage to their home when they were away in Astossky. The house and shed doors had been damaged from Angleo's Death Cords. The heat from the energy whips melted a hole in the metal door of the shed. Drips of melted metal had hardened below the hole.

Baas took one more look at the evening horizon and headed for the house. Inside, Olossky turned off the tele-vid with a remote, then he asked, "What ya been doin'?"

"Oh, nothing much. Just thinking."

"Thinking about what, son?" Olossky asked, wondering what was bothering Baas.

"Mom and grandpa and Karrii-207."

So, that's what's bothering him, Olossky thought.

"I miss them too…just as much as you do, Baas," Olossky said.

"Why? Why?" Baas went on.

"Why? Well, because your grandpa had to find a job, that canister leak was an accident at the Academy of Sciences, and we had to sell Karrii-207 and the other robots for the credits," Olossky said. "If I could have prevented any of it from happening, I certainly would have, believe me."

"I know," Baas said, looking down with sadness.

"I tried to make up for selling Karrii-207 by purchasing many of the robots we now have," Olossky said, putting his hand on Baas's shoulder.

Baas turned around and hugged his father. "I know the last couple of years have been difficult on you too, Dad."

The next day, Baas walked to Kanthas and purchased a bottled carbonated beverage called Sevela. He drank it on his way to the Kanthas Archive Historical Building. He walked along the sand trail and into the building. He saw the old remains of things from the Tarr Kingdom, things that explorers had brought back to the museum— what few explorers there were. He also saw other things of mystery that were found on the desert plains of Kaskoon.

After leaving the Kanthas Archive Historical Building, he thought of how awesome it would be to explore the remains of the Tarr Kingdom and the unexplored landscapes of the southern hemisphere of Kaskoon.

Before he went back home, he walked back to the residential store and bought a newspaper that he had forgot to purchase when he bought his Sevela.

When he arrived home, he gave his father the *Astossky Editorial.* Below the title, it read: "Sandkeens attack Astossky woman," "More skeletons found in Astossky archeological dig," "BlueMar Government getting stricter on Rythell citizens," "A smuggling bust on Zalho's World."

Man, those Sandkeens are getting more aggressive, Olossky thought.

Baas went to his room and turned on some sort of music that bothered Olossky because of its fast sound and its heavy metal/thrash rhythm.

"Turn it down!" Olossky shouted, trying to read the newspaper.

Baas turned it off and would jam later. He turned on some three-dimensional holographic pictures from the planet Sanbor, where his grandpa lived.

A few days later, Roedie came home from Astossky where he had learned about electronics at the Academy of Sciences.

Baas walked from his room down the metal stairs to the living room where Roedie was telling his dad about his experience at the Academy of Sciences. He asked Roedie to come outside for a second. When they were standing in front of the house, Baas asked, "Do you want to go to the Tarr Kingdom?"

"The Tarr Kingdom? Are you *crazy?*" Roedie asked.

"Well, do you or don't you?" Baas asked.

"Ah...sure. When?"

"Today. Right after you see the stuff about the Tarr Kingdom at the Kanthas Archive Historical Building," Baas said.

"I've seen that before."

"Play along with the lie, bro. That's where dad's gonna think we're going," Baas said, lifting his eyebrows.

"Oh, I see," Roedie said. "When are we goin'?"

"Now," Baas said, walking toward the Airglider that sat in front of the house.

"I'll tell dad we're going to Kanthas," Roedie said. He went into the house where he met his dad by the kitchen. "Can we go to Kanthas?"

"You mean the Tarr Kingdom, don't you?" Olossky asked, leaning against the wall.

"How did you know?" Roedie asked.

"I have good ears," Olossky said. "Also, how many times can you go to the Kanthas Archive Historical Building to see stuff on the Tarr Kingdom without me getting suspicious?"

"Can we?" Roedie asked.

"Well, if you take two laser rifles, two laser pistols, and a com with you, you can go to the Tarr Kingdom. I can't tell you where it is, because I don't know. I think it's somewhere around the Southern Sand Ridge. You and Baas had better be careful. Wait a second and I'll get the things," Olossky said as he went to get the lasers and the com.

A minute later, he came back with them and handed the arm full of items to Roedie.

"Thanks," Roedie said. "Bye."

"Be very careful," Olossky demanded.

Outside, Roedie stepped into the Airglider with an arm full of items.

"Well?" Baas asked.

"Well, nothing. He knows. But we can go anyway. Here are the lasers and a com," Roedie said.

"So many?"

"He's cautious."

"That cautious?"

"What can I say?"

"Let's go," Baas said, turning on the Airglider and putting it on automatic.

Soon, Baas and Roedie flew past the Controller and along the sand hills. Kilometers went by as they flew along the dunes and cliffs that made Kaskoon what it was. Minutes stretched into hours. They were traveling very fast and the wind was making their hair fly in all different directions.

"Look! Look, man! The Tarr Kingdom," Baas said, over the sound of the blowing wind.

"It's as badass as they always said it was," Roedie said.

Smaller temples sat on either side of a larger, main temple. They were all surrounded by sand hills. The temple spires seemed to reach up toward the blue sky.

Baas flew the Airglider the rest of the way on manual. They flew behind a large outcrop so that no one could see the Airglider from the sand wastelands—if anyone was around to see it at all. They stepped out of the Airglider and grabbed their weapons and communicator.

"Hey, look at this building," Roedie said, pointing to a building that was directly behind the large outcrop where the Airglider was parked.

"I think—from what I remember at the Kanthas Archive Historical Building—this was used for their ancient armadas," Baas said.

The electronic door was stuck open and the wind had blown sand into the small building. They went inside and looked around.

"Nothing is in here," Roedie said, looking at the one-room building.

"Well, let's explore the main temple," Baas said.

Leaving the building, they went around a large outcrop that was twice the height of themselves and as large as their house in diameter. They went to the front of the main temple. The electronic door struggled, but slowly opened as they approached it. Strangely, it still worked after all those years. They entered and found themselves in a corridor that led to a stairway at the far end. Two other perpendicular corridors led in different directions.

"Let's take the corridor that goes straight ahead first," Baas said.

"This place is big," Roedie said.

"I know what you're talkin'," Baas said.

They went down the corridor to the stairway.

"I wonder where this stairway leads," Baas said, walking up the steps. "Look. It's just a big, empty room."

"This room extends from one end of the temple to the other. This is probably where the throne room was," Roedie said.

"Well, I guess we'd better see what's at the end of the other two corridors downstairs," Baas said.

Roedie saw something out of the corner of his eye. "Wait!" he said.

He bent over and picked up a piece of dust-covered paper that was on the floor of the large room.

"What is it?" Baas asked.

"An old paper. It says, '*I am going to name the first settlement that my explorers develop, Astossky. Signed, Phatom Tarr,*' " Roedie said.

"This is amazing! Maybe the Kanthas Archive Historical Building will buy it from us," Baas suggested.

"Maybe," Roedie said, putting the paper inside a pocket in his beige robe.

They headed back down the stairs to the corridor intersection and then looked at each other.

"Let's take the one on the right first," Roedie said.

"Okay," Baas said.

At the end of that corridor, there was a stairway that went below ground level.

"Hey, look. Another corridor is down there," Roedie said, peering down the steps.

"Man, it's dark down there," Baas said.

"Come on, let's see what's down there," Roedie said.

They went down the steps to the corridor below and heard something fall behind them.

"Did you hear that?" Baas asked.

"Yeah," Roedie whispered.

They hid behind a wall and Baas said, "That was something metallic that dropped on the floor back there."

"I know," Roedie said.

A Sandkeen jumped around the corner of the wall followed by a second one.

"Let's get the hell out of here!" Baas yelled.

They ran the opposite way they had come from, toward another stairway that went down further.

No! We need to go up, Baas thought.

Roedie found another set of stairs that led upward. They needed to keep distance between them and the two Sandkeens. They kept running up the stairs and came out into the main corridor above ground.

"Hey, isn't this the same…" Roedie mumbled as he kept running.

They quickly ran around a corner and out the temple door.

"Let's get into the Airglider," Baas said.

When they ran around the large outcrop, they saw a Fateen Pest sitting in the Airglider.

"Hey, get out of there! Get out!" Baas shouted.

The Fateen Pest showed its teeth and growled, then ran extremely fast from the Airglider. The Fateen Pest looked like a mixture between a wolf and a rat, with pointed ears and a long tail.

"Let's get out of here!" Baas said.

They hopped into the Airglider and took off as the two Sandkeens came around the large outcrop.

The Sandkeens were dressed in gray robes. The red-skinned creatures had two straight, thin, tan tusks at each corner of their mouths. One of the two Sandkeens had a broken tusk at the right side of his mouth. Many Sandkeens then possessed a kingdom that once was the home of the people who created them.

"That was close," Roedie said.

"That was damn close," Baas said. "Call dad on the com."

"I can't."

"What?"

"I can't," Roedie repeated.

"Why?" Baas asked.

"I dropped the com running up the stairs," Roedie said.

"Great!" Baas said, looking at Roedie and then back to the front of the Airglider as it flew along the sands.

Before they went past the Controller, Roedie saw a metal object protruding from the sand where they had been attacked by Sandkeens the first time. The memory of the Angleo's Death Cord hitting his arm made him flinch.

"I wonder what that metal thing could be," he said to himself as the wind blew his blond hair.

"What did you say?" Baas asked.
"Oh, nothing," Roedie said.

CHAPTER FOUR
THE INFORMATION

A MASSIVE BUILDING was located in a forest on the planet Andron. It was the BlueMar Government's main realm. The building was surrounded by an evergreen forest of white pine trees that covered the entire planet. Even the planet's two natural satellites had forests on them. The building and its docking platforms were made from titanium metal, their white surfaces reflecting in the streams of water that flowed through the forest below the immense building. Several docking platforms sat along the front of the building. Lights were located on their flat surfaces to guide ships in. Several ships were fixed on each docking platform, including Silver Dagger fighters. The small, silver, V-shaped fighter ships came to a point at the front. They were the BlueMar Empire's prime fighter ships and were very maneuverable.

Inside the throne room, Quarrel Duelco's robot, Balerox, was standing next to a computer located near the throne. A BlueMar Government Commander, a Realm Commander, a BlueMar Government Officer, and two Realm Guards stood nearby. They were accompanied by four enforcement agent investigators who stood before the empty throne. One of the enforcement agent investigators was Santu. He wore a helmet and all types of electronic equipment on his body for life support. He had no original legs. They were lost in the Battle of Keelonn. Electronic legs replaced the original ones. He was one of the best enforcement agent investigators in the galaxy.

Behind Santu, another enforcement agent investigator stood in a fixed position. He wore a metal suit of armor. Wires and small hoses ran through the mid-section of his suit, connected to hidden weaponry. His name was Zantar. Standing beside Zantar, there was a humanoid insect enforcement agent investigator. He had large insect eyes and a nose that spread out in three different directions. His name was Zaggon. Standing behind Zaggon, there was a quaint looking enforcement agent investigator dressed in a light tan colored robe. He belonged to the Sala Species. The back of his head curved out and up. Three horns were on the top of his head and two tusks were on each side of his small mouth. The horns and tusks were all straight, long, thin, and very sharp. His people were indigenous to both the Qas Star System and his home in the Salano Star System. His name was Salasting.

A black robed figure walked out from a shadow in the dark throne room. It was, the supreme emperor of the galaxy, the tyrant, Quarrel Duelco. His black hair matched his dark robe. He turned and faced Santu and the other enforcement agent investigators. They could see the arrogance emitting from his every move.

"Welcome to Andron. As you may know, since this is a low priority for the BlueMar Empire, we will not be wasting our resources on this investigation. I want you enforcement agent investigators to find a man named Olossky Cantin. All the information you need for the investigation will be on the electronic computer cards that Con will give you. The proposed compensation is also on the cards. Each of you have your own methods, but this is to be a collaborated effort. If you choose to accept, contact Con for further instructions."

A bald figure came out from the shadows. It was Con, holding four computer cards in his hand. He walked over to each of the enforcement agent investigators and handed them a card. Con walked back into the shadows, disappearing from sight.

Quarrel Duelco motioned for two Realm Guards and the BlueMar Government Officer to escort the four enforcement agent investigators to the docking platform. They were led up a few titanium stairs and out of the throne room.

At one of the docking platforms, the enforcement agent investigators agreed to meet at a private cafe to discuss the matter. They entered their ships and flew from the forest planet's surface, like four birds forming a perfect arrow formation.

The four enforcement agent investigators sat at a table in the back of a remote cafe. They finished reading the information from the computer cards.

"I'm out. I don't care for the compensation amount," Zantar said, taking a drink of his beverage. "I can make more mining Lysithium Star Crystal."

"I agree with you, Zantar. It's all yours, Santu and Zaggon," Salasting said, removing the card from his computer. "I'm heading back to the Ipsinittorr Star System."

"I'm in. I need the credits," Zaggon said.

"I was hoping you would agree to this," Santu said.

After finishing their drinks, Zantar and Salasting left the cafe. Santu and Zaggon continued to discuss the matter. They used what data they had from the BlueMar Government and performed some high-tech cross references of their own. After some complex computer searches from private networks that only they had access to, they came up with a hit for Olossky Cantin on the planet Kaskoon.

Santu and Zaggon decided to travel together in Santu's ship. They landed in the Kaskoon desert, ten kilometers from Astossky. Santu set his computer to start sniffing all the network data in Astossky.

"I've got something," Zaggon said.

Santu read the screen. Apparently, Olossky Cantin was the developer and main operator of the Controller that gave power to the city. It also listed his two sons, Baas and Roedie, as authorized operators of the Controller.

"Let's check it out," Santu said.

Santu landed the ship near the Controller. They grabbed their laser rifles and stepped out of the ship. Santu opened a large door on the side of his ship. Inside, there was a large driving vehicle called a Weathertread. It could be driven in snow, ice, sand, forest, swamp, and float in water. He drove the Weathertread out onto the hot, dusty sand and toward the Controller. As they drove the Weathertread, they heard a screech and felt a bump as the Weathertread ran something over. Santu looked on his control panel and saw that he had run over a Fateen Pest. He took his gaze from the screen and looked back out the window. He saw the Controller ahead of them.

So, that's the Controller, Santu thought.

They stopped the Weathertread and stepped outside, looking at the black Controller and all of its settings. He could kill the power to the city and it would lure Olossky or someone close to him out to the Controller. Santu studied the device and looked back at Zaggon. As he turned, he noticed a metal arm protruding from the dusty sand nearby.

"What is that?" Santu asked.

They walked over to the metal object. Santu pulled the arm from the sand and it led to a body. He pulled more and it led to a head. The legs had been severed from the body forming a hardened metal burn on the lower body. Santu looked at his own artificial legs and dismissed the bad memory. He lifted it more, until he saw the other arm pop out of the sand. They brought the robot into the Weathertread. Inside, Santu removed a computer card from a slot in the robot's back. All robots were manufactured with information slots in their backs. Most of the slots were at the top-left corner of the robot's back. Santu put the card into the computer to retrieve the robot's information. The robot's name was TELAX-90. He was the property of Olossky Cantin. His residence was an address just outside of Kanthas at house number 74. Santu liked this option much better than killing the power to the city.

"Well, now we are getting somewhere," Zaggon said.

Santu picked up the robot and set it next to an old, red robot that had been in the back of the Weathertread.

"TELAX-90, meet RX-47," Santu said sarcastically to the two lifeless robots.

Driving back to the ship in the Weathertread, Santu ran over the dead Fateen Pest again, a smile on his face. When they arrived, he drove the Weathertread into the side compartment of the spacecraft and they both stepped out. Soon, the ship swiftly lifted from the dusty sand.

Chapter Five
The Hunters

Quarrel Duelco was pleasantly surprised by the communique that he received from Santu and Zaggon. They had found the location of Olossky Cantin!

"Thank you for the communique, Balerox," Quarrel Duelco said to his robot.

Balerox walked over to Quarrel Duelco's throne. "The planet Kas—"

"Quiet!" Quarrel shouted at the robot. "Tell Santu and Zaggon I'll pay them three times the amount of credits that I was originally going to pay them, if they bring Olossky Cantin back here alive.

"Right away, sir," Balerox said.

"Three times as much?" Zaggon received the message.

Santu's expression seemed bittersweet. He didn't mind bringing him back alive for three times the amount, but he would have enjoyed the kill. The enforcement agent investigators landed just outside of Kanthas at house number 74. As Santu and Zaggon stepped out of the ship, they scanned the vicinity around the Nemnalon house.

Olossky came out of the house to see what was going on. Santu and Zaggon pulled out their laser pistols and started walking toward Olossky.

"Who the *hell* do you think you are?" Olossky looked at them without moving.

Santu walked over and put the laser pistol to Olossky's face.

"Are you Olossky Cantin?" Santu asked.

"Look, I don't know who you are or why you're here, but—"

"Too many questions can get a man into a lot of trouble. I'll tell you why we're here. You left a job with the BlueMar Empire after learning some classified information," Santu said.

"I'll make sure the house is secure," Zaggon said.

He went to the door. It would not open. He stood back and shot the door panel with his laser pistol. It opened. Santu continued to hold Olossky at gun-point outside. Zaggon saw EX-87, TX-2000, EF-7, and GRA-135 in the house, but no people. He destroyed all the robots with his laser pistol and went back outside.

"There were four robots inside, but no one else," Zaggon said.

"Where are your sons?" Santu asked.

"Off-planet," Olossky said.

Baas, Roedie, and KEN-102 were observing everything that was happening from inside the shed, as they peered through the hole in the door that KEN-102 never finished repairing.

Santu looked at Olossky for a long moment. "All right, let's get into the ship," he said, pointing Olossky toward the ship door with his laser pistol.

Once inside, Santu said, "Zaggon, lock the fool up."

Zaggon brought Olossky into the back of the ship. He put him in a small security cell and turned on a laser lock. Blue lasers crossed the doorway, preventing Olossky from escaping. They flew from the surface of Kaskoon.

Baas and Roedie could not believe what just happened.

"Where'd they take him, Roedie?" Baas asked.

The three of them stepped out of the shed and looked into the sky.

"I don't know, but we're gonna find him," Roedie said.

A ship approached the docking platform in the early morning, foggy mists of Andron. Deep within the walls and corridors of the government's main realm, a door swiftly opened to the side and two figures walked down a few steps, escorting a man in shackles.

"Good morning, Quarrel. This is Olossky Cantin who left the BlueMar Empire with your classified information," Santu said.

Quarrel stared at Olossky. "So, we've finally found you…" he said. "Where are your sons, Baas and Roedie?"

Olossky thought for a moment. For the sake of Baas and Roedie, he said, "I don't know what you're talking about."

"You're obviously lying," Quarrel said. He motioned for his Realm Guards. "Lock him up."

Two Realm Guards brought Olossky back up the stairs and out the door. Quarrel Duelco continued talking to Santu and Zaggon as they made themselves comfortable in some chairs.

Olossky was led through a maze of corridors to a cell where he was shoved in. Similar to the cell on the ship, blue colored lasers crossed the door when one of the Realm Guards turned on the laser lock. They stood guard outside the cell. Olossky could hear the echoes of people screaming and shouts of pain.

"Will you two join the BlueMar Government in finding Olossky's sons? And I can assure you, the pay will be outstanding. We would do it ourselves, but we don't have the resources available right now," Quarrel Duelco said to Santu and Zaggon.

They both agreed to the offer.

On Kaskoon, Baas, Roedie, and KEN-102 were taking care of the remaining pieces of the robots on the floor of the house. They stacked them against a wall.

"Baas, Roedie," KEN-102 said, "I have to tell you something about my past."

"Your past?" Baas asked, looking at the robot like he was crazy.

"I have some information," KEN-102 went on, "that you should know about."

"What kind of information?" Baas asked.

"Your father used to work on assignments as an electronic scientist for the BlueMar Government. My creator, Commander Rigid'n Morrwhell, assigned me to work with your father during this time. Your father learned some classified information regarding the BlueMar Empire planning to expand throughout the entire BlueMar Galaxy and eventually the Regulominuss Galaxy as well since they discovered a wormhole," KEN-102 said.

"So, how did you end up with dad?" Baas asked. "I thought he purchased you from someplace."

"That's a story for another time," KEN-102 said.

"Good thing we got in the shed when we saw that ship coming in the distance. I had a strange feeling about it," Roedie said.

"We've got to find the place where they took him so we can get'm back," Baas said.

"I know what the name of the planet is where they took him. After all, I used to work for the BlueMar Empire. The name of the planet is Andron," KEN-102 said.

"Do you know where it is?" Roedie asked.

"No, I don't. They may not keep him there."

"Oh, that's real good. That only narrows it down to the whole galaxy!" Baas said.

"We'll have to get a ship in Astossky and Ikk Sylikyt is a ship dealer. I know where his lot is too," Roedie said.

"Then, I think we'd better start packing," Baas said.

"We're going to need oxygen suits, tanks and masks, coms, laser rifles, clothes, tools, camping gear, food, and water," Roedie said.

"Then, let's get 'em," Baas said.

"Let's go."

They went into the house and started gathering their needs. After they were finished, they put the things into the Airglider. Baas, Roedie, and KEN-102 got into the Airglider and Baas started it up. Looking at their home, possibly for the last time, they headed toward Astossky.

They flew past the Northern Sand Ridge. It was a hot day on Kaskoon to be traveling, but they did not care, because they were on a quest, a quest that would bring them to the farthest stars, lightyears from their star system, thousands of terameters from their home. It was a quest to find their father no matter what.

When the three of them arrived in Astossky, they went to a starship dealer to buy a ship on what credits they had left from home.

A man named Ikk Sylikyt had five starships and a Weathertread at his lot. The first two ships were terrible looking; some parts were smashed and dented up from battles. The third ship was okay, but it was an old model. The fourth and fifth ones were just right for Baas and Roedie. They had five seats in them. There was one for the pilot, one for the navigator, and the other three for passengers. They had deflector shields, anti-gravitation capability, ion laser drives, and capabilities of lightspeed. They picked the fourth ship. It cost almost all the credits they had, including the trade-in for the Airglider.

While Roedie checked everything out on the ship, Baas paid Ikk

Sylikyt. They took their things from the Airglider and put them into the ship. Their supplies included orange, pink, lavender, and green food pills as well as blue and red Sevela and lots of water. Weapons, tools, and the other equipment they had grabbed from home were also loaded onto the ship.

On the side of their new ship, it read, *Zoota 2000.* They stepped into the ship and looked it over together. Baas sat in the pilot's seat, Roedie sat in the navigator's seat, and KEN-102 sat in one of the passenger seats. After studying the controls, Baas started it up. They soon lifted from the surface of Kaskoon. They had a feeling it would be the last sight of their home planet.

Chapter Six
The Island in the Sea

From *The Adventures of Baas and Roedie—*

ROEDIE:

Baas, KEN-102, and I were in the spaceship named *Zoota 2000*. While we were still above the planet Kaskoon, I started the space navigation on the computer. The navigation system was up-to-date with the latest astronomical information. There were several screens to rotate through with all the information needed for space travel. The main screen had a display of the BlueMar Galaxy on it. The system was fairly simple. We just had to choose a star system from the drop-down menu. Once selected, we would then choose the planet or satellite from another drop-down menu. During travel, the ship's computer would automatically avoid gravitational masses. If the selected destination was not environmentally friendly, whether from temperature, atmosphere, radiation, or other hazardous issues, it would automatically stop the ship from proceeding. For each celestial entity in the database, whether it was a planet, a satellite, a star, or whatever, the computer had just about all the information we would need for it.

"Well, is this the other planet that you were talking about, KEN-102?" I asked, pointing to the computer.

"Yes, it is the one," KEN-102 replied.

The planet's information populated on the screen.

"The planet is called Proteron. It is an old sand planet that now has green plants and small seas in some areas. There are several cities on the planet," the computer, named Zoota, stated through a speaker system.

We all watched the computer display the information on its screen.

"Proteron is the planet where another electronic scientist who knows your father is supposedly retired. He may be of some help in locating him. It won't hurt to check," KEN-102 said.

We set a course for Proteron. It was only a short distance from Kaskoon. The flight was fairly quiet as we were occupied with thoughts of our new quest to find our father. Several hours later, we arrived at Proteron.

"Turn on the anti-gravitation and head for the nearest city," I said.

Baas did so and we started descending through the planet's atmosphere at a very slow rate of velocity, on a vector toward the nearest city, Protos.

The *Zoota 2000* landed on sandy ground in the city and we stepped out. I looked around the busy streets and saw many people going about their tasks.

"Let's check that intoxication joint out over there. Ask around and see where we can find an electronic scientist here," Baas said. "There can't be many."

We walked over to the intoxication joint called SeaScape, where two men—both about thirty years old—were standing there in black leather outfits, most likely as bouncers.

"Okay, where do you three think you're goin'?" The bouncer stopped us before we entered.

"We have to ask around for an electronic scientist," Baas said.

"Well, go in…but hurry up. And you won't find one in there," the other bouncer said, motioning them in.

We entered the dimly lit building. As we made our way over to the counter, we noticed the place was filled with many different types of people.

"Well?" I whispered, looking at Baas.

Baas turned from me to the bartender. "Do you happen to know where we can find an electronic scientist around here?" he asked.

"No. No, I don't," the short man behind the counter said.

"Oh. Just askin'," Baas said.

We looked away from the counter and into the rest of the intoxication joint. There were pirates all through the place. I caught two of their names, Siioxx Toon and Teeb Jii. We looked over on the other side of the large room and saw a man tearing at a prostitute's clothes.

"Stop it!" she shouted and jerked away.

"Shove it up your bloody-ragged hole, bitch! I want my credits back!" the man shouted back.

He took a metal bar and smashed her across the teeth. Blood dripped to the floor. I had to turn away.

"I think we better get out of here," I said.

"Me too," Baas said.

We walked outside and down the gravel street. I was trying to get the image out of my head. In front of us, there were two men fighting with long knives. We stepped way around them and stopped by a light pole. There was a man standing there. I looked at Baas and then back to the man.

"Do you know where we can find an electronic scientist around here?" I asked.

"Oh! I did not see you there. What was that? An electronic scientist? I can't remember. Yes. Ah, hmm, there is old Suzue on Suzue Island," the man with bloodshot eyes said.

"Where is that?" I asked.

"You take a Windrider and go across the sea about three hundred kilometers. Oh! Yes, the Windrider. It takes air through its tur— Oh, you don't want to hear that. It's an anti-gravitation transport. It rides on the wind, on the air above the water, if ya know what I'm talkin'."

"Where can we get one?" Baas asked.

"Over there, across the street," the man said, pointing across the dusty, gravel street.

"Thanks," I said.

There was a building with Windriders in its lot. Beyond the building, a very large sea could be seen. Baas, KEN-102, and I walked over to the building and went inside. Baas asked how much it was to rent a Windrider. The man behind the counter told us it would cost five credits for one day. Baas pulled five credits out of the pocket in his silk jumpsuit and gave it to the man. The man gave him the electronic key for the Windrider.

Outside, I asked, "Where did you get those credits?"

"Those are the credits we had left from Sylikyt at the ship lot back in Astossky."

"Oh."

"I'm gonna lock up *Zoota.* I'll be back in a minute," Baas said.

He left. KEN-102 and I got into the Windrider and waited for Baas to return. When he returned, he got into the Windrider and started it up.

"Hang on to your seat, Roedie! Let's see what this thing's got!" Baas shouted.

He turned on the kilometer graph. It would read our distance. We flew from the lot and headed for the water at the beach's edge.

Suzue Island, here we come, I thought.

There was a man standing on a sand beach, gazing at the sea. A small castle was located behind him. He was watching a robot walk on the beach beside him. He looked out beyond the beach at the waves and the sea and saw a small dot above the water. It was growing larger by the minute.

After traveling about 285 kilometers, Baas and I saw an island ahead. It had a castle on it.

"Look. There it is!" I said.

"We've got about fifteen kilometers to go yet," Baas said, looking at the kilometer display.

Fifteen kilometers later, we stopped the Windrider at the beach of Suzue Island and turned it off. When Baas turned it off, the anti-gravitation and thrusters died out and the Windrider slowly dropped to the sandy beach. Baas, KEN-102, and I stepped out.

"Who in these seas are you?" a man on the beach asked.

"My name is Baas and this is my brother Roedie and our robot KEN-102," Baas said.

"My name is Suzue. Can I…do something for you?"

"Are you an electronic scientist?" I asked.

"Yes, I am," Suzue said.

"Did you know our father, Olossky Cantin?" I asked.

Suzue's jaw dropped and he just stared at them for a moment. He turned to KEN-102.

"Are you okay?" Baas asked.

"Ah, yes. Let's go inside," Suzue said as he turned around and headed for the castle.

We went through a door into the castle. The robot that was on the beach with Suzue followed us inside. On the inside, there was a small room with two doorways leading from it, one to the right and one straight. Suzue opened the one that went straight ahead of us and we went inside. After walking through a small corridor, we entered a very large room. On one side of the room, there was an upper level. It had a railing on the edge of it. There was a door toward the end of the railing. Exotic furniture sat in the upper level. A few pieces of exotic furniture also sat in the lower level. In front of us, there was another doorway.

"I'll give you a tour through the castle," Suzue said.

He led us up some stairs to the higher level floor. We went past the exotic furniture and through the door next to the railing. On the other side of the door, there was an office. Another door was located on the right side of the office.

"This is my office," he said. "My quarters are beyond. But this office is where I spend a lot of my time working."

We went back down the stairs after seeing his latest project on the computer.

"Come on, Mot!" Suzue shouted to his robot who was still in the office.

After we waited for the robot to come down the stairs, we went through the door that was along the far wall of the large room. On the other side, there was a corridor. Suzue led us through a door in that corridor. It was dark in the room until Suzue turned on an illuminator. There were shelves of metal junk along the gray stone walls.

"Spare parts," Suzue said. Then he looked at Mot.

We went to another door off from the corridor and Suzue said, "That is the basement where I fix robots."

He said that he would show it to us later. He led us to the last door in the corridor. On the other side, there was another corridor. We followed along the corridor to where it ended at a wall. A door was on the right. There was a computer room on the other side. Suzue told us that he loved computers and needed them in some of his experiments. There was another electronic door that he led us through. This time, it was a large library with many books in it.

"Hey, Baas, I'll show you a neat book on galaxies," Suzue said.

I thought that if Mot was walking into book cases and Suzue was showing Baas and KEN-102 galaxy books, I would slip out of the library for a look at what I saw in Suzue's office.

I went back through the maze of corridors to his office. Again, I saw what I had seen before, a handle on a small book case. I pulled the handle and the book case slid aside. There was a room on the other side of the book case. I entered into the small room beyond and shut the book case door behind me. There was a metal ladder on the other side. The ladder led both up and down. I decided to go up. The metal ladder led to another small room with a lever on the wall. I pulled the lever and a door opened up into a kitchen beyond. I had a quick look and went back down the ladder. Instead of stepping off the ladder where I got onto it, I worked my way down further. The ladder ended in a very small area. There were brick walls around all sides but one. That wall had a door. I opened the door and I saw the outside of the castle. I did not see the beach. It must have been on a different part of the island. In a corner next to the door sat an old pair of BlueMar Government Commander boots with the logo embedded in the leather.

I went back to the library and Suzue was still showing Baas and KEN-102 the books. Mot was still walking into the book cases.

What a strange robot, I thought.

I saw things differently now. Suzue must have been a BlueMar Government Commander at one time and decided to leave and take sanctuary on this island. He must dislike the BlueMar Government.

"Well, that's the last one on galaxies," Suzue said, putting the books back into the book case.

"That one galaxy was shaped neat. What was it called?" Baas asked.

"It's the Regulominuss Galaxy," Suzue said.

"Have we ever been to the Regulominuss Galaxy?" Baas asked.

"No. But the way the government is working at it, we should be there in the next decade," Suzue said.

"That would be exciting to explore another galaxy," I said.

They turned around. "Oh, I forgot you were with us. We're getting so interested in these galaxies," Suzue said. "We are…They are just starting to explore outside the BlueMar Galaxy."

"Are you going to show us the rest of the castle?" I asked.

"Yes. Right away," Suzue said.

He led us through a second door in the library and we entered into a long corridor. The corridor turned on a thirty degree angle twice and ended at a door on the right. We went through the door and into another room decorated with more exotic furniture. A stairway was located to the right. Suzue led us up the stairway and into a kitchen. It was the same kitchen that I had seen from the ladder.

"Do you want something to drink?" Suzue asked. "After all, it is hot out."

"I'll have some Sevela, if you have any," Baas said.

"Yes, Sevela sounds good right now," I said.

"Yes, I have some," Suzue said, getting the Sevela. He handed them the beverages. "Have you guys seen Mot?"

"Not me," Baas said, opening the Sevela.

"I haven't," I said, drinking my bottle of Sevela.

"He is in the library…walking in circles," KEN-102 said.

"That robot! I'm gonna have to fix his circuitry," Suzue said.

After we drank the Sevela, we were led to a stairway next to the kitchen. At the top of the stairway, a door opened to reveal the castle roof. We stood at the tallest point of the castle, overlooking the beach below. Suzue gestured for us to sit in some chairs on the roof patio.

"This is the life," Suzue said, gazing out into the sea.

We relaxed for a few minutes and finished our Sevela.

"So, about our dad…" I said.

"Yes. Follow me," Suzue said, getting up from his chair.

We went back down the two flights of stairs and to the room that led to the basement. Mot found us and followed us down the stairs.

In the basement, Suzue turned on the illuminators to reveal a collection of BlueMar Government Commander paraphernalia.

"I was once a BlueMar Government Commander as well as an electronic scientist. I did not like the direction that we were heading, so I left. That is something they don't take lightly. I've managed to keep below their radar, but if you guys found me, then perhaps I'm not hidden well enough." He smiled. "Yes, I knew Olossky. He was a fine electronic scientist. We outsourced his services through the company that he worked for because I was so busy. I needed the extra help. Your father and I had some good conversations. Unfortunately, he learned some classified information and freaked out. He never returned to the job."

Baas and I looked at each other.

"We had no idea that he worked with the BlueMar Government," I said.

"You," Suzue said, pointing at KEN-102, "were assigned to Olossky. Didn't you belong to Commander Rigid'n Morrwhell?"

"Yes, I did…I left with Olossky. He didn't want me following him, but I insisted," KEN-102 said. "I remember you as well. That's why we're here. There is something you said once that led me to believe you would be here. I did not like my old master and something triggered in me that I should go with Olossky, so I did." He looked at Baas and Roedie. "I didn't have a chance to explain everything to you guys."

"Odd. I've seen this phenomenon before. May I check his computer card?" Suzue asked.

"Yes," I said.

Suzue pulled the computer card from KEN-102's back and looked at it.

"I can't get the information from this," Suzue said.

"Why?" Baas asked.

"Because the computer card that he has is the new Bonvoxx computer card," Suzue said. "I don't have the equipment for it. Well, anyway, I've seen this phenomenon before where the artificial intelligence of a robot takes over and they become more emotional and cognitive. Very interesting," he said, putting the computer card back into its slot.

"So, they sent some agents after our dad and took him away. We were hoping that you may know where he might be."

"I'm sorry. I don't. With the number of prisons and penal colonies the BlueMar Government has around the galaxy, he could virtually be anywhere. I wish I could help more," he said.

"Well, thanks anyway," Baas said.

We headed back upstairs and out of the castle.

"Before you go, I'm going to give you something," Suzue said.

"Mot?" Baas asked.

"No. I'll fix him."

Baas laughed.

"I'll be right back," Suzue said, running into the castle.

We waited. He came back out with a case of both red and blue types of Sevela.

"Here you go. Good luck on tracking down your father," Suzue said.

We thanked him and said our goodbyes.

On the way across the sea back to the city of Protos, I told Baas where I went while they were in the library. I told him about the boots I saw.

Upon arrival, we returned the Windrider and walked back to the *Zoota 2000*. I wasn't quite sure if it was a wasted trip or not. We lifted from the surface of Proteron.

BlueMar Empire Update:

On the planet Andron, Quarrel Duelco sat on his throne. His aide, Con, sat next to him. He felt protected. Not only did his aide and guards protect him, but he had a whole galaxy full of his people to protect him. He smiled.

CHAPTER SEVEN
THE REPTILES OF QUATON

From *The Adventures of Baas and Roedie—*

BAAS:

"Baas, look!" Roedie said. "The ship's burning up! Cut the engines!"

"Shit! What's wrong with it?" I shouted as I turned them off.

"I don't <u>know!</u>" Roedie said.

"Well, can you fix it?"

"I don't know. It looks like it's the engine. It could be the ion-drive system failing. It could be a cathode or maybe even the magnets in the system," Roedie said.

"What's gonna happen?" I asked.

"We won't be able to fly," Roedie said. "We'll just drift."

I looked around the small ship and then started to say something, but I stopped when I caught a view out of the corner of my eye. It was a planet!

"Look out the window!" I shouted.

"Oh, shit!"

"What?"

"We'll be pulled down by the gravitational force of the planet. The anti-gravitation isn't working because of the engine problem."

"Can you fix it before we land?" I asked.

"*Land?* We're not gonna land. We're gonna crash!" Roedie shouted.

"Ah, how long do we have?" I asked.

"Hang on. I'll check the computer," Roedie said, sprinting over to the control panel.

Roedie sat down in the seat in front of the computer and the screen automatically lit up.

"Zoota, give me all the information that you have on this planet," Roedie said.

"It is called Quaton. The BlueMar Government set up a lab on the planet fifty years ago. They left after they studied the planet for five years. There are large reptiles in the southern hemisphere of the planet. The northern hemisphere has a few ground volcanoes and a lot of water vapor. It has forests and swamps scattered across its surface. It is unknown why the reptiles don't live in the northern hemisphere. Humans can survive on the planet only in the northern hemisphere, unless they want to be a reptilian meal. The time we have until impact is two point seven five minutes."

"Thanks for warning us," Roedie said. He got out of the chair and said, "Let's take cover in the back of the ship."

"Okay. Come on KEN-102," I said. The robot walked with us to the back of the ship.

"Zoota, count down till impact," Roedie instructed the computer.

"One minute and forty seconds," Zoota said.

"I hope this doesn't hurt," Roedie said.

"So do I," I said.

We clutched our hands on anything we could hold onto in the back of the ship. Fear ran through all of us.

"Five...Four...Three...Two...One...Impact," Zoota said.

The ship plunged into the trees of Quaton.

A long pause followed. There was a faint electronic chirp.

"KEN-102? ...Baas?" Roedie looked around the darkness of the ship and rested his head against something metal.

No movement followed.

The morning light of the planet Quaton brightened the inside of the *Zoota 2000*. Roedie picked himself up from the floor. Limping, he walked over to me and looked at me. He started to pick me up and was startled by an electronic chirp.

"Yes. I can fix my planet, Olossky. I don't know if the star is a star. What? I can fix my planet, Olossky. I don't know if the star is a star. What? I don't know if the planet is a mist, mist, mist—"

"KEN-102, hey!" Roedie shouted, pushing the robot.

"Oh, Roedie, what happened to me?" KEN-102 asked, looking up from the floor.

"Are you all right, KEN-102?"

"I seem to have cracked a board of Bonvoxx circuits," the robot said. "Roedie, I—Olossky, are you okay? What? Quaton? Olossky! Electron survey is the—be on—Astossky. What? Oh, Olossky, how are you doing?"

"KEN-102, talk to me, man," Roedie said.

"What's going on?" I asked, lying on the floor.

"Baas!" Roedie shouted as he turned toward me.

"What happened?" I asked.

"We crashed," Roedie said.

"Where at?" I asked.

"Somewhere in the northern hemisphere, I hope," Roedie said.

"What's wrong with KEN-102?" I asked.

"I think his Bonvoxx memory integrated circuit board is damaged. I'm not sure if I can repair it," Roedie said. "Are you all right?" he asked me.

Slowly, I moved each limb and answered, "I think so."

Roedie helped me to my feet. He then opened a panel on KEN-102 and looked inside. He adjusted one of the memory cards and closed the panel.

"That was an easy fix. I had to reseat one of the cards back into its slot. How's that, KEN-102?"

"Thank you. I feel much better now," the robot said.

"Good. Let's go outside and see where we landed and assess the damage," Roedie said.

I opened the side door and stepped out. Roedie and KEN-102 followed behind me. Outside, there was a wide path through the forest and swamp that was cleared from the ship crashing. On either side of us, the forest and swamp looked dark and gloomy. Misty fog covered the leafy ground.

"KEN-102, are we in the northern hemisphere?" Roedie asked.

"Yes. If my surveillance sensors are correct, we should be," KEN-102 said.

"Good," Roedie said.

"Now what?" I asked.

"Let's look around for some— Look! A volcano!" Roedie shouted.

"Wow!" I said.

"It's just a small one, almost flat on the ground," Roedie said.

"There must be quite a few of those around," I said.

"Well, I'm going to see what's wrong with the *Zoota 2000*. I'll be back in a minute," Roedie said.

He went to check the ship for damage from the crash and to see if he could figure out what went wrong with the engine. I had a look around the surrounding area near the ship. Soon, he found me and told me he repaired the drive. The magnets in the ion-drive system had become mis-aligned. Apparently, one of the trees that we had struck cut a power link that runs the computer, lights, and other things on the ship.

"It will be a little bit before I can repair the power link," Roedie said. "KEN-102, I need your help with this."

"I can give you a hand," KEN-102 said.

"We should be able to bypass the circuit," Roedie said.

"Yes, we should," KEN-102 replied.

KEN-102 disassembled the ship's metal panels. While Roedie started preparing the wiring on the dead side of the circuit, KEN-102 disabled the power to the live side. When Roedie was finished repairing the terminals, KEN-102 reconnected the power link and enabled the power. He then replaced the ship's panels.

After Roedie and KEN-102 repaired the ship, we were getting ready to leave. Suddenly, we felt very strong vibrations and heard loud thumps on the ground. We all looked through the tall trees and saw a gargantuan reptile coming toward us, breaking trees in its wake.

"Let's run into the swamp and then find a place to hide. We need to lure it away from the ship," Roedie said.

We ran into the dark swamp. There was just enough light to see where we were going. Not knowing how deep it was, we walked on logs with black water on either side. We had to cross clumps of grass and hold onto branches that almost broke in our hands. After going through kilometers of swamp, we came to a ridge. I didn't know how KEN-102 kept up with us through the swamp, but nevertheless he did. On the ridge, we saw several deer run by. The ridge led out of the swamp and up an ascending hill. White pine trees surrounded the immediate area. We saw birds and other animals on the way up the hill. We stopped at a pine grove. Large stones were fixed in several areas among the pine trees. We rested on one of the large stones.

"I was wrong. Now we're in the northern hemisphere. The swamp that we came through is the southern hemisphere. We just passed through the equator," KEN-102 said.

"That means the reptiles can't come on this side of the swamp," Roedie said.

"The reptiles only dominate the southern hemisphere," I said.

"Very strange... I wonder if the reptile that was chasing us did anything to our ship," Roedie said.

"Probably not since it was under a tree," I said.

"They *eat* trees, Baas," Roedie said. "And if it *did* do something to the *Zoota 2000*, we're stuck here for good."

"Well, I don't think it did anything to the ship," I said.

"Well, we have to get to the *Zoota 2000* to find out," Roedie said.

"I like this side of the world better," KEN-102 said.

"I say we go back and get off this hole," I said.

"Well, KEN-102, you're welcome to stay, but we are leaving," Roedie said.

"Okay, let's go," I said.

The robot did not hesitate to follow.

We went down the slopes and into the swamp. We were anxious on the long hike back, but at least we were not running. Upon exiting the swamp, we saw large foot prints on the misty ground. There was no sign of the reptile and the ship was undamaged.

"Good thing you fixed the ship before that thing chased us," I said.

"Yeah. Let's get out of here before it *is* too late," Roedie said.

We got into the ship and started up the engine. Everything seemed to be working fine. We lifted off just in time; a large reptile that was unseen behind the other trees appeared. It knocked down a large tree that landed in the very spot we had been sitting.

Once we were in space above Quaton, we found the engines were working as expected. And we were off to another place. Where? I did not know.

CHAPTER EIGHT
THE CHASE

From *The Adventures of Baas and Roedie—*

ROEDIE:

After lifting from the surface of Quaton, we flew into space and everything was normal. However, we needed to search for a place to land in order to do some diagnostics, which required the engines to be off. In the nearby Fem Glucto Star System, we found a large cavernous rock called Tarlyonn Asteroid. *Zoota 2000* settled next to a creepy area on the asteroid known as The Eerie Caverns of the Damned. It didn't take long, but when the results came back normal, we got out of there quickly.

We then headed for ESSF-2. It was an Energized Star System Field. At each ESSF, there were five different star systems that one could go to with the right sequence on the ship's control panel. We went through the second ESSF and into a star system where cosmic dust brightened the view of space.

We were in the Thisis Star System. A planet called Zalho's World was on the other side of ESSF-2. It was a luxury planet that seemed to always be in the news for its crime. Our heading was beyond Zalho's World to a planet called Vegaluss, a supposedly unpopulated planet. We thought that perhaps a remote planet such as Vegaluss may have been a place where our father could have been held captive in some remote facility. We were traveling through the Thisis System for some time when suddenly I heard laser fire hit the ship.

"What the hell's goin' on?" Baas yelled.

"I don't know," I returned.

"And now you meet Cru Montt!" a voice said over the com.

"What?" Baas shouted.

"I've heard of Cru Montt. It's a space gang," I told Baas.

"There must be fifty ships out there!" Baas said.

"I'll put the ship on lightspeed-plus," I said.

"Go for it," Baas said.

I put the *Zoota 2000* on lightspeed-plus and we were just a streak of light. Lightspeed-plus enabled the ship to travel slightly faster than the speed of light. We ended up on the other side of the star system when we came out of lightspeed-plus.

"That gang kills people for the hell of it," Baas said.

"Think you could get away from Cru Montt?" a voice asked over the com.

"Oh, shit!" I shouted.

I put the *Zoota 2000* on lightspeed-plus again, but they managed to follow us. They chased us to a planet called Xevoui. We landed *Zoota 2000* and ran toward an energy plant nearby. We entered a corridor. There were illuminators fixed along the walls.

"Where are we?" Baas asked.

"In an energy plant," KEN-102 answered.

"Run," I said, "Cru Montt's behind us."

We ran to a speed-lift and stepped in, but the door slammed shut before KEN-102 could join us. The speed-lift went down to another level and the doors opened. Baas and I stepped out onto a titanium catwalk.

A woman came up to us. She had a work uniform and a metal hard hat on. She stared at Baas and I for a moment.

"What are you two doing on level four? This is a restricted area," she said.

"Run!" Baas yelled.

We entered another speed-lift. It sped down to a lower level at an extremely fast speed that left me feeling nauseated. The doors opened to reveal a multi-level excavating system. People were working on the bottom floor, mining some type of resource. The lower level of the energy plant consisted mostly of rock. The caves reminded me of The Eerie Caverns of the Damned. We ran toward an illuminated corridor on our left. The corridor led in three different directions. We looked at each other.

"What about KEN-102?" Baas asked.

"I just hope they didn't catch him," I said.

An alarm started pulsing in the corridors.

"It must have been that lady alerting security," I said.

We ran.

Cru Montt was chasing KEN-102 through the corridor. He was ahead of them by some distance. He ran around a corner and abruptly dropped down a shaft. He landed quite loudly in a small room, which had pipes and wires running along the ceiling. He stood up and headed toward the only door in the room. Beyond, he noticed a crystal art piece in the center of the room. It was a larger room than the one he had come from. There were two other doors in the large room. He went through the door on the right. It was quite dark inside, but KEN-102 kept on going, searching for Baas and I. After exploring through a maze of rooms, the robot became discouraged and sat on a ledge. He started tapping his metal hands on the ledge since there was no use going on. He hoped that Baas and I would hear him tapping.

Baas and I found a closet full of work uniforms. We each slipped into a uniform so we would be less obvious.

"Look! There's a door inside the closet," Baas said.

"Let's check it out," I said.

We went through the door that was at the other end of the long walk-in closet. It opened to reveal a large room on the other side. A crystal art piece stood in the center of it.

"I wonder what that's for," Baas said.

"Let's go through the door across the room," I said.

It opened to a room with pipes and wires that ran along the ceiling. The room had no other exit except a shaft in the ceiling.

"There was another door off from the other room. Let's check that one," I said.

We went back to the room with the crystal art piece in the center. Baas stopped. He heard something.

"Listen. I hear tapping," he said.

Curious, we went through the door and into a dark room. Where was the tapping coming from? We followed the sound through a series of rooms and found KEN-102 sitting on a ledge.

"KEN-102, what's going on?" I asked.

"Oh, it's nice to see you two. I fell down a shaft and found this place. I was hoping you two would hear the tapping," he said.

"I wonder where Cru Montt is now," Baas said.

"We have to find our way back up to the *Zoota 2000*," I said.

After a seemingly endless maze through the energy plant, we found our way back up to the ground level. We only ran into one worker, who did not question us. I'm sure the uniforms helped. In addition, they were looking for two people, not anyone with a robot, especially a labor robot. Eventually, we found our way out to the *Zoota 2000*. Cru Montt had left. They were most likely driven off by the energy plant's alarms.

"Let's get out of here before they come back," I said.

We got inside the *Zoota 2000* and took off. After finding out there was no chance for life or a prison facility on the hot planet of Vegaluss, we went back through ESSF-2 and out of the Thisis System. Our father could not have been held captive there.

BlueMar Empire Update:

On the planet Andron, Quarrel Duelco was expecting a man from the Rednii Alliance named Acatine. He was an expert at tracking families. They planned to discuss the search for Baas and Roedie. While he waited, he checked the status of the work being done at the newly discovered wormhole that would bring the BlueMar Empire to the Regulominuss Galaxy. So much more needed to be done with that discovery, but they were spread too thin throughout the BlueMar Galaxy and Quarrel could not spare the necessary resources that he would have liked to.

There was a sound at the door and Acatine entered the throne room.

CHAPTER NINE
THE SWAMPS OF TUSKA

From *The Adventures of Baas and Roedie—*

BAAS:

We were flying in space so long that I seemed to see aberrations out the observation window. I was flying the ship toward a nearby planet.

"Zoota, switch the ship to automatic," I said.

"Right away, sir," the computer said.

After the ship had been switched to automatic, everything was once again quiet. The faint roar of the ship's engines was the only sound heard.

"What's the name of this star system?" I asked.

"It is called the Tuska Thaxe Star System," Zoota said.

"Can we survive on the planet?" I asked.

"If you couldn't, I would have informed you by now," Zoota said.

"Right. Thanks."

"Are the swamp creatures that live on this planet dangerous?" Roedie asked.

"No, but they do carry staves with them for self protection," Zoota said.

"Do they speak our language, Zoota?" I asked.

"Most of them do, but they also have a language of their own. Their language is called Tuskus, as is their species," Zoota said.

The computer suddenly died and the screen went blank.

"What in the..." I started.

"I know what the problem is," Roedie said. "It's the good thing I know about electronics."

"What is it?" I asked.

"It's the key-fuse that operates the computer," Roedie said.

"Can you fix it?" I asked.

"I can, if the parts I need are in my kit," Roedie said.

"What kind of parts?" I asked.

"Electronic components," Roedie said. "I'm gonna have to look at the key-fuse and a schematic first so I can get the specs for the components."

He opened the computer and looked at the complex circuitry inside. He pulled the key-fuse from one of the boards.

"Every component inside the key-fuse is burned out. I'll check and see if I have all the components in my kit," Roedie said.

Looking at the key-fuse, he then picked up a schematic from a pocket at the side of the computer. He studied the schematic.

"Good. I found the key-fuse on the schematic," he said.

He brought the schematic over to his kit in the back of the ship.

"Yeah, I have them all," he said after checking.

He showed me the schematic. I did not say a word! It was just a lot of complex lines to me. After repairing the key-fuse, he put it into the computer and it lit up like a star.

"All right! It's workin'," I said.

"Are you there, Zoota?" Roedie asked.

"Yes, I am," the computer said.

"Good," Roedie said.

"We will be in Tuska's gravitational force in a few minutes," Zoota said.

"Do you think dad could be on that planet, Baas?" Roedie asked.

"I don't know, but that's why we're here," I said. "From what I read earlier, there is an old penal colony here."

"Are we ready to land?" Roedie asked.

"Shift the stabilizers and head down to an adequate landing area, Zoota," I said.

The *Zoota 2000* landed in a clearing on Tuska. Swamp surrounded the clearing with mossy logs and tree stumps scattered throughout. Vines dangled from tall trees and disappeared into the mist that covered the lurking waters. It was very eerie.

Roedie and I stepped outside and looked around. It was quiet. KEN-102 followed us.

"The whole planet can't be swamp," Roedie said.

"It is, except for one mountain," KEN-102 said.

"I'll head into the swamp a little ways to see if I can find any Tuskus," Roedie said.

He started toward the mossy logs and black waters. Wet vines dangled in his path. He moved them aside as he went onward. A few minutes later, I could barely see him in the dark swamp. After a short time, he turned around and came back out.

"The only thing I see is green, wet moss and black water," Roedie said.

"The Tuskus have to be somewhere. Maybe we landed on the wrong part of the planet," I said.

"They live all over the planet, not just in one area," KEN-102 said.

"Well, we'll just wait," Roedie said.

Behind us, two Tuskus jumped out from the swamp. Horns were on their heads. They looked at each other and then at us.

"Do you speak BlueMar?" I asked.

"BlueMar? What is BlueMar?" one of the Tuskus asked.

"It's the language you're speaking now," Roedie said.

"Oh, I see. What brings you here?" the Tuskus asked.

"We're lookin' for a government outpost. Do you know if there are any facilities on this planet?" Roedie asked.

"Years ago, but not now, not on Tuska-Tew."

"Tuska what?" I asked.

"Tuska-Tew. That is the name of our planet," the other Tuskus said.

"I thought it was just called Tuska," I said.

"That is what outsiders call it," the Tuskus said.

"Oh," I said.

"I knew dad wasn't here," Roedie said.

"Well, we'll just have to search on other planets like we have been doing," I said.

"Yeah, we better be on our way," Roedie said.

"Well, we're sorry that you couldn't find what you're looking for," the Tuskus said.

"Thank you. Bye," Roedie said.

As the two Tuskus walked back into the swamp, another Tuskus flew by on a Swamp Phantom. It had two wing-like engines on each side of its body. Two laser guns were mounted in the front of it. A large pointed wing was at the back of the body. The Tuskus on the Swamp Phantom had a helmet on and a metal staff was hooked on his back. The Swamp Phantom swerved back and forth between the trees. Soon, it disappeared from view.

We got back into the *Zoota 2000* and flew from Tuska.

"What a strange place," Roedie said.

"I guess," I said.

"Not just the place, the creatures too," KEN-102 said.

"They must have some technology. There were lasers on that anti-gravitational transport," Roedie said.

"They probably don't have that much technology," I said.

"What's the next planet that we had in mind, Kenneth?" Roedie asked, looking at the navigation panel.

"*Kenneth?* How extraordinary. But I do prefer KEN-102. And the next planet that we had in mind is called StonRamm," KEN-102 said.

CHAPTER TEN
THE DESERT WASTELAND

From *The Adventures of Baas and Roedie—*

ROEDIE:

After passing the Lost Moon of Lazohsha, we saw StonRamm. It was a desert planet.

"Zoota, let's head down to the planet," Baas said.

The *Zoota 2000* began entering the atmosphere of StonRamm. Like many planets we've visited, StonRamm had an exosphere, thermosphere, mesosphere, stratosphere, and troposphere. As the ship flew through the stratosphere, rust colored clouds swiftly parted. We landed in a sand field. Stepping out of the ship, we walked toward the ruins left from some inhabitants.

"How horrifying. These people's lives were totally destroyed," I said.

"Terrifying, isn't it?" Baas said.

The planet was all rock, sand, and stone. The temperature was comfortable. The sun could barely be seen through the rust colored clouds. The place was very quiet. When we reached the ruins, we looked around the rubble. There were ancient symbols on the stone. A few dead, yellow grass plants were scattered about stone outcrops. There did not seem to be any life on the planet. *Wait!* There was some BlueMar language written on a far wall. It read: *"Our people are dying from the Tabaannaann Plague."* Beside the wall of writing, there was a stairway that led beneath the ruins. We slowly descended the stairs. They led to a room that was made of stone.

"That's what mom died of…" I said.

"I know. I try not to think about it. Wow! Look. There are baby Fem Tatons down here. Aren't they cute?" Baas said.

"Yeah," I said.

The Fem Tatons were furry creatures with blue eyes and a variety of coat patterns. They had short tails and pointed ears. They looked like little wolves.

"Let's get out of here before their mother comes back," Baas said.

I did not bother to say anything back to Baas. I just stared at the baby Fem Tatons. They were so cute.

"I want one of those baby Fem Tatons," I said.

"Are you crazy? We wouldn't make it out of here alive, if you took one of them. And we better get out of here *now,* before their mother *does* come back," Baas said.

"Yeah, I guess so," I said.

We went back up the stairs and out into the ruins. Baas and I were walking toward the *Zoota 2000* when we saw KEN-102 come around from the side of the ship.

"You two better hurry. There is a herd of Fem Tatons coming this way," KEN-102 said.

We ran into the ship and closed the door.

"The species of people that died of the Tabaannaann Plague were called Secors," KEN-102 said.

"It seems like every planet that supposedly has the potential of a prison or facility that may be holding dad ends up with no government outpost," I said.

"We just gotta keep on tryin'," Baas said.

"Maybe this isn't the best way to find him…" I said.

We left StonRamm, on our way to yet another planet. I wondered what we would find next. Would it be more swamp, more desert? Would we find our dad? I *certainly* did find out!

BlueMar Empire Update:

"Bring me the highest commander in rank, Con. I have a mission for him," Quarrel Duelco said.

"Right away, sir," Con said.

Later that evening, Con brought a commander into the throne room.

"What is your name?" Quarrel Duelco asked.

"Rokk Landcorr, sir," the commander said.

"Ah!   ...The famous Landcorr family...famous for war and leadership."

"Yes, sir."

"I will have a mission for you in the future, the Mission to Claderane."

"Mission, sir?" The commander inquired in wonderment.

"Yes. We will talk about it later. Until then," Quarrel Duelco said, pointing to Con, "escort Rokk Landcorr to his post."

"Yes, sir," Con said.

Con led him from the throne room.

"You have something up your sleeve, don't you?" Balerox asked as he stood next to the throne.

Quarrel turned to face the robot. "Don't you have work to do, Balerox?" he exclaimed.

"Yes, sir."

"Then do it, you piece of shit," Quarrel Duelco said.

Now that I know where the resistance is, I'm going to crush them in their wake. I'll let them run a little further on their chain, and then I'm going to choke them with it! Quarrel Duelco thought.

CHAPTER ELEVEN
THE ESSENCE OF TEREENA

From *The Adventures of Baas and Roedie—*

BAAS:

Siitap was our next destination. It was located in the Velkonn Star System. The name of Siitap's star was Velkonn Delta Five. It was a paradise planet with beautiful green-leaved trees and a carpet of grass. Forests beautifully decorated the planet. Sky blue lakes accented the green forests in many locations, some with lush green islands and gray rocks protruding from the water. Siitap's single satellite, SiiLat, reflected the star's light in the sky blue lakes.

"Between KEN-102's knowledge, Zoota's database, and our assumptions, we sure aren't doing too good at finding dad..." Roedie said.

The *Zoota 2000* slowly landed in a clearing in the forest. The sun was shining. Roedie, KEN-102, and I stepped out of the *Zoota 2000* and onto a carpet of grass that covered the clearing.

"This is so beautiful," KEN-102 said.

"Let's set up the tent over there," I said, pointing to some trees that nearly surrounded a thick green carpet of grass. "It will be nice to get out of the ship for a change."

A clear stream of water was flowing next to the half circle of trees. The area was almost out of the line of sight from where we landed.

We brought out a tent from the camping gear that we had packed and set it up on the carpet of grass. We put in two cots, a couple of pillows and blankets, a small table, an illuminator, and a com for communicating with Zoota, if necessary. We put the cots on each side of the tent with the pillows and blankets at each end of the cots. Between the head of the cots, we placed the table. The illuminator and the com sat on the table. We made a place at the end of my cot for KEN-102 to shut down for the night.

After setting up, we talked about our search for a government outpost on this planet. It would be a long search. As day slowly faded into night, the stars began to show in the dark evening sky. Roedie turned off the illuminator and we fell to sleep.

In the misty morning, with fog and mists covering the planet's surfaced carpet of grass and trees, a human appeared by a tree next to the tent. It was a female human, approximately the same age as Roedie, seventeen years old. She was nude. She had beautiful, long, blond hair. Her face was so beautiful and elegant with her fine nose and her brown eyes. She was slim with long thighs and an ass smooth as silk. She walked toward the tent with curiosity, slowly getting closer.

Inside the tent, Roedie and I were still sleeping and KEN-102 was shut down at the foot of the cots. Roedie woke up and sat up on the edge of the cot. He saw a shadow on the outside of the tent. He slowly got up and stepped over KEN-102. He opened the door very slowly and saw the most beautiful girl that he had ever seen before…and she was nude. When he opened the door all the way and stepped outside, she just stood looking at him without running or being startled. And, oh, did he look at her! It may have been love at first sight for both of them…

"Hi," she said nervously.

"Hi," Roedie said in amazement. "Who are you?" He looked at her beautiful figure.

"I am Tereena. Who are you?" she asked.

"My name's Roedie. My brother and our robot are in the tent. Why aren't you wearing any clothes?" he asked.

"I appeared on this planet—which I call Ersent—about seventeen years ago and grew up here. I didn't think there were any reasons to wear them. There was no one else on this planet till now. I was raised by my nanny robot. She taught me to speak and basically taught me my whole education. My Nanny has really been my entire world. Sadly, she stopped working a couple years ago. I'm not sure, but I think her power supply ran out," she said.

"Appeared?" Roedie's eyes got big.

"Yes, I appeared here mysteriously," Tereena said.

"Are you sure?" Roedie asked.

"As far as I know," she said. "As I got older, I asked Nanny a lot of questions, but she didn't know the answers. She was only programmed to take care of me and educate me."

"You said there were no other people on this planet?" Roedie asked.

"No one until you," she said. "Someone probably just left me here when I was a baby with the nanny robot to care for me."

"Then my dad isn't here" Roedie said, looking down with defeat. He looked back at Tereena. "But I would like to stay and get to know you a little better."

"I would like to get to know you better too," she said with a shy smile. "And what is this about your dad?"

"We've been searching for our dad all through the galaxy, because the government took him away," Roedie said.

"That sounds dangerous," she said.

"Yeah, it is. Ah…would you like to come with us?" he asked.

"You mean, look for your dad with you? I don't know. I'll think about it while I am here with you," Tereena said.

"You're so beautiful, Tereena," Roedie said, trying not to become aroused.

"So are you, Roedie," she said.

She slowly walked toward him, her bare thighs ever so noticeable. She put her long arms around him. Slowly, she moved her lips toward his. They kissed, their tongues merging together like a surge of lightning.

I woke up and saw that Roedie was gone. I got up and slowly opened the tent door, to see my brother with a nude girl!

"Holy cosmos!" I gasped.

I turned to get KEN-102 and tell him. When KEN-102 and I looked out the door, they had already disappeared together into the forest.

"They're gone," I said.

After Tereena showed Roedie some of her favorite sites, they returned to the tent.

"Where did you go, Roedie?" I asked. "Who are you?"

"This is Tereena," Roedie said.

Roedie explained her situation to me.

"Where did you two go?" I asked.

"She showed me some cool sites," Roedie said, smiling.

We all went into the tent to talk. Of course, I couldn't help but look at her fine figure as well.

"Do you want to come with us to look for our dad?" I asked.

"Roedie asked me the same thing. I have thought about it. There is nothing for me here anymore. Nanny is gone. Yes, I will go," Tereena said, "but I have to get some of my things from where I stay in the forest. By the way, what is the real name of this planet?"

"It's called Siitap," Roedie said.

"Does the moon have a name too?" she asked.

"Yes. The satellite is called SiiLat and the star is called Velkonn Delta Five," I said.

"Oh," she said, getting up.

Roedie stood up along with her.

"We're gonna go get my things now," Tereena said.

KEN-102 and I stayed in the tent while Roedie and Tereena left for her home.

They walked along a path through the forest, which mostly consisted of large white pines with some other assorted trees. The trail curved and went by a large maple tree. Brush and leaves were along either side of the trail. Tereena stopped and picked some berries from a plant on the side of the trail. She ate some of the berries and gave some to Roedie.

"These are delicious," she said.

"Mmm… They are," he said as he ate the berries.

They continued along the trail. Ahead of them, there was a small yard and a house built from trees, branches, and leaves.

"You built this all by yourself?" Roedie asked in awe.

"Yes," she said, turning her face toward him with a sparkle in her eye.

She grabbed a vine necklace that hung from a tree branch hook. She then walked over to a log chest and opened it, pulling out a scanty pair of grass shorts.

"I made these a long time ago. Should I wear them?" she asked.

"No!" Roedie said. "I mean, I have a silk jumpsuit in the ship that you can wear."

"Okay," she said. She turned her attention elsewhere. "Goodbye, Nanny…" She looked at the motionless nanny robot that was positioned against a wall of logs.

When they arrived back at the camp, KEN-102 and I had the tent and other stuff in the *Zoota 2000*. Tereena turned away from us and looked back into the forest for a long time.

"KEN-102 and I will leave you two lovers alone and go talk to Zoota," I said.

Tereena finished a heartfelt farewell to the only place she's ever called home. She and Roedie stepped aboard the *Zoota 2000*. We flew from the surface of Siitap, but maybe not for the last time…

Tereena sat in one of the passenger seats and smiled at Roedie. He found some of his clothes for her to wear and then sat with her.

CHAPTER TWELVE
THE ESCAPE OF SEPHEENA

From *The Adventures of Baas and Roedie—*

ROEDIE:

The *Zoota 2000* swiftly landed on the snow-ice planet of Zonia. We landed in one of the many evergreen forests where the snow was very deep.

Although we did not have any winter gear, we did put on some warm clothes. Grabbing our laser rifles, we stepped out of the ship and into the deep snow.

"Sorry about this diversion, guys, but as I told you, my memory circuits tell me that I've been here before. When I saw the planet name appear on the screen, I recalled the situation here. There is a dictator here named Zantorra. His queen is Quinell. Zantorra's aide is Sethonia. There are also Zonia Guards to watch out for. But most important, there is Sepheena and Alaress, two girls that would be about your age by now. They're Zantorra's slaves," KEN-102 said. "I really don't think your dad is here, but we need to help these girls."

"Where is this place?" Baas asked.

"It is in a forest like this. My sensors tell me that it is not far from here," KEN-102 said.

"Let's rescue the two girls," Baas said.

"Yeah," Tereena said.

"Okay," I said.

The snow was knee-deep, and it was very cold. Wading through the snow, we headed through the white pine forest to where Zantorra's palace was located. It seemed like it was getting deeper as we went further into the thicket. We were well into the forest when the snow was up to our hips. I looked up into the sky to discover a storm was building. When we arrived at Zantorra's palace, we approached cautiously and peered at the palace entrance through the pines. Lights ran along the palace parameter, revealing two Zonia Guards that stood next to the palace entrance.

"We can't get through there," I said.

"I know where we can get into the palace," KEN-102 said. "When I worked here, I learned of an entrance to the palace through a cave that starts over there." He pointed to a small stone ledge covered mostly with snow and ice.

KEN-102 led us to a metal door that was built into the stone ledge.

"We can go through this door to get into the palace," KEN-102 said.

We opened the heavy door and went inside to discover the cave that KEN-102 had mentioned. An eerie squeak echoed throughout the cave as we closed the door behind us. We made it through to the end of the dark passageway. Another metal door was located at the other end of the passage. After entering, we were in a room with several metal doors leading from it. We opened one door and it led to an empty storage room. We checked all of the rooms and finally found the way into the palace. It was a long corridor with old, rusted metal doors on either side of it. We opened some of the doors, but there was no sign of the girls. The rooms were all dungeons, filled with gallows and other tormenting devices to terrify victims of Zantorra. There were vices and cells filled with skeletons strung up by chains. One skeleton was on the stone floor, its skull crushed under a large sledgehammer. Hundreds of people must have been slain by Zantorra over the years. We went through the door at the end of the corridor, which led to an upward staircase. We went up the stairs to another level of the palace. At the top of the steps, we entered a room on the left. From there, a spiral staircase led upward once again. KEN-102 mentioned that the last time he was here, Sepheena and Alaress were located in that area of the palace. At the top of the stairway, there was a corridor. It had illuminators built into the walls. Electronic doors were along the sides of it. All we had to do was find Sepheena and Alaress's room. We stood in front of a door. It opened. A computer room was on the other side. All types of electronic components and printed circuit boards were setting on metal racks along the wall. We entered the room and looked around. A door was in the back of the room, hidden behind a wall of computers. We opened it and looked inside. A ladder that led down a shaft was located in the small, dark room. What was at the bottom of the shaft? A death trap waiting to kill us all? Zantorra's dungeons? We left the room and closed the door.

"Let's check some of the other rooms in the corridor," Baas said as we left the computer room.

"That's the first time we said anything to each other since we entered the palace," Tereena said.

"What's there to say? Those dungeons were sick," I said.

"Yes, they were," she agreed.

"Let's check this room," Baas said, entering a room across the corridor. It was a storage room.

Moving along, we checked the last door in that corridor. It opened to reveal an empty room. After studying the empty room, KEN-102 quickly turned to us as he recalled the palace layout.

"Their room is just down the corridor and to the left," he said.

We went around the corner to another corridor. There was a door to the left. The door automatically opened. The room was beautifully decorated. It had colorful flowers and a lot of other beautiful accents in it. It seemed like it would have been fit for Queen Quinell, but it was not the queen's room. It was Sepheena and Alaress's room. We went inside.

"Who are you?" one of the girls asked. It was Alaress.

"We came to rescue you two," Baas said.

"Oh. Aren't you the robot that used to bring us food a couple years ago?" Alaress asked.

"Yes. I was assigned here by the BlueMar Government as a favor to Zantorra. I was then reassigned on short notice to work with someone named Olossky Cantin. I soon left the government with Olossky. I went to the Kaskar Star System to the planet Kaskoon and resided outside of a small town called Kanthas. Olossky is the father of these two gentlemen, Baas and Roedie. The BlueMar Government took Olossky away because he found out some classified information about them. We are now looking for their father. On the last planet that we checked, we found Tereena here…or rather, she found us. And now we have stopped here, because I remembered you two young ladies. So, here we are to rescue you. Believe me, I would have escaped with you two before, but there was nowhere to go on this planet. And I couldn't get access to a ship," KEN-102 said.

"At least you brought us good food when you were here," Sepheena said, a smile on her face.

Sepheena had long, brown hair that was in several thin braids at her temples. She had green eyes that sparkled in the light. She wore a white suit.

"But the important thing is that you remembered us…Thank you," Alaress said.

The two girls grabbed some of their clothes and other belongings and quickly put them into a bag. Tereena looked at their clothes hanging in the closet.

"Hey, I'm wearing Roedie's clothes. Do you think I can get some girls' underwear from you?" Tereena asked with a smile.

Sepheena and Alaress looked at Tereena and then looked at each other. Alaress grabbed some panties, bras, and a couple outfits and put them into another bag for Tereena.

"Thank you," Tereena said.

"You're welcome," Alaress said.

The two girls grabbed their coats.

"Let's go," I said.

We all left the room and entered the corridor. We were spotted by two Zonia Guards who came running down the long corridor with laser rifles in their hands.

"Holy cosmos!" I shouted.

We ran around the corner and into the other corridor just before the guards fired their rifles. The blue beams of energy blasted holes in the illuminated wall. A shower of sparks filled the corridor.

"In here," Baas shouted.

We ran into the computer room and opened the door located behind the wall of computers.

"Where does this shaft go to?" Alaress asked.

"I thought you'd know," Baas said.

"I don't," Alaress replied.

Baas looked at Sepheena.

"Neither do I," Sepheena said. "We were told to never go into this area."

"Well, we'll find out," I said, starting down the ladder.

They all followed me. The shaft led to an underground cave. We went through the cave until it ended.

"A dead end?" Sepheena was disappointed.

"Not quite," I said. "Look down."

They did so. There was a hole in the cave's floor with another cave beneath.

"It's our only chance. Let's go," Tereena said.

She jumped down, her long, blond hair flying upward. We quickly followed her. The cave below was the same cave that we entered the palace in. We ran to the end of it and opened the metal door. Suddenly, a blue laser beam was fired from the other end of the cave. The intense laser beam blasted into Aaress's side. She fell to the ground, just outside the metal door, into the knee-deep snow. It was ice cold now and snow was falling rapidly. The freezing wind blew through our hair. I repeatedly fired back into the darkness of the tunnel.

"Is she all right?" Baas asked as my teeth chattered.

Sepheena had a sad look on her face as a tear dropped from her right eye and froze on her lips.

"The guards are coming up the tunnel," I said.

We picked up Alaress and ran behind a large white pine tree.

"She's dead!" I shouted over the roar of the ice cold wind.

"Oh, no. No!" Sepheena cried.

Tereena had a frightened look on her face.

"We must go," KEN-102 said.

"We have to get out of here," Baas said in a soft voice.

We left Alaress behind the white pine tree. Her black hair set out against the white snow. Flakes of snow fell onto her closed eyes, her face motionless.

Blue beams of laser fire flew directionless through the whiteout of the storm. We ran for our lives through the snow and pines, not bothering to look behind us. The storm was very bad and we could barely see the trees in front of us.

"Why don't we warm up under the boughs of a white pine tree?" Baas suggested after we had traveled some distance.

"Yeah, but only for a moment," I said. "They might be following us."

We went under the shelter of a large white pine's branches. All the branches were covered with snow and ice. The only sight of the outside was through the small opening that we entered from. When the storm died down some, the forest became visible again.

"Ready to go?" I asked.

They all agreed it was time to move on. We went back out into the snow.

"How far is it now?" I asked KEN-102.

"The ship is just over the next hill," he said.

"Good," I said.

When we finally arrived at the *Zoota 2000*, we were thankful for the warmth of the ship. We took off from Zonia as quickly as possible. Not far from the planet, a Zonia Fighter Ship appeared from out of nowhere and followed us. Bright flashes of blue energy brightened the darkness of space as it fired its weapons at us. Baas maneuvered the ship around on a 180 degree angle and cut his speed. The Zonia Fighter Ship was in front of us now. Baas fired the ship's lasers and the Zonia Fighter Ship exploded with a blinding light.

"Thanks for rescuing us," Sepheena said, "even if Alaress didn't make it." She choked back her tears.

"You're more than welcome," Baas said. "Slavery and trafficking cannot be tolerated."

Sepheena went over to Baas and kissed him with her sweet lips. She took his hand and pulled him up. "I need to talk to you. I'm— I don't even know where to start. Alaress was an amazing friend…"

"Roedie, do you want to fly this thing now?" Baas asked. "We're going to go talk."

"Sure thing," I said, moving to the pilot's seat.

Tereena joined me, sitting in the navigator's seat.

Baas and Sepheena went to the back of the ship to talk. He tried to comfort her the best he could as she told him about Zantorra's sex trafficking practices. She mentioned that even Queen Quinell was a slave before he made her his queen. The only other slave concubines at the time were Alaress and Sepheena, but they had learned of plenty more slave girls that where there before them.

KEN-102 announced our next destination. It was the Castles of Oryonite.

BlueMar Empire Update:

"What did you get from the eighth level, Con?" Quarrel Duelco asked.

"An old book that I thought you might be interested in," Con said.

"Oh?"

"It's called, *The Wicked Mission of the Marazos*. It's about a mission that took place in the time of Hellion Hex Halberd ("Satan the Second"). He was the sixth emperor of the BlueMar Empire. He was only an emperor for one year, from 229982 SA to 229983 SA. I just thought you may be interested in it," Con said.

"That's nice, but you thought wrong. Now, go get Commander Rokk Landcorr," Quarrel Duelco commanded.

"Yes, sir," Con said as he walked up the steps and through the electronic door.

When Con returned to the throne room without Rokk Landcorr, Quarrel Duelco had an angry look on his face.

"Where is he?" he shouted.

"Right here, sir," a voice said from the entrance.

It was Rokk Landcorr. He was dressed in a new type of uniform. It was an off-white, one-piece uniform with gold trim. Multiple stripes were below his left shoulder. They were the stripes of command. He wore the highest that any of the BlueMar Government Commanders could get.

"Well, well, we're looking spiffy, aren't we?" Quarrel Duelco replied.

"Thank you, sir," Rokk Landcorr said.

"You can carry out your Mission to Claderane now," Quarrel Duelco said.

"Yes, the mission we talked about in great detail yesterday afternoon? Well, I estimated it. It will take a little time to get the logistics prepared, but I will be on my way as soon as possible," Rokk Landcorr said.

"Good," Quarrel Duelco said, "I knew you would." A smile spread across his face as he expressed great confidence.

Chapter Thirteen
The Castles of Oryonite

From *The Adventures of Baas and Roedie—*

Baas:

"If that was a government outpost, there would be all kinds of ships surrounding the castles," Roedie said.

"I'm not so sure about that," I said.

"All Zoota knows about this place is that it is referred to as the Castles of Oryonite," KEN-102 said. "Oryonite is supposed to be unexplored."

"Well, somebody explored the planet. The castles don't look that old," Roedie said.

"Maybe someone built them and left for some reason," Tereena said.

"Why would they do that?" Sepheena asked.

"I don't know, but we can't just hover here forever," Roedie said.

"Well, why don't we land on the docking platform?" I asked.

"Are you crazy?" Roedie asked.

"Let's just land there. What do we have to lose?" Tereena asked.

"Our lives." Roedie smiled sarcastically.

"We'll find out what we have to lose when we get down there," I said.

"Roedie, you gonna land?" Sepheena asked.

"Yes, that's what everybody wants," Roedie said reluctantly.

He landed on the smooth surface of the docking platform. I stepped out of the ship. From out of nowhere came a squad of troops, all in their teens. They held laser rifles in their gloved hands. Their leader stepped forward. He was about the same age as I.

"You wouldn't happen to be in the BlueMar Government, would you?" I asked, my smile fading.

"Ah…no," the leader said.

"Good… Let me explain. You see, my dad was taken prisoner by the BlueMar Government and we're looking for him. If this isn't a BlueMar Government outpost, then what is it? Is there a BlueMar Government outpost on this planet?" I asked.

"There are no outposts of any kind on Oryonite…except the castles here," the leader said.

"I see," I said.

"No outposts?" a voice asked from inside the ship. Roedie stepped out.

"Can you take us to your leader?" I asked.

"We will take you to Queen Amorra," the leader of the troops said. "Perhaps she will know what you people are talking about. Would you and your crew like to talk to her about this government stuff?"

"Yes, that would be great," I said.

Hearing the conversation from within the ship, Tereena, Sepheena, and KEN-102 also stepped out onto the smooth surface of the docking platform. The squad of troops escorted us toward the castles, looking at Tereena and Sepheena all the while. We were led up a long winding stairway that was connected to one of the outside castle walls. It led high above the smooth docking platform. Half way up the castle wall, the stairway ended at a door. We went through the door and into the castle. A long corridor was before us. We were led down the corridor and through a maze of other corridors. We went up another stairway that opened up into the throne room. A woman sat on a throne to the left of the stairway. She was in her twenties. An electronic fan was blowing fresh air toward her. I felt like asking her what her life story was. I wondered how she had come to power at such a young age. But I was too intimidated to ask.

"Welcome to the Castles of Oryonite. You may be seated," she said, gesturing toward a number of seats next to the stairway.

We all sat down as the troops went back down the stairs.

"What brings you here?" she asked.

"We're looking for our dad, Olossky Cantin. The BlueMar Government took him away to one of their outposts…we think. We're trying to find it," I said.

"The BlueMar Government has many outposts. I'll tell you something. I know where there are some BlueMar Government officials located right now, but I don't know if it's an outpost where your father would be," Queen Amorra said, her black hair and brown eyes shining from the light that came through a window in the ceiling.

"Where are the officials at?" I asked.

"I'm no lover of the BlueMar Empire, but I do expect something in return," Queen Amorra said.

Roedie and Tereena looked at each other and looked around the large room.

"What do you want in return?" I asked.

"Let me think of something," she said. "How about a schematic of your robot?"

I looked at KEN-102. "Can you give us a schematic of yourself?"

"I can program it into an empty memory card or a computer, if there is a computer around here," KEN-102 said.

"I do happen to have a computer around here," she said, getting up from her throne. She walked over to us. "Follow me."

She led us down the stairway and through another maze of corridors. We ended up at a room where there was a small computer on a table.

"Do your stuff," Queen Amorra said to KEN-102.

"Your memory card would have to have a total of 984 gigabytes in it for me to program my entire circuitry into it," KEN-102 said.

"The computer has a capacity of 999 exabytes," Queen Amorra said.

"Well, I guess that won't be a problem, then," KEN-102 said.

KEN-102 walked over to the computer and plugged something from his chest panel into an information slot on the computer. The computer screen lit up with a number of different schematics. KEN-102 disconnected the cable and put the connector back into his chest panel.

"Can I built a robot with those schematics?" she asked.

"Yes, if you have someone who knows about electronics," KEN-102 said.

"I know someone."

"So, where are these BlueMar Government officials located?" I asked.

"They're on a planet called ThornZozaa, which is the twin planet of Conbokkestor. Conbokkestor has no life on it. They're both just beyond the Oryonite Star System," Queen Amorra said. "They are attending a grand opening ceremony for a new facility they built there."

"What's the name of that star system so I can program it into our computer?" Roedie asked.

"It is the ThornZozaa Star System," she said.

"Okay," Roedie said, lifting his eyebrows. She had better be right.

"Thanks," I said.

We were escorted back down to the *Zoota 2000*. Roedie started up the ship and we swiftly lifted from the smooth docking platform of the Castles of Oryonite. We were on our way to the ThornZozaa Star System.

CHAPTER FOURTEEN
THE RESCUE

THE *ZOOTA 2000* flew through the ThornZozaa Star System.

"We're almost there. We only have ten lightminutes," Roedie said, sitting in the pilot's seat.

Tereena sat in the navigator's seat next to Roedie.

"That's a long way," Baas said.

Baas sat in the back of the ship next to Sepheena, her arms draped around him.

"It's a complicated course," Roedie said.

He set the computer for a 20 degree angle to the port side, down onto the elliptic plane of the star system. The ship was traveling 299,792.458 kilometers per second.

"This standard year 230929 SA hasn't been a very good one," Baas complained.

"Yes, but we take the good with the bad," Roedie said as he looked into Tereena's eyes.

Two planets appeared through the ship's observation window. Roedie cut the ship's engines and they drifted.

"They must be ThornZozaa and Conbokkestor," Baas said, referring to the planets looming ahead.

"Zoota, which one of those planets has life on it?" Roedie asked.

"The one on the starboard side," the computer said.

"Okay," Roedie said.

Roedie ignited the ship's engines and they left that part of space far behind. They entered ThornZozaa's atmosphere. Thick gray clouds blocked the view of the planet for a brief moment.

"Zoota, what are the chances of us being detected?" Roedie asked.

"One in seven," the computer answered.

They landed in a small field.

"My sensors pick up three very large metal objects on the other side of that ridge," KEN-102 said, pointing out the window to a ridge on the right.

Everyone followed the robot's gaze.

"Zoota, what are those metal objects that KEN-102's talking about?" Roedie asked.

"They appear to be three BlueMar Government ships," Zoota said.

"Holy cosmos." Roedie's jaw dropped.

"Let's go check it out," Baas said.

"Yeah," Roedie said, turning toward Tereena, Sepheena, and KEN-102. "You guys should really stay here."

"But—" Tereena started.

"Really, you should. It could be dangerous," Roedie said. "I don't want anything to happen to you two…ever."

"Okay," Sepheena said, "but we don't want anything to happen to you two either."

"I know," Roedie said.

Baas grabbed his arm com. Roedie grabbed two laser rifles.

"We'll be back in a while," Baas said. "Don't worry about us."

Baas and Roedie walked up to the peak of the ridge. Roedie gave Baas one of the two laser rifles.

"Let's go down for a closer look," Baas said.

"Yeah," Roedie said.

They went down to the ships that were fixed between two ridges. Baas lifted his right arm with the attached com and turned it on. "Zoota, are there any life forms aboard these three ships?"

"Yes, but only a couple officials on each ship. It's not quite a skeleton crew. However, there are all kinds of people beyond the other ridge," Zoota said over the com.

"There are what?" Roedie asked.

"We're gonna check it out," Baas said into his com.

"Let's have our laser rifles ready just in case of any trouble," Roedie said.

They grabbed the laser rifles that were slung over their shoulders and walked up the next ridge. There was a government celebration at a new facility on the other side of the ridge. A lot of officials could be seen moving about the facility grounds and going to and from the entrance.

"You must go!" a voice said behind Baas and Roedie.

They quickly spun around and pointed their laser rifles toward the old man standing there.

"Don't shoot!" he said.

"Who are you?" Roedie asked.

"My name is Klat Morrel. You must go before they catch you. I was a prisoner for them, but I just broke free," he said, showing them his dangling chains.

"You did?" Roedie asked.

"Do you know an Olossky Cantin?" Baas asked.

"Yes, I do. You two must know him." Klat stared at Baas and Roedie for a long moment as if he recognized them.

"He's our father," Roedie said with a smile on his face.

"Where is he at now?" Baas asked.

"Over there…beyond the ships with the rest of the slave prisoners. They're in chains. They're chopping away at the ridgeside to make room for a landing area. I will take you to him."

I wish I could tell them more right now, but it's too soon, Klat thought.

He led them down the ridge and beyond the parked ships to where a group of men were working. One man looked up and saw them coming. It was Olossky. He threw down his pickax.

"Holy cosmic shit! Baas! Roedie!" he shouted.

They ran to him and hugged him.

"How did you two find me?"

"We bought a ship and started a quest to find you. We've searched a lot of planets," Baas said.

"KEN-102 wasn't in the house when they came for me. Where is he?" Olossky asked.

"In our ship on the other side of that ridge. He's with Tereena and Sepheena," Baas said.

"Who?" Olossky asked.

"Our girlfriends. We met them on our search for you," Baas said.

"A man named Nikk Eneb Oszon, who was an intelligence agent for the resistance on the mining asteroid of Zyvor, told me there is a resistance group on a planet called Claderane in the Claderane Star System. We have to go there and help them destroy the BlueMar Empire. During my captivity, I also found out the BlueMar Empire has a small ally called the Rednii Alliance that has their back," Olossky said.

"These ships are virtually empty. We can take them. There's barely a skeleton crew aboard each ship," Baas said.

"They are?" Olossky asked. "Get these chains off me and we'll borrow a few ships. Since we're all locked in chains, they didn't even bother leaving a guard."

Roedie used a tool to release the chains and shackles that were on Olossky. At last, he was free.

"What about us?" the other prisoners asked.

They began releasing the chains and shackles from the other slave prisoners and told them to wait there. The old man waited there as well.

Olossky, Baas, and Roedie ran over the first ridge toward the *Zoota 2000*. They opened the side door.

"Who are you?" the girls asked in unison.

"Olossky!" KEN-102 shouted in excitement.

"That's your dad?" Tereena asked Roedie.

"Yeah, we found him," he said, a smile on his face.

"Hi," Sepheena said.

"We're gonna take the big ships on the other side of that ridge," Baas said.

The girls glanced at each other with worried looks on their faces.

"What?" Sepheena asked.

"That's suicidal," Tereena said.

"No, it isn't. There are only two officers in each ship. The rest are all over another ridge having a party," Baas said.

Baas started the *Zoota 2000* and flew over the first ridge. He flew into the docking bay of the large ship called *Quasar*. They all exited the *Zoota 2000* and glanced around the docking bay.

The large ship had a wing with four small engines in it at the top and either side of the ship. The back of the ship was connected to the front of the ship by a metal neck. The other two ships looked similar to the *Quasar*.

"It's odd there are no Silver Dagger fighter ships on board. Anyway, I'll fly this ship along with KEN-102," Olossky said.

"Tereena and I will fly the one on the starboard side of this ship," Roedie said.

"Sepheena and I will fly the one on the port side of this ship," Baas said.

"They're easy to fly. I've been on the bridge of this one before when I worked for the BlueMar Empire," Olossky said.

"I hope the other two are as easy as this one," Baas said.

"When you find the bridge, let me know over the com on the panel," Olossky said.

"We'll tell ya," Baas said.

The freed prisoners also boarded the *Quasar* at a nearby entrance to the docking bay. Olossky grabbed a laser rifle from a docking bay locker.

So, where are these two officials located on this ship, Olossky thought.

Before Olossky could complete the next thought, the two officials rounded a corner and walked right into the tip of Olossky's laser rifle. They reached for their own weapons, but not fast enough. Olossky was quick to take them both down. He threw the two officers from the edge of the docking bay to the ground below. His audience of former prisoners stared at him in shock.

Baas, Roedie, Tereena, and Sepheena went back into the *Zoota 2000* and flew into the docking bay of the ship on the port side of the *Quasar,* the *Light Avenger.* Baas and Sepheena stepped out.

"Good luck," Roedie said.

"Yeah," Baas said.

Roedie then flew the *Zoota 2000* out of the *Light Avenger's* docking bay. He flew around the *Quasar* and into the docking bay of the *Galactic Explorer.*

Olossky had a group of former prisoners staring at him in the docking bay of the *Quasar.*

"Well, are you people coming to the bridge with me, or are you gonna stand there?" he asked.

They all followed Olossky and KEN-102 to the bridge of the *Quasar.* When they arrived, Olossky turned on the com.

"Sepheena and I found the bridge. Everything looks easy as the *Zoota 2000,*" Baas said over the com. "I kicked out a couple of government officials. They jumped from the docking bay edge."

"Tereena and I are on the bridge as well. Everything looks about the same as the *Zoota 2000* here too," Roedie said. "Only one of the two officials had the sense to drop his weapon. The one who is alive, jumped from the docking bay and limped away. I shot the other one who raised his weapon at me and he fell from the docking bay edge to the ground below. I never killed anyone before and…I feel beside myself."

"It would have been you or him, Roedie. I'm sorry, but we need to go. Okay, get ready to start the engines," Olossky said.

"We're ready," they said.

"Start them now," Olossky said, igniting the *Quasar's* engines.

The ships lifted from the planet with a loud, thunderous roar. They flew toward the sky. The government's celebration came to an abrupt halt as troops, guards, and commanders ran up the ridge to see their transportation disappearing within the gray clouds of the sky. The stranded government officials looked at each other with blank faces.

Chapter Fifteen
The Flight to Claderane

"Lasers in the hundreds of terawatts, stabilizers, turbo rocket engines, lightspeed-plus capability, deflector shields, reflector shields, nano-state electronic drive systems, pico-state central communication system, key-fuse power core, anti-gravitation, ion drives, liquid nitrogen cooling systems—" Baas was cut off.

"Look at these controls!" Sepheena said.

"It may be as easy to fly as the *Zoota 2000*, but it's way more complex," Baas said.

The three vast ships flew toward the Claderane Star System. Supposedly, the Claderane Resistance was there, according to Nikk Eneb Oszon.

"There's an object on my scanner," Olossky said into the com, which was set for local distances only.

"I see it, Dad," Baas said.

"Just be cool for a minute," Olossky said.

Another ship came up beside the three. It looked similar to the three ships and was just as large. Olossky looked out the bridge window and read the name of the ship as *BlueMar Empire Two*.

I wonder who is commanding that ship, Olossky thought.

"*Quasar,* do you read? This is *BlueMar Empire Two,*" an unknown voice said from the other ship.

"Roger, *BlueMar Empire Two,*" Olossky said.

"*Light Avenger,* do you read?"

"Yes, we copy you," Baas said in a deep voice. Baas waited.

"Good. *Galactic Explorer,* do you read?" the voice asked.

"Yes, sir," Roedie said, looking at Tereena with wide eyes.

"Now, listen here. We are to go to the Claderane Star System, to the planet Claderane, as assigned. However, we're not going to warn them of our attack as planned, but we are to strike with surprise. That is an order straight from Quarrel Duelco himself," the voice said.

"Roger," Roedie said.

"Roger," Olossky said.

"Roger, *BlueMar Empire Two,*" Baas said.

"Good. I take it things went well at the celebration for the new facility on ThornZozaa. I hope your updated Silver Dagger fighters were brought back in a timely fashion. This is Commander Rokk Landcorr and I will lead the fleet to the Claderane System. This is an important major assignment for me, given directly by Quarrel Duelco: *The Mission to Claderane.* I don't want anything to go wrong. If somebody makes a mistake, they're gonna die! Got it?"

The *BlueMar Empire Two* took the lead in front of the *Quasar.* As it slowly flew past, Olossky could see many Silver Dagger fighter ships in the docking bay, their silver V-shaped bodies reflecting the illuminators above them.

You just made the mistake! Olossky thought.

Olossky looked at the ship's large engines through the window, and then he looked down at the control panel. He smiled, studying the front laser controls. There were seven switches that controlled twenty-two different terawatt lasers. There was a power switch, a safety switch, a power level variable control, a power boost switch, and a trigger switch for all twenty-two lasers. The twenty-two lasers also had a master switch and a coolant switch. Olossky flicked on the master switch, turned off the safety switch, turned the power level variable control to full power, turned the power boost switch on, and turned the power switch on. The lasers energized and built up power. As they heated, Olossky enabled the coolant. On the control panel, the heat LEDs turned from green to red, the danger point. Olossky flicked the trigger switch. As the red LEDs dropped back to the green level, twenty-two lines of intense blue lasers flashed by the window. They hit in the middle of the *BlueMar Empire Two's* ion engines. The *BlueMar*

Empire Two burst into a ball of blinding light, disappearing into energy and space dust.

"Okay," Olossky said, "everything is all right. Just keep on flying."

Later, they entered the Claderane Star System.

"Okay," Olossky said, "we're gonna have to cut the ships' engines here. Cut them on my mark…Now!"

All three ships cut their engines and slowly drifted at a crawl.

"Why did you want us to stop?" Roedie asked over the com.

"Because we're in BlueMar Empire ships. The Claderane Resistance will shoot at us. But if you take your small ship—what do you call it?" Olossky asked.

"*Zoota 2000*," Baas said.

"If you take the *Zoota 2000* to Claderane and tell them about us and these ships, they won't shoot at us," Olossky said.

"I see," Roedie said. "Okay, I'll go right now."

Roedie stepped away from the com and turned to Tereena.

"I'll have to stay and run the ship," she said.

"Yeah," Roedie said. He turned back to the com. "Turn the coms on long distance range so I can hear you from Claderane. But don't talk on long distance range until I talk to you first."

"Okay," they said.

They turned the coms to long distance range.

Roedie kissed Tereena. "Bye," he said.

"Bye. Be careful," she said.

"I will," he said, leaving the bridge.

In the docking bay, he stepped aboard the *Zoota 2000*. He engaged the engines and flew out into space.

Roedie entered Claderane's atmosphere and landed on the surface below. The ship rested on a large landing pad that Zoota had recommended. A small group of people approached the *Zoota 2000*. Roedie stepped out.

"Who are you?" one of the men in the group asked.

"Hi. I'm Roedie Cantin. A man named Nikk Eneb Oszon told my dad, Olossky Cantin, there was a Claderane Resistance here on Claderane. My brother and I rescued my dad from the BlueMar Empire. We took three BlueMar Empire ships and came here. The three ships are still in space, not far from here. I came here in this ship so you wouldn't think we were the BlueMar Empire and start shooting at us. We want to help destroy the BlueMar Empire. Are you with the Claderane Resistance?" Roedie asked.

"Yes, we are. Mr. Oszon was an officer in the Claderane Resistance undercover on the Zyvor mining asteroid until the BlueMar Empire caught him. I don't know if he's dead or alive. Yeah, we have another enemy that we have to destroy too: the Rednii Alliance. They're allies with the BlueMar Empire. By the way, my name is Rikks Kyton. I am the leader of the Claderane Resistance. These are my officials," Rikks Kyton said, gesturing toward the group. "Lighrt Rhign, Saalarlic Don'ador, and Falaskk Malakite. We are familiar with your family name. If you want to tell your people in the ships to land, a com is located in this building behind me."

"Yeah, I better let them know," Roedie said.

I wonder why my family name sounds familiar to him, Roedie thought.

"Follow me, then," Rikks said, walking into a building next to the landing pad. "And welcome to Claderane City."

Roedie, along with Rikks's officials, followed Rikks into the building. The building was connected to a series of other buildings. It was part of a small city.

They came to a com. Rikks switched it to long-distance range.

"Roedie to the *Quasar,* do you read?" Roedie asked.

"Loud and clear," Olossky said. "Can we land on the planet?"

"Yeah. Follow the same course I did," Roedie said.

"Okay," Olossky said.

The three ships headed toward Claderane. Upon arriving, they landed behind the *Zoota 2000.*

"I'll have our maintenance robot look the three ships over," Rikks said. He went to a door on the right of the com. "Karrii-207, we need your help."

A robot came from the room. It was Karrii-207, the robot the Cantins had owned when Baas and Roedie were small.

Roedie looked at the robot. "Is that you?" he asked.

The robot looked at Roedie.

"You know him?" Rikks asked.

"Roedie!" he shouted in excitement.

"Yeah. He was our robot when we were younger," Roedie said.

"Well, he's yours," Rikks said.

"Oh, my… Thank you so much!" Roedie said.

As they exited the building, they noticed Olossky, Baas, Tereena,

Sepheena, KEN-102, and the former prisoners standing next to the *Zoota 2000*.

"This must be your father," Rikks said.

"Yeah," Roedie said.

"Hi," Olossky said. "We came to join the Claderane Resistance."

"Well, you're welcome to," Rikks said. He introduced himself. "There is currently a special council meeting in progress that was called on by the council members. They will be voting on when to start the destruction of the BlueMar Empire. The meeting should be over shortly. As leader of the resistance, I'm not allowed in the meeting because it may influence someone's vote. We'll either start the military campaign tomorrow or sometime in the near future."

"If we wait, it will be impossible to destroy the BlueMar Empire. Before too long, they will defeat us. As it is, we destroyed the *BlueMar Empire Two* battleship en route to Claderane. It was full of Silver Dagger fighters and headed for this planet to destroy the Claderane Resistance...to destroy us. They know where we are now," Olossky said.

"Most of my people know that. I just hope they vote for the campaign to begin tomorrow," Rikks said.

"So do I...So do I," Roedie said.

"Why wait? What is the significance of that?" Olossky asked.

"Some think it will take longer to build up our forces. But I know we don't have that kind of time. And now with these three ships, I think we're in good shape," Rikks said.

"Baas do you remember Karrii-207?"

Baas looked at the robot, remembering him now.

"Karrii-207!" he shouted.

"Well isn't it a small galaxy," Olossky said, looking at the robot. "It seems like I just sold you because we needed the credits."

"Who are these people?" Rikks asked, pointing toward the former prisoners.

"They are former prisoners from the BlueMar Empire," Olossky said.

"Oh. Do any of you know if Nikk Eneb Oszon is alive?" Rikks asked.

The old man, Klat Morrel, stepped forward. "He's dead. They killed him," he said.

Rikks looked down for a long moment. He looked back up at the crowd. "Do any of you want to join in the destruction of the BlueMar Empire?" he asked.

Klat Morrel, who had broke free from his chains on ThornZozaa, looked like he was about to say something, but hesitated and remained silent. None of the former prisoners answered, except Olossky.

"My family is totally in this fight," Olossky said.

A long moment of silence followed.

"Okay, I understand the rest of your decisions. You've all been through a lot," he said. "If you want to live here on Claderane, you're welcome to."

The group of former prisoners quickly agreed to take Rikks up on his offer.

"Lighrt, Saalarlic, Falaskk, can you three escort them to the housing section?" Rikks asked.

"Yeah," they said. They led the former prisoners into the building.

"Karrii-207, can you look over the three ships, complete any modifications that need to be done, and make sure everything is in order?" Rikks asked.

"Right away," the robot said.

"Now, who haven't I met here? You two lovely ladies and you," Rikks said, pointing to Baas.

"This is my son Baas. You've already met my other son Roedie. This is Sepheena, Baas's girlfriend, and this is Tereena, Roedie's girlfriend," Olossky said.

"I'm glad to meet you all," Rikks said.

"You forgot somebody," KEN-102 said.

"And I'm glad to meet you as well," Rikks said to KEN-102.

A man came out of the building. "They voted for the destruction of the BlueMar Empire to begin tomorrow," he said.

"Okay," Rikks said, "so tell as many people as you can. Announce it over the central communication system."

"Yes, sir." The man ran back into the building.

Rikks turned to Olossky. "Follow me. I'll find you guys a place to sleep."

After entering the building, they were led down a long corridor. It took ten minutes of walking through corridors and stairways to reach the housing section. Rikks found them a place to stay for the night.

"I'm going to get the fleet ready for tomorrow," Rikks said. "I'll see you in the morning."

He left them and walked back down the corridor.

By morning, the fleet was ready to go. Fifty men in tan colored uniforms were assigned to Baas's ship, Roedie's ship, and Olossky's ship. A large number of white colored Kalaar robots were put on each battleship to pilot the Star Knight fighter ships in battle. A number of the Star Knight fighters were also assigned to each of the three battleships.

Star Knights were manufactured by a corporation on Claderane, exclusively for the Claderane Resistance, and distributed to all of their outposts in the galaxy. The same manufacturer also produced the special Kalaar robots to pilot the Star Knights. Although the fighter ships could be piloted by humans, the use of robots kept human casualties down during battle. The Star Knights had long bodies that came to a point in the front. Lasers were mounted on either side of the body. Highly modified swept wings angled toward the back of the fighter, then angled inward before angling back outward again. A sleek pointed stabilizer sat at the upper back end of the ship.

A number of other large battleships joined the *Quasar, Light Avenger,* and *Galactic Explorer* as the fleet proceeded toward the planet Andron at lightspeed. The campaign was a synced and collaborated effort with other divisions of the Claderane Resistance across the galaxy. Each fleet had their own part in the large military campaign.

Chapter Sixteen
The BlueMar War

Quarrel Duelco was inspecting his new personal spaceship that he had the best engineers in the BlueMar Empire build. It was a golden colored ship called *Aurulent.* He stepped inside and tested a few things. He made sure everything was designed to his specifications. When finished, he stepped back onto the docking platform and admired the ship from the outside. He was very satisfied with the results. He turned his attention toward the view of the forest nearby.

I could use a nice walk through the forest, Quarrel Duelco thought, *and then I will test my new ship.*

Quarrel often walked through the forest to clear his mind. He walked to the edge of the docking platform and down a flight of metal stairs. He stepped onto a metal grate walkway, which led across a stream and through the forest. He disappeared into the foliage.

An extreme disturbance shook the planet Andron. Multiple explosions shook all structures on the planet. Five other ships from the Claderane Resistance accompanied the *Quasar, Light Avenger,* and *Galactic Explorer.* Together, they continued to bomb the structures until they were leveled.

It is the end of the ruthless tyrant, Quarrel Duelco, Olossky thought.

The Claderane Resistance ships moved back from the planet. Olossky looked out the bridge window of the *Quasar.* He thought he saw a golden colored ship in the distance of space, but dismissed it.

Sepheena stayed on Claderane during the BlueMar War. The war only took a few months to complete. It was surprisingly short...much shorter than expected. Successful reports started flowing in from the other divisions across the galaxy. After returning from battle, Tereena found Sepheena pacing the landing pad.

"It's nice to finally have you guys back. I was so worried about you all," Sepheena said as she gave Tereena a hug.

"The others will be here shortly. They are finishing up some matters at one of the other landing pads," Tereena said.

"You look exhausted," Sepheena said.

"I am. We just arrived. Let me tell you some of the highlights of the war," Tereena said as they slowly walked along the landing pad.

"Yes, I'd like to hear that," Sepheena said.

"After destroying the facilities on Andron, we flew to the next BlueMar Empire outpost in the Andron System to a planet called Aaldabron. We destroyed the outpost. The final outpost in the Andron System was on the planet Advolon. We destroyed it as well. We then headed to the Iasesheenia Star System with another surprise attack in mind. Up until that point, we had the advantage of surprise. We thought they wouldn't be expecting us. However, the word must have gotten out. A battleship was waiting for us. The battleship, *Cosmic Metal,* started to fire its lasers at the fleet. Many of the BlueMar Empire's Silver Dagger fighters were launched to attack us. They were no match against our Star Knights and were quickly eliminated. We took some damage, but we fired back heavily. After an intense fight, the battleship exploded. We suffered only minor damages. We destroyed all of the government facilities on the planet of Iasesheenia. There were many other Claderane Resistance divisions fighting other battles across the galaxy. I don't know any of those details.

"Baas mentioned over the com that he had a debt to take care of in the Zonia Star System. He explained the long story to Olossky about who Zantorra was. He told Olossky that he would meet us back here on Claderane. That left us with a fleet of seven ships. I know he's back, so don't worry. Baas flew the *Light Avenger* to Zonia and hovered in front of Zantorra's palace for quite some time. He then shot all his lasers at the palace, leveling it. Fire rolled into a cloud, leaving the palace destroyed and in rubble. He avenged Alaress for you…for all of us. And he retrieved her frozen body so that she could have a proper burial," Tereena said.

Sepheena looked into Tereena's eyes, tears flowing down suddenly.

"Oh, Tereena, I miss her. She was my best friend. What Baas did was wonderful. I will help with the funeral arrangements," Sepheena said. "I'm so thankful that KEN-102 remembered us from when he worked there."

"Yes, me too. Anyway, Olossky announced that we were heading to the Rednii Star System. And Rikks Kyton made a speech. He said if the divine have to defeat the evil in war, they must. It's war. It's life. He said none of us are perfect, but some of us try to do what's right and those who do what's right know who they are. He went on to say that other people may have different opinions. The speech was quite impressive.

"The Rednii Alliance was waiting for us. There was a fleet of Rednii battleships and fighters that attacked us when we arrived. The Rednii's Fire Striker fighter ships started attacking our seven Claderane Resistance battleships. The Kalaar robots, flying in our Star Knights, were launched. The fast, maneuverable Star Knights came thundering out of our docking bays. They intercepted the Fire Strikers.

"The inside of a Star Knight is so cool. I was able to fly one on a test run. The dash boards have illuminated screens with foreground scans and curved side-scans where the XYZ axes can be seen. They have long-range detection on the left side of their dash boards. Next to them, there are energy level LED displays and digital speedwave systems.

"Anyway, there were twenty-two Fire Strikers and thirty-five Star Knights. The Kalaar robots fired on the Fire Strikers and four of them exploded. The Star Knights looped around on a tight angle and headed straight for the rear quadrant of the Fire Strikers and repeatedly fired again, destroying three more of them. The Fire Strikers intercepted the Star Knights and blew up thirteen all at once. The Star Knights then trailed off and back around firing on five of the Fire Strikers. The five Fire Strikers disintegrated. The Fire Strikers fired back on seven more Star Knights, blowing them into space dust. Fifteen Star Knights intercepted and fired on the remaining Fire Strikers, their lasers sabering the ships into cosmic material. The battle was over. Not much was left of their battleships after the dogfight. The remaining fifteen Star Knights returned to our ships. All seven of our battleships started toward the planet Rednii and we destroyed them there. Then we flew to the other two planets in that system, Cynann and Fibrooyon, where other Rednii Alliance outposts were located. They didn't expect our onslaught.

"The BlueMar Empire and the Rednii Alliance are no longer threats to us. We left the Rednii Star System and headed back here for a victory celebration. We met up with Baas along the way," Tereena told Sepheena.

"So, let's celebrate," Sepheena said.

PART TWO
THE EXPLORATIONS

CHAPTER SEVENTEEN
THE VOYAGE BEGINS

TWO YEARS LATER, the Claderane Resistance had its government set up throughout the BlueMar Galaxy. It was called the Claderane Government, but some people referred to it as the New BlueMar Government. The people of the BlueMar Galaxy could finally live free without a dictator, for Quarrel Duelco had been dethroned. It was a long, hard struggle to set up the new government, but it was well worth it. The capital of the Claderane Government was on the planet Claderane. Rikks Kyton was the president of the free galaxy.

The BlueMar War of the year 230929 SA was over. It was now the beginning of the year 230931 SA. In the BlueMar War, there were many significant battles that basically won the war. The resistance division from Claderane were responsible for the Andron Onslaught, the Aaldabron Onslaught, the Advolon Onslaught, the Battle of Iasesheenia, the Onslaught Upon Zantorra, The Battle at Rednii, the Rednii Onslaught, the Cynann Onslaught, the Fibrooyon Onslaught, and the Attack of Zyvor. There were many other significant battles across the galaxy from the other divisions as well.

Roedie, Tereena, and Sepheena were all twenty years old that year and Baas was nineteen. They had been through a lot over a few years.

Roedie and Tereena along with Baas and Sepheena had been married at an elegant double wedding ceremony shortly after the war.

Since the war was over, the government wanted to explore the different planets in the BlueMar Galaxy that had never been explored and some that had never been charted. They selected a group of people to accomplish the explorations, including Olossky, Roedie, Tereena, Baas, Sepheena, KEN-102, and Karrii-207. They also had a crew assigned to them that consisted of many Kalaar robots, engine crewmen, doctors, and other personnel. The mission was expected to take approximately five months.

A number of Star Knights were delivered to each ship that was selected for the voyage. The *Quasar, Light Avenger, Galactic Explorer,* and five other Claderane Government Ships (CGS ships) were chosen for the voyage. And of course, there was the old *Zoota 2000* aboard the *Galactic Explorer,* as Roedie used it most of the time. As a fleet, the eight CGS ships were called the Claderane Government Explorers. Some vacation time was given to each of the crew members before they were sent out to explore the unknown regions of space.

Roedie and Tereena went to Siitap for their vacation, Tereena's home planet. They enjoyed the beautiful scenery there. They stayed for a few days. Of course, she just had to be nude, so Roedie followed suit. It was the best time of their lives. It was so peaceful. They walked through the forest naked. They talked for hours in the home she had built. They rolled in the green grass meadows. It seemed like an eternity went by as they kissed and made love for most of their stay there. They wanted to stay there longer, but they knew they would soon have to get dressed, walk back toward the *Zoota 2000,* and fly back to Claderane.

Baas wanted to show Sepheena his home planet of Kaskoon for their vacation, at least for a few days before they were sent out to explore, but they did not get a chance. Instead, they spent their time printing data papers for ships' logs and overseeing logistics. While Baas was in the government offices finishing some paperwork, Sepheena was taking a break outside along one of the many stone terraces that overlooked the city. She leaned against the elegantly designed stone railing. Sepheena remembered when she was in Zantorra's palace. She had been taken away from her family and then her family was killed. She was so lonely, so sad. She missed Alaress, her best friend. She had given her a wonderful funeral ceremony. As she remembered these things, she felt sadness in the cool autumn air of Claderane. Her loneliness was gone now. She had Baas now and everything was all right. But still, there was the presence of sadness in the chilling air.

The Claderane City lights were bright in the distance. Conditions were just right for the ice crystals in the atmosphere to create beautiful light pillars of white and blue light that extended vertically into the starry night sky. When Roedie and Tereena arrived on Claderane, they noticed Sepheena looking out over the city. Her gaze did not break as Roedie and Tereena approached.

"They're beautiful, aren't they?" Tereena said to Sepheena, looking at the light pillars.

There was no response.

"What's wrong?" Tereena asked.

Tereena already knew the answer. Sepheena was still grieving Alaress's death. Sepheena did not say a word as tears rolled down her face, her gaze still upon the city. Tereena put her arm around Sepheena and turned her around to face them.

"Oh, honey, we don't want you to feel sad. I know you've been through a lot. I can't image what it's like to lose a friend. I know it's not easy to let go. We love you and we don't want to see you this way.

"Before Baas and Roedie came along to Siitap, I was so lonely. When Nanny died, I wanted to commit suicide, but I didn't. Who in the hell is gonna remember me stuck on some planet in the middle of nowhere? Whoever abandoned me there when I was an infant— parents or not—are... Oh, it angers me. Anyway, just know that each morning is a new day. We are always here for you," Tereena said.

Sepheena's tears stopped rolling down her sweet cheeks.

"Where is Baas?" Roedie asked.

"Getting things ready to go for tomorrow," Sepheena said.

"I'll go get him. You need him right now," Roedie said. "Seriously... you two could have used a good vacation instead of working."

Baas later came out of the building with Roedie and went over to comfort Sepheena. Roedie and Tereena left them together on the terrace as they searched for Olossky to have a discussion.

In the morning, they were ready for their voyage. Thanks to the extra efforts of Baas and Sepheena, all the logistics were complete. They all had their farewells and started the voyage, a voyage that would take them to the farthest reaches of space.

CHAPTER EIGHTEEN
THE TASKII INCIDENT

THE CLADERANE GOVERNMENT Explorers were flying at lightspeed toward an unexplored part of deep space, near the edge of the BlueMar Galaxy. They encountered a spaceship that flew by so fast, all they saw was a white streak of light out the observation window. It went off their scanners a second later. Their computers did manage to capture a screen image of the streak of light and reduced it to a slower speed. It was a long, rectangular ship, which came to a point in the front. There were four pointed, star-shaped spire-type structures in the front and in the rear of the ship. The front spires had lasers mounted at all four points. There were also pointed wings and a stabilizer at the back of the ship.

"I wonder where that came from," Olossky said over the com.

"I don't know. Could there be any BlueMar Empire officials left?" Baas asked.

"It's a possibility, but I don't think so, especially in something that fast," Olossky said.

The pilot of the *Quasar* turned around and looked at Olossky. After the BlueMar War, Olossky was made a commander and captain of the *Quasar*. He was also assigned as admiral of the Claderane Government

Explorers.

"This part of the BlueMar Galaxy has never been explored before. It could be another civilization of people," Olossky said.

"There is a planet on the scanner, sir," Kahgn Zign Lightign, first officer of the *Quasar*, responded.

"That could be the home planet of the ship that flew by," Olossky said.

"The streak of light didn't even go toward the planet," Kahgn Zign Lightign said.

"Interesting," Olossky said.

"It's uncharted, Admiral. It doesn't have a name yet," Kahgn said.

"Well, let's check it out. I want the fleet on full alert. We don't know what could be on that planet," Olossky said.

"Yes, sir," Kahgn said.

The fleet flew closer to the planet.

"I want this fleet to stay in orbit with full stabilizers on," Olossky said through his com in the captain's chair.

His seat overlooked the control panel where Kahgn Zign Lightign was posted.

"Have the computer check all main life forms on the planet," Olossky said.

"Although there isn't much information to record, the planet has a lot of plains and tundra on it. The only creatures on the planet are cannibals and eat their own kind. There is nothing else in the food chain, except the grass in the plains. But for every one that is eaten, one is born. They are very reproductive creatures. Their current population growth is approximately zero, according to the computer. The creatures have heads that curl upward, little eyes, and a nose that spreads from their eyes to their long mouths. They are about twice the size of humans. There are millions of them on the planet," Kahgn said, showing Admiral Olossky an electronic image of one of the creatures.

"Well, look at that red textured, leathery skin. That's not the prettiest thing I've seen in the galaxy. Record all the information that we get from the planet. As admiral of this fleet, I have been commissioned to name the uncharted planets. It will be called Taskii. And the star system will be the Taskii Star System," Olossky said, spelling the name out for Kahgn.

"Okay, sir," Kahgn said.

Kahgn recorded all the information regarding Taskii and also put a memory card into a slot in the computer panel for archival purposes.

"Those are some repulsive creatures. There's nothing much here.

We've recorded what we can. We can exit orbit and move on to the next location," Olossky said over the com.

"I wonder where the home planet is for the fast ship that flew by us," Kahgn said.

"I don't know, but I would like to find out. We may even find it yet. That incident with the ship was very strange to say the least. If we do locate them, I hope the people there are not hostile," Olossky said.

"I hope not too," Kahgn said.

They exited their orbit at Taskii and went back into deep space. The distant stars emitted light to the Claderane Government Explorer ships. It was very peaceful in space. Sometimes it could get lonely, but other moments were filled with interest and excitement. The more interesting places that could be found, the more excitement that was shared by the entire fleet. The fleet flew onward to a set of twin planets, also in the Taskii Star System. They were not prepared for the devastation that lay ahead.

CHAPTER NINETEEN
THE LAST OF A CIVILIZATION

THE FLEET ARRIVED at a set of twin planets that were found at the edge of the Taskii Star System. After investigating the twin planets with drones, they discovered they were called Kethe and Karrah. They studied the two civilized planets and recorded their information. Strangely, they didn't detect anyone alive on either planet. There were two large ships plunged into the desert surface of Kethe.

"Roedie, I want a team from your ship to go down and check out those two ships that impacted on the surface of Kethe," Olossky said into the com.

Roedie sent a team to investigate the two ships. The team had their coms on and ready to use them if necessary. Three Star Knights landed on the surface of Kethe next to the two ships that had crashed into the sand.

"Hey, Makan, come here for a second," the first man said as he walked into one of the two ships.

"What did ya find, Galikel?" Makan asked.

"There are *dead* people in here. The stench of death lingers in the air. I would like to know what happened to them," Galikel said.

"Holy cosmos! Look over there," the third man said.

"What is it, Tokens?" Makan asked.

"This man's head is here in the corner and his body is right there by you," Tokens said, pointing toward a corner of the ship.

"What killed them?" Galikel asked.

"I don't know and I wouldn't like to find out," Tokens said.

"Let's check out the other ship and get off this planet," Makan said.

When they investigated the second ship, horror followed. A creature jumped out from the inside of the ship. It had been hiding in a dark corner of the open entryway. It had a curled up head, little eyes, and a nose that spread from its eyes to its long mouth. It opened its large, red, leathery mouth with three sets of razor-sharp teeth in it. With a quick rip, the creature decapitated Makan and then Galikel. Tokens ran for his Star Knight and got in just in time.

When he returned to the *Galactic Explorer,* Tokens headed straight for the bridge and told Roedie and Tereena what had happened.

"One of those reptilian creatures from Taskii was down there in one of those ships. It killed all the people aboard the ships and it killed Makan and Galikel. I barely made it back to my ship in time to get out of there with my life," Tokens said in a panic.

"Holy cosmos. What did it do to them?" Roedie asked.

"It bit off their heads," Tokens said, still in shock.

"I'll tell the admiral about this," Roedie said, reaching for the com.

Over the com, Roedie told Olossky what had happened.

"Oh, no," Olossky said. "All right, we won't be sending a team down to Karrah to check that gargantuan robot out. There is a very large robot just outside of an abandoned settlement that appears to be inoperative. The planet is a desert just like Kethe anyway."

"I think we should check out the space station above Karrah, though," Roedie said.

"If you think it's important. I just hope there aren't any of those reptiles on that space station," Olossky said.

"Baas and I will go. It looks like a small city in space," Roedie said.

"It looks like someone or something tore it apart," Baas said.

Roedie temporarily assigned Tokens to be in charge of the *Galactic Explorer.* He headed to the docking bay with Tereena. They flew the *Zoota 2000* over to the docking bay of the *Light Avenger* to pick up Baas and Sepheena.

"We are bringing laser rifles, right?" Roedie asked.

"Yeah, it could get dangerous," Baas said.

"Of course, we're bringing them," Tereena said in the back of the ship.

"Let's go," Baas said, closing the ship door.

The *Zoota 2000* left the *Light Avenger's* docking bay and flew toward the space station that was orbiting Karrah.

"Be very careful," Olossky said over the com.

"Don't worry, Dad, the Sandkeens won't get us here," Roedie said over the com.

"No, but something else might," Olossky said.

"Thanks for the encouragement," Roedie said sarcastically.

They landed in the docking bay of the space station and had the computer check the air pressure. After finding it was safe, they stepped out of the *Zoota 2000*.

"This place looks like something big crashed into it," Roedie said.

"Yeah. Leave your com on continual transmit, so they can hear us," Baas said.

They started toward a long corridor and went up a flight of stairs to the next level. They soon came to a small ladder well and climbed upward. They came out in a large metal tunnel that ended at a metal grate. They opened and passed through to the other side.

"There is no one here," Roedie said.

"Well, with our tracer here, we won't lose our way back to the ship," Baas said.

"Wait. I'm reading a single life form on the scanner," Roedie said.

"Look!" Tereena said, pointing to an open door located at the far end of the room.

"Another corridor…" Baas said, walking through the door.

"This reminds me of Zantorra's palace. It's like a maze," Sepheena said.

"Let's go," Roedie said.

They went down the corridor that ended at another room. Inside the room, there was an old man with gray hair and a white beard. He looked up at them.

"Who are you people?" the old man asked.

"We are members of the Claderane Government," Baas said.

"Why are you here?" The man was visibly confused.

"Our fleet of eight large ships has been exploring uncharted regions of space in the BlueMar Galaxy," Baas said.

"Well, you don't want to explore the reptiles," the old man said.

"We already have," Roedie said.

"Oh, no! You did? Where?" the old man asked.

"On the planet where two ships are crashed," Roedie said.

"They are destroying our civilization or they already have," he said.

"You're the only one left," Baas said.

"So, I'm the last of a civilization? Huh."

"There is another planet. It has a large robot on it," Roedie said.

"Yeah, the people built him to kill off the reptiles who we are trying to exterminate," the old man said.

"*Were* trying to exterminate. It's over," Roedie said.

"Not till they kill me, it's not. We should have never went to their planet in the first place," he said.

"We saw their home planet as well, but we didn't land there. They aren't going to kill you, because *you* are going to be saved. We can bring you back to the fleet with us," Baas said.

"All right, if you insist," he said.

"What's your name?" Tereena asked.

"It's Shamalon Kanar," he said.

"I'm Baas Cantin, captain of the *Light Avenger*," Baas said. "And this is my wife, Sepheena Cantin."

"My name is Roedie Cantin, captain of the *Galactic Explorer*. This is my wife, Tereena Cantin."

"It is *very* nice to meet you all. Are you brothers?" Shamalon asked.

"Yes. Our father, Olossky, is the admiral of the fleet," Roedie said.

"I see," Shamalon said.

"Well, let's go," Sepheena said.

They found their way back to the *Zoota 2000*. They all stepped aboard and Roedie flew it to the *Light Avenger*. After dropping off Baas, Sepheena, and Shamalon, he and Tereena returned to the *Galactic Explorer*.

Shamalon was in his assigned quarters on the fifth level when he was called to the bridge of the *Light Avenger* by Sepheena. When he arrived on the bridge, Shamalon stood before Sepheena.

"Yes?" he asked.

"Thanks for responding so quickly," Sepheena said.

"My father would like to speak with you over the com," Baas said.

"Hi, Shamalon," Olossky said. "I am Admiral Olossky Cantin."

"Hi. How can I help you?" Shamalon returned.

"We did a very thorough search on both planets with our scanners and you *are* the only one left alive. The reptiles apparently killed off the civilization. That robot was put out of commission somehow. I'm sorry about all this, but nevertheless we are happy to have you among our fleet," Olossky said.

"Thank you, Admiral Cantin," Shamalon said.

"You are more than welcome to visit our lounge and meet some of the crew when you feel up to it," Baas said.

"Thank you. Perhaps soon, but for now, I just want to be alone. Thank you," he said.

He walked back to his quarters.

CHAPTER TWENTY
THE SEARCH GOES ON

"…THREE…TWO…ONE…Lightspeed engaged," a voice said.

Five ships streaked across the star system, fading from sight.

"They're on their way now," Kahgn said.

"Good. Have my son Roedie come to this ship immediately," Olossky told Kahgn.

"I'll get right on it," Kahgn said. He turned on the com and said, "*Quasar* to *Galactic Explorer*, this is Kahgn. Admiral Cantin would like to see Captain Roedie Cantin aboard the *Quasar* as soon as possible."

"We read you. I'll send for him right away," Tokens said from the bridge of the *Galactic Explorer.*

He tried the com, but there was no answer. He turned around to see if there was anyone on the bridge behind him. An officer was standing by the entrance.

"Hey, will you please go to the second level and get Roedie from his quarters and get him up here on the bridge?" he asked. "He's not answering the com."

"Yes, sir," the officer said and went out the bridge door.

• • •

"Oh, I love you, Roedie," Tereena said, stepping out of the shower in their quarters.

"I love you too," Roedie said.

She walked over to him and put her arms around him.

"You're getting my clothes soaked," Roedie said. "You're such a nudist."

"I'll dry off in a minute," she said.

Roedie kissed her lips and they both dropped to the couch.

"Roedie! Watch it," Tereena laughed. "Roedie, stop tickling me."

His touch changed from the playful tickling to slow, smooth caresses, as he massaged her breasts.

"Roedie, make love to me," she moaned as he kissed below her sensitive navel.

A pulse came from the door in their quarters.

"Who is it? Tell them to go away," Tereena said.

"Wait a second," Roedie said to Tereena.

He went into the foyer and answered the door. An officer stood at the entrance.

"Commander Roedie, Admiral Cantin would like to see you aboard the *Quasar* right away."

"He's busy!" Tereena's voice came from the other room.

"I'll be up in a few minutes," Roedie said.

The door shut and Roedie walked back into the other room.

"Do you have to go?" Tereena asked, sitting on the couch with an innocent look on her face.

"Yeah, but I'll be back," he promised, raising his eyebrows.

"Yeah, Tokens, what's goin' on?" Roedie asked.

"Your dad would like to see you on the *Quasar,*" Tokens said.

"I know. What's this regarding?" Roedie asked.

"I don't know. You can ask him on the com," Tokens said.

"Nah, that's all right. I just thought you might know. I'll just go to his ship. If Tereena comes up here to the bridge, tell her where I went," Roedie said.

He headed for the docking bay.

In the docking bay, Roedie got into the *Zoota 2000* and started it up. He flew into the darkness of space and over to the *Quasar.* After landing in the docking bay, he headed for the bridge. In a corridor, Roedie saw KEN-102.

"How's it goin'?" Roedie asked.

"Okay," the silver robot said. "Olossky wants to see you."

"That's where I'm headed. Are you coming along?" Roedie asked.

"No. I have to help Karrii-207 with some things down in the engine room," KEN-102 said.

"Oh. Tell him I said 'hi,' " Roedie said.

"I will do so. Bye," KEN-102 said.

"Bye," Roedie said, walking toward the bridge.

He went through the doorway of the bridge and walked down a few steps to where Olossky sat in the captain's chair.

"Oh, good. You're here."

"Hi. What's up?" Roedie asked.

"The five CGS ships just headed off in space at lightspeed to explore two planets that were out of our way. They should be back as soon as their mission is complete. Perhaps we'll find that ship that flew by us like a streak of light," Olossky said.

"Why do you want me here, then?" Roedie asked.

"Baas was busy so I decided to get you—"

"How do you know that I wasn't busy?" Roedie cut him off.

"Were you?" Olossky asked.

"As a matter of fact, I was," Roedie said.

"I'm sorry," Olossky said.

"That's all right. Now, what did you want?" Roedie asked.

"We just entered a star system with three planets and I want you to see the information on them," Olossky said.

"Okay," Roedie said.

"The information on the three planets is coming up on the computer now," Kahgn said.

"What is it?" Olossky asked.

"The first planet has no life and no atmosphere. What do you want to name it?" Kahgn asked.

"Ah...call it Ekka," Olossky said, spelling it out.

"Okay, I'll record all the information," Kahgn said.

"How do you come up with these names?" Roedie asked.

"I use my imagination," Olossky said with a smile on his face.

"The information on the second planet will be on the screen in a moment," Kahgn said.

"What's on the planet?" Olossky asked.

"There is no intelligent life there. However, there are some interesting animals that have three horns on their faces. There are other small mammals similar to foxes and wolves as well. It has mostly bushes, shrubs, and tall grass. It has quite a few water systems. What do you want to call it?" Kahgn asked.

"Call it Tarras," Olossky said, once again, spelling it out for Kahgn.

"Okay," Kahgn said, recording the information.

Roedie looked at the computer screen. "There's more information on the screen," he said.

Kahgn looked at the computer screen. "Holy cosmos! It's confirmed that the third planet has humans on it. There are five villages on the planet," Kahgn said.

"Okay," Olossky said, "Roedie, can you send Tokens down there?"

"I'll get back to the ship and let him know," Roedie said.

Roedie headed toward the docking bay of the *Quasar* and back to the *Galactic Explorer.*

Tokens landed his Star Knight on the planet. As he climbed out of his ship, a crowd of people gathered.

"Greetings. I am here to—" Tokens was cut short.

"Hey! Hey, man, who—"

"Hey! Are ya come ta Rikkett ta kill us, man?" a man shouted, his old white cloth robe fluttering in the wind.

A man with white hair and a white beard moved forward to the front of the crowd. He wore a tan cloth robe. "Get off our planet," he said.

"Ya come ta get us?" another old man shouted as he bent over in his brown cloth robe to pick up a large stone.

The crowd started beating on the Star Knight with clubs and they threw stones at it. Tokens quickly climbed back into the cockpit and started the Star Knight. He had a similar reception at the other four villages. He gave up and left the savage planet. On his return to the *Galactic Explorer,* he told Roedie over the com about what had happened on the planet the natives called Rikkett.

"Well, we really can't accommodate those who cannot conduct themselves properly. It would put the fleet at risk," Olossky said after hearing what had happened.

Kahgn agreed and then turned back around to the computer to record the planet name and what had transpired there.

"Sir, there is another one of those fast objects on the screen! It's like the one we saw several months ago," Kahgn said.

"Where did it come from? Where is it going?" Olossky asked, looking concerned.

"It came from the planet that just appeared on our long-range scanners, but it's too fast to find out where it's going," Kahgn said.

"I want to head for that planet at lightspeed. Is there any word from the other five CGS ships that left to check out the two planets?" Olossky asked.

"Yes. They're right behind us. They said that there is nothing on the two planets. What do you want to name them?" Kahgn asked.

"Litheh and Myzerh." He spelled the names out for Kahgn.

Kahgn recorded the information very quickly.

"If I'm not mistaken, this area we're headed for is the last uncharted region of the BlueMar Galaxy that's on our agenda before we head back to Claderane. Okay, inform the fleet to head for that planet on the long-range scanners at lightspeed," Olossky said.

Kahgn did so.

Chapter Twenty-one
The Kameron

"THE SEVEN PLANETS in this system are highly technologically advanced worlds," Kahgn said.

"That first planet is where that ship came from?" Olossky asked.

"Yes," Kahgn said.

"Are the people on these planets dangerous?" Olossky asked.

"I don't know. There is no record of any kind of beings advanced as these," Kahgn said. "Hey, that ship is returning."

"Try to communicate with the ship," Olossky said.

Kahgn enabled the communicator and they waited. A fast blur of words came from the communicator.

"Slow the message down to our speed level," Olossky said.

Kahgn did so.

"You are invading Kameron space," the voice said again at a slower speed.

Decelerating from lightspeed, a group of Kameron military battleships appeared on either side of the other Kameron vessel.

"Send them a message from us. Tell them we are no threat to them and we are searching for uncharted regions of space. And ask them to slow down their message speed," Olossky said.

Kahgn did so.

"Where did your eight ships come from?" the voice asked.

"We are from the Claderane Government," Olossky said. "Where did *you* people originate from?"

"We originated from the Mazits and came to this part of the galaxy. We stayed here and shut out the rest of the galaxy. We understand that a peaceful government is now in control of the galaxy. We have thought about reaching out to you and introducing ourselves, but have refrained because of the uncertainties," the voice said.

"We understand," Olossky said.

"A few years ago, we started exploring these three colony planets in the Kameron Star System, however we are now preparing to explore another galaxy," the voice said.

"That would be interesting," Olossky said.

"Definitely," Kahgn said.

"I see. With the discovery of your star system, we are pretty much finished exploring the uncharted regions of this galaxy. Can we join together and explore unknown space in this other galaxy you mentioned?" Olossky asked, hopeful. "But if we did, how could we get across the stretch between the two galaxies?"

"If you can come aboard my ship, *Keen Saber,* I can answer that question and many more. My name is Sintos and I am the leader of the Kameron," he said.

"Would you mind if my sons, Baas and Roedie, join me?" Olossky asked.

"Ah, sure that would be great," Roedie said with a nervous voice.

"Yeah," Baas said.

"Yes, that is fine. Well then, if you just give me your coordinates, I'll port you aboard the *Keen Saber,*" Sintos said.

"Port us aboard?" they asked perplexed.

A functional docking bay was unnecessary on the *Keen Saber* since they used porting for their method of arrival to and departure from the ship.

Aboard the *Keen Saber,* Olossky, Baas, and Roedie were walking down a corridor with a large, bald man named Sintos. After learning more about the Claderane Government Explorers, Sintos had just agreed to let the fleet join with his ship on the journey.

"I can have my technicians modify your ships so they can travel the speed of time with our tac-time engines. It's up to you," Sintos said.

"The speed of time?" Baas looked amazed.

"That's an interesting concept," Roedie said.

"Timespeed is more than a concept. It's a reality," Sintos said.

"Could I ask what timespeed is exactly?" Olossky asked.

"Yes, I'll tell you. I'm not like some people that think you wouldn't understand it because it is more advanced than your current knowledge. If someone even makes an attempt of trying to understand something, it's better than not trying at all."

"I agree," Olossky said.

"Initially, we thought timespeed was lightspeed squared; however, we now know that was incorrect. As you know, lightspeed is 9,460,730,472,580.8 kilometers per year, also known as one lightyear. When referring to spaceships, it is an extremely fast speed. However, lightspeed times one million—as we now know—is referred to as timespeed. It is one million times faster than the speed of light. So, basically timespeed is 9,460,730,472,580,800,000 kilometers per year. We traveled that speed during testing for the tac-time engine, but it was determined that our maximum speed should only be used at 83.3 percent of timespeed, which is 7,880,788,483,659,806,400 kilometers per year. Since our close neighbor, the Regulominuss Galaxy, is 624,750 lightyears away or 5,910,591,362,744,854,800 kilometers, it will only take us approximately .75 year or nine months to arrive at our destination. Even at 83.3 percent of timespeed, we still consider it as timespeed. That is because at that velocity, it is great enough to change time. As we have discovered during our timespeed testing phase, if the tac-time engines are programmed to rotate clockwise, you will travel into a future time frame. And likewise, if the tac-time engines are programmed to rotate counter-clockwise, you will travel into a past time frame. We discovered that it is not possible to stay in the present time frame when traveling at timespeed.

"All the while one is traveling at that velocity, the size of all matter traveling at that speed decreases rapidly until it disappears from one time frame to the next. However, when the ships decelerate out of the timespeed range, they return to their normal size. It is a fascinating phenomenon.

"Future time frame dates and past time frame dates can be programmed into your ships' computers. There is a warning, however: If you try to find out what infinity will be like by traveling into the future or past without stopping within the time/date limit that your computers give you, you will be dealing with unknowns. You may never return to the normal time frame. But don't worry, computers will be programmed with the appropriate data for time/date limits and other important code. Also, all ship's engines will be synchronized when starting or stopping timespeed so they stay together. But you mustn't get the speed/time/distance formula of space travel confused with the future or past achievable dates of time travel. Although they are related, they are two different things. With time travel at timespeed, one month is equivalent to approximately two hundred and twelve years. We chose to travel in past time frames to the halfway point between galaxies and then switch to future time frames for the other half of the journey in order to ensure we arrive at the same present time frame as the BlueMar Galaxy. We will need to stop periodically on this nine-month crossing, about every three months, so we can do routine maintenance on the tac-time engines," Sintos said.

Olossky, Baas, and Roedie did not say a word.

"I see you are getting all this," Sintos said. "I'll just continue, then…

"Our three colonies here, Kameron I, Kameron II, and Kameron III are just the beginning. On Carron, our home planet, they developed teleportation—which we refer to as porting—and also reflector shields for our ships. With porting, the molecules in our bodies break down and get converted into a digital signal, sent through a maser beam to a specific location, and then converted onto a virtual collector and our bodies reform. It can work with objects as well. With reflector shields, any laser fired at the ship's hull will reflect off and go into another direction. They also reflect scanner signals, keeping the ships stealth," Sintos said.

"We also have reflector shields, but certainly not porting," Roedie said.

"Do you want the technicians to install the tac-time engines, then?" Sintos asked.

"Well, that would only leave one problem," Olossky said.

"And what might that be?" Sintos asked.

"The galaxy charts and mapping programmed in our ships' databases only contain the BlueMar Galaxy," Olossky said.

"We can fix that. The other code I was referring to was just that, the mapping of both the BlueMar Galaxy and our projected calculations of the Regulominuss Galaxy," he said.

"Okay…you may install the tac-time engines and reprogram the computer mapping," Olossky said.

"Okay," Sintos said. "I'll have my teams work on all eight ships starting within the hour."

Their conversation went on for quite some time. Sintos was very impressed with their Star Knight fighter ships. While Sintos's technicians began modifying the eight CGS ships above Kameron I, the *Keen Saber* and two Star Knights headed across space toward Carron. Sintos wanted to showcase the fighter ships because he was so impressed with them. Baas and Roedie volunteered to fly the Star Knights with the *Keen Saber*.

Sintos was ported down to one of the many cities under the ocean planet of Carron. He told his people they were going to begin the voyage to the Regulominuss Galaxy. He also told them about the new people that came to the Kameron System and Sintos had them view their Star Knights.

The planet Carron was a brilliant blue color from space with darker blue sections of deeper water visible. It was an ocean planet with an oxygen and nitrogen atmosphere. It had a single gray satellite.

When Sintos finished his business at Carron, the *Keen Saber* and Star Knights flew to other colonies in the system to notify them of the news. They arrived at a large gaseous planet with light greenish-gray bands of gases. It was called Tibis.

Sintos was ported down to the planet's satellite, Cibtar, where he was greeted by another man that looked similar to himself.

They met in a field near the man's home. Fixed before them was a most spectacular view. Across a lake, mountains and white pine trees could be seen, their brilliance reflecting in the water. A sky view revealed Tibis in the background with its light greenish-gray bands. Beyond Tibis, the dark blue Carron could be seen with its single gray satellite. The light blue planet of Rialerson was visible beyond Carron, decorated by its frozen ring of ice. Rialerson's four satellites were visible surrounding the planet. Many beautiful, bright blue stars decorated the darkness of space. And Sintos's destination, the Regulominuss Galaxy, could also be seen further out in space, but still very visible from where they stood. The barred spiral galaxy was the masterpiece of the sky.

Orbiting the moon of Cibtar, the *Keen Saber* drifted overhead. Baas and Roedie flew by in their Star Knights.

"Sintos, glad to see you," the man said.

"I've got news. We are going to explore the Regulominuss Galaxy. And we also have new friends that will be traveling the great distance with us. I wanted to show you their Star Knight fighter ships," he said, pointing to the sky. "I am most impressed with them. They came from a part of the BlueMar Galaxy that we've avoided because of the former BlueMar Empire."

"Being apprehensive about reaching out is understandable. Those fighter ships are very nice and they actually look very similar to your *Keen Saber.*"

"Hmm…perhaps that's why I like them so much," Sintos said.

"I'll miss you, brother," the man said.

"I will miss you as well, Larsinn," Sintos said. "But I must hurry because I want to personally give the news to the other colonies."

"I hope ya make it, Sintos. Bye," Larsinn said.

"Bye, brother," Sintos said, a tear dripping down his cheek.

He gave his brother a long hug before porting from the surface of Cibtar and he was back aboard the *Keen Saber* with his crew.

The *Keen Saber* and two Star Knights left the planet Tibis and headed for two other colony planets. The first was the light blue colored Rialerson, with its frozen ring of ice. The planet was full of life. It had thousands of different types of plants and animals. Once again, his stay was brief. They moved on to the last colony in the Kameron System. The colony was located on a satellite called Nori Masyn. It was the single satellite of the planet Rella. Rella was decorated with stripes of blue and black gases. After Sintos informed the people of Nori Masyn, they left the outer colonies of the Kameron and returned to Kameron I.

"Everything is all ready to go," Olossky said over the com.

"Good," Sintos said. "My team is fast and efficient."

They soon started the count-down to timespeed when all of the sudden, out of nowhere, two ships appeared. They were flown by Santu and Zaggon, two enforcement agent investigators who were out for revenge. They were after the Cantins.

"When we wiped out the BlueMar Empire, I think we forgot those two," Roedie said, immediately recognizing Santu's ship.

"Not them!" Olossky shouted.

Yes, *them,*" Baas said.

Ignoring what Olossky, Baas, and Roedie were talking about over the com, Sintos said, "Five seconds until timespeed."

Santu and Zaggon began firing on the nine ships.

"Three…two…one…timespeed engaged," Sintos's voice faded.

In a second, the nine ships were the image of a flash of light.

They were gone…gone to another galaxy…gone to the Regulominuss Galaxy.

"Where did they go?" Santu asked.

Zaggon did not answer the question as the Kameron military came to the defense of the departing fleet and destroyed the two ships in an instant.

Part Three
The Regulominuss Galaxy

MESOLOGUE
DARK DREAM

ADMIRAL OLOSSKY CANTIN slept in his quarters aboard the *Quasar* and dreamed. In his dream, he floated in the space between galaxies, just drifting. Suddenly, a blinding light surrounded him and he shielded his eyes. Then, everything went black. The darkest of dark was all that existed. He woke up and took a deep breath, covered in sweat.

What the hell was that? he thought.

Chapter Twenty-two
A Drifting Planet

THE FLEET WAS three months into their journey to the Regulominuss Galaxy. They were temporarily out of timespeed. The hot tac-time engines of the nine large ships needed to cool so routine maintenance could be done by Sintos's technicians. His technicians also instructed their counterparts from the Claderane Government Explorers on the procedures for the maintenance on the tac-time engines.

Traveling between ships during timespeed was a sure death sentence. Any ship leaving the docking bay would immediately be left far behind in space and time with only lightspeed capabilities. There would be no planets around and they would never reach their galaxy in their lifetime…which would only be a couple weeks without food and water. They took the opportunity of being stopped for maintenance to meet.

Eight people sat at a long table in the briefing room aboard the *Quasar*. Sintos sat at one end of the long table and Olossky sat at the other end. Roedie, Tereena, and Tokens sat on one side of the long table while Baas, Sepheena, and Kahgn sat on the other side. Olossky was talking about old times.

"The new galaxy may have a planet that looks similar to Kaskoon," Olossky said. "I miss our little house outside of Kanthas."

"So do I. Too bad we can't go back," Roedie said, holding Tereena's hand.

"If that Quarrel Duelco could have kept to his own business, we would still be there. Those enforcement agent investigators that he sent after us were all that I could take from those fools," Baas said, an angry look on his face.

"If there would have been dictators like that in our government, we would have kicked their asses out too," Sintos said in a deep voice.

"My father met Quarrel Duelco a long time ago on the planet 'Schytion in the year 230881 SA. Quarrel and that bitch he was with cut my father with a knife because he wouldn't give them two credits to pay for their drinks. They were in an intoxication joint. This was before Quarrel was an emperor for the BlueMar Empire. Tetra Reab was emperor at the time. That was *way* before I joined up with the Claderane Resistance. Now look at me…I'm on my way to a different galaxy," Tokens said.

There was an announcement over the com stating the technicians were finished with the maintenance on the tac-time engines and timespeed could be initiated once again.

"Well, I better get back to my ship," Sintos said.

Sintos punched a code into the advanced com on his arm. He turned into small particles of energy and was ported to the *Keen Saber*. Everyone else flew back to their own ships.

"Okay, start the tac-time engines," Sintos said.

The pilot turned to the panel aboard the *Keen Saber* and started the procedure for timespeed.

"Five…four…three…two…one…timespeed engaged," the pilot announced.

The fleet was a flash of light as the nine ships left that part of space and time.

Several days had passed since they started timespeed after the first maintenance. The technicians aboard the *Light Avenger* had to repair a valve on the ship's tac-time engine that was missed during the earlier maintenance. Going forward, everything seemed to work properly. Of the nine months that it would take them to reach the Regulominuss

Galaxy, they would need to disengaged timespeed every three months for routine maintenance as well as the halfway point to switch from past time frames to future time frames. During the second maintenance stop, at the sixth-month mark, they double-checked everything to be sure there would be no more valve issues.

Two months after their second maintenance stop and eight months into their trip, something special happened. Baas, Sepheena, and a few doctors from their ship were in a delivery room. Dr. Matzon was monitoring the delivery of Sepheena's child while Dr. Elzi and Dr. Xexioux delivered the child. Sepheena was on a minimal amount of pain medication. She did very well with her breathing and her focus. It took several hours before the happy moment came for Sepheena and Baas. She saw her newborn son.

Although there were communications among the fleet during their journey, Baas was apprehensive about telling his father about the baby because he was afraid of his father's reaction. Approximately a month later, Olossky found out about the baby. Over the com, Olossky and Baas had a private discussion. Olossky was in his quarters aboard the *Quasar* and Baas was somewhere on the *Light Avenger.*

"I don't see why you're upset with me!" Baas said in a sharp voice.

"You didn't even *tell* me she was pregnant. She was on that ship for I don't know how many months without communicating with anybody except you," Olossky said.

"Should that be a surprise?" Baas asked.

"It *sure* is," Olossky said. "I'm just concerned about babies and children with the dangers that we face."

"It's like you're not even happy to be a grandpa! And she got pregnant a month before the trip. I only—"

"Of course, I'm happy to be a grandpa. I'm just concerned about the child's safety. We really didn't have any clear-cut rules about that before we left. When can I see my grandson?" Olossky asked.

"Olossky, to the bridge. I think you should see something," Kahgn's voice came over the com.

"Baas, we'll have to finish this discussion later."

"What is it?" Olossky walked through the electronic door of the bridge.

"Sintos said that we're out of timespeed permanently until we return to the BlueMar Galaxy," Kahgn said. "It is a coincidence that when we disengaged timespeed, a planet appeared on our long-range scanners. That system seems to be drifting out from the Regulominuss Galaxy."

"Can Sintos make anything out on the planet yet?" Olossky asked.

"I contacted him and he said he couldn't get anything on the planet from this far away," Kahgn said.

"Okay. Keep me posted. I'll be in my quarters," Olossky said, walking off the bridge.

"Oh, Admiral?" Kahgn swirled around quickly in his chair.

"Yes?" Olossky turned around before going through the door.

"The technicians are scheduled to do the post-timespeed maintenance on the tac-time engines."

"Yes, I know," Olossky said as he left the bridge.

"Hi," Sepheena's weak voice said to her small boy. "Do you like the name Reminall?" Sepheena stroked his little cheeks.

"Hi," a voice came from the door.

Sepheena looked up.

"Oh, hi, Shamalon. I haven't seen you in a while. Are you doing better since we rescued you from that space station?"

"A lot better. I see you had a boy. Did you name him yet?" Shamalon asked.

"Yeah. His name is Reminall," she said.

"Oh, I like that," he said.

"Where is Baas?" Sepheena asked.

She looked exhausted with glassy green eyes.

"I think he's on the *Quasar.* I'm not sure," Shamalon said.

"Okay. Thank you," she said.

In the darkness of space, blue-tinted cosmic dust drifted along the Claderane Government Explorer ships' outer hulls. The fleet anxiously awaited their arrival upon the new galaxy.

On the bridge of the *Quasar,* Kahgn sat gazing at a distant sky-blue colored star. Its grayish-white planet had an asteroid-like moonlet. It was a lost star system that had drifted out from the Regulominuss Galaxy.

"We're coming upon the planet now," Kahgn said into the com.

Moments later, Olossky walked onto the bridge. "Scan the planet for any life forms," he said.

I wonder what could be on that planet, he thought.

"You won't believe this, sir," Kahgn said, amazed at what he had found.

"Probably not. What is it?" Olossky leaned forward in his chair.

"There are two humans on the planet, sir," Kahgn said, managing a smile.

"Holy cosmos. Let's send the *Zoota 2000* and two Star Knights to the surface," Olossky said. "I want to check that out."

Roedie was in his quarters aboard the *Galactic Explorer*. He was standing next to his electronic closet door using a hex set wrench on the door panel. He removed four bolts and the panel came off from the wall. Several wires were connected to the panel. He took a wire link and hooked it to two red wires and the closet door moved aside and stayed in the wall without closing.

He took a larger hex set wrench and removed four bolts from a floor plate. Using a titanium bar, he pried the metal plate from the closet floor. When he removed the metal plate, he noticed a small rectangular opening. A metal ladder led down to a walkway far beneath the closet floor.

This is so bitchin', he thought.

He enjoyed the lower levels of his ship ever since he discovered them. It was the place he went to escape the stresses of his job, his man-cave of sorts. He found this section was isolated from other lower levels in the ship. Unlike this section, the other lower levels could be accessed easily from other areas.

He made his way down a metal ladder to the grated catwalk below. He turned to the left and started walking, the sound of his steps against the grooved metal grating echoing throughout the lower levels. The catwalk turned right and he made his way up a set of metal stairs that were long and high. When he reached the top of the steps, he turned right, then left, then left again and came out high above the original walkway.

My metal underworld, he thought.

The illuminators gave adequate lighting to the area. He turned left and came to a stop at a three-way intersection, then he turned left again. Several meters down, he turned to his right and went into a ladder well. Climbing up the ladder, he reached another metal catwalk. Roedie was now several levels up from his quarters. He went down the catwalk to his right and passed a grille vent located against a wall. He came to a door, which swiftly slid aside as he approached. He entered a computer room and sat in a chair in front of the computer.

"Okay," he said to himself.

He punched several keys on the keyboard and the computer read: *Code procedure?* He punched in several more keys and entered a password. Across the room, a storage compartment slid out from inside the wall. Roedie went over to the compartment and took out a crate of particle beam laser rifles. The particle beam laser rifles were a bit different from the normal laser rifles that were usually used. They penetrated an object and exploded the objects from within. He removed four of the particle beam laser rifles from the crate and put it back into the compartment. He had previously tested the rifles and was satisfied with the results.

This should do, he thought.

He headed back to his quarters.

"I'll be back as soon as I can. We just have to check out this planet," Baas said as he kissed Sepheena, her mouth warm with passion.

"Bye. Be careful," Sepheena said, looking worried.

"I wish you could come," Baas said.

"I told you, I'm still bleeding," she said, tilting her head.

"I know. Take care of Reminall," Baas said, kissing his son on the forehead.

"I will," she said, waving after him as he left the room.

"Okay, I'll be joining you three in the *Zoota 2000* in a few moments. We will be escorted down to the planet by two Star Knights. ...See you three in the docking bay," Olossky said, waving Baas, Roedie, and Tokens off the *Quasar* bridge.

In the docking bay, Baas, Roedie, and Tokens each had a particle beam laser rifle slung over his shoulder. Roedie also had one for Olossky.

"What's the difference between these rifles and our regular ones?" Baas asked.

"They explode things from within. They're a little extra protection in case anything happens down there," Roedie said.

"Couldn't our regular laser rifles be good enough?" Tokens asked.

"I made these. They are a hell of a lot better than the other laser rifles. I've also tested them to my satisfaction," Roedie said.

"I see," Tokens said.

"Oh, by the way, how are Sepheena and Reminall doing?" Roedie asked.

"Fine," Baas said. "How's Tereena?"

"She sprained her arm helping me fix our broken couch," Roedie said with a smile on his face.

"...Kind of like on Siitap when I couldn't find you two," Baas said.

"Hey, she was showing me sights," Roedie said.

"I'm *sure* she was..." Baas said.

Below the third-level observation deck that overlooked the docking bay a set of doors opened.

"Here comes Olossky," Tokens said, pointing toward the other end of the docking bay.

Two Kalaar robots followed behind Olossky, their white plating reflecting the illuminators high above. The robots climbed into two Star Knights on the right side of the docking bay.

"Ready?" Olossky asked, putting his hands together.

They all nodded. Baas gave him a stare-down, as he was still upset from their earlier conversation.

They landed the *Zoota 2000* at a location on the planet where the computer indicated there was a clearing near the two humans. The Star Knights swiftly landed on either side of the *Zoota 2000*. They stepped out of the ship. It was dark outside, but they were able to make out the trees and forest around them.

Roedie was at the edge of the forest looking for signs of the two humans when he heard a sound in the nearby trees. He turned to look and a furry, gray creature jumped at him. Roedie stepped out of the way just in time. The animal turned its head toward Roedie, its eyes glowing red in the dark. Roedie pointed his particle beam laser rifle at the creature. The creature opened its mouth and growled, saliva dripping to the ground. The growl seemed to come from deep within the creature. More saliva dripped from its mouth, flowing past its sharp, pointed teeth. Before the creature could jump at him, Roedie shot it with his new rifle. A lavender colored beam of light cut through the darkness of the night and hit the creature. Spurts of light red liquid burst from the creature's body. It fell over dead.

"That was a Geeyi Wolf," an unknown voice said from behind Roedie.

He jumped and spun around.

"Who are *you*? Oh! Hey, I found one of them!" Roedie shouted.

Olossky, Baas, and Tokens ran to the edge of the forest where Roedie stood. The two Kalaar robots remained guarding the ships.

"Who is it?" Olossky asked, coming to a halt next to Roedie.

Olossky saw a woman standing next to a tree.

"What do you people want? You're not from the Rexxian Empire, are you?" the woman asked.

"*Who?*" Olossky had a strange look on his face.

"If you don't know of the Rexxian Empire, then you're not from it. Good! Who are you, then?" she asked.

"Wow, you speak our language. Your ancestors must have migrated here somehow. We came from the BlueMar Galaxy. We're searching for new life forms and exploring other worlds. We're headed for the Regulominuss Galaxy," Olossky said.

He looked up and pointed to the edge of the Regulominuss Galaxy, which loomed in the night sky, partially hidden behind the planet's moon.

"You mustn't go there! There is an empire there, the Rexxian Empire. They are evil people who clone, enslave, and murder.

This planet, Kalerson, used to be in the Regulominuss Galaxy until it drifted outward. The entire star system has drifted outward. This is the only planet in the star system. We have a star, a moon, and this planet. Rwaji named the moonlet Sandtilian. This planet used to be part of a slave operation set up by the Rexxian Empire. They slave the Syclones on the four Ovlon planets," the woman said.

"Ovlon planets? Who is Rwaji?" Olossky asked.

"*I am.* What's this all about, Taila? Who are these people?" a man asked as he exited the forest.

They all turned to him in surprise.

"They are searching for life on other worlds. They're going to the Regulominuss Galaxy," she said.

"My name is Rwaji and she is Taila. If you are going to go to the Regulominuss Galaxy, you better be prepared for a battle with the Rexxian Empire," Rwaji said.

"This is Roedie, Baas, and Tokens. And my name is Olossky."

"We are prepared," Tokens said, "if we have to fight."

"Would you like to join us on our ships?" Baas asked.

"No. We've had enough of the Rexxian Empire and we've been here too long to leave now," Taila said.

"That's understandable," Olossky said.

"No. This is our home. We will grow old together here," Rwaji said.

Rwaji and Taila gave them all the information they knew about the Rexxian Empire.

"Okay. We better get back to the ships and get prepared for a battle, then," Olossky said. "We wish you two good luck."

"Thank you. We wish you luck also," Rwaji said.

When the fleet knew what they were going to face upon arrival at the Regulominuss Galaxy, they hesitated a bit, remembering the short, but deadly war with the BlueMar Empire.

"Okay, start engines at lightspeed and head for the Regulominuss Galaxy," Sintos said over the com.

The nine ships left the Kalerson Star System, headed for the Regulominuss Galaxy.

Chapter Twenty-three
Operation Ovlon

A few weeks later, they were very close to entering the new galaxy. There was curiosity among the fleet regarding what they would find on the four planets of Ovlon. Most of the people in the fleet had been training as a contingency plan in case they ran into any trouble when arriving at the Regulominuss Galaxy.

Baas, Roedie, Sepheena, Tereena, Tokens, and several of the Claderane Government Explorer officers were preparing in a training room of the *Quasar*.

"Hey, Baas, try this," Sepheena said, spinning on her side and diving over a metal shield, firing her laser pistol, and hitting the target.

"It's too difficult," Baas said sarcastically as he smiled at Sepheena.

"Ha, ha." She looked at him, hands on hips.

"Okay. Here goes!" Baas did the same thing that Sepheena did, but he missed the target and put a hole in the wall.

Tereena made her way up an artificial mountainside with her finger tips in the cracks of the stones.

"Oh, shit! I'm slipping."

Tereena hung to the side of the artificial mountain with one hand. She fell from the mountainside, two point five meters high, and landed hard on the floor of the ship. She lay still.

"Tereena! Tereena!" Roedie ran over to her.

"I'm all right. It's the good thing this padding is here," she said, standing up.

She put her arms around Roedie.

"Are you okay?" he asked, looking into her eyes.

Looking down toward her leg, she said, "Yeah, I just hurt my leg."

Tokens ran over to the artificial mountainside and looked at Tereena.

"Thank God, you're all right!" Sepheena said.

"That was high up," Baas said.

"She's all right," Roedie told Tokens.

"I think this is enough training for today," Tokens said.

"More like a week," Tereena said, rubbing her left hip and thigh.

"Okay, training's over for the day!" Tokens shouted to the officers.

They left the training room. Baas, Roedie, Tokens, and the male officers went to the showers on the right side of the corridor. Sepheena helped Tereena as she limped along. They joined the women officers in the showers on the left of the corridor.

They were finally entering the Regulominuss Galaxy. Admiral Olossky made an announcement to all the commanders of the fleet: Commander Sintos of the *Keen Saber,* Commander Roedie Cantin of the *Galactic Explorer,* Commander Baas Cantin of the *Light Avenger,* Commander Encelidia of the *CGS 1,* Commander Sanatoma of the *CGS 2,* Commander Roklarr of the *CGS 3,* Commander Mawjawi of the *CGS 4,* and Commander Tykonis of the *CGS 5.*

The luminous light of billions of stars brightened the view of the fleet. They were on the edge of a new galaxy. Olossky gazed out the bridge window.

"Punch in the coordinates that Rwaji gave me," Olossky told Kahgn.

"Completed. We should be within the Ovlon Star System in approximately five hours, sir," Kahgn said.

Roedie was alone in his quarters when he heard the news. They were finally entering the new galaxy. A vibration shook the *Galactic Explorer* and Roedie fell to the floor.

"What the *hell* is going on?" he shouted.

Tereena ran through an illuminated corridor toward the bridge.

Another vibration shook the ship. Tereena stopped running when she tripped down some stairs and landed on her right cheekbone in a corridor intersection. She screamed and lay on her back, her left leg flat on the floor and her right leg slanted upright. She held the right side of her face.

Roedie ran out of his quarters toward the bridge. He saw Tereena lying on the floor of the corridor intersection.

"Oh, Tereena!" Roedie went to her side.

"Roedie!" Tereena sat up and hugged him. "Whatever jarred the ship the second time made me trip and fall. I was goin' to see what's happening," Tereena said, still hugging Roedie.

"I'm on my way to the bridge as well. Where does it hurt, Tereena?" Roedie asked.

"My cheekbone…I landed on it," she said.

"This sure ain't your day, is it?" Roedie asked.

"No, it isn't. Shall we go see what the hell is going on?" Tereena said as she got up from the floor.

On the bridge, crew members punched buttons and flicked switches, controlling the ship's lasers.

"What's going on?" Roedie asked.

"We're in an asteroid field. Two asteroids already hit the ship. One hit the top set of ion engines and the other one hit below the left docking bay," Tokens said. "We're shooting the asteroids with our lasers."

"Can the ship be repaired?" Roedie asked.

"Yes. Our technicians are working on it now," Tokens said.

"How did we get into this asteroid field? Where is the rest of the fleet?" Roedie asked in a loud voice.

"We had to maneuver around a large asteroid to save the ship and everybody on it, but we ran into a lot more of them. The rest of the fleet is safe," Tokens said.

"That's good," Roedie said.

"We're using the lasers to blow up the asteroids. If our deflector shields weaken too much, we're dead," Tokens said.

"Well, just keep on firing," Roedie said.

Two of the best technicians in the fleet were on board the *Galactic*

Explorer. Along with their teams, they quickly replaced electronic components and patched walls with metal plates.

"Hey, Silva Grid, how are you doing with the walls?" one of the technicians asked as he replaced the titanium floor plates.

"Okay, Thalaghen. How are you doing?"

"All right," Thalaghen said. "We'll be done with these repairs sooner than I anticipated."

"We're out of the asteroid field," Tokens announced with a smile on his face.

"Good," Roedie said.

"We'll catch up with the rest of the fleet in a few minutes," Tokens said.

Tereena kissed Roedie. He found that her mouth was bleeding and spit her blood into a trash can on the side of the control panel.

"I'm sorry. I didn't know my mouth was bleeding," Tereena said.

"That's all right. Let's get you to see the doctor," Roedie said.

"The *Galactic Explorer* has caught up with us, sir," Kahgn said.

"Good," Olossky said. "Ask them again if everything is all right."

"Yes, sir," Kahgn said. He pressed a button on the com. "This is the *Quasar* calling. Is everything all right?"

"Outside of minor damages that are being repaired now, yes," Tokens said.

"We're glad to hear you're okay," Kahgn said.

"Sorry we couldn't answer your earlier inquiry. We were a little busy firing on asteroids. It was pretty intense for a while there," Roedie said.

"I'm just glad you're okay," Olossky said.

"Oh, sir, we are entering the Ovlon Star System now," Kahgn said.

"Okay, scan the planets," Olossky said.

Kahgn turned on a display after scanning the planets. He punched several buttons on a keyboard. On the screen, there was a city. Many technologically advanced semis drove along roads in the city. Ships flew in the atmosphere of the planet. Clones were working with heavy, metal boxes and containers. The clones looked human, except they all looked alike. Kahgn put on a headset and listened for a while.

"These are called Ovlon Freight Transporters," Kahgn said, pointing to a ship on the screen. "Those are Syclone slaves, ruled by the Rexxian Empire."

Kahgn took off the headset and turned off the display.

"It looks like humans can survive on that planet," Olossky said.

"Yes. The Syclones are similar to humans. I take it that the people in the Rexxian Empire are human as well," Kahgn said.

"Okay, I want Roedie, Baas, Sepheena, Tereena, KEN-102, and Karrii-207 to go down and investigate things a little," Olossky said.

"Karrii-207 isn't available. He is dismantled," Kahgn said.

"What happened?" Olossky demanded an answer.

"He fell off a five hundred meter high catwalk in the engine room," Kahgn said.

"Shit! Okay… Well, have the others investigate, then," Olossky said.

After picking up KEN-102 from the *Quasar* and then Baas and Sepheena from the *Light Avenger,* Roedie and Tereena exited the docking bay and headed for the planet of Ovlon IV.

CHAPTER TWENTY-FOUR
OVLON IV

THE ZOOTA 2000 reflected the sun, Olevine, from its shiny hull as it swiftly cut through the grayish-white clouds in the atmosphere of Ovlon IV.

"Dulos Exceltii will have your ass, if you don't fire on that incoming craft!" a man named Syats shouted. He stood next to another man in the Rexxian Empire Building in the city of Purenaan on Ovlon IV.

"I'll send a message on the com and deploy White Star fighters," Cordellex Fiilo said.

Two white colored fighter ships flew above the forest of Ovlon IV. The White Stars had low profile, long, rectangular shaped bodies. They tapered to a point in front of the cockpit canopy. The cropped delta wings were level with the bottom of the ships, their angles straightening briefly before continuing to angle toward the cropped back portion. A sleek stabilizer was fixed at the rear of the ships. Two ion engines sat on either side of the tail and two lasers were mounted on either side of the wings. There was a Rexxian Empire symbol on each wing. The symbol was in the shape of the Regulominuss Galaxy. The two White Stars fired their lasers at a target on their screens.

Laser flashes came from two ships in the distance, hitting the *Zoota 2000* and disabling the deflector shields. The ship sparked and smoke began pouring from it. It started to go down into the forest of Ovlon IV.

"We're in a shipping lane and, as I understand, there is a Cyyro Liner coming toward us. The Cyyro Liner is five lightminutes away," Kahgn said.

"Uh, okay, report to the *Zoota 2000* that we are going to head away from Ovlon IV until traffic clears up. And then let's get out of this shipping lane," Olossky said.

Kahgn turned on the com and called for the *Zoota 2000*. He received no answer.

"There's no answer and I'm not getting a reading on the ship," he said.

"They're probably in the city somewhere. Okay, let's head out," Olossky said.

"Yes, sir," Kahgn said.

Kahgn punched a series of buttons on the computer keyboard and the *Quasar* headed away from the Ovlon IV shipping lane. Kahgn informed the rest of the fleet to follow the *Quasar*.

"What in the hell hit us?" Baas shouted.

"Zoota says that the two fighters following us hit us with their lasers," Sepheena said.

"We're going down," Roedie said.

"Hang on!" Tereena shouted, as the *Zoota 2000* plunged through the high trees and down into thc brush of Ovlon IV.

"They're gone," one of the White Star pilots said.

"Let's head back to the base. That's what Cordellex Fiilo commanded," the other pilot said.

"Should we check out the wreckage?" the first White Star pilot asked.

"Cordellex said nothing about checking the wreckage. He was relaying an order from Syats," the other pilot said.

"Yeah, we should not deviate from orders," the first pilot said.

"We don't want to anger Syats's commander. Emperor Dulos Exceltii doesn't take any shit," the other pilot said.

There was an explosion.

Fire blazed from the *Zoota 2000* with intense flames. They caught the high trees around them on fire.

Sepheena was separated from the rest of the crew. They were on the ground, away from the burning *Zoota 2000*, when the blast occurred. Sepheena screamed as the force of the blast pushed her over a ledge without any control over herself.

"Sepheena!" Baas cried out, reaching into the hot air.

Tears started rolling down Baas's face. He started running toward the distant ledge with the intent of jumping after her. Roedie ran after him and grabbed him. They both fell to the ground near the edge of the cliff.

"You can't jump after her!" Roedie shouted over the noisy blaze of the crackling fire.

"Let me go, you fucking idiot!" Baas punched a hard fist into Roedie's face.

Roedie's nose started bleeding. Baas started for the cliff once again. Roedie grabbed Baas's ankle again and he fell to the ground. Tereena ran over to them.

"Don't you see? Why have two people die? Isn't one bad enough?" she said.

Baas stayed on the ground this time. The gaze of his watery eyes looked so distant. He kept them fixed over the cliff's edge. He started sobbing heavily. Tereena and Roedie cried with him and they hugged each other tight.

"What are we gonna do now?" Tereena asked, looking toward the burning *Zoota 2000*.

Roedie stared up at Tereena's beautiful face, dirt-smudged rosy cheeks, and blond hair.

"I don't know, Tereena. I just don't know," he said.

Sepheena fell from a high ledge. She landed on a smaller ledge below in the greenery of small bushes and brush. She hit her head hard on a small rock hidden at the bottom of the bushes. She lay still.

A tall grayish-brown skinned creature popped its head around a corner near the ledge and looked at Sepheena's unconscious body. The tall creature went back around the cliff. He talked to some other creatures around the cliff wall. Two other tall creatures came around the corner and picked up Sepheena by the arms and legs and took her away from the ledge and around the rock wall.

"Hey, look," Tereena said, pointing to KEN-102 under a tree. They all ran over to the tree. KEN-102 was not moving.

"Are you all right?" Baas asked.

"Yes," KEN-102 said.

The robot got up from the ground and one of his silver arms fell off and onto the ground where he had been sitting.

"Oh, KEN-102, your arm!" Roedie picked up the arm. Smoke came from KEN-102's shoulder. Wires hung from the dismantled limb.

"I can fix it," Roedie said. "I didn't take that electronics course at the Academy of Sciences for nothing."

Holding KEN-102's arm up to his shoulder, Roedie twisted some wires together between the two openings. He snapped the arm into place, where it remained. Roedie opened a plate on the upper part of KEN-102's arm and flicked a few switches and then put the panel back into place.

"Thanks," KEN-102 said.

They found some of their supplies from the ship scattered on the ground. Baas picked up a medical kit and put it in his pocket. They found their rifles and some food bars. Most of the other ship contents were destroyed.

"All right, let's start out this way," Roedie said, heading for some trail.

"Why that way?" Baas asked.

"Why any way? To get out of here, that's why," Roedie said.

They followed Roedie on the trail. There were high trees and low bushes all around them. As they walked along the trail, cracking sounds were made when they crunched small twigs and dry leaves under their feet.

Sepheena awoke to see the forest around her. She sat on a rock with green bushes on either side of it and a tree to her back. She could hear the distant sound of running water from some unseen stream. She felt a bandage on her head. A voice interrupted the sound of the stream.

"You must lead us against the Walaa Kontis."

A grayish-brown skinned creature stood in front of her. She noticed that he spoke her language.

"Who are you? *What* are you?" Sepheena asked.

"I am Riecha'l'adoss of the Phathrit Kai," the creature said.

"Riecha'l'adoss? What's that?" Sepheena asked.

"That is my name. I am the leader of the Phathrit Kai," the creature said.

"What is Phathrit Kai?" Sepheena asked.

"Phathrit Kai is the name of my people as one. It is another name for our army against the Walaa Kontis."

"Who are the Walaa Kontis?" she asked.

"They are our enemies. Their leader is Gawanel'storn'l. It's the good thing we found you first. The Walaa Kontis would have killed you."

"Why?" she asked, holding her head with both hands.

"Our legend says that a queen-warrior would appear out of nowhere and that she would lead us against the evil Walaa Kontis. The Walaa Kontis don't believe the legend and would have killed you," Riecha'l'adoss said, looking at Sepheena with a gaze.

Sepheena started thinking about the day before she awoke. She could not remember. Her head was pounding. She *did* remember hitting her head on something hard at the bottom of some bushes and shrubs.

"We have a meeting with the Walaa Kontis tomorrow. It is supposed to be a peaceful one. I will bring you along," Riecha'l'adoss said. "The legend says that after the first meeting with the Walaa Kontis—when the queen-warrior appears—she will lead us from that point forward."

"Oh…Where does this legend come from?" Sepheena asked.

"Thou doesn't know about the legend?" Riecha'l'adoss asked, stepping back in amazement.

"No," she said.

"Oh, yes, the legend says that the queen-warrior would know little about our ways when she appears. The legend was passed down through the generations of my people. It says that it was written by a lost Syclone, but we never knew what that meant," Riecha'l'adoss said.

Sepheena looked at Riecha'l'adoss.

The legend, it's only a story, written by a Syclone. His people went on for generations thinking it was real. Is it? I did appear. I can't remember anything from the other day or before that. I don't know who I am! Sepheena thought.

"The legend says the queen-warrior should have a name,"

Riecha'l'adoss said.

"I don't know who I am!…I can't remember," Sepheena said.

"Pick a name. You are the queen-warrior," Riecha'l'adoss said.

"I can't remember! I can't remember!" she screamed, putting her hands on her head.

"But the legend says—"

"I don't give a damn about your legend," Sepheena shouted, cutting Riecha'l'adoss off.

After awakening under a large white pine tree where they had slept during the night, Roedie, Baas, Tereena, and KEN-102 made their way down a steep slope. The morning air was fresh and there was a mist on the ground that covered their feet along the trail.

When they reached the bottom of the slope, Baas said, "I have a feeling we're being followed."

Roedie slowly looked up the slope that they had just come down. He heard a twig break at the top of the slope.

"We are definitely being followed," Roedie said.

"If someone wanted to attack us, they could have done it while we were sleeping," Tereena said, looking at Roedie and then to the top of the slope.

"Maybe they just want to follow us…to see what we're going to do," Roedie said.

"Well, let's get out of here," Baas said.

Green plants brushed against their legs as they continued to walk along the trail. They stepped over a log lying across the trail. When they came to a bend in the trail, Roedie stopped.

"I don't think they're following us anymore."

"That was probably their territory—whomever they are—and they wanted to see if we would leave," Tereena said.

"Probably," Baas said.

Baas went ahead of Roedie and stepped in something. He looked down. *Dung!* He remembered stepping in Fateen Pest dung back on Kaskoon.

Sepheena awoke in some sort of tent. She found that she still could not remember anything from before. Her bandage was removed, revealing a slight bump. A face popped in the tent door. It was not Riecha'l'adoss.

"Riecha'l'adoss will see you now," the creature said.

She slowly got up and went out the tent door to find out what

Riecha'l'adoss wanted. Mist covered the ground. Riecha'l'adoss stood by the tree that she had sat by when she awoke the morning before.

"Yes?" she asked.

"It is time to go to the peaceful meeting place. You will carry this," he said, holding out a staff with a pointed end.

"Syta'l'omis and Taweeb'l are the two warriors that will be joining us."

Sepheena took the staff. Riecha'l'adoss turned and started into his tent, stopped. He turned back around to Sepheena.

"I will be out shortly," he said.

"Okay," Sepheena said.

She waited. When he came out, he called two warriors. They came down a hill from their guard duty. Two other warriors took their place.

"Syta'l'omis, Taweeb'l, we are going to the meeting place now," Riecha'l'adoss said.

Sepheena, Riecha'l'adoss, Syta'l'omis, and Taweeb'l stood on a trail when three gray skinned creatures came around a bend to face them.

"Gawanel'storn'l, we have our queen-warrior like the legend says," Riecha'l'adoss said.

The leader of the Walaa Kontis stared at Sepheena.

"There is no legend. We saw three others like her this morning and a strange one too."

"We have proof that there is a queen-warrior. She stands here before you," Riecha'l'adoss said.

"Yes, I see that," Gawanel'storn'l said, looking at Sepheena.

"You have no proof of these other four," said Riecha'l'adoss.

"If you want proof, I'll get you proof. We will meet here tomorrow at the same time and I will have the four others," Gawanel'storn'l said.

"Tomorrow, then," Riecha'l'adoss said.

He turned and started back for the camp followed by Sepheena, Syta'l'omis, and Taweeb'l.

Before Gawanel'storn'l and his two warriors left the meeting place, he turned around and took one last look at Sepheena as she walked away.

Walking on the trail back toward the camp, Riecha'l'adoss asked, "Do you know of any others like yourself around here?"

"I can't remember," she said.

In space above Ovlon IV, the fleet waited for an answer from the *Zoota*

2000. They received none.

"Still no reading?" Olossky asked.

"No, sir."

"I hope nothing happened to them," Olossky said, very worried.

"I hope not," Kahgn said.

"I'll wait a day or two longer and then I'm going to send a team down to the planet," Olossky said.

"I think something will turn up," Kahgn said.

"We'll see," Olossky said. "We'll see."

Roedie grabbed for his laser rifle at his side and aimed it at some creatures that stood in front of him. Baas and Tereena held their laser rifles up as well.

"Can those hurt the Walaa Kontis?" one of the gray skinned creatures asked.

They noticed the creature spoke their language.

"They can hurt anything that gets in our way. And what is the Walaa Kontis?" Roedie asked.

"It is our tribe, our people," the creature said.

The creature started moving his hands toward the laser rifle that Roedie held. Roedie jumped back and pointed the laser rifle straight at the creature's face. The creature jumped back.

"Don't try anything funny," Baas said.

"'Cause if you do," Tereena said, pointing her laser rifle toward a tree beside the creatures and firing it, "we'll have to hurt you."

The laser beam struck the tree and splinters of wood flew from it as it fell to the ground with a loud crash. The creatures turned and started running down the trail.

"We have to follow them to see who their leader is and what he wants from us," Roedie said, running after the creatures.

The others followed him.

"We could be running into a whole mess of trouble," Tereena said.

"It won't be the first time," Roedie said.

Gawanel'storn'l waited for his warriors to return with the three people and the strange one. His warriors ran to him, almost stumbling.

"Where are the others? Did you find them?" Gawanel'storn'l asked.

"Ah…no. They found us," one of the warriors said.

Roedie, Baas, Tereena, and KEN-102 stopped running when they saw the creatures had stopped.

"What do you want from us?" Roedie asked, pointing his laser rifle at the creatures.

"We are a people called Walaa Kontis. There is another tribe called Phathrit Kai. Phathrit Kai is our enemy. They have a person like you with them. They say she is their queen-warrior from their legend," Gawanel'storn'l said.

"Did you say 'she'?" Baas asked.

"Yes, it is a female of your species," Gawanel'storn'l said.

"Could it be Sepheena?" Baas looked at Roedie and Tereena.

"I doubt it," Roedie said.

"Then again, we didn't find a way to the bottom of the cliff to search for her either," Tereena said.

"True," KEN-102 said.

"Where is the female you speak of?" Roedie asked.

"We have a meeting with the Phathrit Kai leader, Riecha'l'adoss, tomorrow. He will bring her to the meeting place," Gawanel'storn'l said.

"Tomorrow?" Tereena asked.

"It is not wise to travel at night. We have shelter for you four for tonight," Gawanel'storn'l said.

They cautiously agreed to wait until morning and took them up on their offer for shelter.

Sepheena awoke in her tent. Riecha'l'adoss came through the tent door. He walked over to Sepheena and grabbed her.

"You are now our leader," Riecha'l'adoss said. Take us to meet with the Walaa Kontis."

"Are you ready to go?" Sepheena asked.

"Yes," he said.

They went through the tent door. Outside, Riecha'l'adoss called Syta'l'omis and Taweeb'l again and they started out for the meeting place.

"Where are they?" Roedie asked, standing at the meeting place.

"They will be here," Gawanel'storn'l said.

Sepheena, Riecha'l'adoss, Syta'l'omis, and Taweeb'l came around the bend in the trail.

"They're here," Gawanel'storn'l said.

Baas, Roedie, Tereena, and KEN-102 saw three grayish-brown skinned creatures come around the bend.

"Sepheena!" Baas ran to her and hugged her.

"What are you doing to our leader?" Riecha'l'adoss asked.

"Who are you?" Sepheena asked Baas.

"Sepheena, you know who— What happened to you?" he asked.

"She may have lost her memory," Tereena said.

"Yes, she must have," Baas said.

"I told you, there were four more, Riecha'l'adoss," Gawanel'storn'l said.

"Yes, I see. You know her?" Riecha'l'adoss asked, looking at Baas.

"Yes," Baas said. "She is my wife and the mother of my child, Reminall."

"I can explain everything to these leaders," Roedie said. "Baas, Tereena, Sepheena, KEN-102, and I are from a fleet in space. We are here to investigate the Syclone slaves. We were shot down and our ship exploded. Sepheena was pushed off from a cliff from the force of the blast. She must have hit her head and lost her memory."

"*Syclone!* That is who created our legend!" Riecha'l'adoss shouted.

"I do remember hitting my head on a rock," Sepheena said.

"Then there is no legend," Riecha'l'adoss said. "Who will lead us against the Walaa Kontis?"

"You will need no leader," Gawanel'storn'l said. "The only reason why we fought in the first place was because of your legend. And if you don't have a legend anymore, there can be peace between our two peoples. The Phathrit Kai and the Walaa Kontis can be at peace."

"I still don't remember you," Sepheena said.

"I think you have a concussion. You will remember," Baas said, "after I give you some medicine to help with your memory."

He took a small medical kit from his pocket and searched through it.

"Oh, no! Is there not an amnesia treatment pill in here?" He rummaged through the medical kit contents. "Wait, there it is."

He removed a package that came standard in every medical kit and opened it. A pill came out into his hand. He gave it to Sepheena and she took it and swallowed it.

"Okay, how long does it take for this to work?" she asked.

Sepheena started to fall and Baas grabbed her and lowered her to the ground. He knelt next to her.

"I hope this works," Baas said.

The complex medication heavily stimulated the brain neurotransmitters that triggered memory formation and recall. It also contained high doses of specific vitamins and herbs. They anxiously waited for the medicine to work. Within an hour, she opened and closed her eyes.

"Baas?" she said, looking into his eyes.

"Did I ever tell you that you have the most beautiful green eyes," Baas said as he kissed her warm lips. "Thank You, God."

"That leaves one problem," Roedie said.

"What?" Riecha'l'adoss asked.

"We have to find the city," Roedie said.

"Problem solved," Riecha'l'adoss said. "I know the way to the city called Purenaan."

"Good," Roedie said.

Riecha'l'adoss led them on a journey through forest, swamp, and wilderness. They followed a trail that brought them by beautiful trees, across a small stream, and deep into the forest. Shadows from the trees surrounded them. They traveled as close to the city as Riecha'l'adoss was comfortable with. He then went back to his home, back to his place in the wilderness. After all, he had a lot of peaceful things to talk about with the Walaa Kontis. After he left them, they traveled onward toward Purenaan by themselves. Soon, the forest thinned and the distance between the trees grew.

"Hey, look. A road," Tereena said.

They walked up a bank and onto the road. Further down the road, the city of Purenaan could be seen.

"There it is," Roedie said.

"Yes, and here comes our ride to the city," Baas said.

"An Ovlon Semi."

The Ovlon Semi came toward them at a steady speed. It was headed toward the city. The semi had an innovative design and included some of the Rexxian Empire's most advanced technology. On the side of the semi, the mirrored glass window glared from Ovlon IV's sun, Olevine. The wheels moved with swiftness. There was a square power core next to a liquid cooling tank toward the bottom of the semi. On top of the semi, the roof tilted upward. On the tilted surface, two mirrored windows glared from Olevine's bright light. The Ovlon Semi was hauling a tanker trailer.

"Get out your laser rifles," Roedie said.

They stepped out onto the road and pointed their laser rifles straight at the front window of the approaching semi. The semi slowed to a stop a few meters away from them. Roedie carefully walked to the driver's door. The rest followed him, looking into the front window of the cab. Roedie motioned with his laser rifle for the man inside the cab to step out. Slowly the door opened and the driver stood before them. He looked human, for the most part. He was bald and muscular.

"What's this thing haulin'?" Roedie asked.

"I'm transporting part of a chemical formula the Rexxian Empire uses on the metal for their laser cannons. But if you're from the Rexxian Empire, you should know that," the man said.

"We are not from the Rexxian Empire," Roedie said. "Are you a Syclone?"

"You're not from the Rexxian Empire? Well, you sure ain't a Syclone. All Syclones look alike, because we are clones. Who are you, then?" the man asked, fear running through his voice.

"Are you a Syclone?" Roedie repeated.

"Yes. Where do you come from?" the man asked, trembling in fear.

"We are from a fleet in space. We come in peace and we are here to help you. We plan to set all Syclone slaves free, but we are here to investigate things first," Roedie said.

"You are the ones! There has been talk going around in Purenaan about a ship being shot down into the forest by the Rexxian Empire. You are the ones!" the man said.

"Yes, our ship was shot down," Baas said.

"I will help you. There is a place where you people can stay and hide. All of the Syclones look the same. The women look all the same and the men look all the same. You people can't be seen in public," the man said.

"What is your name?" Sepheena asked.

"Quee-A3/B6," the man said.

"What?" Roedie asked.

"Quee-A3/B6. That is my name. The Rexxian Empire names all Syclones with codes and numbers when we are born," he said.

"How terrible. The damn evil bastards," Sepheena said.

"Not really. I like it," Quee-A3/B6 said.

"Let's go," Baas said.

"Okay, there are only two seats in the front of this semi, but you other four can stay in the sleeper," Quee-A3/B6 said.

"We *all* should stay in the sleeper in case someone looks inside," Roedie said.

"Okay. Let's go," Quee-A3/B6 said, getting into the driver's seat.

The others went to the other side, got in, and went into the sleeper.

"Where we goin'?" Tereena asked.

"I have to drop this load off at a station and then we can head to the place where you can stay. When we get to the laser equipment station, stay down," Quee-A3/B6 said.

"Okay," Baas said, peering out the front window.

Quee-A3/B6 started the Ovlon Semi. He shifted it through a few gears. It had tubes and wires connected from the shifter rod to the floor. Below the driver's feet, there were four metal petals. He pressed some buttons on the dashboard while the semi started moving.

The dashboard had many LEDs and digital displays on it. There was a digital speedometer, an LED power display and an LED coolant display. A computer and keyboard was built into the dashboard on an angle.

They all introduced themselves and had a good conversation. After traveling several kilometers, they arrived at the station. It was located some distance off from the main road.

"There it is," Quee-A3/B6 said.

Later in Purenaan, the city was dark as night set in. An Ovlon Semi tractor stopped in back of a building in the dark. Quee-A3/B6 turned off the rectangular LED headlights. They all stepped out of the semi.

"This is it," Quee-A3/B6 said.

"Thank you for doing this," Roedie said.

"There is another Syclone that I will be sending here tomorrow. He will look just like me, but he's not me. His name is Bees-K4/S7," Quee-A3/B6 said.

"Did you say earlier that there is a com in this place?" Baas asked.

"Yes," Quee-A3/B6 said. "From what you were saying earlier during our conversation, it should be similar to your coms."

"If we get the right frequency, we can communicate with the fleet," Roedie said.

"I have to go check in at the Rexxian Empire Building," Quee-A3/B6 said. "I'll try to come back tomorrow with the other Syclone."

"Okay," Roedie said.

Quee-A3/B6 got back into the Ovlon Semi and left while the others went into the building.

Inside, they found the com. Roedie sat down and turned it on.

"See if you can turn it to the com frequency that we use," Baas said.

Roedie turned a dial and digital numbers changed on a display. He turned it until it came to the com frequency they used.

"—ossky calling the *Zoota 2000*. Please come in," Olossky's voice came over the speaker.

Roedie pressed the transmit button and said, "This is Roedie. Come in, *Quasar*. Do you read?"

"Yes. What happened? We've been trying to contact you," a long worried voice said.

"The *Zoota 2000* was shot down by the Rexxian Empire. It blew up. We had a few difficulties. We are stranded here, but we have help. A Syclone is helping us," Roedie said.

"Good. Do you want us to send down a rescue ship?" Olossky asked.

"Not yet. We're in a building for the night. It's safe," Roedie said.

"Okay. We had to move away from the planet because we were in a shipping lane."

"Okay. We'll keep in touch. Roedie, out," he said and turned off the com.

Baas looked at Roedie for a long moment. "I'm sorry I punched you in the face."

"We crashed, you thought you lost your wife, you weren't thinking clearly… I was only trying to help," Roedie said, giving his brother a hug. "I love you, Baas."

"I love you too, Roedie."

There was a knock on the building door the next morning. They were all asleep, but Roedie heard it and woke up. He grabbed his rifle and slowly walked to the door and opened it.

It was Quee-A3/B6. No, it was someone that looked like him.

"Hi. I am Bees-K4/S7. Quee-A3/B6 sent me here," he said.

"Come in," Roedie said.

The Syclone stepped into the building.

"Quee-A3/B6 couldn't make it," Bees-K4/S7 said.

"Why?" Baas asked, getting up from where he slept.

"Because Cordellex Fiilo sent him to Ovlon I for a job. I can't help you get the information you want for your investigation, but I can get you off this planet."

"How?" Roedie asked.

"If we break into the Rexxian Empire Building, I can get you people Rexxian Empire suits to wear. If you wear them, you will be thought of as one of them because they are not clones," Bees-K4/S7 said. "If you go to Ovlon I, you might be able to find Quee-A3/B6. He can help you a lot more than I can. The Rexxian Empire isn't so strict on Ovlon I as it is here. Are you ready to go?"

"Are you crazy?" Sepheena asked, getting up from where she had slept.

"The only way to get you off from this planet is to go to the Rexxian Empire Building. Sure it's a risk, but it's the only way," Bees-K4/S7 said.

"He has a point," Roedie said, "if you know what I'm talkin'. If the fleet sends us a rescue ship, our element of surprise with the Rexxian Empire will be gone."

"I won't go," Sepheena said, hands on hips.

Sepheena made her way along a corridor in the Rexxian Empire Building along with Roedie, Baas, Tereena, KEN-102, and Bees-K4/S7.

"I'll bring you to the White Star fighter ships," Bees-K4/S7 said. "Oh, by the way, you were shot down by White Stars."

"I hope the ships convert to the coordinates that dad gave us over the com before we left the building," Roedie said.

"They will," the Syclone said.

They made their way around a corner and through an electronic door. A large docking bay was on the other side. The building had no personnel working at that hour.

"I'll show you how to run them," he said.

They walked over to a group of White Stars and climbed inside one of them. Bees-K4/S7 showed them the White Star control panel. They slipped into the Rexxian Empire suits given to them by Bees-K4/S7. The suits had the Rexxian Empire symbol of the Regulominuss Galaxy on either shoulder.

"You sure you won't get caught?" Baas asked Bees-K4/S7.

"Yes, I'm sure," he said.

They each went to their own White Star and started the ship, like the Syclone had shown them. The five White Stars took off into the atmosphere of Ovlon IV through an opening in the docking bay. The White Stars were not as maneuverable in aviation as the Star Knights that they were used to flying.

Bees-K4/S7 started toward the door of the docking bay. The door opened and two Rexxian Empire Troops stood in front of him with laser pistols drawn.

"What do you think you are doing, Syclone?" one of the troops shouted.

Bees-K4/S7 did not answer. The man who had asked him shot his laser pistol at the Syclone. He fell dead to the metal floor.

CHAPTER TWENTY-FIVE
THE REXXIAN WAR

AFTER ROEDIE AND the others returned to the fleet, they had a small celebration aboard the *Quasar*. The fleet was very happy to see them all back safely. The celebration took place in a medium-sized room. A long table sat in the center of the light gray room with several snacks and refreshments at one end. Illuminators were fixed along the ceiling, brightening the room very well.

Roedie and Tereena sat on a couch drinking Sevela. Baas, Sepheena, and Reminall sat at the table along with Olossky, Kahgn, and Sintos. Tokens and Shamalon were standing by an air system vent having a conversation. Some of the other CGS commanders were present as well.

"The Syclone that we have to talk to is on Ovlon I. His name is Quee-A3/B6," Baas said.

"While you were gone, we made some Syclone connections with their computers. We can find out where any Syclone is working," Olossky said.

"Why would the Rexxian Empire want to enslave the Syclones? No one deserves to be a slave. That is just wrong and evil," Kahgn said.

"Well, from the information that was available on their computers in the Rexxian Empire Building, we know that the Rexxian Empire was originally formed on the planet Rexx. They were too lazy to do work themselves and so they created and slaved the Syclones in the Ovlon Star System," Sintos said.

"If we knew where the planet Rexx was, we could go there and destroy them there," Sepheena said, holding Reminall in her arms.

"We don't know how large the Rexxian Empire actually is," Kahgn said.

"If we can get in touch with Quee-A3/B6, we can find out," Baas said.

"Now that we've hacked into their system, I can look him up on the computer," Kahgn said.

"I know he's somewhere on Ovlon I. That's all I know," Baas said.

"When we're finished here, we can get started on looking him up in the computer," Olossky said.

Next to the air system, Tokens and Shamalon were talking about the five White Star fighters that were now in the *Quasar* docking bay.

"I wonder what we'll do with them," Shamalon said.

"They aren't as advanced as our Star Knights," Tokens said. "I've seen them in the docking bay."

"I'll probably go down there myself to check them out when I get a chance," Shamalon said.

Roedie and Tereena cuddled on the couch, kissing each other. It was a wonderful feeling to be on cloud nine. Their passion for each other was very evident.

Olossky and Kahgn stood at the computer. They were looking for Quee-A3/B6 in the list of Syclone names on the screen.

"Here he is," Kahgn said, pointing to a name on the screen.

"Good. Find out where he is located," Olossky said.

Kahgn selected the name on the screen. It changed the display and the screen read: "*Quee-A3/B6, Ovlon I, Taanii-Taanii, Rexxian Empire Building, 256.*"

"From the information I get, he is on Ovlon I, in a city called Taanii-Taanii and he is currently working in Rexxian Empire Building number 256," Kahgn said.

"He's working now? Good. I'm going to send Baas and Roedie to Ovlon I to get Quee-A3/B6 and bring him back here to the fleet," Olossky said.

• • •

Baas and Roedie were sitting in two White Stars, ready for departure to the planet Ovlon I. Olossky gave them the coordinates to Taanii-Taanii. The two ships flew from the docking bay of the *Quasar* and into space.

"With these White Stars, the Rexxian Empire will not suspect us," Roedie said into his com that was tuned to their special frequency.

"Smooth flying," Baas said into the com of his White Star.

They flew toward Ovlon I. When they reached the atmosphere of the planet, they headed toward the city of Taanii-Taanii.

"I'll check the computer to see the exact location where Quee-A3/B6 is," Baas said.

Silence followed.

"Well?" Roedie asked.

After punching some buttons, Baas said, "He's working at the only chemical plant in this city. It's over there."

Baas looked out the window to a large plant that had tanks and pipes within and around it. They landed at the plant and stepped out of the White Stars. They were wearing the Rexxian Empire uniforms they had received from the Rexxian Empire Building in Purenaan on Ovlon IV. They walked toward the building where Syclone slaves were working.

Roedie walked up to one of the Syclones. The Syclone backed away, noticing that Roedie and Baas were not Syclones.

"Where is Quee-A3/B6?" Roedie asked.

Assuming they were from the Rexxian Empire, he was very cooperative.

"Over there," the Syclone said.

Roedie and Baas walked to where the Syclone had pointed and saw Quee-A3/B6 putting a pipe into a large container and then turning some type of handle.

"Hey," Roedie shouted.

Quee-A3/B6 jumped. He looked over at the other Syclones in the building and then back to Roedie.

"Don't scare me like that, Roedie," Quee-A3/B6 said.

"Sorry. We have to bring you to the fleet so my dad can talk to you regarding the Rexxian Empire," Roedie said.

"About what?" Quee-A3/B6 asked.

"We'll get into the details later. Right now, we have to hurry," Roedie said.

They quickly walked toward the door. A laser beam hit Baas in the middle of his back. He fell hard to the floor. Roedie and Quee-A3/

B6 turned to see where the shot came from. It was the Syclone that showed Baas and Roedie where Quee-A3/B6 was.

"What the hell do you think you're doing?" Quee-A3/B6 asked.

"I'm getting tired of the Rexxian Empire pushing us around," he said.

"These aren't Rexxian Empire officials. They're here to help us. They come from a fleet in space," Quee-A3/B6 said.

"You expect me to believe that?" the Syclone asked.

"Yes. It's true. We are trying to find out information on the Rexxian Empire to free you Syclone slaves. We took these uniforms and those White Stars from the Rexxian Empire Building in Purenaan on Ovlon IV," Roedie said.

Baas stirred on the floor.

"How can he move? He's dead," the Syclone said, looking at the laser pistol in his hand.

"Check your power level switch," Quee-A3/B6 said.

"Oh," the Syclone said, "it was on stun. But, don't think I wouldn't have changed it, if I had known."

"Do you believe us or not?" Roedie asked.

"Yes. Okay, I believe you. But why are you taking Quee-A3/B6?" he asked.

"We are taking him up to the *Quasar* to help us find out more information on the Rexxian Empire," Baas said, standing up now.

"Oh," the Syclone said.

"That hurt. If you had killed me, my brother would have taken you out," Baas said.

"I like your fighting spirit. Just save it for the upcoming war. We will set you slaves free. We just need information right now," Roedie said.

"I'm sorry. My name is Soph-T9/X3. I hope you will be all right."

"I'm okay," Baas said. "But we must hurry."

They left the building. It was cramped, but Quee-A3/B6 squeezed into the back of the White Star that Baas flew. The ships lifted from the surface of Ovlon I.

After questioning Quee-A3/B6, much information was revealed about the Rexxian Empire. Their scientists had developed the race of clones over two hundred years before, in order to have free labor. Many slave operations were set up. Those who opposed the movement were killed.

"We need to know where the planet Rexx is located. We are going to take the Rexxian Empire by surprise and destroy them, if we can,"

Olossky said.

"Before you destroy the Rexxian Empire, you must seek approval from the Keeper of this galaxy. His name is Mara-Harcheit," Quee-A3/B6 said.

"Why do we have to ask him—whomever he is?" Roedie asked, standing next to Kahgn on the bridge of the *Quasar*.

"Because he is a very powerful wise man. He's a mysterious authoritative figure with a spiritual connection to the galaxy. You could say, he has all the answers, according to our legend," Quee-A3/B6 said.

"How do you know him?" Olossky asked.

"Oh, I don't know him. I've never met him. I only know *of* him and where he is located…sort of. We have a lot of legends. But if any of them are true, it's this one," Quee-A3/B6 said. "We have to go there. Believe me, he *will* tell you the right thing to do."

"Where is he?" Roedie asked.

"He is on a planet called Yibon. If he says that you can destroy the Rexxian Empire, he will tell you where Rexx is located," Quee-A3/B6 said.

"Do you know the coordinates to Yibon?" Olossky asked.

"Kind of. The location is also part of our legend, and has also been confirmed, because some have gone there to seek his wisdom. You have to go through the Galactic Channel that you found on your scanners and you must have the correct signal to transmit into the Galactic Channel or you may come out into a star or deep space. The Galactic Channel naturally cycles through gateways to different sections of the Regulominuss Galaxy. The signal that is sent will lock in to the timing sequence for the correct section of space that we seek," Quee-A3/B6 said.

"That's similar to the ESSFs back in the BlueMar Galaxy," Baas said.

"Do you know the right signal code?" Olossky asked.

"Yes. Have your computers send a signal into the Galactic Channel to lock into the correct cycle. Send signal code 22F7," Quee-A3/B6 said.

"Okay, punch that into the computer and send the signal into the Galactic Channel, as Quee-A3/B6 mentioned," Olossky said to Kahgn.

Kahgn did so.

"Okay, have the rest of the fleet follow suit," Olossky said.

"After the signals reach the Galactic Channel, we have exactly twenty-nine point nine minutes to get through it before it cycles," Quee-A3/B6 said.

"Okay," Olossky said. "Kahgn, inform the rest of the fleet to follow us at lightspeed. Then I want you to bring the *Quasar* through the Galactic Channel at lightspeed."

Kahgn informed the rest of the fleet over the com and prepared the engines for lightspeed.

"We won't have much time for the correct opening. Let's go," Olossky said.

"Ten...nine...eight...seven...six...five...four...three...two... one...lightspeed engaged," Kahgn said over the com.

The fleet left that area of space near the Ovlon planets and flew deeper into space, near the edge of the star system.

"We'll be there in twenty-five minutes," Kahgn said.

"There may be pirates in the area too," Quee-A3/B6 said.

The fleet arrived at a part of space that was tinted with a bright purple color. The *Quasar* went through an opening inside the purple tinted area and exited into another part of space.

"Our timing was way too close to its next cycle. Check and see if all the ships made it through the Galactic Channel," Olossky said.

"Okay," Kahgn said. "It's difficult to get a reading on the ships with all the space dust interference."

Kahgn called all the ships over the com and asked them to report.

One by one, the ships started to report in. First, Commander Sintos stated the *Keen Saber* made it through. Tokens reported in from the *Galactic Explorer*. Shamalon, who had been helping out on the bridge of the *Light Avenger*, stated they were also through. Next came reports from Commander Encelidia from *CGS 1*, followed by Commander Tykonis from *CGS 5*, Commander Sanatoma from *CGS 2*, and Commander Mawjawi from *CGS 4*.

"The *CGS 3* did not report in, sir," Kahgn said to Olossky.

"Check on them," Olossky said.

"*CGS 3*, are you all right? Do you copy?"

There was no response.

"Commander Roklarr of *CGS 3*, do you read?" Kahgn asked after a pause.

A faint static signal came over the com. "...we're heading into a star. The Galactic Channel cycled as we entered," the faint voice of Commander Roklarr said as static overtook the signal.

"Holy cosmos!" Kahgn shouted.

"...the ship's burning up!" Commander Roklarr screamed.

The sound of screams was followed by an explosion. The static signal went dead.

"They're dead!" Kahgn said, his face a pale white.

Olossky made the announcement over the com. "This is Admiral Olossky. I regret to inform the fleet that we have lost *CGS 3* and her crew. Please take a moment of silence to remember their sacrifice."

Since Quee-A3/B6 was not fully certain of the exact location of Yibon, Roedie was sent out to investigate a nearby planet to rule out that possibility. The flight of his Star Knight flashed through the darkness of space at the speed of light.

You bastards! he thought.

Two ships were following him, firing their lasers. Roedie checked his computer to see if the area was clear ahead of him so he could travel slightly faster than the speed of light. It was clear. He flicked a switch and the Star Knight went to lightspeed-plus.

When Roedie slowed the ship back to lightspeed, the two ships that were chasing him were left far behind. He sent a signal back to the fleet with his findings and headed in that direction.

"We're getting a signal in from Roedie," Kahgn said.

"What is it?" Olossky asked.

"Listen," Kahgn said.

"I was chased by two ships. They were firing their lasers at me. I put the ship on lightspeed-plus and managed to get away from them. The planet I checked out wasn't Yibon because it didn't have any life forms on it. I'm heading for the fleet at lightspeed now," Roedie said over the com.

"Thank God, he's all right," Olossky said.

"Let him know we found Yibon on our long-range scanners and with a little of Quee-A3/B6's help," Kahgn said.

"The ships that were firing at him must have been pirates," Quee-A3/B6 said, sitting on the bridge of the *Quasar* along with Kahgn and Olossky. "They are known to be in the area."

"We don't need more problems," Olossky said.

The fleet entered the Zasreen Star System and proceeded toward Yibon.

"Roedie, I want you, Baas, KEN-102, and Quee-A3/B6 to go down to Yibon in the new *Zoota 2001*. It was designed by our scientist and engineer, Mas Treeb, and built by two of our finest technicians, Silva

Grid and Thalaghen. Inside a compartment in the ship, there will be an Airglider that you will need. I want you to find the Keeper on Yibon. When you do—*if* you do—I want you to make an official request to destroy the Rexxian Empire. And ask him where the planet Rexx is located," Olossky said as they stood in the docking bay of the *Quasar*.

"Okay," Roedie said.

Sepheena was holding Reminall in her arms. She walked over to Baas and Roedie along with Tereena. Tereena kissed Roedie and stepped back, holding his hands. Baas kissed Sepheena and gave Reminall a kiss on the forehead.

After they had their farewells, Baas, Roedie, KEN-102, and Quee-A3/B6 entered the new *Zoota 2001*.

"This looks exactly like *Zoota 2000*," Roedie said amazed.

"It has a compartment below the floor that holds an Airglider and it's a lot larger," Baas said.

"Talk about large…this ship, *Quasar*, and the rest of the fleet are the biggest ships I've ever seen in space. I've never seen the Rexxian battleships. I've only heard about them," Quee-A3/B6 said.

"They programmed the computer to sound just like the old Zoota and they filled the memory circuits with all the things the other Zoota knew and a lot more," KEN-102 said.

"What other Zoota? I am the *only* Zoota. I am *Zoota 2001*," the computer said.

"They programmed it with everything except the crash on Ovlon IV," KEN-102 said.

"I guess the computer *is* more than the other one was," Baas said.

"Again, I ask you, what other computer?" Zoota asked.

"It's a long story," Roedie said.

"I have all eternity," the computer said.

"No, you don't. We have to go on a mission right now," Roedie said. "And don't get smart or I'll pull your plug."

The new *Zoota 2001* flew from the *Quasar* docking bay and headed for the distant planet Yibon.

When they reached the planet, Roedie flew the ship through the sky blue colored atmosphere. They hadn't detected any structures, but Quee-A3/B6 had a strong feeling to land near a trail they saw in the distance. Roedie landed the *Zoota 2001* in an open area near a rocky hillside next to the trail. They all stepped out of the ship and onto the flat, stone surface. Strands of golden grass grew up from within the cracks of the stone.

"Okay, let's get the Airglider out from that compartment and get going," Roedie said.

After removing the Airglider from *Zoota 2001's* compartment, they stepped in. Roedie started it up. Slowly, it rose from the ground with a hiss and they took off.

"Where the Xyinna Wolves howl is where the Keeper's castle is located," Quee-A3/B6 said. "That's what the legend says anyway."

"You Syclones rely on your legends too much," Roedie said with a grin on his face, the wind catching his hair.

"Don't you have legends?" Quee-A3/B6 asked.

"I guess we do, but we don't rely on them. I'm going to follow this trail up that high hill over there," Roedie said, pointing to the hill in the distance ahead.

The sun was shining bright as they ascended up the trail and into a wooded area. Many different types of trees decorated the forest. The trail went through a series of twists and turns. On their left, a hill set high above them, topped with tall trees. Beautifully colored leaves decorated the tree tops. A brief clearing on the right of the trail revealed a distant canyon with sheer rock cliffs. The trail went straight for some distance before turning again. They had traveled at least five hundred kilometers by the end of the day. The Airglider was much faster than the one they had used back on Kaskoon.

It was getting dark on Yibon and Roedie stopped the Airglider and turned it off. It lowered to the ground where there was another large bluish-green slab of stone with a large crack running through it.

"It looks like the trail ends just ahead of us and we haven't seen a castle or heard any wolf howl yet," Roedie said.

"Maybe we should have taken that trail that ran perpendicular to this one, which we passed back aways," Baas said.

"We've gone five hundred and twenty-five point four kilometers already. Checking that trail back there is worth a try," Roedie said with a sigh.

"We should stay here for the night, though. The legends say that there are dangerous creatures at night on Yibon," Quee-A3/B6 said.

"You and your legends, I don't know about them," Roedie said.

"How are we going to sleep here in the Airglider? There is no protection from whatever Quee-A3/B6 is talking about," Baas said.

"For one thing, there is a laser shield on *this* Airglider to protect from the elements or other dangers," Roedie said, turning on the laser shield. "And for another, there is nothing going to come and bother us in the night. I just want to go to sleep."

A few minutes later, there was a loud growl in the forest next to the Airglider and then there was a movement. A large creature came running toward the Airglider. It hit the laser shield and a loud crackling sound could be heard. The creature ran back into the forest.

"On second thought, I'll stay up," Roedie said.

"That must have been a Stirlaxeen," Quee-A3/B6 said.

"Oh," Roedie said.

Soon, they all closed their eyes, trying to get some sleep. Even Roedie's eyelids became too heavy to stay awake. As the night settled in, the forest noises came alive. A couple of Xyinna Wolves could be heard in the distance.

Roedie's eyes opened wide.

The morning was very misty. They awoke in the Airglider one by one. As the sun rose, the mist cleared and the shiny glare of the morning sunlight reflected from the front of the Airglider.

"What in the *hell* are we doin' in this damn place? Oh, how I'd love to be back on Kaskoon right now. I'm getting sick and tired of traveling through space. It seems like it's been an eternity since we left Kaskoon in the *Zoota 2000*. I'm wasting valuable time. I'm wasting my life. For what? Remember that girl, Sanalia? We dated. She was so special to me. She's the one that lived in Kanthas. I mean, I love Tereena, I just don't understand why anything is the way it is. I just want to leave. I just want to go home. Damn it!" Roedie said.

"What the hell is going on with you all of the sudden?" Baas asked.

"Did you know that I wanted to be an electronic scientist, like dad? You wanted to be an explorer. You're doing what you want. And do you know what else?" Roedie asked.

"What?" Baas asked.

"Tereena's pregnant," Roedie said. "I'm not ready for this…"

Baas looked at Roedie. "So, that's what's bothering you? Roedie, when Sepheena was pregnant, I could not have been happier. I didn't know the first thing about being a father, but I learned real quick. I take it that you and Tereena did not plan this."

"It was a contraceptive failure," Roedie said.

"You should be happy for her, happy for your child. It *will* be Reminall's cousin, you know? It's nothing to be anxious over. You will be a great father, Roedie," Baas said.

"Do you think so?" he asked.

"I know so," Baas said, giving his brother a hug.

After watching the whole thing, Quee-A3/B6 and KEN-102 looked at each other.

"Well, I think we better go find that other trail back there, don't you?" Roedie asked.

"Yeah, after we eat something," Baas said, getting out the food they had brought.

As they sat in the Airglider, they enjoyed crunchy fruit and grain bars and bottled water they had brought with them. After finishing, they were eager to go.

"Let's go, bro," Baas said.

Roedie turned off the laser shield and turned on the Airglider. It rose up with a hiss.

When they arrived at the perpendicular trail they had passed approximately 50 kilometers back the day before, Roedie turned the Airglider to the left and headed down the trail. This new trail displayed many tall pine trees on either side. Several kilometers beyond the turn, the pines faded to reveal a small field of tall, greenish-yellow grass that decorated the edge of a canyon. It was evident that it was another section of the same canyon they had seen earlier the day before. As they approached, Roedie stopped the Airglider. Ahead of them, there was a single tree on the edge of a cliff. A large gray stone rested at the foot of the tree. Where the trail ended at the cliff, an old wooden bridge made of logs extended outward over the canyon. Not far past the edge, the logs and posts ended and were broken. They had collapsed on the left side of the bridge. Across the two kilometer wide canyon, the logs and posts dangled from the other side of the broken bridge as well. They hung down to the nothingness below. The trail on the other side began with a tunnel that was cut through a small mountain that overlooked the canyon.

"How do we get across that canyon?" Baas asked.

"I'll turn the anti-gravitation up all the way and the ground at the bottom of the canyon will counter it. When we get to the other side, I'll turn it back down," Roedie said.

"What if there is no bottom to the canyon?" Quee-A3/B6 asked.

Roedie looked from Quee-A3/B6 to the canyon. "I'll check," he said.

Roedie turned off the Airglider and hopped out. He went to the edge of the cliff and looked at a sign next to the tree. A slight breeze blew over the top of the cliff. Xyinna Wolves once again howled in the distance, the sound echoing through the canyon.

"Verction's Canyon," he read. "There's a bottom all right. It's about five kilometers down. That's all right. The Airglider can handle a depth of seven point five kilometers. I won't quite have to turn it up all the way."

Roedie stepped back into the Airglider and engaged the engine. He turned the anti-gravitation up almost all the way and it started to quickly rise above the trail as he flew it over the edge. It then lowered back down below the trail level and bounced a little until he made some fine-tune adjustments. The flight across the canyon was then smooth.

KEN-102 looked over the side of the Airglider. "Baas, look," he said, pointing to the dark bottom of the canyon.

Baas looked over the side from the front seat of the Airglider, his grip tightening on the seat. "I think I'll just focus on the other end of the canyon," he said.

Quee-A3/B6 peered over the side. "Oh, my…I wouldn't like to fall from here," he said.

"Me either," Roedie said.

When they reached the other side of the canyon, Roedie turned the anti-gravitation back down. They were on the small section of wooden bridge that remained. A tunnel leading into the side of the cliff was before them. A sign was posted next to the tunnel entrance that read: The Keeper, Mara-Harcheit.

"We're going the right way," Quee-A3/B6 said.

Roedie flew the Airglider into the dark tunnel. When the Airglider was completely inside the dark tunnel, illuminators automatically lit up on the Airglider. They all saw a dot of daylight at the other end of the tunnel. When they reached the other end and exited the tunnel, the trail twisted and turned through a forest. They came around a sharp curve in the trail. Roedie stopped the Airglider and stared at something.

"What is it?" Quee-A3/B6 asked.

"Look," Baas said, pointing to what Roedie saw.

Across a golden field of grass, a castle stood on a distant hill. It looked almost as if it were an image. It was made of gray stone. Green vines wrapped around the ancient stone pillars. It looked as though it had not been occupied for centuries.

"That's got to be the Keeper's castle," Quee-A3/B6 said.

"Okay," Roedie said, turning the Airglider toward the castle.

When they reached the castle, Roedie turned off the Airglider. They stepped out onto the ground and walked toward a set of wide stone steps at the front of the castle. Green moss slightly overlaid the light gray steps. The dry moss crunched under their feet as they went up the stairs to the terrace that ran along the front of the castle. They slowly walked between two of the ancient pillars and disappeared into a dark atrium.

"This place reminds me of the Eerie Caverns of the Damned," Baas said.

"It reminds me of our adventures at the Tarr Kingdom," Roedie said, slowly walking to a staircase in the dark atrium. "Let's go up there."

"Why?" Baas whispered cautiously.

"I can see light up there," Roedie whispered back.

They walked up the stone steps toward the dim light. At the top of the stairway, they saw a very strange looking skeleton with a knife in its ribs. It certainly was not a human skeleton.

"I wonder who killed him," KEN-102 said.

"*I* did," a voice to their right said. A man with a white robe stood there. One of his eyes was missing. Only an empty socket remained. He had black hair with gray throughout.

"Who are *you?*" Baas asked.

"I am Kortha, the Keeper's aide. Do you seek Mara-Harcheit?" the man asked.

"Yes," Quee-A3/B6 said.

"Follow me. If you are wondering why I killed that creature with the knife in its ribs, it is because he was trying to kill us. Long ago, there were people that tried to overtake this castle. They were trying to kill Mara-Harcheit. They were called Yithas. That skeleton was one of them. Their evil species is dead now, at least here in the Regulominuss Galaxy. The Xyinna Wolves helped us finish them off here. Their species came from the Nyctogluktoouss Galaxy," Kortha said as they walked along.

They were led through a corridor made of gray stone. They soon entered a large throne room. An old man with long, white hair sat on the throne. His white hair draped over the red robe he wore. A white beard matched his hair.

"You may be dismissed, Kortha," the man on the throne said.

The man in the white robe left the large throne room.

"Are you the Keeper?" Roedie asked.

"I am Mara-Harcheit of Yibon, the Keeper of the Regulominuss Galaxy, the galaxyologist of Yiblos," the man said.

"We need to know if—" Roedie was cut off.

"I know everything that you want to ask me before you speak," the

Keeper said.

"You do?" Baas asked. "Are you some sort of prophet?"

"Something like that. The Rexxian Empire has made me very angry for a long time…about five hundred years to be exact. I've grown tired of their slavery of the Syclones. I can see you've brought one with you." He looked at Quee-A3/B6. "You have my blessing to destroy the Rexxian Empire. There is one small problem however: The Rexxian Empire battleships are much larger than the battleships in your fleet. But there is a chance to win. I'm sorry you lost one of your ships on the journey here. The planet Rexx is located in a star system of the same name, the Rexx Star System. Your ships' computers should be picking up the coordinates right about now," the Keeper said.

"How?" Roedie asked.

"I just planted them there," the Keeper said.

Roedie gave the Keeper a strange look.

"Thanks for your help," KEN-102 said.

"Thank *you*," the Keeper said.

"So, what is Yiblos?" Roedie asked.

"Yiblos is the name of our two galaxies as a whole. Your BlueMar Galaxy and my Regulominuss Galaxy together are called Yiblos. We are very close neighbors," Mara-Harcheit said.

"You seem really connected with the universe," Roedie said.

"I am…" he said. "You all have a blessed trip back to your fleet."

They all thanked him and left the throne room. They met Kortha in the corridor by the stairway. He led them down the steps and out to the terrace.

"Well, you all take care," Kortha said.

"You too. Bye," Baas and the others said as they walked down the mossy steps.

When they returned to the fleet, they found the coordinates to Rexx were indeed planted into the computers by the mysterious Mara-Harcheit. The fleet had been in the Regulominuss Galaxy for about a month and could now travel to the planet Rexx.

In the distance of space, the planet Rexx was shining like a star. Closer to the planet, there were two long, narrow, triangular battleships that tapered to a point at the front, like a shim. They were larger than any one of the ships in the fleet of Claderane Government Explorers. One of the two Rexxian battleships was three times the length of the other.

The longer ship had four engines fixed along the back, stepped across on a 30 degree angle from port to starboard. Each of the ships had two docking bays on either side of their lower sections.

The fleet came upon the planet Rexx at sub-lightspeed, ready for battle.

Emperor Dulos Exceltii of the Rexxian Empire was a tall military man with light gray hair. He towered over the commander on the bridge of the *Rexxeltii*, the larger of the two Rexxian battleships. Commander Siitelaxx Tonn read the information on the screen.

"Emperor Exceltii, there are eight ships approaching us at sub-lightspeed. They are all larger than a Cyyro Liner but smaller than the *Felis*," the commander said.

"Have Commander Extallon of the *Felis* send out ten White Stars and send ten from here on the *Rexxeltii*. Also, have Commander Extallon prepare his men for this incoming party. I'm pissed as it is that he let White Stars—I don't know how many—be stolen from Ovlon IV under his command," Dulos Exceltii said.

"We have twenty White Stars coming at us, Olossky," Kahgn said.

"Okay, send out Kalaar robots in forty Star Knights," Olossky said.

"That's two Star Knights for every White Star," Kahgn said.

"I know," Olossky said. "Let's follow the Star Knights in toward the two large ships. Find out where the main drives of the two large ships are. That's where I want to focus and concentrate our laser fire. I want five ships of the fleet to fire on the largest Rexxian ship and three of our ships to fire on the smaller Rexxian ship. On my mark, have the other ships in the fleet and the *Quasar* fire *all* of our lasers at the same time. After that, split up the remaining Star Knights. Send half to the surface of Rexx to destroy the military headquarters and anything else down there that could be a threat to the fleet. Send the other half to help us destroy the two large ships."

Kahgn turned on a screen. It displayed the two large Rexxian ships. He punched a few keys on the keyboard and a scrambled picture appeared.

"I can't find out where the main power drives are because they are scrambling our scanner signals," Kahgn said.

"Is Commander Sintos able to do any better?" Olossky asked.

Kahgn checked with Sintos.

"Not exactly, but he seems to think the rear of the ship would be a likely target for the power drives," Kahgn said.

"Okay. Have the ships fire toward the rear, then," Olossky said.

"Okay. What if the two ships have deflector shields?"

"Between all of our laser power and their own lasers reflecting back at them from our reflector shields, I would think it will weaken any deflector shields they have in place," Olossky said.

Kahgn quickly completed the task. He explained to the fleet what had to be done.

The eight ships of the fleet followed the forty Star Knights in toward the Rexxian ships. When the White Stars and Star Knights intercepted each other, the fleet went around the two groups of fighters and headed straight for the two Rexxian ships.

Olossky launched additional Star Knights to help destroy the two large Rexxian ships.

"Okay, Siitelaxx Tonn, send out the rest of our White Stars," Dulos Exceltii said. "I want these two ships turned around to face the oncoming threat. Fire all lasers at them. Send a message over the com to have the forces on Rexx send out White Stars."

Of the twenty White Stars that Dulos Exceltii initially deployed, there were only five left. Of the forty Star Knights that Olossky deployed, there were thirty-five left.

Three Star Knights smashed straight into three White Stars, making three soundless explosions in space. The two remaining White Stars exploded when two Star Knights cross-fired on them, sending four blue laser beams to form a double "X".

Half of the remaining Star Knights flew to the surface of Rexx to destroy the military base and anything else that could be a threat to the fleet. The other half of the remaining Star Knights flew in behind the fleet to aid them in destroying the two Rexxian ships.

On the planet Rexx, the sixteen Star Knights intercepted a group of White Stars and several different types of military ground vehicles. One of them looked like an Ovlon Semi, but it had lasers on it and it was firing at the incoming Star Knights. The other ground vehicles had eight dual wheels on them and they all had large particle beam laser cannons fixed to them. One laser beam slashed through two Star Knights as they swerved from left to right. The remaining fourteen Star Knights finished off all of the White Star forces except for one that headed toward space.

The Star Knights turned toward the ground vehicles and fired. Blue streaks of high powered energy struck the ground vehicles. The military vehicles' engines made several loud vibrations and then exploded into thousands of metallic pieces. A large piece of the metal shrapnel flew up and struck a Star Knight as it flew by, causing it to explode. It sent a shower of fire over a small town.

The thirteen remaining Star Knights destroyed other military targets on Rexx before flying back toward space to help the fleet.

"What the hell is Inyurooh Saa-Atlom and Shasatoga Borr doing down there? Tell them to send up more White Stars!" Dulos Exceltii shouted.

"There is no response, sir," Siitelaxx Tonn said.

"Damn!" Dulos Exceltii shouted.

The two Rexxian ships, *Rexxeltii* and *Felis,* were swarming with Star Knights. The second wave of White Stars came from the two Rexxian ships. The White Stars and Star Knights battled between and around the Rexxian ships.

Three White Stars plunged straight into *CGS 1, CGS 4,* and *CGS 5.* The three fleet ships lost control and impacted into the side of the Rexxian ship, *Felis.* The *Felis* exploded, taking with it the three CGS ships and several fighter ships from both sides.

"Did you see that?" Dulos Exceltii shouted, looking through the observation window onboard the only remaining Rexxian battleship.

"Our lasers are just reflecting off their ships like they would reflect from a mirror," Siitelaxx Tonn said.

"Impossible!" Dulos Exceltii shouted.

"If we fire our lasers one more time at that remaining Rexxian ship, it will be enough power to overload their deflector shields and destroy the ship. But we're too close to the ship," Kahgn said.

"How long will it take for the ship to explode when our lasers hit it again?" Olossky asked.

"About one minute," Kahgn said.

"Okay, tell the fleet and remaining Star Knights to disengage and head toward the Ovlon Star System at lightspeed after we fire at the ship," Olossky said.

Kahgn did so.

The lasers hit the *Rexxeltii* and the fleet and Star Knights left at lightspeed. The *Quasar* was the last ship out.

The *Rexxeltii's* deflector shields were disabled and the ship's engines exploded, causing it to lose control. It raced uncontrollably toward Rexx's gravitational force. The ship fell down to the surface of Rexx and impacted into an antimatter power reactor. There was a bright flash as the planet cracked up into trillions of disintegrating asteroids.

"Did you see that flash?" Kahgn asked.

"Yes, the whole planet exploded somehow. If we were any closer to it, we would have had it," Olossky said.

After discovering the Rexxian Empire was not as large as they had assumed, there was much relief among the remaining fleet. Other than the military headquarters on Rexx, there were only a couple small command posts and the slave operations at the Rexxian Empire Buildings in the Ovlon Star System. The trained officers of the fleet along with many Syclones helped in those campaigns. The Syclones were then left to form their own system of government, a new government that would be free from oppression.

A few months after the destruction of the Rexxian Empire and the fleet's subsequent explorations in the Regulominuss Galaxy, the *Zoota 2001* landed in the city of Purenaan on Ovlon IV. Baas and Roedie had their farewell with Quee-A3/B6.

"I'm sorry about Bees-K4/S7. At least we took care of the Rexxian Empire and the officers in the Rexxian Empire Buildings on all of the Ovlon planets. The Syclone slaves are finally free. How is the formation of the new government going? I understand many of the Syclones would like to have their main capital be on the planet Olbah, the innermost planet in this system. Is Olbah really just one large megacity?" Roedie asked.

"Things are going good. Olbah is kind of one large megacity. There are only a few small undeveloped areas. It has been the only free Syclone planet, since the Syclones there overtook it. The Rexxian Empire couldn't get through their own deflector shield that surrounds the planet. And there are so many laser weapons mounted on it that the Rexxian Empire didn't dare go near it after the overthrow. Of course, none of the rest of us could get in either," Quee-A3/B6 said. "We are making major progress in forming the new government."

"Now that you've contacted the people on Olbah, they will agree to help set up the new government?" Baas asked, standing next to a desk in Quee-A3/B6's new office.

"Yes. The new government will be called the Ovlon Government. And I am a representative for Ovlon IV. The other four representatives are on Ovlon I, Ovlon II, Ovlon III, and Olbah. One president will preside over the entire Ovlon Star System. I hope to be the president someday," Quee-A3/B6 said.

"You will, Quee-A3/B6, you will," Roedie assured him.

"Thanks. I'm glad you had a ship retrieve Rwaji and Taila from the planet Kalerson that is drifting outside the edge of the Regulominuss Galaxy as well," Quee-A3/B6 said. "They are grateful, as we all are, that you have destroyed the Rexxian Empire. We understand the loss that you've taken with ships and lives destroyed…Again, thank you."

"You're welcome," Baas said. "And don't forget about being good stewards to the two tribes outside of Purenaan, the Walaa Kontis and the Phathrit Kai."

"I'm glad you mentioned that. I have a meeting with their leaders next week to bring them some much needed supplies."

"Awesome. The Ovlon Government may only be in this star system, but I'm sure that the rest of the Regulominuss Galaxy will be watched by Mara-Harcheit, somehow. Don't let pirates or any other despots destroy a good thing. Always be vigilant," Roedie said.

"Well, we'd better get going, Roedie," Baas said.

"Yeah, I guess so. Bye, Quee-A3/B6. You take care," Roedie said.

"Bye," Quee-A3/B6 said.

Baas and Roedie walked through an electronic door and outside the office. They made their way to the *Zoota 2001* and headed for space. Above Ovlon IV, they landed in the docking bay of the *Quasar*.

PART FOUR
THE FINAL MISSION

Chapter Twenty-Six
End of the Quest

Baas and Roedie had just returned from their farewell with Quee-A3/ B6 on Ovlon IV.

After the brief Rexxian War, the Claderane Government Explorers had explored several star systems with Sintos over the course of a few months. There was approximately 85 percent of the Regulominuss Galaxy yet to be explored. Sintos wanted to explore those uncharted regions of the galaxy in his ship, *Keen Saber*. That was his original mission when he and his crew left the Kameron, but it was the end of the quest for the rest of the fleet. The fleet decided to return to Claderane. They *did* have a lot of information recorded regarding the Regulominuss Galaxy to present to their government.

In space above Ovlon IV, they had their farewells. Sintos and his crew aboard the *Keen Saber* flew toward the edge of the Ovlon Star System. Their destination was the unexplored regions of the Regulominuss Galaxy. They even planned to visit the Keeper, Mara-Harcheit, to obtain more information about the Regulominuss Galaxy.

As the *Keen Saber* departed, its hull glistened with a shine that came from the nearby star of Olevine. Soon, the ship disappeared into the distance of space. The rest of the fleet left the Ovlon Star System, bound for the edge of the Regulominuss Galaxy. There were only four ships left in the fleet, *Quasar, Galactic Explorer, Light Avenger,* and *CGS 2.* The small fleet would soon approach the gap between the two galaxies.

"I really need some Sevela," Roedie said, walking to the mess hall on the *Galactic Explorer.*

Tereena followed him down the illuminated corridor. "So do I," she said. "But I think our supply is running low."

They turned a corner and entered the mess hall. There were a couple other crew members eating at one of the tables. The refrigerator was straight ahead of them. Roedie opened it and grabbed two bottles of blue Sevela. He gave one to Tereena and sat at a table in the middle of the room. She sat at the table with him.

"I felt him kick inside my womb today," Tereena said.

"Or her," Roedie said with a smile.

"You're right. It could be a girl," Tereena said. "We didn't want to know the gender."

"It's gonna be a long voyage back to the BlueMar Galaxy," Roedie said, opening the two bottles of blue Sevela.

They both took a long drink of the carbonated liquid.

"When are we going to start timespeed?" Tereena asked.

"I don't know. I'll be informed as soon as dad has a briefing with Kahgn," Roedie said.

"Okay," Tereena said, taking another drink of her Sevela.

After finishing their beverages, they walked the long corridors toward the bridge. Tokens was at the control panel.

"Oh, hi, Roedie, Tereena," Tokens said.

"Hi," they said in unison.

"We're just waiting for a message from the *Quasar* to start timespeed," Tokens said.

"It will be nice to go home," Roedie said.

Baas and Sepheena stood on the bridge of the *Light Avenger,* along with Shamalon. They awaited orders to start the tac-time engines.

"Well, I have to take a piss. I'll be back up on the bridge in a few minutes," Baas said as he left the bridge, the electronic door sliding shut behind him.

Reminall was in a crib next to Sepheena on the bridge. Sepheena was happy that Tereena was pregnant and Reminall would have a cousin to play with.

Baas soon returned to the bridge and they waited for the message over the com.

"Attention, all fleet ships. This is Admiral Olossky Cantin. We are ready to enter timespeed. We are going to change it up a bit for our return trip. We'll be going into the future to the halfway point and then switch to the past, which is the opposite of what we did on our trip here. Kahgn will send you all the information and coordinates to arrive at the correct time and place in the BlueMar Galaxy," Olossky said.

Kahgn sent the other ships the information and coordinates. On Kahgn's mark, the fleet engaged their synchronized tac-time engines and flew toward the BlueMar Galaxy. The voyage between the two galaxies would take approximately nine months at timespeed.

The fleet had options for the return-date programming of the tac-time engines. They could have gone to a time frame that was shortly after they had left, making it seem like they were not gone long. However, after a brief meeting held earlier between the fleet officials, a decision had been made to return to a time frame that reflected the actual time they were gone in real-time. The computers were programmed for the third month of 230933 SA, which—including the return trip—will have been two years and three months total from when they left Claderane in 230931 SA.

Four ships traveled from the Regulominuss Galaxy at timespeed. One month into the trip, they witnessed the BlueMar Galaxy and its bright spiral shape become an extremely bright flash of light, extending out from the galactic center. The flash was so large, it reached the outer edges of the galaxy. Then the BlueMar Galaxy was gone. Only a bright burning core remained. After a short period of time, the core faded out as well.

This galactic outburst event disturbed those in the fleet very much. They knew something happened to the BlueMar Galaxy, but they did not know what. They recorded the information but kept advancing ahead at timespeed into the future toward the halfway point between galaxies. Their first three-month maintenance stop for the tac-time engines went well. Upon reaching the halfway point, they switched the tac-time engines to the past for the remainder of their journey. The empty darkness in which they were headed reminded Olossky of the dark dream he once had.

. . .

Five months into the trip, Tereena had a baby girl. The excitement of the new born child was shared among the fleet over their coms.

A month later, the fleet was stopped for their second three-month tac-time engine maintenance for the return journey. Although Reminall was only 11 months old, the Cantins took the opportunity of being out of timespeed to celebrate Reminall's upcoming first birthday. As they gathered aboard the *Light Avenger*, it was also a chance for the rest of the family to see the baby for the first time.

Soon after the celebration was over and they each returned to their own ships, the fleet started timespeed for the final increment of the voyage back to the BlueMar Galaxy. They were almost home, but it would take another three months to arrive.

Roedie and Tereena sat in their quarters aboard the *Galactic Explorer*. Tereena held their baby girl in her arms.

"I can't believe she is three months old and we still haven't settled on a name," Roedie said.

"I made my final decision last night," Tereena said. "Is she cute or what?"

"She's very beautiful," Roedie said. "So...?"

"How about Phasheena?" Tereena said.

"Phasheena... That's the one I liked," Roedie said. "I'm glad we settled on that one."

They had thought about many names for the child before the decision. Roedie gave Tereena a hug and took Phasheena into his own arms. The baby started to cry. He gave her back to Tereena.

"She wants her mommy," Tereena said.

"I see that," Roedie said with a grin. "My dad wants to see her again as soon as he can."

"I know," Tereena said, looking at the child.

"Since I also have other things to take care of on the bridge, let's go up there and call him over the com, see if he's busy," Roedie said.

"Okay," she said, getting up from the couch. "The last couple of months sure have been nice, being completely healed from the delivery."

"I know they have, and you did wonderful during delivery, Tereena," Roedie said as they left their quarters.

On their way to the bridge, they encountered two officers who were arguing in the corridor.

"Hey, that's about enough!" Roedie shouted. He looked at Tereena and Phasheena. "You two go up to the bridge. I'll be up there shortly," he said, turning back to the two officers, who were now waiting for a lecture.

"Why are you two grown men fighting?" Roedie asked.

"He stole my laser rifle from the table in the mess hall earlier. He says it's his," one of the officers said.

"It is mine. I was in the mess hall before you even—"

"Okay, that's enough. You've got to be joking. All you have to do is check the assigned serial number. Look, we're all tired of being on this ship. Just settle down. We're almost home, so have some self control. We'll deal with this later," Roedie said, taking the laser rifle from the officer.

He left them, heading for the bridge. The two officers gave each other dirty looks and took off in opposite directions.

On the bridge, Roedie set the laser rifle down and called for Olossky over the com.

"Yes?" Olossky answered.

"Would you like to see our little girl?" Roedie asked.

"Why, I sure would," Olossky said.

Since Olossky had already gone through one child being born during the voyage under his command, he was not as concerned about the second child, especially since they were returning home. He still wished Baas would have told him sooner. He absolutely loved being a grandpa…and he was a grandpa again.

Tereena put Phasheena up to the screen.

"Oh, she's so cute," Olossky said. "What did you name her?"

"Phasheena," Tereena said.

"Oh, I like that name," Olossky said.

Suddenly, the darkness of space became extremely bright with light from a burning galactic core that appeared out of nowhere in the distance of space. In a short period of time, there was another flash. This time, the brightness was so extreme they had to shield their eyes from the observation window. Tereena covered Phasheena's eyes until the brightness dimmed. The BlueMar Galaxy appeared out of nowhere.

"That's the opposite of what happened when we left the Regulominuss Galaxy, going into future time frames. Previously, it exploded instead of re-forming," Olossky said over the com. "I'll get back to you guys later."

. . .

Olossky switched off the com.

That is like my dream, he thought.

"Kahgn, I want the information on the reappearance of the BlueMar Galaxy recorded and backed up on a memory card," he said.

"Yes, sir," Kahgn said, doing so.

When finished, Kahgn put the memory card in the file with the rest of the growing collection from their voyage.

One month later, Olossky stood on the bridge of the *Quasar.*

"We will be entering the BlueMar Galaxy in a few minutes. We should turn off all tac-time engines now and switch to lightspeed," Kahgn said.

"Inform the fleet to stop all synced tac-time engines on your mark," Olossky said.

Kahgn did so.

The fleet came out of timespeed and switched to lightspeed. They flew from the edge of the BlueMar Galaxy to the Claderane Star System, the capital of the Claderane Government.

Soon, the four fleet ships slowly settled on the surface of Claderane. Their long voyage was finally over. They would need to schedule the post-timespeed maintenance on the tac-time engines.

Admiral Olossky Cantin, Commander Roedie Cantin, Commander Baas Cantin, and Commander Sanatoma organized their crews and slowly, one by one, they all stepped out of the ships. Rikks Kyton, the leader of the Claderane Government, stood by the nearby building to greet them. Rikks shook hands with Olossky as he greeted the man.

"Long time, no see," Olossky said.

"What took you guys so long? It's been over two years," Rikks said.

"Boy, have we got a lot to tell you," Olossky said.

"There shouldn't be that much to tell. You were just assigned to explore the only part of the BlueMar Galaxy that had never been explored before, just a little corner of the galaxy. I'm surprised it took so long. And where are the other CGS ships? Why is there battle damage to these ships?" Rikks Kyton asked, looking past the crew members to the ships beyond. "Who are these two children?"

"It's a long story," Olossky said, "a real long story."

"Well, I'm listening," Rikks said.

Olossky turned around to see where Kahgn was in the crowd of people that had exited from the ships.

"Kahgn, do you have the memory cards?" Olossky asked.

"Yes, Admiral," Kahgn said, stepping through the crowd toward the front with a metal container of filed memory cards. "I have them right here."

"Let's go take a look at these memory cards," Olossky said. "I'll tell you what happened first."

"Okay," Rikks said. He turned toward the crowd. "You can all go back to where your old quarters were before you left, if you'd like. Nothing has changed in the buildings since you left. We'll be having a celebration later in the main hall building." He turned back to Olossky. "Let's go."

Olossky and Rikks entered the government building, followed by Roedie, Tereena—holding Phasheena—Baas, Sepheena—holding Reminall—Kahgn, Shamalon, and KEN-102. Slowly, the rest of the crew from the fleet dispersed and went to their old quarters in the different buildings. Olossky introduced Shamalon Kanar to Rikks Kyton.

Deep within the small city of buildings, Olossky told Rikks Kyton what had happened on their voyage.

"Yeah, we explored the part of the BlueMar Galaxy that hadn't been explored before. We'll give you the details when we show you the memory cards. After that, we came to the Kameron Star System, where there is a highly technologically advanced people. They are humans as well. But anyway, they were just about to start exploring in space too, only they were going to go to another galaxy and explore. Well, we asked them if we could go to explore in the other galaxy with them. They said we could. So, they equipped our ships with tac-time engines, engines that go one million times faster than lightspeed, which is considered timespeed. With timespeed, you can only go into future time frames or past time frames. So, we traveled toward the Regulominuss Galaxy for nine months…nine hundred and fifty-four years into the past and then another nine hundred and fifty-four years back into the future. We arrived in the Regulominuss Galaxy in the same time frame as the BlueMar Galaxy," Olossky said.

"Really?" Rikks asked with a blank look on his face.

"Yeah."

"Don't you think it would have been a good idea to contact me for approval to go there?"

After a long pause, Olossky said, "You know, I was so excited about exploring another galaxy, it didn't even cross my mind. But, yes, it would have been a good idea. I apologize."

"Continue…Admiral."

"Then, we encountered a drifting planet outside the Regulominuss Galaxy. To our surprise, there were two people on it. They warned us about a Rexxian Empire. They said the Rexxian Empire was slaving Syclones—which are a race of clones. So, we went to the Ovlon Star System and found out a lot of information on the Syclone slaves. A Syclone showed Baas and Roedie where there was a mysterious prophet of sorts, who authorized us to destroy the Rexxian Empire and set the Syclones free. So, we were in a war while we were gone. And we won the Rexxian War. We set the Syclones free. And they set up a new government.

"We did some exploring in the Regulominuss Galaxy as well, but then decided to come home. The highly technologically advanced people continued to explore in the Regulominuss Galaxy.

"Three of the CGS ships were destroyed in the war with the Rexxian Empire. The other CGS ship didn't make it through the Galactic Channel's correct sequence in time and the ship exited into the wrong part of space, straight into a star.

"On our return trip, we decided to do the opposite and went into future time frames to the halfway point and then switched into past time frames. About a month out from the Regulominuss Galaxy, we witnessed the BlueMar Galaxy explode and then there was nothing. On the other half of the return trip, going into the past, we were about a month from our destination and we saw a bright flash of light and the BlueMar Galaxy reappeared from out of nowhere," Olossky said. "We programmed the tac-time engines so we would arrive in real-time. And here we are, two years later."

Rikks did not say anything for a long time, contemplating all the information.

"We are especially concern with the information about the BlueMar Galaxy exploding when we flew into a future time frame," Olossky added.

"And the children?" Rikks asked.

"Baas and Sepheena had a child, Reminall. And Roedie and Tereena had a child, Phasheena," Olossky said, introducing his two grandchildren.

Kahgn handed Rikks the metal container of memory cards. One by one, Kahgn showed the information to Rikks on a computer.

"I would like to know what made the BlueMar Galaxy explode. It seems to be some type of special bomb that will go off at some point," Rikks Kyton said.

"I know. It disturbs me very much," Olossky said.

"Whatever it is, this means the BlueMar Galaxy will explode in the future," Roedie said.

"And I can give you an exact date on that," Kahgn said, selecting a specific memory card and inserting it into the computer. "Let's see… it will be in the year 231145 SA. Since it is 230933 SA, we have exactly two hundred and twelve more years."

"Just great," Rikks said. "Well, I don't think there's much we can do about it. We can't take a whole galaxy full of people and move them to another galaxy."

"That's for sure," Baas said.

"Why don't we have a meeting concerning this later? I think you guys need a vacation," Rikks said. "How would you like to go back to Kaskoon for a vacation?"

"We'd love it!" Roedie and Baas said together.

"Okay, you can leave as soon as you want. You are more than welcome to stay for tonight's celebration," Rikks said. "Mr. Kanar, we can find you a place to live here on Claderane, if you would like."

"Yes, I would be very grateful," Shamalon said.

"Okay, Kahgn, can you find Mr. Shamalon Kanar a place to live and then come back here when you're finished?" Rikks Kyton asked. "I have an assignment for you to go to the Kameron Star System—which you guys mentioned is where the technologically advanced people are from—and let the people know the status of Sintos and his crew. I also want you to give them a personal invitation to join our government, if they so choose."

"Sure," Kahgn said.

"See you guys when you are back from your vacation," Shamalon said.

"Yeah, see you later, unless you're not staying for the celebration," Kahgn said to the rest of them.

"We might stick around for it," Olossky said as Kahgn and Shamalon left the room.

"Well, did you know that later this year, I will be out of office?" Rikks asked.

"No," Olossky said.

"Yeah. Do you remember Lighrt Rhign? Well, he's going to take my place," Rikks said.

"Oh," Olossky said.

"When you leave for Kaskoon, I need you to leave the government ships here. You do still have the *Zoota 2000,* don't you?" Rikks asked.

"No. It exploded on Ovlon IV. But I had some people build a new one. It's called the *Zoota 2001,*" Olossky said, getting up from the chair.

"Well, contact me if you need anything," Rikks said. "Take care. I hope to see you at the celebration tonight."

"Yeah, I think we'll be there," he said.

They did stay for the celebration. It gave time for Sepheena and Baas to visit Alaress's tombstone and pay their respects. Near dark, there was a fireworks display, a lot of food, and a great time of music, dance, and fellowship. Awards were presented to the admiral and commanders for all they had done on the mission. Honorable mention and a moment of silence was given to the commanders and crew who lost their lives during the mission. Afterward, Olossky, Roedie, Tereena, Phasheena, Baas, Sepheena, Reminall, and KEN-102 went into the *Galactic Explorer* and headed for the docking bay. They stepped into the *Zoota 2001* and Roedie started the engines. He flew it from the docking bay of the *Galactic Explorer* and up into the atmosphere of Claderane. They were on their way to a long awaited vacation. They were on their way home to the warm sands of Kaskoon.

Chapter Twenty-seven
Quarrel Duelco's Revenge

The *Zoota 2001* entered the Kaskar Star System. The Cantins flew past the three Kelson Asteroid Belts and the three planets of Kelsar. They headed toward the planet Kaskoon, which was the closest planet to the star called Kaskar.

Kaskoon had one satellite called Kasmarr. From space, both Kaskoon and Kasmarr looked like two spheres of sand. The small ship entered into the atmosphere of Kaskoon. They flew toward their home, just outside of Kanthas.

Particles of sand slammed into the front window of the *Zoota 2001*. They could see the endless stretch of sand and rock hills. Further, they saw the orange-red horizon over the far hills of sand in the distance. The ship descended toward the sandy ground in front of the Nemnalon house and shed. When the ship landed, Roedie turned off the engines. They stepped out of the ship and onto the soft sand that long awaited their return.

"Man, it's been a long, long time, Roedie," Baas said.

"Too long," Roedie said.

"It hasn't changed much," Olossky said, walking toward the house.

"It looks like somebody has been here," KEN-102 said. "Look at the tracks in the sand."

"Yeah, I wonder who was here," Roedie said.

Olossky came over and looked at the tracks.

"It was probably the Sandkeens," Baas said.

Tereena walked over to look at the tracks, Phasheena in her arms. Sepheena was right behind her, holding Reminall's hand.

Reminall was 14 months old. He was walking now and he was just starting to talk.

"Yeah, they must be Sandkeen tracks," Olossky said.

"Let's go inside the house," Roedie said.

The door panel was destroyed and the door was partially opened with wind-blown sand spread into the living room. They entered the house, the door struggling to shut behind them. Their old robots were stacked against a wall, completely destroyed.

"Don't mind the mess. This is the result of the people who took me away," Olossky said. "KEN-102, I want you to recycle the robots and fix the door when you get a chance."

"Yes, sir," KEN-102 said.

"I can't believe you lived here on a sand planet," Sepheena said to Baas.

"Well, at least it's warmer than the planet you lived on when you were younger, before you were taken to Zonia," Baas said.

"That's true. I lived on a small snow planet in the Sno-Pleednii Star System. It was the farthest planet from our star, Endreen. The name of the planet was Ithoce. It didn't have a satellite. We lived in a warm cave where there was a hot spring and some good soil for a small garden. But outside of that cave, it was damn cold. The average temperature outside was always well below freezing. I didn't like it at all," Sepheena said.

"I don't think I'd like it either," Olossky said.

"I'm glad that you've opened up more about your past. I know it has been painful for you," Baas said.

"Alaress and I were good friends. Her family lived in an adjacent cave…of course until we were both abducted and our families killed by Zantorra. We went from one frozen planet to another," Sepheena said.

"Well, I'm gonna check the 'frigerator," Roedie said, walking into the kitchen.

He opened the refrigerator door. There were two unopened bottles of Sevela and a very, very bad smelling pile of slime that was once a kahsaah. After all, it had been setting there for about five years. Roedie grabbed the two bottles of Sevela and shut the refrigerator door before the whole house started to smell.

"Let's all have some Sevela," Roedie said.

"Several years old Sevela…that sounds good. Not!" Tereena said.

"I think you better get that rotten food out of the refrigerator and throw it outside," Olossky said.

"Okay," Roedie said.

He threw away the two bottles and the rotten kahsaah mess. Discarding it into the garbage can outside, he held his breath until he was away from it. He went back into the house.

Tereena and Sepheena sat with the children on their laps in the two chairs next to the east wall. Baas sat in the chair next to the small table against the south wall. KEN-102 sat on the steps that led up to Baas's room and Roedie's room. Olossky and Roedie stood in the doorway to the kitchen. They all stared at each other with blank faces.

"Well, why don't I show you the house…what little there is to show," Baas said to Tereena and Sepheena.

He showed them Roedie's room, his own room, the kitchen, the bathroom, Olossky's bedroom and the closets. After that, they went back into the living room.

"Well, why don't we take you to Astossky and show you around. I have to buy some food anyway," Olossky said. "First, we'll show you around Astossky and then we'll go to the store."

"You should check out Kanthas too," Baas said as they headed toward the door.

"While we're there, I want to find out who's been operating the Controller while we've been gone," Olossky said, walking outside.

"Do you want to take the Airglider that's within the ship or do you just want to take the ship?" Roedie asked.

"Let's take the ship," Baas said.

They all boarded the ship. Roedie started its engines and they flew toward Astossky.

Roedie landed the ship in one of the free parking ground docking areas in Astossky. They all stepped onto the worn concrete. Roedie and Baas removed the Airglider from the ship and locked the ship. They all stepped into the Airglider.

"Well, where to?" Roedie asked as he sat at the controls of the Airglider.

"Well, why don't we start at the southeast end of Astossky and go to all the sites until we get to the northwest end of Astossky?" Olossky said.

"Sounds good," Baas said.

They headed toward the southeast side of Astossky.

He had been on Kaskoon for over four years. Since then, he traveled the desert sands to relieve his boredom. In the four year period, he had gone to the Tarr Kingdom, the old Controller, the Southern Sand Ridge, the Northern Sand Ridge, the Kahreen Sea of Sand, the Great Plain of Shoon, the Jiikuryon Caves, and the Nycove Sand Bog. He was almost tempted to go down into the Caverns of the Sandkeens, but if he had, he would have never made it out. He already had an encounter with a Sandkeen that resulted in a scar across his face.

He was in his golden colored ship, headed toward the house where he stayed while he was there on Kaskoon. When he reached the house, he noticed that someone had been there. It could not have been the Sandkeens, because there were signs of a ship that had landed there.

There was only one other explanation. He knew who was there. A smile spread across his scarred face. At last, Quarrel Duelco could get his long awaited revenge on the Cantins. He had waited for his revenge long enough. He drew out his laser rifle, laughed to himself, and waited in the living room of the Nemnalon house for the Cantins to return.

The Cantins had gone to half the sites in Astossky when they stopped at a restaurant to eat. It was the Sand Star restaurant. They made themselves comfortable at a table next to the window and the waiter came by and gave each of them a menu, except for KEN-102.

"Prices have dropped considerably since we destroyed the BlueMar Empire four years ago," Olossky said.

"I see that," Roedie said, looking at the menu.

"Well, what sounds good?" Tereena asked.

"I don't know about you, but I'm getting a nice big steak and vegetable soup with some Sevela," Roedie said.

"I'm going to try the kahsaah," Sepheena said. "I'll get some soup for Reminall."

"I'll get some soup and salad for myself and some fruit puree for Phasheena," Tereena said.

"Well, I'm getting some chili," Olossky said.

"I'll get some kahsaah and soup," Baas said.

The waiter was attending several tables in the large dining room. He stopped by, took their orders and the menus, and disappeared around a corner to enter the orders.

"I guess I'll have some electrons," KEN-102 said.

They all laughed.

"Do you have enough credits to pay for the meal?" Olossky asked Baas and Roedie in a joking manner.

"Well, if they don't have enough credits to pay for our meal, they'll be in back with the robots washing dishes," Tereena said.

"I had a dream that I was a dishwasher once," Roedie said.

The waiter came back with their food. They ate their hearty meals and finished looking at the sites in the other half of Astossky.

Olossky stopped at the Kaskoon government office. He went in to find out whom was operating the Controller while they were gone. He found out that Astossky and Kanthas had installed their own separate automatic Controllers a few years ago.

Afterward, they went to the store to purchase some food and head back toward Kanthas in the *Zoota 2001*.

In Kanthas, they went to the Kanthas Archive Historical Building and looked around for a while. Baas and Roedie showed the others a note that was on display. It was a note from Phatom Tarr regarding the development of Astossky. They had turned it in for some credits after finding it on their adventure to the Tarr Kingdom four years earlier. After they were finished at the Kanthas Archive Historical Building, they headed for the house.

Ahead of them, Roedie saw a golden colored ship parked in front of their house.

"Hey, somebody's at our house!" Roedie said.

Olossky looked out the front window of the ship.

"I've seen that ship before. I just don't know where I saw it," Olossky said.

Roedie landed the ship in front of the house next to the other ship. They all stepped out of the ship and headed toward the house door. Roedie had his particle beam laser rifle in his hands as he headed toward the house door. The others followed him at a distance.

The door struggled and slowly opened. A laser was fired. Roedie fell to the living room floor, a severe wound in his right thigh. The laser rifle in Baas's hands was on stun. He fired it at Quarrel Duelco who was in one of the living room chairs next to the east wall. Quarrel Duelco fell to the floor next to Roedie.

"It's Quarrel Duelco," Olossky said as they all went over to check on Roedie. He was not moving. "We need to take him into Astossky right now."

Quarrel Duelco groaned on the floor. Baas turned around and stunned him with the laser again. He fell back onto the floor. Baas and Olossky lifted Roedie and brought him out to the ship.

"That's where I saw the ship. It was leaving Andron when we destroyed the government facilities on the planet," Olossky said, looking at the golden colored ship. "Okay, Baas, can you stay here and make sure he stays in a stunned phase?"

"Yes," Baas said, "but keep in touch over a com. I want to know how Roedie's doin' at the Med-Center."

"Yeah, I'll keep in touch with ya," Olossky said.

Olossky, Sepheena, Reminall, and Tereena—holding Phasheena—stepped aboard the *Zoota 2001*. They flew Roedie to the Med-Center in Astossky. Reminall was scared and started crying. Sepheena comforted the child.

Baas and KEN-102 stayed and guarded Quarrel Duelco. Baas grabbed the laser rifle that Quarrel Duelco shot Roedie with.

At the Med-Center, several doctors and medical robots examined Roedie's unconscious body. The laser beam that was fired from Quarrel Duelco's laser rifle came very close to hitting an artery in Roedie's thigh. It was a severe wound.

Olossky was concerned as they waited in the waiting room. Sepheena and Reminall were sitting in some chairs next to Olossky.

"If he dies…" Tereena broke off as she started to cry.

"I hope they can do something for him," Olossky said, holding Phasheena in his arms.

They sat quietly for a long time. A sense of deja vu came over Olossky.

"I'm gonna take a little walk," Tereena said.

She stood up from her seat and left the waiting room. Sepheena and Olossky looked at each other as she left the room.

"Think she'll be all right?" Olossky asked.

"I don't know. I better go talk to her. Can you watch Reminall?" Sepheena asked.

"Yeah," Olossky said.

"I'll be back in a while, honey. You stay with grandpa," Sepheena said as she left the room.

Reminall looked up at Olossky with a smile.

. . .

Sepheena caught up with Tereena in the corridor. She walked with Tereena in silence for some distance, trying to find the right words to say. Tereena had comforted her on more than one occasion and now she was at a loss for words to return the favor.

"I don't want anything to happen to Roedie either, Tereena," she finally said.

"I know."

Tereena stopped and leaned against the wall, staring at the red carpet. Sepheena put her arm around Tereena and she looked up.

"Why don't we go see how he's doin'?" Sepheena asked.

"Yeah…let's go," Tereena said.

They walked toward the office.

"Is he doing any better?" Baas asked over the com.

"I don't know. I haven't heard anything yet," Olossky said into the com on his arm as he sat with his two grandchildren.

"Well, let me know when you hear something," Baas said.

"Okay," Olossky said. "What's Quarrel Duelco doing?"

"He's still on the floor," Baas said. "Every time he stirs, I stun him again."

"Okay," Olossky said.

Baas set down the com and started to say something to KEN-102 when Quarrel Duelco stirred on the floor.

"Don't shoot again." He looked up from the floor. "I have to show you something that I found."

"What is it?" Baas asked.

"It's a document that I found at the Tarr Kingdom," Quarrel Duelco said.

"Let me see it," Baas said.

"Not quite so fast. I'll let you have it if you set me free," Quarrel Duelco said.

"Give it to me before I blast your face off," Baas said.

"No," Quarrel Duelco said, getting up from the floor.

Baas shot Quarrel Duelco with the laser on stun again. The dethroned and conquered emperor of the long dead BlueMar Empire fell to the floor once more.

Baas turned to KEN-102 once again. "As I was about to say before the rude interruption: Do you think it would be nice to have Kaskoon be the capital of the galaxy instead of Claderane?"

"Yeah, that would be nice," KEN-102 said.

Baas went over to Quarrel Duelco to search for the document that he was referring to. He found it and read it.

"It tells about a missile the Tarr Kingdom sent out somewhere into the galaxy, because they were afraid that some of the other people in the galaxy might take over the Tarr Kingdom in the future—which did happen in 230655 SA. But they didn't foresee a good government taking over the bad government that took them over. The missile was set to detonate many years later in the future. KEN-102, this is it!"

"Is what?" KEN-102 asked.

"Do you remember when the galaxy exploded when we went into future time frames, going timespeed and when it re-formed back together when we went into past time frames?" Baas asked.

"Yes," KEN-102 said.

"Well, what made the galaxy explode must have been the missile the Tarr Kingdom sent out somewhere into the galaxy. The document says that the missile can destroy the whole galaxy. It says it's called the Xalgoma Stride. I think I better keep this document," Baas said.

Sepheena and Tereena found out from the office that Roedie would be fine. After the doctors and medical robots were finished, there was no sign of a scar on Roedie's leg where he had been hit.

When Olossky heard the good news, he told Baas over the com. Roedie entered the waiting room and everyone hugged him.

They took care of the papers with Lu Bluestar. She was the same person that helped them years before when Roedie was hurt. After Olossky paid the Med-Center, they stepped into the *Zoota 2001* and Tereena flew it toward Kanthas.

Tereena landed the *Zoota 2001*. They all stepped out and went into the house.

"How do you feel?" Baas asked.

"All right," Roedie said.

"Listen. I got something to tell you," Baas said.

He told them about the document that he took from Quarrel Duelco. He told them what it meant.

"We should take that to the capital and show Rikks Kyton," Roedie said.

"We also have to take Quarrel Duelco in to be dealt with," Olossky said.

"Well, what are we waiting for?" Sepheena asked.

"Before we go, I have to put these bags of food away," Olossky said. "I bought some things that won't spoil."

Olossky put the food items into the cupboard.

Baas gave Quarrel Duelco one more stun with the laser before they took him into the *Zoota 2001*.

KEN-102 repaired the house door and recycled the old robot remains at a facility in Kanthas. They locked the house up and stood outside. The cool night air swiftly drifted by.

"What are we going to do with his ship?" Baas asked.

"Blow it up," Olossky said.

"I'll get right on that," Baas said.

Baas put one of the explosive charges they kept in the *Zoota 2001* onto Quarrel Duelco's golden colored ship. They all took shelter behind the *Zoota 2001* before Quarrel Duelco's ship, *Aurulent*, exploded.

"Well, let's go," Olossky said.

They stepped into the *Zoota 2001* and lifted from the surface of Kaskoon.

On Claderane, the Cantins met with Rikks Kyton regarding the document that Baas retrieved from Quarrel Duelco.

"Well, that was a short vacation," Rikks said.

Before taking care of the document matters, Rikks Kyton had Quarrel Duelco executed.

"That should have been done over four years ago," Rikks said as they entered a small meeting room.

"I agree," Olossky said.

"We have to find out where in the galaxy the Tarr Kingdom sent this missile called Xalgoma Stride," Rikks said.

"Yes, but how?" Baas asked.

"I know. We could use one of our ships that has a tac-time engine installed and go to a past time frame to the Tarr Kingdom. We can land the ship far enough away from the kingdom so that no one will detect it. We'll have to dress up just like them, though," Roedie said.

"That sounds like a good idea," Rikks said.

"Yeah. We can find out where they sent the missile," Olossky said.

"When you guys find out where they sent the missile, I want you to return to the future time frame—our present time frame—to where the missile is located and disassemble it, if you can," Rikks Kyton said. "It will be your final mission. After it's complete, we won't have any other missions for you and you will be retired from the government.

Your retirement compensation is paid for life. Just think, you can do whatever you want. Olossky, you can even become leader of the Claderane Government, if you run for that position."

Olossky laughed. "I'll pass on that one. And what if we run into any problems?"

"Just do the best you can. I know it will take a while, but do the best you can," Rikks said.

"Okay," Olossky said.

"Oh, that's right. When you guys were on Kaskoon, a man named Klat Morrel was looking for you. I'll give you his house number. It's not too far into Claderane City here," Rikks said.

He wrote down the house number and gave it to Olossky.

"I remember who Klat Morrel is," Roedie said. "He was the man that came up behind us on that ridge on the planet ThornZozaa and showed us where you were, Dad." Roedie looked at Olossky.

"Why don't we go see what he wants?" Olossky asked.

They all stood up.

"I'll have the *Quasar* ready for your mission when you return from talking with Klat Morrel. It will be parked on the same landing pad where the *Zoota 2001* is now."

"Okay," Olossky said. "Bye."

"Bye," Rikks said.

They left and went to find Klat Morrel.

Chapter Twenty-eight
Klat Morrel's True Identity

The walk through the city of buildings was quite a long one. There were so many corridors connecting the various buildings that it took ten minutes to get to the housing section.

"I think this is it," Roedie said.

"Yeah, it is," Olossky said.

Olossky pressed the door sensor. After a long pause that seemed like forever, the door slid to the inside of the wall. A man stood in front of them. It was Klat Morrel.

"Oh, yes. I would like to talk to you," Klat Morrel said. "Please come in."

They entered his home.

"Make yourselves comfortable," he said, gesturing toward a couch and chairs in front of them.

Sitting quietly, they all looked at Klat.

"Now, what I have to tell you is going to probably startle you. I'll go get you all a Sevela," Klat Morrel said.

He left the room and returned with six bottles of Sevela. He handed one to each of them and opened one for himself.

"Okay, here I go," he said. "I'm gonna start way back and tell you from the beginning. The BlueMar Empire was growing strong throughout the galaxy. But they were soon fighting a resistance that started in 230736 SA. At that time, the emperor of the BlueMar Empire was Thytan Xenex.

"Thirty years later, the leader of the resistance was the son of Iver Arra and Lyhn Mikbo. His name was Tahles (Arra) Cantin. The family name changed from Arra to Cantin for some reason. At that time, the emperor was Zonvhel Thine I. Then Tahles and Nikhi Cantin's son, Nomlu Cantin, became leader of the resistance in 230802 SA. At that time, Zonvhel Thine II was the emperor of the galaxy. Then Nomlu and Kahthi Cantin's son, Knighr Cantin, became leader of the resistance in 230832 SA. At the time, Tetra Reab was the emperor of the BlueMar Empire. Knighr and Teetana Cantin's son, Serenitol Cantin, became leader of the resistance in 230862 SA. And at that time, Tetra Reab was still the emperor of the galaxy," Klat Morrel said.

"Serenitol is our grandpa," Baas said.

"Yes, he is. And he wanted to drop in rank in the resistance and change his name to an alias. He was still in the resistance, but there was a new leader that took over. But he never told you, Olossky, that he was in the resistance, because he didn't want you to be involved…even over your mother's arguments. Yes, the late Medess Cantin argued with Serenitol about telling you, Olossky. He moved to the planet Kaskoon to live near you, not letting you know that he was in the resistance. People in the resistance knew him by his pseudonym. He said he was moving to the planet Sanbor for a job, but really he got into further actions with the Claderane Resistance. On future missions, he disguised himself so that you or Baas or Roedie wouldn't recognize him," Klat Morrel said.

"How do you know all this stuff?" Olossky asked.

"Yeah," Roedie said.

"Serenitol's pseudonym is Klat Morrel," Klat Morrel said, taking off a wig, a pseudo beard and a few layers of pseudo skin on his face.

"Why didn't you tell us?" Olossky asked.

"It was for your protection. But I just did," Serenitol Cantin said.

Olossky, Baas, and Roedie got up and hugged Serenitol.

"It's been a long time," Olossky said.

"Too long, son," Serenitol said.

"I've got stories of my own that you don't even know about," Olossky said.

"Yeah?" Serenitol inquired.

"I found out some vital information about the BlueMar Empire planning to conquer the remainder of the BlueMar Galaxy and the Regulominuss Galaxy as well. The most classified part of the information was their discovery of a wormhole to the other galaxy. They were just on the verge of that discovery and did not want the information known to anyone. I did not find out the location, but only that they knew. I'm happy they were never able to complete their work with that discovery. I left my assignment with them and didn't return. KEN-102 insisted on coming with me. Quarrel Duelco eventually found me on Kaskoon and they took me away. That's when I met your Klat Morrel character," Olossky said.

"So, the resistance is in the blood," Serenitol said, laughing.

"That must be why Rikks Kyton said he was familiar with our family name when I first met him here on Claderane, back before the BlueMar War," Roedie said.

Olossky, Baas, and Roedie stood back as Serenitol pointed at Tereena, Phasheena, Sepheena, and Reminall.

"I still have to meet you guys," Serenitol said.

"This is my wife, Tereena, and our little girl, Phasheena," Roedie said, putting his arm around his wife.

"Hi," Tereena said. She took Phasheena's hand and waved it. "Say, 'hi, Great Grandpa.' "

"I'm not that old," Serenitol said with a smile.

"And this is *my* wife, Sepheena, and our son, Reminall," Baas said, pointing to Sepheena and Reminall.

"Say, 'hi,' Reminall," Sepheena said.

"No!" Reminall said with a mean look on his face. He turned away.

"*Well...*" Serenitol said.

"Hey, now that we know your true identity, why don't we have a little celebration before we go on our final mission as government officials?" Roedie suggested.

"Yeah, why don't we?" Olossky asked.

Serenitol went back into the kitchen and brought out a bottle of Grenagaihn export white wine with the year 230826 SA printed on the label. It was 107 years old. He went back into the kitchen and brought out some wine glasses. He carefully opened the wine and poured it into the glasses, giving each one a glass.

"Here's to a successful final mission," Serenitol said, holding his wine glass high in the air.

The others followed suit, holding their glasses in the air with him. They carefully clinked their glasses together and took a drink.

. . .

Later, they left Serenitol's home and headed for the *Quasar.* Tereena, Sepheena, the two children, and KEN-102 were going to stay on Claderane, while Olossky, Baas, and Roedie went on the mission.

After their farewells with Rikks Kyton and their families, they proceeded to board the *Quasar* and engage the ship's engines. It would be just a skeleton crew, but that's all they needed for the mission. Olossky was going to pilot the *Quasar* while Baas and Roedie helped on the bridge with navigation and time calculations. It would take a couple months of circling the galaxy to reach the correct time frame and a couple months to return.

The ship slowly lifted from the surface of Claderane and headed for space. Roedie programmed the tac-time engine with the date to arrive at Kaskoon at the appropriate time.

"Ready for timespeed?" Olossky asked.

"Any time," the two brothers said together.

The ship disappeared, going into past time frames, to the year that was printed on the document that Baas took from Quarrel Duelco, to the year 230532 SA. It was a time when Ci'is Moro'oe was ruler of the Tarr Kingdom.

Chapter Twenty-nine
Kingdom in the Sands

The *Quasar* came out of timespeed in the Kaskar Star System. They headed for Kaskoon at lightspeed.

"So, we're in the year 230532 SA and Ci'is Moro'oe is the ruler of the Tarr Kingdom," Baas said.

"Yes, we've gone four hundred and one years into the past. And it is the first month of the year. The document says that they sent the missile out in the second month. That gives us one month to find out where they're going to send it," Roedie said.

"Yeah, we have one month to find out, but I want to be out of there in less than a week. Got it?" Olossky said.

"I hope that's not a problem," Roedie said.

"So do I," Olossky said.

The *Quasar* entered the atmosphere of Kaskoon. Olossky landed the ship where their Nemnalon house will be located in the future. Shutting down the ship, Olossky stood from his chair.

"Now, we have to make some plans," Olossky said, looking at Baas and Roedie. "We are going to take one of the Airgliders that's in the Star Knight construction room off from the docking bay and go just close enough to the Tarr Kingdom to get a good look at the type of clothes they wear. When we find out, we're gonna have to come back here and make some outfits that look exactly like theirs. Then we'll go back and stash the Airglider. We'll kind of drift in with the crowd so we aren't noticed, if you know what I'm talkin'."

"What about weapons?" Roedie asked.

"For this scout operation, we'll each carry a laser rifle. But when we infiltrate the kingdom, we'll have to keep the laser rifles in the stashed Airglider," Olossky said. "We should probably have concealed laser pistols when we go in. I'll grab a camera as well."

"Rikks Kyton left three new lasers over here on the counter," Baas said, walking over to a counter on the bridge of the *Quasar*. "There's a note here. I read it earlier. It says that these lasers are new ones just developed by one of Rikks's engineers. It says they are automatic particle beam laser rifles that have twice the power of regular particle beam laser rifles. They emit twenty laser beams per second."

"Now that's an impressive laser weapon," Olossky said.

Grabbing the automatic particle beam laser rifles and camera, they headed for the docking bay. After walking down the stairs from the third level, they entered the Star Knight construction room off from the docking bay.

The construction room itself was modified by Karrii-207 when the Claderane Resistance received the ship from Olossky and KEN-102, after they had acquired it from the BlueMar Empire. The other two ships, *Light Avenger* and *Galactic Explorer*, brought in by Baas, Sepheena, Roedie, and Tereena, were also modified by Karrii-207 at the time, the evening before the launch of the BlueMar War.

Among the spare pieces for constructing Star Knight fighter ships and other things, there were a few Airgliders and Weathertreads. Olossky, Baas, and Roedie managed to get one Airglider out into the docking bay and start it up. They checked to be sure it was operating properly. After a brief moment, the Airglider's engine stopped and it fell to the metal docking bay floor with a loud, echoing clang. Baas was inside it at the time. He stepped out and walked toward Olossky and Roedie, his back crouched. He straightened his back up.

"That hurt," he said.

Olossky and Roedie started to laugh.

"Very funny," Baas said. "So, what do you think is wrong with it?"

"I don't know, but we could try the other two Airgliders in there with that other junk," Roedie said. "I can't understand why Rikks Kyton didn't have a good Airglider ready for us."

They all looked at each other and started walking back to the Star

Knight construction room. After bringing out the other two Airgliders, they tried them. The first one did not start at all and the second one fell apart when they tried to start it. They brought them both back into the room of cluttered metal.

"We'll just have to repair the first one we got out of here," Olossky said.

They walked back into the docking bay. Baas went over to the Airglider and opened a panel at the front of it. He looked inside at all the electronic components and circuitry on a number of circuit boards.

"Roedie, I think this is a job for you," he said.

Roedie walked over to the open panel and looked inside. He removed all twelve plug-in boards and examined each of them. One of them had two components burned out. He put all of the printed circuit boards back into place, except for the bad one.

"What is it?" Olossky asked.

"There is a burned-out resistor and a burned-out diode on this board," Roedie said.

"The other Airgliders are the same model. Let's hope the components on the same board from one of the other Airgliders aren't burned out as well," Olossky said.

"I hope not," Roedie said, going back into the Star Knight construction room to check the other circuit boards.

On the first Airglider he checked, all components were fine. He pulled the board out of its terminal. He discarded the bad board into the pile of metal junk. He came back out into the docking bay with the good board, replaced it in its slot, and closed the panel.

"Okay, try it again, Baas," Roedie said.

"Oh, no, not this time," Baas said.

"Come on. It's not going to fall again," Roedie said.

Baas stepped into the Airglider and started it up. It rose from the metal floor with a hiss and stayed up this time.

Baas looked at Roedie. "You're lucky," he said.

"Ha, ha," Roedie said.

Olossky and Roedie stepped up into the Airglider where Baas was.

"Did you make sure that the ship's door was locked, Roedie?" Olossky asked.

"Yeah, it's locked," Roedie said.

"Good. Let's go," Baas said, flying the Airglider toward the docking bay exit.

"Stop!" Olossky said.

Baas stopped the Airglider.

"What's under that tarp against the docking bay wall?"

"I don't know," Baas said as he turned off the Airglider.

Olossky stepped out and walked over to the docking bay wall. Beneath a yellow and black striped, metal stairway that led to the upper level observation deck, a tarp covered what Olossky had suspected. He removed the tarp to reveal a brand new and improved Airglider.

"I didn't think Rikks would leave out any details," Olossky said.

"Let's take *that* one," Baas said.

After returning the old Airglider to the Star Knight construction room, they stepped into the new Airglider. Olossky started it and flew the Airglider out of the *Quasar* docking bay. The docking bay exit portal was ten meters up from the sandy ground. As they dropped, they bounced a couple times without touching the ground before the Airglider stabilized.

The wind was still. Ripples of sand stretched across the hills. They flew toward the Tarr Kingdom. Flying over a hill, they passed two Sandkeens who just looked at each other and went back to stabbing a Fateen Pest. They passed where the original Controller will be located in the future. Just an outcrop was there now with dark brown rocks spread across the beige sand. They passed the Nycove Sand Bog and then noticed the kingdom in the sands, the Tarr Kingdom.

"Hey, there it is," Baas said, pointing to the temples in the distance.

Olossky slowed the Airglider. He flew it behind a large outcrop nearby and came to a stop. They stepped out and grabbed their automatic particle beam laser rifles.

"We'll have to hide behind these outcrops that are scattered across the sand toward the Tarr Kingdom," Olossky said.

They made their way toward the temples, hiding behind each outcrop. They proceeded, getting closer and closer to the temples.

When they were approximately two hundred meters away from the closest temple, Olossky retrieved the camera from his pocket.

"Okay, that's far enough. I'll get some pictures of the people's clothes, so we know how to replicate them."

"There's two of them now," Roedie said.

They all looked across the stretch of sand to see two men dressed in black suits. They had chains around their waists and wrists. Fingerless gauntlets covered their hands. They both had knives that rested at their right sides. In their hands, they held metal staves. One man looked to be about twenty years old, while the other looked about thirty. The two men stood on either side of the temple door.

"They must be guards," Baas said.

Olossky snapped a few pictures. He assigned the word "guard" to the pictures on the camera.

They looked back across the stretch of sand. A man came out of the temple door. He wore a white robe with gray trim. He looked to be around the age of thirty years. The man said something to one of the guards and the guard left his post and went into the temple. The man in the white robe walked down a tan set of stone steps and over to an older man who wore an all gray suit. The man in the gray suit gave him an order.

"At your service, ruler's aide," the man in the white robe said, quite loudly.

They could not make out the rest of their conversation. Olossky took a couple more pictures and labeled them "ruler's aide servant" and "ruler's aide".

"Okay, you two can be guards and I will be a servant for the ruler's aide. Let's head back to the Airglider," Olossky said.

They started back toward the Airglider, hiding carefully behind each outcrop. When they finally reached the Airglider, they got in and flew back to the *Quasar*.

Olossky, Baas, and Roedie stood on the bridge of the *Quasar*. Rikks Kyton had left a variety of materials in many different colors and patterns inside a closet off from the bridge of the *Quasar*. They brought out the variety of materials from the closet and laid them out on the counter.

"You two can start making your guard suits and I'll make my servant's suit," Olossky said.

"What we need is a seamstress robot," Roedie said.

"I agree," Baas said.

Baas and Roedie grabbed some black material from the pile in a metal container. Olossky took some white and gray material.

They cut and sewed for about two days before there was any resemblance to the clothing in the pictures on the camera.

After some much needed sleep, they met on the bridge to finish up the clothing.

"How's this?" Roedie asked, holding up the black suit.

"That looks exactly like the ones the guards were wearing," Olossky said.

"What about this?" Baas asked, holding up his black suit.

"That looks convincing to me as well," Olossky said.

"Now we have to put the finishing touches on the gauntlets and find a couple of knives and staves," Roedie said.

"Well, I'll go to the weapons room and see if I can find something close while you finish up on the gauntlets," Baas said, leaving the bridge.

By the time Baas returned with two knives, two staves, and some chains that looked similar to the pictures on the camera, Roedie and Olossky had finished the gauntlets and white robe with gray trim.

"Where have *you* been for the last few hours?" Olossky asked.

"I thought I'd let you guys finish the rest of the things," Baas said.

"You suck! At least you could have finished your own gauntlets, if you would have come back here in time," Roedie said.

"Let's not argue," Olossky said, handing the pair of fingerless gauntlets to Baas.

Baas handed Roedie a knife, a staff, and some chains.

"It did take me a while to find these," Baas said.

"Okay, let's put these outfits on," Olossky said.

They all changed into their outfits. Baas and Roedie slipped on their fingerless gauntlets. They attached the knives to their right sides, put on the chains, and grabbed the staves.

"Ready?" Olossky asked.

"Yeah," Roedie said.

"I'm a bit anxious," Baas said.

"We need to synchronize our digital time displays and meet at exactly twenty-two hundred hours behind that same outcrop where the Airglider will be. Learn as much as you can. And try to fit in," Olossky said.

They left the bridge and headed for the docking bay. After stepping into the Airglider, they exited the *Quasar*.

Hiding behind each outcrop, they made their way toward the temple once again. At the last outcrop, they looked at each other.

"Okay, I'll go in first," Olossky said. "You two come join in about five minutes."

"Okay," Baas and Roedie said.

When it was all clear, Olossky stood up and walked toward the temple. He walked behind a large outcrop that was next to a building where armadas were assigned missions. Baas had told him about the armadas from what he learned at the Kanthas Archive Historical Building. Olossky went around the rock and toward the first temple. Fear ran through him at the thought of being discovered as an intruder.

Baas and Roedie had that same feeling as they walked toward the temple five minutes later. A man in a gray suit walked out the temple door. It was Ci'is Moro'oe's aide.

"Hey, Whimthiw Servant, I need your help back in the science building. We have to make sure the Xalgoma Stride's fuel isn't leaking again," the ruler's aide said to Olossky.

"Yes, sir," Olossky said.

"You will call me Gleesinoss. My name is Gleesinoss Mhythewn. Why do you Whimthiw Servants persist on calling me 'sir?' I told you guys about that before," the ruler's aide said.

"Sorry about that, Gleesinoss," Olossky said.

"That's more like it. Now, let's go to the science building. Oh, and you two Sand Knights," Gleesinoss Mhythewn said, pointing at Baas and Roedie who stood by the outcrop, "go over and give a hand to the Whimthiw Servants in the armada building. They're moving some heavy equipment."

Baas and Roedie looked at each other as Olossky and Gleesinoss took off toward the back of the second temple. Walking toward the armada building, memories came back from when they had explored there.

"Where in all these sands have you Sand Knights been?" a Whimthiw Servant asked.

"Gleesinoss just told us to come here a second ago," Roedie said.

"Well, let's move this stuff. If you Sand Knights don't get your act together, you'll be sent to Astossky," the Whimthiw Servant said.

Baas and Roedie looked at each other.

What do they do to people in Astossky? That's not even a city yet, Baas thought.

They started to help move the heavy equipment across the room of the armada building. It was going to be a long day.

At twenty-two hundred hours, they managed to meet at the Airglider behind the far outcrop without being seen.

"Okay, tell me everything that you found out today," Olossky said.

"We were together all day. We found out that if you don't do as they say, you'll be sent to Astossky. Phatom Tarr, the first ruler of this kingdom, developed Astossky into a town. They must do something to the people they send there," Roedie said.

"I do remember reading in the *Astossky Editorial* that they had found skeletons in an Astossky archeological dig. So, is that all you've learned today?" Olossky asked.

"That's all we learned that's worth mentioning," Baas said.

"Okay. What I learned is that they want to send the Xalgoma Stride off from this planet as soon as possible. But from the document, we already know the date they're going to launch it. It's set to detonate in six hundred and thirteen years. And I also learned a lot of technical information about the Xalgoma Stride," Olossky said.

"Then we still don't know where they're gonna send it," Baas said.

"Hopefully, I can find that out tomorrow," Olossky said.

"Why don't we just follow the missile to its destination? Roedie asked.

"Hey, I never thought of that," Olossky said. "Great idea."

"Why don't we do that?" Baas asked.

"We will," Olossky said, getting into the Airglider.

Baas and Roedie also stepped into the Airglider. They flew back to the *Quasar* docking bay and parked the Airglider.

"We can either wait here a month or fly a month into the future," Olossky said.

"Let's go timespeed into the future," Roedie said.

"Okay," Olossky said, starting up the *Quasar*.

The ship lifted from the sands of Kaskoon and headed toward the night sky. Olossky programmed the computer for timespeed. It only took about seventeen minutes to go one month into the future at timespeed.

"What time is the missile set to launch?" Olossky asked.

"According to the document that I retrieved from Quarrel Duelco, it is the second day of the second month of 230532 SA at zero seven hundred hours," Baas said.

"We have eight hours yet. I'm gonna sleep for six hours. I'll set my alarm," Olossky said. "I'll also leave the ship orbiting the planet."

"I think I'll get some sleep too," Roedie said.

"Yeah," Baas said. "But instead of going to the quarters section to sleep, I think we should stay on the bridge."

"Yes," Olossky said.

They all found a place on the bridge to sleep.

Olossky woke up.

"Hey, Baas, Roedie, the missile's gonna launch in ten minutes. I must not have heard my alarm," Olossky said.

Baas and Roedie quickly got up. Olossky flew the *Quasar* in space above the Tarr Kingdom.

The Xalgoma Stride launched.

CHAPTER THIRTY
THE XALGOMA STRIDE

THE XALGOMA STRIDE flew past the *Quasar* at an increasing speed. Olossky followed right behind it.

"Looks like it's heading toward the Tuska Thaxe Star System," Roedie said.

A minute later, the Xalgoma Stride turned on a 60 degree angle, 30.64 degrees from the galactic plane.

"I guess it's not heading there," Roedie said.

"We'll find out where it's heading when it gets to its destination," Olossky said.

They entered the Rotooth Tanis-Sintex Star System. It was a star system that consisted of five giant, gaseous planets: Aoraaian, Aaroseekk, Delfooyion, Leista, and Eraanio-Sintex Fygaborr. The system's star was called Rotooth.

When the BlueMar Empire was in power, they used the Rotooth Tanis-Sintex Star System primarily for the mining of titanium and Lysithium Star Crystal on some of the gas giants' satellites.

When it left the Rotooth Tanis-Sintex Star System, the Xalgoma Stride changed trajectory again, on a 31.57 degree angle and matched the galactic plane exactly. They followed it.

"It's heading for the center of the galaxy," Olossky said.

"That's it!" Roedie said. "If you put an explosive device in the middle of something, it will blow to the outer edge when it explodes if it is powerful enough—"

"Yeah," Baas said.

"And the Xalgoma Stride has the power to blow up the entire BlueMar Galaxy. It seems strange that the thing has enough force and is fast enough to expand its energy across the vacuum of space to every bit of matter in the galaxy," Roedie continued.

"Well, it's the most powerful explosive device made in history. I'm surprised that the Tarr Kingdom could make such a weapon," Olossky said.

"So am I. But I am thinking that it has to be something that's far beyond nuclear," Baas said.

"Definitely...I did not find out what they manufactured it with when we were at the Tarr Kingdom," Olossky said. "The missile's slowing down now. It slowed down to exactly four hundred kilometers per hour."

"Wait a minute. Look at the screen," Roedie said. "The engines just stopped on the missile. It's just drifting now."

"Yeah, we're only four terameters from the center of the galaxy," Olossky said.

"We're coming upon masses of stars now," Baas said.

"Yeah, and it's gettin' kinda hot in here. You wanna turn up the air conditioner?" Roedie asked.

Olossky stopped the *Quasar* immediately.

"Look at the radiation level," Olossky said.

Olossky pressed a button and a protective shield covered the observation window.

"We can't go any further unless we use the reflector shield," Roedie said.

"Yeah, but even then, the radiation will cause the reflector shield to decay," Olossky said.

"Do you still have the missile on the scanners?" Baas asked.

"Yes," Olossky said. "It stopped."

"Where?" Baas asked.

"It's in a space where there's a large gap between stars. The radiation there will be low," Olossky said. "I know Rikks wanted us to destroy the Xalgoma Stride in our normal time frame, but we're here now. Let's just do it."

"If we are able to get through the high radiation to where the missile is, we can disassemble it," Baas said.

"Well, if we keep the reflector shield on and go through the high radiation area at lightspeed-plus, we might be able to do it," Olossky said.

"Why don't we try it?" Roedie said.

"Okay," Olossky said, "here goes."

He activated the reflector shields and they flew through the high radiation area at lightspeed-plus.

"We did it," Baas said.

"Yes, but one engine in the tail end of the *Quasar* went out. There's a hole in the reflector shield where that engine is," Olossky said, looking at the screen in front of him.

"Is the radiation low enough here so it doesn't penetrate a spacesuit?" Roedie asked with a look of concern on his face.

"Yes, the level is low enough here," Olossky said. "Since both you and I know about electronics, Roedie, we'll go out and disassemble the Xalgoma Stride together. Baas, I need you to stay here on the bridge in case anything else happens."

"No problem," Baas said. "Be safe."

"Okay, let's go put on our spacesuits and rocket packs, Roedie," Olossky said.

Olossky and Roedie left the bridge and went to the docking bay. In the docking bay, on the opposite side of the Star Knight construction room, there was a closet containing spacesuits and rocket packs. After they put on their suits and rocket packs, they collected some tools from a cabinet in the docking bay and went into the airlock. Moments later, they were in space. With the tool containers attached to their arms, they maneuvered their rocket packs toward the Xalgoma Stride.

From a distance, the Xalgoma Stride looked like a large cylinder that narrowed toward the front and came to a point.

"Since the missile was exposed to high levels of radiation from the stars, it's the good thing these suits can withstand those high amounts," Roedie said through the com in his spacesuit helmet.

"Yeah," Olossky said. "When I saw the missile at the Tarr Kingdom, the panel that had the electronics in it was down by the engines."

They drifted toward the aft of the Xalgoma Stride and stopped, holding onto the missile's tail fins. Olossky opened the panel with an instrument from the tool container and looked inside. The illuminator mounted on his helmet brightened the inside of the panel.

"Here's the power core," Olossky said.

He pulled out the power core circuit board.

"I just pulled its first power source," Olossky said.

He pulled out two more power core circuit boards and handed them all to Roedie, who put them into his tool container.

"Now, its timer is powered with the auxiliary power core. I found out from one of the scientists at the Tarr Kingdom that it also has proximity sensors. If its sensors detect that it's not in the correct location from where it should be after it reaches its destination, it will detonate," Olossky said.

"What gives it the power to explode, if we pulled all three power cores?" Roedie asked.

"There's a fourth one inside the auxiliary section and is surrounded by radioactive material. We can't get to that one, but there are wires leading out from it that control its power. If we cut those wires, it won't detonate," Olossky said.

"Where are the wires?" Roedie asked.

"They're up toward the apex of the missile," Olossky said.

They carefully drifted to the other end of the Xalgoma Stride, first moving to the middle wings and then making their way to the canards at the front. There were several red LEDs flashing near the apex. Olossky opened a panel at the tip of the missile. Inside, there were several wires.

"Which one do we cut?" Roedie asked, wire cutters in his hand.

"Two are the wires leading from the fourth power core circuit board in the auxiliary section and the other wires control the proximity sensors. If we cut the proximity sensor wires, it will give false location information and detonate. We have to cut the correct wires. The larger wires should control the power," Olossky said.

"*Should?*" Roedie asked.

"It is a bit difficult to tell them apart. I see two large red wires. The other red sensor wires are a smaller gauge," Olossky said.

"Why don't you cut both power wires at the same time as I cut the group of sensor wires?" Roedie asked.

"That would be the only logical thing to do. *Now* you're using that brain of yours," Olossky said.

Roedie gave his father a serious look. "Now's not the time to be funny. We're about to die."

They both started laughing.

Olossky sighed. "Okay, are you ready?"

"Yes," Roedie replied.

Olossky and Roedie reached into the panel and cut the two groups of wires simultaneously. There was a small vibration that came from the Xalgoma Stride and then it was still and its red LEDs went out.

"We did it," Olossky said.

"Yes, we did. We saved the galaxy," Roedie said.

"Let's get back to the *Quasar* and hit this 'shell' with the laser cannons," Olossky said.

They made their way back to the *Quasar*. After entering the docking bay through the airlock, they took off their spacesuits and rocket packs. They headed for the bridge.

"Did you do it?" Baas asked.

"Yeah. Now it's your turn. I want you to hit the tail end of that missile with the laser cannons. Theoretically, since it has been disarmed, hitting it should not blow up the galaxy. But make sure it's the aft section, just in case," Olossky said.

"Okay...no pressure," Baas said.

Baas sat at the computer and pressed a series of buttons. The ship turned on a 90 degree angle toward the Xalgoma Stride. He shot the aft of the missile and it disintegrated into cosmic dust and energy.

"We did it!" Olossky said. "Now, let's head for Claderane in the future."

Olossky took over the captain's chair that Baas sat in.

"Yeah, let's go," Baas said.

"Ready to go through the high radiation area at lightspeed-plus?" Olossky asked.

As they brought the *Quasar* back through the high radiation area, they kept a careful watch on the display.

"Oh, man! This time, the whole back end of the reflector shield decayed," Olossky said. "But all of the ion engines are still working except for the one that was damaged the first time we went through. It did not affect the tac-time engine."

Olossky turned off the reflector shield and programmed the timespeed calculation into the computer to return to Claderane at the appropriate date. It would take a couple months of circling the BlueMar Galaxy as they advanced through future time frames.

Two months later, on Claderane, they stepped out of the *Quasar*. Rikks and their family were there to greet them. Baas told everyone what had happened. They had the largest celebration ever. All of Claderane City celebrated with a festival. It became a galactic holiday.

• • •

Later that year, Rikks Kyton left office and Lighrt Rhign took his place. There were to be other leaders in the future: Treten Ce'disee, Resin Oslevol, Ianil Sturnlhen, Brias Moght, and others.

The Claderane Government did not manufacture any more tac-time engines for timespeed travel, nor did the people of the Kameron. The tac-time engines that were already in service were removed and destroyed, except for one. The general consensus was that they could be dangerous to possess, for a terrorist could go into a past time frame and change the future by altering an event. The only tac-time engine that remained was at the request of Roedie for the *Galactic Explorer,* which he had purchased from the Claderane Government. Permission was granted.

The Cantins lived on Kaskoon after their service with the government was finished. Olossky died just a year after their final mission, in the year 230934 SA. And the following year his father, Serenitol, died.

After Olossky's death, Roedie was not himself. He changed to a person that Tereena did not know. But they both loved each other very much and worked through things until their happiness returned.

Baas did not feel as emotional with his father's death. Baas and Sepheena lived a long, good life on Kaskoon after the troubled times.

Phasheena and Reminall grew tall and proud.

The BlueMar Galaxy was saved from the destruction of the Xalgoma Stride. The future generations could now live in peace. At least that's what they thought...

Epilogue
Futuristic Dimensions

After their daughter, Phasheena, was raised, Roedie Cantin traveled into future time frames with his wife, Tereena. It relieved his tension. It was something that would not be possible if the Xalgoma Stride was not destroyed.

He changed the name of his ship from *Galactic Explorer* to *Time Explorer*. Going into future time frames with the *Time Explorer*, they were able to see what other people would never see: the future generations of their family and many other things of interest.

To be continued…

LIGHTYEARS
APPENDICES

GALACTIC HISTORY

For eons of time, there drew a line to historical records,
but some still remain, or I could not make this claim of
galactic history...

—Recorded from the Keeper, Mara-Harcheit.

Mara-Harcheit lived on the planet Yibon in the Zasreen Star System in the Regulominuss Galaxy. He was known as the Keeper, the ruler of the Regulominuss Galaxy. He studied both the Regulominuss Galaxy and its close neighbor, the BlueMar Galaxy. Mara-Harcheit named both galaxies together as one, Yiblos. He became galaxyologist and wrote the galactic history, the history of Yiblos. How he came to know much of the historic events in Yiblos remained a mystery:

The first known historic record of humans was on the paradise planet of Kylon in the Kytos Star System. They mysteriously appeared from some distant galaxy. Human historic records before that time could not be found. The distant galaxy from which they came was unknown. It was 200,000 years before they became advanced enough, once again, for space travel. The system of time in that period was known as BSA (Before Space Age). Kylon was also populated by the indigenous Cliedis Reptiles.

Eventually, the humans were forced to flee from the paradise planet of Kylon when the Cliedis Reptiles started attacking the humans. The humans fled to three planets in a distant star system in the year of 224050 SA (Space Age). To differentiate the advent of space travel, only the suffix of the time system changed from BSA to SA, not the numbering sequence. They settled Kelson I, Kelson II, and Kelson III in the Kaskar Star System, where they remained for 1402 years.

Then a super nuclear war began that lasted approximately three years. The Kelson War, fought with super nuclear missiles, caused the three planets to crack apart and turn into asteroids. Later, it became known as the Kelson Asteroid Belts. Before the destruction of the planets, most people fled to Kelsar I, Kelsar II, and Kelsar III—the next three planets that were closest to the star, Kaskar. They were all sand planets, also located in the Kaskar Star System. They remained on the Kelsar planets for 3715 years, until the radiation from the Kelson War reached close to Kelsar II and Kelsar III. All of the people migrated to Kelsar I and remained for 603 years.

When the people thought the radiation reached Kelsar I, some people took off across the galaxy in search of a new life. They became known as the Mazits, or "migrating people." Some of those people became advanced in technology, such as the people from the Kameron Star System, some became emperors of large empires, such as the Rednii Alliance and the BlueMar Empire, which was founded in the year 229776 SA. Some of the Mazits went to other galaxies, presumably through a forgotten wormhole. Not only did some travel to the Regulominuss Galaxy, but also some may have gone to the Nyctogluktoouss Galaxy, which was located beyond the Yiblos set of galaxies.

When the radiation finally did reach Kelsar I in 230326 SA—the farthest that it would ever reach—the remaining people on Kelsar I migrated to Kaskoon, the closest planet to the star. Meanwhile, the BlueMar Empire was growing strong throughout the galaxy.

Some of the Mazits that left Kelsar I and settled on Kaskoon eventually established the Tarr Kingdom. The man that founded the kingdom in 230332 SA was named after it. He was Phatom Tarr. While the Tarr Kingdom grew, the Mazits that fled out among the stars also grew. Because of this, there was a fear that one of the strong Mazits people would come and overthrow the Tarr Kingdom. The fear grew strong and Ci'is Moro'oe, the fourth ruler of the Tarr Kingdom, along with his scientists, developed a missile called the Xalgoma Stride. They sent it to the center of the BlueMar Galaxy in 230532 SA.

In the year of 230655 SA, the Tarr Kingdom's fears became a reality when the BlueMar Empire seized control over the Tarr Kingdom. Nyton Radell was the emperor of the BlueMar Empire at that time. The BlueMar Empire took over most of the BlueMar Galaxy during that period. There were many dictators in the history of the BlueMar Empire. They were soon fighting a resistance that began in 230736 SA. The resistance destroyed them in the BlueMar War of 230929 SA.

Two years after the BlueMar War, the Claderane Resistance had its government established throughout the BlueMar Galaxy. It was known as the Claderane Government or the New BlueMar Government.

The Claderane Government sent a fleet out on a mission to search for new worlds in uncharted regions. The fleet discovered the scientifically advanced people in the Kameron Star System. They teamed up to do their exploring in the Regulominuss Galaxy by traveling there at timespeed.

When the fleet reached the Regulominuss Galaxy, they were informed about a slave operation being handled on the four planets of Ovlon. The Rexxian Empire was slaving Syclones. One of the Syclones helped the fleet find the planet Yibon, seeking the Keeper, Mara-Harcheit. They sought approval to destroy the Rexxian Empire and free the Syclone slaves. Approval was granted and the Rexxian Empire was defeated in the Rexxian War. The Syclones were set free to form a new government.

The advanced people from the Kameron remained in the Regulominuss Galaxy to continue exploring, while the Claderane Government Explorers returned to the BlueMar Galaxy. On their return voyage to the BlueMar Galaxy—traveling into future time frames to the halfway point—they saw the BlueMar Galaxy explode. It was the result of the Xalgoma Stride. And the fleet witnessed the BlueMar Galaxy reappear on the second half of the return trip—traveling into past time frames.

The Claderane Government sent three of their commanders on a mission into the past to find and disassemble the Xalgoma Stride. Because they were successful, the BlueMar Galaxy had a future to look forward to—whether it was a bright one or not remained to be seen.

Galactic History Addendum Chronology of Leaders from Select Governments

The 27 Emperors of the BlueMar Empire

1.	Rhast Ler Reigtz	229776 SA—229819 SA	43 years
2.	Eilian Ter Fhyrool	229819 SA—229900 SA	81 years
3.	Jurlis Maar Satiton	229900 SA—229910 SA	10 years
4.	Tech Exx Nitonell	229910 SA—229942 SA	32 years
5.	Moht Phen Saclada	229942 SA—229982 SA	40 years
6.	Hellion Hex Halberd ("Satan II")	229982 SA—229983 SA	1 year
7.	Stan Kes Bohlevinaah	229983 SA—230039 SA	56 years
8.	Phiik Zheloviix	230039 SA—230064 SA	25 years
9.	Reminten Sijen	230064 SA—230110 SA	46 years
10.	Rubyhd Garahelz	230110 SA—230134 SA	24 years
11.	Lous T'y Kiij	230134 SA—230212 SA	78 years
12.	Keeba Tewh	230212 SA—230223 SA	11 years
13.	Qaasz Arnspii	230223 SA—230279 SA	56 years
14.	Trem Krytec	230279 SA—230313 SA	34 years
15.	Sern Errhd	230313 SA—230359 SA	46 years
16.	Erttan Ytterkade	230359 SA—230432 SA	73 years
17.	Terrh Spinem	230432 SA—230448 SA	16 years
18.	Vuhl Tumethio	230448 SA—230470 SA	22 years
19.	Siih Loh	230470 SA—230516 SA	46 years
20.	Meto Pernh	230516 SA—230561 SA	45 years
21.	Eth Aseodymion	230561 SA—230652 SA	91 years
22.	Nyton Radell	230652 SA—230678 SA	26 years
23.	Thytan Xenex	230678 SA—230736 SA	58 years
24.	Zonvhel Thine I	230736 SA—230800 SA	64 years
25.	Zonvhel Thine II	230800 SA—230816 SA	16 years
26.	Tetra Reab	230816 SA—230886 SA	70 years

27.	Quarrel Duelco	230886 SA—230929 SA	43 years

The 6 Rulers of the Tarr Kingdom

1.	Phatom Tarr	230332 SA—230395 SA	63 years
2.	Kelis Torb	230395 SA—230453 SA	58 years
3.	Webler Dicott	230453 SA—230500 SA	47 years
4.	Ci'is Moro'oe	230500 SA—230544 SA	44 years
5.	Ricot Lomana	230544 SA—230590 SA	46 years
6.	Vela Dor'bist	230590 SA—230655 SA	65 years

The 17 Leaders of the Claderane Resistance

1.	Tarkh Thoom Malist	230736 SA—230741 SA	5 years
2.	Goltzh Eoleeurt	230741 SA—230747 SA	6 years
3.	Seshena Fiilot	230747 SA—230756 SA	9 years
4.	Leebon Aanstor	230756 SA—230762 SA	6 years
5.	Aaron Cibtel	230762 SA—230766 SA	4 years
6.	Tahles (Arra) Cantin	230766 SA—230802 SA	36 years
7.	Nomlu Cantin	230802 SA—230832 SA	30 years
8.	Knighr Cantin	230832 SA—230862 SA	30 years
9.	Serenitol Cantin (Klat Morrel)	230862 SA—230869 SA	7 years
10.	Anisterr Kaal	230869 SA—230879 SA	10 years
11.	Bran Logh	230879 SA—230891 SA	12 years
12.	Tannis Zygens	230891 SA—230899 SA	8 years
13.	Wanil Thewn	230899 SA—230903 SA	4 years
14.	Taal Myh Reaeb	230903 SA—230911 SA	8 years
15.	Thes Whiten	230911 SA—230918 SA	7 years
16.	Kentaal Flimtos	230918 SA—230924 SA	6 years
17.	Rikks Kyton	230924 SA—230929 SA	5 years

First 6 Presidents of the Claderane Government

1.	Rikks Kyton	230929 SA—230933 SA	4 years
2.	Lighrt Rhign	230933 SA—230937 SA	4 years
3.	Treten Ce'disee	230937 SA—230941 SA	4 years
4.	Resin Oslevol	230941 SA—230945 SA	4 years
5.	Ianil Sturnlhen	230945 SA—230949 SA	4 years
6.	Brias Moght	230949 SA—230953 SA	4 years

CANTIN FAMILY TREE
VERSION 1

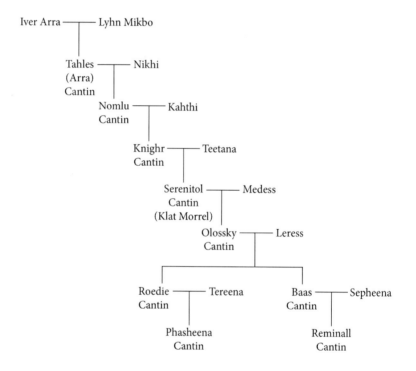

LIGHTYEARS
TERMINOLOGY INDEX

A

B

C

L

M

C7   Quaton
C24   Quee-A3/B6
C13   Queen Amorra
C12   Queen Quinell

R

C1   Radell, Nyton
C22   Reab, Tetra
C4   Realm Commander
C4   Realm Guard
C16   Rednii
C8   Rednii Alliance
C17   Rednii Onslaught
C16   Rednii Star System
C15   reflector shield
P   Regulominuss Galaxy
C21   Rella
C25   Rexx
C25   Rexx Star System
C25   *Rexxeltii*
C22   Rexxian Empire
C24   Rexxian Empire Building
C24   Rexxian Empire Troop
C26   Rexxian War
C15   Rhign, Lighrt
C21   Rialerson
C24   Riecha'l'adoss
C20   Rikkett
C23   Roklarr, Commander
C30   Rotooth
C30   Rotooth Tanis-Sintex Star System
C2   Rrijial Star System
C22   Rwaji
C4   RX-47
C3   Rythell

S

C25   Saa-Atlom, Inyurooh
C4   Sala Species

C4 Salano Star System
C2 Salasting
C1 Sanalia
C23 Sanatoma, Commander
C3 Sanbor
C29 Sand Knight
C1 Sand Star
C1 Sandkeen
C22 Sandtilian
C2 Santu
C22 'Schytion
C6 SeaScape
C10 Secor
C12 Sethonia
C1 Sevela
C11 SiiLat
C11 Siitap
C4 Silver Dagger
C21 Sintos, Commander
C27 Sno-Pleednii Star System
C25 Soph-T9/X3
C1 Southern Sand Ridge
C1 Space Age (SA)
C2 speed-lift
C16 speedwave systems
C15 Star Knight
C25 Stirlaxeen
C9 StonRamm
C30 Sturnlhen, Ianil
C6 Suzue
C6 Suzue Island
C9 Swamp Phantom
C1 SX-94
C24 Syats
C22 Syclone
C5 Sylikyt, Ikk
C24 Syta'l'omis

T

C25 Taanii-Taanii

U

V

C8   Vegaluss
C11 Velkonn Delta Five
C11 Velkonn Star System
C25 Verction's Canyon
C2   Vess, Tryl

W

C24 Walaa Kontis
C4   Weathertread
C29 Whimthiw Servant
C24 White Star
C6   Windrider

X

C27 Xalgoma Stride
C28 Xenex, Thytan
C8   Xevoui
C22 Xexioux, Dr.
C25 Xyinna Wolf

Y

C25 Yiblos
C25 Yibon
C25 Yitha

Z

C2   Zaggon
C3   Zalho's World
C2   Zantar
C12 Zantorra
C25 Zasreen Star System
C12 Zonia
C12 Zonia Fighter Ship
C12 Zonia Guard
C6   Zoota (computer)

Lightyears II
Intragalactic Terrorism

Dedication

This book is a tribute to my dear cousin Heidi, who gave me inspiration on a mystic past for the character Tereena. I love Heidi and her son, Richard II, very much. I will miss them.

—Troy Wymer
September 8, 1988

Lightyears II
Intragalactic Terrorism
Contents

Chapter One
After the Battle of Shoon

A MAN STOOD in the heat of the desert, staring at the distant horizon without flinching an eye. Anger was visible in his facial expression. His name was Destin Cantin. He wore a titanium metal suit of armor. There were laser scorches on the surface of his armor. On his hands, he wore fingerless gauntlets with spikes on the back surface of them. In one hand, he held a battle helmet that had automatic particle beam lasers mounted on either side of it. In the other hand, he held a particle beam laser rifle.

He was a leader in the Civil Resistance. He was also the last one of the resistance that was still alive on that planet. All of his friends and companions on that planet were killed by the troops of the Immortal Cantin Empire. It was an empire ruled by his distant relatives. If he was lucky, his wife, Arcacio Cantin, would still be alive when he returned to the cavern in which they lived. If they killed her, he would fight till death to avenge her. She was the only person he had left. And his love for her was as large as the universe itself. Sure, there were still Civil Resistance members on other planets and at locations throughout the galaxy, but no one was as close to him as his wife was.

His father, Thatril Cantin, died when he was yet a boy. His mother,

Merisa Cantin, got remarried to a rich bastard who was the leader of the Kaskar Terrorist Organization. Why she fell in love with him and left the Civil Resistance, Destin would never understand. The terrorist organization was one of his many enemies. His sister, Aarin Cantin, along with his great grandmother, Phasheena Cantin, were killed during a battle in space. That battle was against one of his other enemies, the Thisis Militia. Cantin was his great grandmother Phasheena's maiden name. She kept the same name for her son, Jerell, because she was not married to Jerell's father, Rik Binel. She would not have kept her son's name, Cantin, if she had known that her cousin, Reminall Cantin, was going to give shame to it.

Reminall Cantin gave shame to the Cantin name by becoming president of the Claderane Government—the government in power of the entire galaxy at the time—and then, once he was president of the Claderane Government, declaring himself emperor of the BlueMar Galaxy. He turned the Claderane Government—a government of democracy—inside out with his pseudo promises. He went as far as to move the capital of the galaxy from the planet Claderane to the planet Kaskoon—which was later renamed to Kas. He seated the capital right were his grandfather's house had been—just outside of the town that was known as Kanthas. The Cantin Empire soon changed its name to the Immortal Cantin Empire. It later began its Reign of Terror campaign that destroyed the only two developments on Kaskoon, Kanthas and Astossky. Reminall wanted the whole planet for himself. The empire then turned on the people of the galaxy. It took many years for new cities to be re-developed on Kas.

Reminall's parents, Baas and Sepheena, his aunt and uncle, Tereena and Roedie, as well as his cousin, Phasheena and her partner, Rik Binel, were all against his concepts when he became emperor. Some people went as far as to compare Reminall Cantin with the ninth emperor of the old BlueMar Empire, Reminten Sijen, and its last emperor, Quarrel Duelco.

Reminall Cantin then started a revolution of terrorist organizations throughout the galaxy. After a number of years, he sold galaxy territory to select terrorist organizations for a profit. Some of the terrorist organizations began to form their own totalitarian governments.

Later, the leaders of the Immortal Cantin Empire—Reminall's descendants—had just one terrorist organization under their "metal claw," the Kaskar Terrorist Organization. The Immortal Cantin Empire started expanding its space boundaries to the Tiosoon Star System. The territory the Immortal Cantin Empire owned was approximately five star systems—its territorial boundary being a rough line, separating them from the many terrorist organized governments. Because of this, there were many ungoverned territories throughout the BlueMar Galaxy.

The largest counterterrorist organization was the Civil Resistance— all terminated on the planet Kas, with the exception of Destin Cantin.

Destin continued to stare at the distant horizon. He stood on the sand of what was known as the Great Plain of Shoon. It was one of the many plains of sand on the planet Kas. He had just left the Battle of Shoon. In the battle, all of the Civil Resistance members on Kas—including his grandparents Jerell and Kareen Cantin—perished. They did manage to wipe out all of the Immortal Cantin Empire Troops in that battle, however. They were known as ICE Troops. Since Destin was the last of the Civil Resistance on Kas, he had to get his wife and leave as soon as possible. The only way he could get through the planet's deflector shield defenses was to obtain a code from a secret backdoor hack in a city run by the Immortal Cantin Empire.

Dressed in one of the Immortal Cantin Empire Troop's suits that he got from one of the men on the battlefield, Destin made his way toward the city of Krymoss. He stood on a sand hill, an outcrop on either side of him. He looked toward the distant city, its advanced structures intriguing him. The white and silver surfaces and the different angles and levels of the city reflected the sun's light, like a mirror. It was very quiet where he stood. The only sound was gusts of wind blowing across the surface of the sand. Destin sat down on a large boulder next to the outcrop on his left. The warm wind blew through his light brown hair. He could see small brown rocks scattered across the beige sand. An oasis of plant life thrived among the two outcrops. Was the desert planet finally beginning to have some plant life? Destin had been there for a long time and that was the first time he had ever seen green plant life. He had been there all those years, and because of the situation, he had to leave. He thought about his wife, Arcacio. If he was not successful in getting the coded information from the city of Krymoss to open the deflector shield defenses, he and his wife would be doomed.

I can't afford to fail, he thought.

He stood up from the boulder and walked toward the distant city of Krymoss.

. . .

Destin entered the parameter of the city of Krymoss. The sand ended where pavement began. As he walked along a paved walkway, he was amazed to see plants and flowers on either side. The sun's light dimmed as the walkway led to some doors under a white cement roof. The electronic doors swiftly slid aside as he entered an atheneum. There was a wide assortment of books throughout the atheneum. He walked from a section with many book shelves over to the main counter.

"Hi," Destin said, looking at a blonde woman at the counter.

"Hi," she said. "Do you need any help?"

"Yeah," Destin said.

"What can I help you with?" the woman asked.

"I was just transferred from the Tuska Thaxe Star System a week ago," Destin lied, "and I need to know where the information center is located."

"Oh. Well, you take the walkway to your left and go down about five doors. Then you'll see a sign that—I think—says, 'Information Complex.' After you go through those doors, you have to go up a stairway to the information center. Do you have your safety personnel card to get in?" the woman asked.

"Yeah," Destin said. "Thanks a lot."

"No problem. If you ever need anything else, you just come and see me," she said with a seductive smile.

"Okay. Thank you," Destin said.

She seems very friendly, he thought.

On his way to the information center, he checked his borrowed suit for a safety personnel card. There was none. He waited for someone to walk out the electronic doors and he quickly stepped in before the doors closed.

He stepped into a large room with a white and black marble floor. Offices were located in the center of the room, busy with personnel. A winding stairway—made from the same type of marble stone as the floor—led to the upper level. Destin followed the stairs, as the blonde woman had explained. The upper level was considerably smaller and had a similar marble floor. There were a couple larger, adjacent rooms leading from the small room.

Oh, great. I'll never find it at this rate. Shit. Which room is it? Destin thought.

Destin entered the first room. On the far side of the room, there were several long, rectangular observation windows where one could look out over the city of Krymoss. Destin could see many levels of the city through the observation windows. Ports and landing platforms could be seen out on the far side of the city. Approximately two kilometers across the city, he saw a ship settle onto one of the docking platforms.

How can our civilization be so advanced in science and technology, yet so uncivilized toward each other? Destin thought.

Destin checked the other room. There was a winding stairway in the center of the room identical to the first set of stairs. He started up the marble steps to the third level. At the top of the steps, he found a large room with many people in it, accomplishing different tasks. Most of them sat at computers, tapping keys on the keyboards.

Ah...the information center, Destin thought.

He walked over to an empty chair in front of a computer and sat down without anyone paying any attention to him.

I should be able to get the coded information needed to disable the planet's deflector shield defenses from this hack, Destin thought as he sighed.

He punched in several logic functions and waited. The backdoor hack had worked for other Civil Resistance members in the past.

Holy cosmic shit! Destin thought.

The secret information for the planet's deflector shield defenses rolled onto the screen.

7DSD241SO. That's it, Destin thought.

He memorized the code and cleared the screen. He left the city of Krymoss, heading toward his home.

Destin stood on a sand hill. At the top of the hill, he could see desert for kilometers. He was headed toward Kahl's Plain. He would have to pass Kamerst Low, which was a sandy low land. He would also have to pass Tuviex Korr, a large outcrop near Kamerst Low. Then he would stop at Keestoon, a small trading settlement approximately five kilometers away from Kamerst Low. He had to purchase some food at Keestoon with the credits that he took from the dead ICE Troops in the Battle of Shoon. Credits were hardly worth anything. In Keestoon, it was barely possible to trade or buy anything with low valued goods or the low valued credits.

On his way to Keestoon, he thought of how the Civil Resistance wiped out one terrorist organization since they were founded. They destroyed the Thisis Militia. But the Thisis Star System was only taken over by another terrorist organization called the Knights of Stygian. The

Civil Resistance might have only wiped out one terrorist organization at that point, but they made many other terrorist organizations weak with their many assaults and battles.

When Destin arrived at Keestoon, he walked to the food market section. It consisted of a series of connected tables with various food items on them. He looked the tables over and picked up a bottle of mixed vitamins, a small package consisting of five pieces of bread, a small jar of mixed nuts, and two pieces of fruit. That pretty much left one of the tables empty.

Keestoon received many of its supplies from the Immortal Cantin Empire's city of Antiqueech, from "reliable sources."

The owner of the food market section walked forward to the tables. "Are you trading or using credits?" he asked.

"I'm using credits," Destin said.

"Okay, let's see," the man said, getting out a calculator. "The vitamins cost ten credits, the bread cost fifteen credits, the nuts cost ten credits, and for every piece of fruit, it cost twenty credits. So, that would be forty credits for the fruit. And with ten percent Keestoon tax, five percent personal tax, and the new two point five percent table service tax, and of course, the ten percent distribution tax for Antiqueech, the total is ninety-five point six three credits."

A door opened at a small shack that was next to the man. A woman came out with an old laser rifle in her hands. She pointed it at the food market owner.

"You know the new policy, honey, so use it," the woman said before going back into the small shack.

"Oh, yes. We have a new policy here: the total credit tax policy. With this policy in effect, your total is multiplied by one point five. Your new total is...one hundred and forty-three point four five credits," the man said.

Destin looked in his pocket and pulled out some credits.

"All I have is one hundred and twenty-five credits. Take it or leave it," he said.

"You'll have to put something back," the man said.

"I'll get it all or I'll get nothing and you'll get zero credits," Destin said.

The woman yelled out the shack door. "We'll take it," she said.

Destin gave the credits to the man, took his things and left. On his way out of Keestoon, Destin was being watched by a dark figure in the shadows of a building.

• • •

It was approximately ten kilometers from Keestoon to Destin's home at the caverns. Ironically, Destin and his wife lived in the Caverns of the Sandkeens, the caves in which the Sandkeens used to live when their species was alive. Sandkeens became extinct approximately fifty years before Destin was born. Since the violent creatures that used to roam the sands of Kas had become extinct, it was possible to hunt Fateen Pests for meat. Fateen Pests were creatures that looked like a mixture between a wolf and a rat.

A man dressed in black stepped into Blackie II Cantin's office. His office was located inside the Immortal Cantin Empire's royal domain. Blackie II was a middle-aged man with some gray mixed in with his black hair.

"Well, Alarquen, did you see which way he left Keestoon?" Blackie II asked.

"Yes, Blackie. He was headed toward the old Caverns of the Sandkeens," Alarquen said.

"So, part of the Civil Resistance is staying there. We lost a lot of troops in the Battle of Shoon today. They thought they could wipe us out. What a mess that's going to be to clean up. Well, thank you, Alarquen. I'll see you later," Blackie II said.

"See you later, Emperor Blackie," Alarquen said.

As Alarquen left his office, Blackie II gazed at the picture on his office wall of his great uncle Blackie, who he was named after. Surprisingly, he resembled his great uncle, with black hair and a husky build.

Many of the Cantins in that branch of the family named their children with second generational suffixes.

Destin stepped down into a small, hidden trench that led underground. There was no sign that anyone else had come down into the caverns since he had left. He followed the cave to where it ended at an underground room.

"Arcacio?" Destin looked around the large room.

"Destin!" Arcacio ran to him, her long, blond hair flowing behind. Destin hugged her tight. She pushed her slender body tight next to his.

"Oh, I love you, Arcacio. I love you so much," Destin said.

"I love you too. I've missed you," Arcacio said.

Destin kissed her. Her warm tongue felt soft against his.

"I heard a group of troops go by above ground today," Arcacio said.

"I was afraid they would come this way. Good thing they didn't find the caverns…" Destin said.

"Where's grandpa and grandma and the rest of the resistance?" Arcacio asked.

There was a long pause.

"They're all dead. I'm the last one left in the resistance on Kas," Destin said, "besides you."

"No!" Tears came from Arcacio's eyes. "Why? Oh, God, why?"

Tears then rolled from Destin's eyes. They hugged again. It was a long embrace. They only had each other at that point. Destin wiped the tears from her eyes.

"I brought some food," Destin said.

He set the bag of food on a table nearby.

"Good," said Arcacio, wiping her eyes.

"I got some information from the city of Krymoss today," Destin said.

"You went there?" Arcacio's jaw dropped. "No one saw you sneaking around, did they?"

"I don't think so," Destin said.

"Let's hope not," Arcacio said.

"As soon as I finish building the ship, we can get through the planet's deflector shield defenses with the code I found," Destin said.

"Good," Arcacio said.

Destin turned around and was practically run down by his wolfdog.

"Well, hi, boy. How's it goin', Cosmos? Huh?" Destin petted the wolfdog as he wagged his tail. "I'm glad I have you for a friend, 'cause they sure don't make robot friends like they used to, do they? Are you enjoying the cooler air down here in the caverns?"

Cosmos's bark turned into a howl. The wolfdog had the most beautiful blue eyes and his coat was an elegant white and grayish-black.

Destin grabbed some water from a counter and took a long drink to quench his thirst. They both ate some of the food that he had brought home.

"I'm going to put the finishing touches on the ship," Destin told Arcacio.

"It's almost all assembled, isn't it?" Arcacio asked.

"Just about," Destin said.

The ship was in a part of the caverns where the floor was a little deeper down than in the room in which they stood. The ceiling above the ship was an artificial one. It could be opened to the ground above with a switch that was located in the room in which they stood.

Arcacio looked through the rest of the food that Destin purchased.

"Be ready to leave in the morning," Destin said.

"The morning? Wow...I guess you *are* almost finished," Arcacio said.

"Yeah," Destin said.

He walked to where the ship was located. The only thing left to do was connect the computer and the device that sent out a signal to bypass the planet's deflector shield defenses. Destin went to work.

Destin walked into the room where Arcacio was.

"It's pretty late," Arcacio said. "Are you tired."

"Yes. It's been a long day. I've fought in battle and done a lot of walking in this heat," Destin said.

"I packed everything," Arcacio said.

"Good. At least we won't have to do that in the morning."

"But we have to leave some supplies behind, since we only have so much room on the ship," she said.

"That's fine," Destin said.

Arcacio walked over to Destin and put her arms around him.

"Are you too tired to make love to me tonight?" Arcacio asked.

"What do you think?"

"With everything that's happened, I just need to escape. I just need you right now," she said.

Arcacio smiled and kissed Destin. They soon lay nude in bed, their tan bodies adding contrast against the white sheets. Destin kissed Arcacio with erotic passion, her lips warm against his. He kissed along her neck to her ear. Her shiny, blond hair emitted a sweet fragrance. He kissed down her neck to her breasts. They expressed their passionate love for each other as the night progressed. Soon, they were both exhausted. They fell asleep where they lay, arms embracing each other.

In the morning, they got cleaned up and put their things in the ship.

"Are you ready?" Destin asked.

"Yeah," Arcacio said.

"Come on, Cosmos," Destin said.

The wolfdog ran into the ship. Destin flicked the switch that opened the artificial ceiling above the ship. Destin and Arcacio stepped into the ship and closed the electronic, air-lock door. Destin strapped

Cosmos in and then they strapped themselves in.

"Okay, here we go," Destin said.

He started the ship and turned on the anti-gravitation. The ship began to rise with a loud noise. It rose from the caverns with a swift motion, causing sand particles to whirl in the wind. Destin punched into the computer the code that he had memorized, 7DSD241SO. Kas's deflector shield defenses were suddenly bypassed as Destin headed for space.

"What should we name her?" Destin asked.

"The ship?"

"Yeah."

"How about *Initial Voyage?*" Arcacio suggested.

"Sounds good to me," Destin said.

In the Immortal Cantin Empire's royal domain, alarms began to go off. One of the government officers was informed about the planet's deflector shield defense situation. He reported to Blackie II.

"Get that shield back up. *Now!*" Blackie II Cantin yelled.

"We're trying," a man said as he left the office.

Another man walked into Blackie II Cantin's office. "There's a call for you on the com," the man said. "I think it's your sister."

"Okay," Blackie II said. "Put her through."

"Blackie, I heard the shield was down."

"Yeah, Reignbo, it is. It's being taken care of as we speak," Blackie II said.

"I'm worried, Blackie," Reignbo II Cantin said.

"So am I. Hang on a minute… What is it?" Blackie II asked a woman that came into his office.

"The shield's back up. A ship escaped," she said.

"Send ICE fighter ships after it!"

"Yes, sir," she said, leaving his office.

"I'm back," he told his sister on the com. "The shield's back up. One ship escaped. I have a feeling it's what's left of the Civil Resistance on this planet. Our troops failed to find the location of the old Caverns of the Sandkeens after searching twice."

"It's that computer vulnerability that you guys haven't been able to figure out, isn't it? Well, at least the shield's back up," Reignbo II said.

"Yeah. Well, can you inform the rest of the family about what has happened?" Blackie II asked.

"Yeah," Reignbo II said. "I'll talk to you later."

"Bye," Blackie II said, turning off his com.

He slammed his fist onto his desk. *Damn them,* he thought.

Chapter Two
The Search for the Lost Queen

Far into the past, there was a royal monarchy on a planet called Neo Terra. It was the Monarchy of Obritess. The people of the Monarchy of Obritess had technology advanced enough to make the planet totally disappear, cloaking it from outside eyes. That is the reason why the old, evil BlueMar Empire could not find and destroy them. On through the years, they kept the planet hidden, even though there were some good governments on the outside. They were glad they kept the planet isolated, because they were currently surrounded by terrorist organizations.

Long ago, the Monarchy of Obritess was ruled by King Baman and Queen Shehlly. On a mission out from the planet's stealth shield to another distant planet, they were chased by a BlueMar Empire ship. They managed to hide on a planet called Siitap. It was a paradise planet covered with lush green forests and carpeted with fluffy grass. Sky blue lakes and streams complemented the many beautiful trees. It was an excellent place to hide out. There were only three people aboard the ship: King Baman, Queen Shehlly, and their daughter Tereena, queen-to-be. Baman and Shehlly could not risk their daughter being killed by the BlueMar Empire if it caught up to them in space. They decided that it would be best if Tereena remained on the paradise planet of Siitap until they returned from their mission on a distant planet. Before they left Siitap, they instructed a nanny robot to watch over Tereena and educate her while they were gone. Nanny had a homing device in her, tuned to a specific frequency. They left the planet on their mission. It was quite a long time before they completed the mission and were able to return to Siitap. When they did, King Baman could not get a reading from the homing device module in the nanny robot. They organized search parties and searched for many weeks and still there was no sign of Tereena or Nanny. They gave up the search and headed for their home planet of Neo Terra. They had planned on her becoming queen of the Monarchy of Obritess when she got older. They were very, very sad for a very long time.

King Baman knew that his daughter was still alive somewhere. If she was not on that paradise planet, then she was somewhere in the galaxy, held captive by the BlueMar Empire. Before King Baman and Queen Shehlly died, they set forth a plan. In the plan, it stated that there would be a period of interregnum without a queen, until their daughter was found. When she was found, she would become queen automatically. The plan stated that until she was found, there would be a civil rule of democracy by the people. Many people left Neo Terra in search of Tereena.

Many years later, the searchers found that Tereena had been rescued from the planet Siitap by two boys and a robot. Tereena, the two boys, and the robot left the planet in search of the boys' father who was captured by the BlueMar Empire. After searching for their father on many planets, they finally found him, and they helped him escape from the BlueMar Empire. After they escaped, they joined the Claderane Resistance. Soon, the Claderane Resistance took over the BlueMar Empire and set up a democracy throughout the BlueMar Galaxy.

After the galaxy was at peace, the new government asked some select people to go on a mission. Among those select people was Tereena and her husband Roedie—one of her rescuers from Siitap. The mission was to explore the uncharted regions of the BlueMar Galaxy. On their mission, they discovered a technologically advanced people. It was decided that the people on the mission, along with the technologically advanced people, would travel to another galaxy and explore. The only way it was possible for them to travel to another galaxy was to use the technologically advanced people's tac-time engines. They were engines that enabled the ships that had them installed to travel timespeed, about one million times faster than the speed of light. With timespeed, they could go into past time frames or future time frames.

After they reached the new galaxy, they found a race of clones that were being slaved by an evil empire. They destroyed the empire and set the slaves free. After that short war, it was decided that the fleet would return to the BlueMar Galaxy—with the exception of the technologically advanced people, who stayed in the new galaxy to explore further.

Later in Tereena's life, she traveled time with her husband Roedie. Tereena's searchers from the Monarchy of Obritess found this out. So, with the possibility of her being in a future time frame, they decided to keep searching for her, generation after generation.

At a time frame, approximately five generations from King Baman and Queen Shehlly, many searchers roamed the galaxy looking for clues to the whereabouts of Tereena.

The determination that it took for a hidden government to search for a single person year after year throughout the entire BlueMar Galaxy was extraordinary. Two of the best searchers from the Monarchy of Obritess were looking for Tereena near the Immortal Cantin Empire's territory. They had to exercise extreme caution around the Immortal Cantin Empire's borders in space. An invisible line between an asteroid mass and a star was not exactly the best way to judge the empire's border either.

The two searchers were in a small ship called *NTMO-191 (Neo Terra Monarchy of Obritess-191)*. The pilot—a male with brown hair—was entering a degree heading into the computer. The navigator—a female with long, curly, black hair—was reading a space map on the computer screen.

"How ya comin' with that map, Tia," the pilot asked.

"Oh, the damn thing keeps skipping a section of space," she told Saven.

"Yeah, it was having that problem before we left Neo Terra. I thought it was minor, but I guess we're gonna have to replace the circuitry. We can replace it with a Bonvoxx circuit duplicate that's in the storage room. We received those from outside of Neo Terra. The main problem is going to be removing the liquid nitrogen tubes from the circuits. We can't shut down the liquid nitrogen, because the computer will slow down to a rate in which we will be in trouble if we run into any unfriendly ships," Saven said.

"So, how we gonna fix it, then?" Tia asked.

"Well, I guess we'll just *have* to shut down the liquid nitrogen. I'll get right on it," Saven said.

He went to the storage room in the back of the ship and retrieved a flexible, paper-thin, Bonvoxx printed circuit. Tia shut down the liquid nitrogen. They opened a panel on back of the computer and a cloud of frosted air puffed out at them.

"We're gonna have to let the circuitry and tubes warm up first so we don't freeze our fingers," Saven said.

When the inside of the computer was warm enough, they disconnected the tubes and removed the old printed circuit from its connector. They replaced it with the new Bonvoxx one, after taking it out of its grounded casing. After it was installed and connected, they hooked up the liquid nitrogen tubes and put the panel back in place.

"I'll turn the liquid nitrogen back on," Tia said.

She did so and went back over to the computer.

"Well, let's see if it works now," Saven said.

They checked the screen.

"Yeah, it's there now," Tia said.

They looked at each other. Their eyes met for a long pause. Their lips came together in a passionate kiss.

"Wow. That was unexpected, but very nice," she said.

"It's been a long time since our last sleep period. Would you like to sleep with me?" Saven asked.

"We've been on this ship searching for Tereena for a long time. I was hoping this would happen a long time ago. I've always admired you, Saven, but I just never said anything. Even back on Neo Terra, I thought you were hot and should have said something," Tia said.

"You know, I've always admired you too. Back on Neo Terra when I saw how very beautiful and sexy you were, I also should have said something," Saven said.

"Well, here we are." Tia smiled.

They kissed once more and headed for her bed.

"We can check out the planet that you were tracing on the screen after sleep period is over," Saven said.

"Have you ever had sex at lightspeed?" Tia asked.

"No, but I've had it with the artificial gravitation turned off," Saven said.

"Now that's an idea," Tia said.

They both enjoyed the long overdue intimate play together as their mounting sexual tensions were finally released.

. . .

Upon waking, they took showers and got back to the computer. They set the computer to observe a planet just outside the Immortal Cantin Empire's territory. It was one of the few free democratic governments throughout the BlueMar Galaxy. The computer would go through all of the planet's telecommunications and extract any information that had to do with Tereena, if there was any.

"*Holy cosmic shit!* There was just a bit of data that rolled by the screen. It said something about a Tereena and Roedie Cantin making a comment about some food at a high class restaurant. You know that all comments and suggestions at most restaurants are stored via artificial satellite to the main office's computer. The name of that restaurant is Celestial Orchard. We have to go down to that city, to that restaurant and see if we can find her," Saven said.

"Did you see her last name. It's the same as the Immortal Cantin Empire's family name. I hope this doesn't mean trouble," Tia said.

"We'll find out," Saven said.

He maneuvered the *NTMO-191* toward the planet. The ship drifted through the gray and white clouds of the planet Perytion. It was cold and raining as they landed in the city of Sparsburg. They landed the ship on a local docking platform. With coats on, they stepped out of the *NTMO-191* and started walking toward the restaurant. The rain poured down hard and it was very cold. They entered the restaurant.

Inside, there were people sitting at most of the tables. They made their way to the counter. Saven asked a person at the counter to check the waiting list for Tereena's name.

"There was a Roedie and Tereena on the waiting list about two hours ago. Which means, they probably left here about an hour ago," the waitress said after checking.

"Shit! Maybe we can catch up to them," Saven told Tia.

"I don't know," Tia said.

They left the restaurant in a hurry. When they reached the *NTMO-191*, they checked the computer to see if any ships had left the planet in the last hour. They found that a ship did leave the planet forty-five minutes earlier. It also fit the description on file of Roedie and Tereena's ship.

"We have to catch up with them," Saven said.

"Yeah, let's hurry," Tia said.

They left the planet of Perytion and headed for the darkness of space.

"That ship's just leaving our long-range scanners. This ship can't go any faster. We may not catch up with them now," Saven said.

"Well, at least we know what direction they went in," Tia said.

"Yeah. Now the problem is finding them," Saven said with a sigh.

They headed in the direction of Roedie and Tereena's ship. They had no idea how long it would take to find them, but they knew they had come very close.

"I would have liked to eat at that restaurant back there," Saven said.

"I know. Me too. But…we have a job to do and we have to do it," Tia said.

"Yeah."

"Should we send a message back to Neo Terra, telling them how close we came to catching up with Tereena?" Tia asked.

"I don't know. They like results, not talk. Why don't we wait and see what happens first?" Saven said.

"Okay."

Chapter Three
The Immortal Cantin Empire

It was an ordinary day inside the Immortal Cantin Empire's royal domain. Many tasks were slowly being accomplished. There was a lot of information from the empire's computers that had to be stored on back-up drives. After all, they were gaining a new star system to their territory. With the addition, the Immortal Cantin Empire claimed seven star systems. Every bit of new information on the gained acquisition had to be stored. Had they not sold their territory to various terrorist organizations several generations back, in the early days of the Immortal Cantin Empire, they wouldn't be in their current situation.

Blackie II Cantin walked down a corridor that was dimly lit with illuminators located within the walls. He made his way toward the nearest information center. He had to find out what was happening at their new star system. He had been hearing rumors about the Finitte Star System being a worthless star system with useless asteroids and large, unwanted gaseous planets. He wanted to find out the details for himself since the information was just in.

He entered the information center. The floor was covered with a fluffy coating of carpet. There were many computers in the large room. Blackie II walked over to one of the computers and sat down in a comfortable chair. There was a sense of tension in the air. Blackie II could feel it. He looked around the room. A few of the other people in the room quickly looked back down at their computer displays when Blackie II discovered they were staring at him.

There's got to be something wrong. I know that now, Blackie II thought.

He punched a few keys on the computer keyboard. There was a slight pause. He received the data on the screen. It was just what he feared. The Finitte Star System was nothing more than a place of asteroids and gaseous planets. He stood up from the chair and looked around the room. After a long stare, he left. In the corridor outside the information center, Blackie II leaned up against the illuminated wall. He had to make a decision.

Should we keep the Finitte Star System…even if it's shitty and useless? Or should we pull our claim on it? Blackie II thought.

He made his decision. The rest of his family in the Immortal Cantin Empire had to be informed. He decided to tell them all personally. He had not visited with any of them in a while, anyway. He made his way down the corridor toward his cousin's quarters. After he had gone through the long maze of corridors, Blackie II reached Reminall II Cantin's quarters. He rang for Reminall II. The electronic door swiftly slid aside to reveal his cousin. He had light brown hair, a beard, green eyes, and an average build.

"It's been a while, Blackie," Reminall II said.

"Yeah, I know," Blackie II said.

"So, what brings you here?" Reminall II asked.

"Did you hear what the Finitte Star System consists of?" Blackie II asked.

"Yeah. I just received a message regarding it about five minutes ago," Reminall II said.

"I've made my decision on the star system. As long as you agree on it, we can put it into effect," Blackie II said.

"What was your decision?" Reminall II asked.

"I decided to keep the star system, but not have an outpost in it. Perhaps just a periodic patrol would be adequate," Blackie II said.

"You know you don't need my approval, but I appreciate that. I'll agree with that. Go ahead and put it into effect," Reminall II said.

"So, how have you been?" Blackie II asked.

"Oh, not too bad. How 'bout yourself?"

"Oh, I've been busy."

"Yeah?"

"Yeah. Well, I'll catch you later, Reminall," Blackie II said.

"Yeah, see ya later," Reminall II said.

Blackie II left his cousin's quarters. He thought about how he and Reminall II used to get along better when they were younger. As kids, they used to make different shapes, such as sand castles, from the sand in the desert courtyard parameter. They used to fly fighter ships together in space. As they grew older, they became distant. Blackie II thought that it might have been because of the busy times in recent years. The empire was trying to expand quickly—perhaps too quickly. Blackie II thought about Reminall II's mother—his aunt. Her name was Cathia Cantin. She had not been married to Reminall II's father, Liroown Teeks. In fact, Cathia killed Reminall II's father for unknown reasons. Perhaps it had something to do with moving up in the empire. But she never moved to any higher position in the empire than she already was. Later, she lived alone in a remote corner of the Immortal Cantin Empire's royal domain, as a recluse. She rarely talked to anyone else in the family because of other unknown reasons. It may have had something to do with Reminall II and Blackie II not getting along well these days. Who knows? No one ever questioned Cathia Cantin about anything, if they knew what was good for them. It was all left a mystery that no one cared to solve.

Cathia's parents, Quarrel and Lita Cantin, only had two children. The other was 'Bastel Cantin, Blackie II's father. Blackie II and his sister Reignbo II seemed to get along fairly well. When they were younger, they fought a lot, but now they were closer. Their mother and father did not get along all that well. Their mother's name was Sheena Cantin.

Blackie II was on his way to tell his mother and father his decision about the Finitte Star System. When he reached their quarters, he told them his decision and visited them for a while.

Everyone seemed to be respecting his decision thus far. Being the highest ranking person in the empire was not easy. The empire was handed to him, so these decisions were his responsibility.

Next, he had to tell his sister, Reignbo II. He walked through another maze of corridors until he came out into the corridor where Reignbo II's quarters were. He rang for her. There was no answer. After a long pause, he decided to come back later.

He headed for a distant cousin's quarters. Her name was Widoweve II Cantin and she was his first cousin once removed. Her late mother and father, Reignbo Cantin and Tiik Veltii, had not been married.

Widoweve II was married to a man named Art Thorr. They had a daughter named Tam' Thorr. Art Thorr was presently in another star system taking care of some empire business. Blackie II's second cousin, Tam' Thorr, lived on her own in different quarters.

Blackie II came to Widoweve II's quarters. He rang at the door. It opened automatically. There was no one in the living room. Blackie II looked around. There did not seem to be anyone around. Walking by the bedroom, he noticed Widoweve II and some other woman lying nude on the bed, having oral sex. They seemed to be having quite a time. Blackie II smiled and quickly left.

Wow! Blackie II thought.

After leaving Widoweve II's quarters, he gathered his thoughts. Perhaps she was simply enhancing her already great sexual relationship with her husband Art… After all, what Widoweve II and this other woman did was not Blackie II's business.

Blackie II went on to the quarters of Widoweve II's daughter, his second cousin, Tam' Thorr. When he reached her quarters, he told her his decision about the Finitte Star System.

"Yeah, it's good to keep periodic patrols through the star system, so some terrorist organization doesn't also try to claim it," Tam' said.

"Yes. That reminds me…I have to find out some information about the Kaskar Terrorist Organization," Blackie II said.

"Are they up to something now?" Tam' asked.

"I don't know yet. But I'll find out. So, how have you been doin'?" Blackie II asked.

"Oh, pretty good. I've been waiting for my friend to come back from my mom's. She was just supposed to get a recipe. How are you doing?" she asked.

"I'm sure your friend will be a while. You know how women are once they start talking about eating. Anyway, I'm doing okay. So, when's your dad coming back from the Tuska Thaxe Star System?" Blackie II asked.

"I don't know. Why?" Tam' asked.

I was just wondering," Blackie II said. "Well, I better be going."

"Well, it was nice seein' you. Stop by again," Tam' said.

"Yeah, I will," Blackie II said.

He left Tam' Thorr's quarters and walked toward his own. There was no one else he had to inform about his decision except his wife, Kathell, his sister, Reignbo II, and his distant cousin, Widoweve II. He would contact them later.

He entered his quarters.

"Kathell?"

"Hi, Blackie. Where ya been?" Kathell asked.

She was a beautiful, tall woman with long, black hair.

"I went to the information center and found out the Finitte Star System consists of a bunch of shit," Blackie II said.

"What shit?" Kathell asked.

"Asteroids…gaseous planets…nothing we can put to use. So, I decided to keep a claim on the star system and have it patrolled periodically," Blackie II said.

"Sounds good to me," Kathell said.

"Yeah? So, what have you been doing all day?" Blackie II asked.

"Sittin' around doing nothing. It's so damn boring around here. There ain't nothing to do."

"Well, would you like to take a trip with me to Kas Voya?" Blackie II asked.

"Sure. For what?" Kathell asked.

"I think the Kaskar Terrorist Organization is up to something. I don't know what, but I'll find out. I can get the information that I need to know from Kas Voya, the scum city," Blackie II said. "We'll leave tomorrow."

He walked over to his personal computer center. He programmed the information and his decision about the Finitte Star System into the computer. His orders regarding the periodic patrols of the system would be carried out by select empire officials. Blackie II stood up from the computer center.

"Blackie…I did my pregnancy test today," Kathell said.

"You did? What were the results?" Blackie II asked.

"It was positive," Kathell said.

Blackie II and Kathell embraced each other.

"Oh, I love you, Kathell," Blackie II said.

"I love *you*, Blackie," Kathell said.

They kissed. Kathell was excited about having a child, but also frightened. It would be her first.

"If it's a girl, we'll name her, Arriel. How does that sound?" Kathell asked.

"Sounds fine to me," Blackie II said.

"And if it's a boy, we'll name him after you. How does that sound?" she asked.

"That sounds fine too," he said.

"I was looking through the genealogy records on the computer today. Reminall I and Widoweve I had three children: Quarrel Cantin,

Reignbo I Cantin, and Blackie I Cantin. I wonder why Blackie I did not have any children," Kathell said.

"He didn't get married, because he couldn't keep one woman. He always had to have a different woman. He probably does have children roaming around the galaxy somewhere. But if so, none that are recorded in our genealogy records," Blackie II said.

"Oh, really. I didn't know that," Kathell said.

"Yeah…Well, I'm tired. I think I'll get to bed early tonight," Blackie II said.

"Yeah, I'm tired too. Do you want to go to bed right now?" Kathell asked with a big smile.

"Yeah," Blackie II said.

He grabbed her ass and walked toward the bedroom. She had firm breasts, her nipples noticeably protruding from her loosely fitted shirt. She followed, removing her loose shirt. When she reached the bedroom, she took off her skirt. Her long thighs were covered with black fishnet stockings that matched the color of her lace panties. She slowly rolled down the fishnet on either leg. She pulled off her black lace panties. Blackie II could see her smooth vulva and the parted labia. He became erect with the arousal. He slowly removed his clothes. Their nude bodies were soon embraced together, as they made love.

The Immortal Cantin Empire's royal domain docking bay was quite busy with many ships arriving and departing. Blackie II and Kathell Cantin walked down an illuminated corridor toward the docking bay. They entered the upper level of the docking bay that overlooked the main floor. As Blackie II received ship clearance, Kathell stood next to the black and yellow railing high above the docking bay floor. As soon as he was finished receiving ship clearance, they walked to a stairway located toward the back of the upper level, which led down to the busy docking bay floor. They entered one of the ships and flew from the docking bay through a rectangular opening at its far end. The opening was approximately fifty meters above the sandy ground outside. Although Kathell was a great pilot, Black II usually piloted the ship when they were together. They flew across the hills of sand and rock that Kas was famous for. They flew toward the city of Kas Voya.

Upon reaching Kas Voya, they landed in its docking bay. They were greeted by a stocky man in a green uniform. It was, Perrin Isp, Kas Voya's main official. After the greeting, Blackie II and Kathell went to the far edge of the city to get some information from a particular source. It was exactly as Blackie II had suspected. He made some quick orders to his troops over his com. Blackie II and Kathell headed for the Kaskar Terrorist Organization's main headquarters in the city of Kas Voya. After what seemed like an endless maze of corridors, they entered the KTO headquarters.

"I'd like to speak with Tharr Istraxx," Blackie II said.

"He is in his office with his wife, Merisa. He noticed you arrived and asked for me to send you in," a man at the desk said, gesturing toward the door.

Blackie II and Kathell entered Tharr Istraxx's office. A man with salt-and-pepper hair sat at a desk along with a brunette woman.

"Blackie? What brings you here?" Tharr asked.

Kathell followed Blackie II toward Tharr's desk where he sat. Tharr's wife, Merisa, sat in a comfortable chair next to the desk.

"I'll tell you what brings me here. I want to know what the hell the Kaskar Terrorist Organization is up to. You're trying to fuck up my empire. You're trying to take it over," Blackie II said.

"How the hell did you get that information?" Tharr asked.

Tharr started to call for assistance over the com. Blackie II quickly pulled out a particle beam laser pistol and shot the com. It disintegrated as a puff of black smoke rose upward.

"You actually thought you could get away with this?" Blackie II asked.

"It ain't over yet," Tharr said.

"I'm afraid it is. As we speak, your terrorists are being killed throughout the empire. They're all dying fast. You will be tried. And there's no need for these headquarters any longer. Troops!" Blackie II yelled.

A squad of Immortal Cantin Empire Troops charged into the office and shackled Tharr and his wife, Merisa. They also found Tharr's guards located in a room beyond his office.

"I'll see you at the trial," Blackie II said.

Blackie II and Kathell left the ex-KTO headquarters. Back in Tharr's office, Tharr's guards and office personnel were killed. Tharr and Merisa were the only two people left alive in the entire Kaskar Terrorist Organization, as Blackie II's orders to annihilate were carried out at all KTO locations. Tharr and Merisa's time would come soon.

The trial came within days. The room was full of people from various places throughout the empire. The entire Cantin family from the empire was present with the exception of the recluse, Cathia. The judge sat high on a throne-like chair at the far wall. Tharr and Merisa sat below the judge, on his left. There was a guard on either side of them. Blackie II stood in the large room, directly in front of Tharr and Merisa. The trial was almost finished. In actuality, it was not a trial at all. It was a ceremony to humiliate Tharr and his wife.

"You stand accused of attempting to destroy the Immortal Cantin Empire. I sentence both of you to death by means of laser bed. You have one last request," the judge said. "What will it be?"

There was a quick silence in the room. A long pause followed.

"I wish for you to spare my wife," Tharr said.

"Your wish is under consideration by Emperor Blackie II Cantin," the judge said.

Tharr looked from the judge to Blackie II.

"I think that can be arranged," Blackie II said.

"Now, Tharr, it is time for you to die," the judge said.

Blackie II gave the guards a signal. They took Tharr to the laser bed termination room. Blackie II told one of his main officials to take Merisa out into the desert.

In the laser bed termination room, Tharr lay facing upward on top of a laser beam absorbing bed. He was strapped down to the bed. Above him, there was a laser device mounted to the low ceiling. The laser beam turned on and hit the bed between his feet. It slowly moved toward the other end of his body. It first cut into his genitals, then his stomach, then his chest, and finally his face, completely cutting Tharr's body into two pieces.

A main official from the Immortal Cantin Empire had Merisa tied to the hot, sandy ground in the desert of Kas. She was nude. She was faced downward on her hands and knees, which had been tied to stakes driven deep into the ground. The warm wind blew sand across her bare skin. Despite her cries and pleas for him to stop, the man raped her and left her there to die in the hot sun.

When the main official returned to the empire's royal domain, he informed Blackie II of Merisa's fate, as if Blackie II would be grateful for his extra efforts. Blackie II pulled out a laser pistol and killed the man.

"I told you to leave her in the desert, with a chance to get to a city and survive. I did not tell you to rape her and leave her to die!" Blackie II told the corpse on the floor.

He immediately went into the desert to find Merisa. When he found her, she was barely alive. He brought her to a medical center in the royal domain. She survived and when she got a chance, she escaped from the empire and lived in some caverns out in the desert of Kas. Ironically, it was the same caverns that her son Destin lived in with his wife Arcacio before they left Kas. This fact was very evident to her from the supplies that were left behind.

Chapter Four
A Leader from the Past

The *Time Explorer* swiftly flew through the darkness of space. It was the only ship left in the galaxy with timespeed capabilities. It had the ability to travel the speed of time, which was about one million times faster than the speed of light. The ship had been through two wars and other skirmishes, but despite its age, it still ran smooth.

Roedie and Tereena Cantin didn't have a crew for their ship, other than a robot that Roedie built, named KEN-103.

Roedie built KEN-103 after his other faithful robot, KEN-102, was destroyed by a space gang. KEN-102 had been in a Star Knight fighter ship traveling through a war zone, returning to the *Time Explorer*. On his return, the space gang shot the Star Knight with a laser cannon and blew it—along with KEN-102—into cosmic dust. KEN-103 was made to look, act, and think like KEN-102. All of KEN-102's memories were stored into KEN-103's memory module from a back-up computer that contained the information.

Roedie and Tereena's normal time frame was five generations back into the past. They traveled time because they enjoyed doing so. They used to bring things back from the future to their normal time frame when they would visit their daughter, Phasheena. However, even if they were careful not to affect time by bringing the things back, they stopped doing so out of fear. They could potentially erase themselves from existence by doing the wrong thing. In fact, they had not been back to their normal time frame in years.

Everything was quiet on the bridge of the *Time Explorer*. The faint sound of the engines could be heard.

"Do you want to go back to that restaurant that we were at last month, the Celestial Orchard?" Tereena asked.

"It was a nice place and they have excellent food, but Perytion is too close to the Immortal Cantin Empire's space border. We don't know that much about that part of our family descendants. They don't know who we are. It's too dangerous," Roedie said.

"Yeah, I guess it is," Tereena said.

"Don't worry. We'll find another nice place like that," Roedie said.

"You know, sometimes I get tired of traveling time. Sometimes I long for home and family," Tereena said.

Roedie walked over to Tereena and he put his arm around her. "You know something? So do I," he said.

"Maybe we should just stop roaming through time and space and go home to Kaskoon," Tereena said, complaining.

"Maybe."

"Well, I think I'm going to go get some rest. I'm tired," Tereena said.

"All right. I'll be on the bridge," Roedie said.

Tereena kissed Roedie and left the bridge.

He looked at the lights on the control panel. They were bright against the dimness of the bridge. Roedie sat down in one of the chairs at the control panel. He put his head down on the panel and let out a sigh. KEN-103 was also on the bridge. He walked over to Roedie.

"Life's a bitch, isn't it?" KEN-103 said.

"Several bitches, KEN-103, several bitches," Roedie said.

"Yeah, that too," KEN-103 said.

Just then, a beeper started going off. Roedie looked up, flicked a switch and it stopped.

"We're coming upon a planetoid," Roedie said.

"Another one of those?" KEN-103 replied.

"Yeah."

Through the observation window, they could see a planetoid covered with snow and ice. It was white and gray with patches of sky blue. Around the planetoid, there were very small moonlets of rock and ice.

"It is beautiful, though," KEN-103 said.

"Yes, it is. That's one of the things I love about space travel," Roedie said.

The planetoid passed out of sight as the ship moved on at lightspeed.

"Well, KEN-102—I mean KEN-103—I'm going to go to my quarters to see Tereena. Watch the bridge, will ya?"

"Yeah. See you later, Roedie," KEN-103 said.

Roedie left the bridge through the electronic door. He walked down the illuminated corridors of the *Time Explorer*. Minutes later, Roedie reached their quarters. The electronic door moved aside. He entered the foyer, went passed the living room, and walked into the bedroom. Tereena was sleeping comfortably on the bed. Roedie was also very tired. He undressed, lay in bed, and quickly fell asleep.

Roedie awoke, surprised to find Tereena on top of him thrusting her hips and moving up and down with a steady pace. Tereena was evidently in a very erotic mood. Roedie smiled at her and his arousal intensified.

Some time later, they both exploded with another exciting orgasm that sent them both to the floor. They continued with their intense, heated sex for most of the night. At some point, they climbed back onto the bed and fell asleep. It was a long sleep.

All was quiet as Roedie flew through space in one of several Star Knight fighter ships that were aboard the *Time Explorer*. The LEDs for the Star Knight's roll, pitch, yaw, and speed could be seen on the display. Roedie was out flying the Star Knight because he wanted to get away to think for a while. One thing he wished he could do was go into a past time frame and warn his mother, Leress Cantin, about a canister leak in a lab where she was a student, to prevent her death from the Tabaannnaann Plague. He wanted to see her again. She was taken from him too early in his life. But he knew he could not save her because it would affect the time continuum. He thought about going back to their normal time frame. It was interesting living in the future, but he missed things back in his normal time frame. Roedie thought about those things for a long time. He slowly fell asleep.

Later, Roedie awoke to find himself in an asteroid mass.

"Holy cosmic shit!" he said.

He quickly maneuvered the Star Knight away from an asteroid that would have destroyed him. He kept swerving back and forth, missing asteroids by meters. He saw that there were no asteroids above him. He quickly pulled the Star Knight upward. Doing so, he almost collided with another large asteroid.

Damn, that was a close one, he thought.

He turned on the scanners and located the *Time Explorer.* He had to travel lightspeed-plus in order to catch up with her.

Tereena was on the bridge of the *Time Explorer.* She checked the scanners to find Roedie's location. She found that he was way off course.

"KEN-103, look at this," Tereena said.

KEN-103 walked over to the scanners where Tereena sat.

"Something must have happened. Do you want me to take a Star Knight out to see what happened to him?" KEN-103 asked.

"Yes, KEN-103. Thank you," Tereena said.

KEN-103 quickly left the bridge. He was in the docking bay before too long. He went down the flight of stairs from the observation deck. When he reached the lower level, he quickly got into a Star Knight and headed toward Roedie's location.

While KEN-103 went after Roedie, Tereena slowed the *Time Explorer* down to sub-lightspeed.

A figure moved in the dark shadows of the *Time Explorer's* lower levels. It moved toward a metal stairway that led upward. There were several illuminators above the stairway. The light revealed the figure. It was a man with a laser pistol in his hand. He proceeded up the stairway to a metal catwalk located on the first upper level of the ship. There were stairways and metal platforms throughout the lower levels of the *Time Explorer.* When the man reached the first level, he entered into the main part of the ship and started walking down a corridor, headed for the bridge. He came to a corridor intersection. Each corridor intersection set slightly lower than the corridors themselves. A few steps were located on all four sides with a common landing. He went down the few steps, turned to his left, and went up the few stairs into another corridor, which led straight to the bridge.

KEN-103 located Roedie.

"Hey, KEN-103, am I glad to see you," Roedie said through the com.

"What happened?" KEN-103 asked.

"I fell asleep at the controls and went off course. I ended up in an asteroid mass. I got out of that and checked my scanner. Now, I'm heading toward the ship," Roedie said.

"Tereena noticed that you were off course, so I came out to see what the problem was. Haven't you been getting enough sleep?" KEN-103 asked.

"I suppose not. Thanks a lot for coming out here, KEN-103," Roedie said.

"No problem," KEN-103 said.

They proceeded toward the *Time Explorer* at lightspeed-plus.

The man with the laser pistol entered the bridge of the *Time Explorer*. Tereena turned around and screamed.

"Shut up, bitch," the man said, smacking her across the face with his fist.

Tears came to her eyes as she landed on the floor of the bridge.

"Who are you?" she asked.

"I've been on this ship ever since the last time you and Roedie left Kaskoon. I don't know how many years ago that was. I've been monitoring the ship, who comes, who leaves. With just one person aboard, my chance is finally here," the man said.

"The chance for what?" Tereena asked, still on the floor.

"What do you think? My chance to take over the only ship left with timespeed capability. I've been waiting a long time for this. Now, get over in that corner," the man said, pointing toward the corner next to the control panel.

He hit her in the mouth again and she started to bleed. She crawled to the corner on her hands and knees. When she reached the corner, he removed some ropes that were looped in with his belt and tied her to the control panel. The ropes were so tight, her wrists and ankles started bleeding.

"I don't want you to try anything funny," the man said.

He walked up to her and stroked her breasts and her vulva through her clothes.

"Get your fucking hands off me, you creepy bastard," she said.

The man pointed the laser pistol at her vulva.

"What did you say?"

She flinched and a tear rolled down her left cheek.

"What's the matter?" he said.

He grabbed her jaw and twisted her head sideways, banging it on the control panel. She let out a yelp of pain. A sound started beeping on a device at the man's side.

"Ah, they're back. They'll have a little surprise when they get to the bridge. And if you yell out anything, I'll kill your precious Roedie," the man said with a snarl.

Tereena tried very hard to loosen the ropes. The pain was so intense, but the ropes were slowly loosening.

Roedie and KEN-103 stepped out of their Star Knights and looked at each other.

"Well, KEN-103, let's go see what Tereena's up to, shall we?" Roedie said.

"Yeah, let's go," KEN-103 said.

They headed up the stairs and toward the bridge.

The man on the bridge stood in a spot where Roedie and KEN-103 would not be able to see him as they entered. Tereena had the ropes loose. She was waiting for the right moment to slip her very sore wrists and ankles out of the ropes. The bridge door slid aside. Roedie and KEN-103 walked onto the bridge. Roedie saw Tereena in the corner with blood on her. He ran over to her, followed by KEN-103.

"Oh my God, Tereena, what happened?" Roedie asked.

"Don't move!" the man yelled.

Roedie turned around in surprise. He stared at the man for a moment.

"Did you do this to her? You! Don't I know you? You're the one who used to sell ships in Astossky. We bought the *Zoota 2000* from you. You fuckin' idiotic bastard. What the hell do you want?" Roedie asked.

"Like I told your precious bitch...I want this ship. It's the only one left with timespeed capabilities. I've waited in the lower levels of this ship for several years, just for this moment. When you used to go back to Kaskoon with your goods from the future, you should have secured your ship a little better," the man said.

"Now that your *moment* is here, what the hell you gonna do?" Roedie asked.

"Kill you all and take the ship," the man said.

"Look, Ikk Sylikyt, you don't even know the first thing on how to run the damn tac-time engine," Roedie said.

"That's why you're gonna show me before you die," Ikk Sylikyt said.

"The first thing *I'm* gonna do is get my wife out of your fucking ropes," Roedie said, turning around.

"One more step and I'll melt a hole through your back," Ikk said.

Roedie stopped, turned around, ran toward Ikk Sylikyt, and kicked him in the face. Ikk fell backwards to the floor, the laser pistol still in his hand. He rose it toward Roedie and pressed the trigger switch. KEN-103 jumped in front of the beam, the blast blowing his metal body apart. Tereena slipped out of the ropes and limped toward Ikk. Ikk could not see her through the smoke of the blast. She walked up behind him and kicked the laser pistol from his hand. It slid across the room. He got up and charged her and they both fell to the floor. Roedie picked up the laser pistol and pointed it toward them. They were rolling around too fast for him to shoot. Ikk pushed Tereena's head to the floor with a cracking blow. She shook her head and got his neck between her legs. She tightened her thighs with all her might and crushed his throat. With a roll of the eyes, he fell backwards. She lay to the floor, exhausted. Roedie ran over to her, picked her up, and hugged her tight.

"Oh, Tereena."

She was too limp to hug him back. He laid her down by the panel. He turned around to see what was left of KEN-103. Looking through the parts, he picked up the memory module and sat it on the counter near the control panel.

"To think he's been on this ship all that time… Wow… I thought there was food missing now and then. The ship really is a security risk of sorts…at least to those in the past that know of its capabilities," Tereena said.

"He had plenty of opportunities to take it while we were in restaurants and such, but he needed one of us to show him how to operate it," Roedie said.

"Very scary," she said.

"Well, now that we have Ikk Sylikyt gone, and KEN-103's mess cleaned up, what are we going to do?" Roedie asked.

"I wanna go to an intoxication joint. I need a drink," Tereena said.

"Yeah, so do I," Roedie said.

He walked over to the control panel and punched several keys on the keyboard. The *Time Explorer* changed course and moved toward the nearest planet that had an intoxication joint on it.

"Okay, we'll go get that drink, babe," Roedie said.

Tereena walked over to Roedie and kissed him. "That's for being my man," she said.

Roedie kissed her.

"What's that for?" she asked.

"That's for not only being my woman, but being the best woman in the entire galaxy," Roedie said.

Roedie walked back over to the control panel and put the ship on automatic control. He walked over to Tereena, picked her up in his arms, and they went to their quarters.

Chapter Five
The Flight to Forestica

The *Initial Voyage* flew from the Kaskar Star System at lightspeed. Destin and Arcacio sat at the controls. Cosmos lay on the floor next to them. They were being chased by fighter ships from the Immortal Cantin Empire. Destin activated the aft laser cannons. The laser beams sliced through two of the four Immortal Cantin Empire fighter ships. The silent explosions brightened the darkness of space for an instant. The two remaining ICE ships flew to either side of the *Initial Voyage* and fired their lasers. Destin swerved upward just in time. He did a loop and ended up behind both ICE ships. He fired and hit one of the two ships. The last ship shot its aft laser cannons at the *Initial Voyage*. The beams reflected from the ship's reflector shield and flew into a different direction. Destin fired and missed the last ICE ship. He fired again and hit the ship, causing it to explode into cosmic dust and energy.

"That was a close one," Arcacio said.

"Yeah, it was," Destin said.

They both looked at each other.

"Oh, no!" Arcacio exclaimed.

"What?" Destin asked.

"According to the scanners, there are about ten more ships coming," Arcacio said.

"Oh, shit," Destin said, "let's get the hell out of here."

Destin switched the ship to lightspeed-plus and flew in the direction of a place that his grandfather, Jerell Cantin, once brought him to when he was younger. He remembered the coordinates vividly. It was a star system that had one planet orbiting a yellow star. The planet had two satellites. One of the two satellites was an airless piece of rock, but the other satellite was much different. It was covered with lush forests and it had air. It was the perfect hideout. The special thing about that satellite was that—from space—it looked exactly like the other satellite of the planet—an airless piece of rock. The planet that both satellites orbited was an ocean planet. There was no land or islands on the entire planet. It was all water. Both the atmosphere and the water were poisonous to humans. Ocean creatures lived in the water, immune to its toxicity. From space the planet had an aqua-bluish color to it. The planet's name was Oceanic. The satellite that did not have an atmosphere was called Grandust. The official name of the satellite with the forest was Grandust II. Destin and Arcacio were the only two people alive that knew that Grandust II was really a forest satellite. Long ago Destin's grandfather, Jerell, built a house on the satellite. Jerell once told Destin that he named the satellite Forestica. That is the name that Destin and Arcacio referred to the satellite as. It was located in the Xerica Star System.

"We left those ICE ships far behind. We'll be well hidden on Forestica by the time they get to the Xerica Star System," Arcacio said.

"Yeah. We should be there in a little while," Destin said.

Destin looked down at Cosmos and the wolfdog howled at them both. They started laughing. They continued to fly at lightspeed-plus until they reached Forestica.

The *Initial Voyage* moved through the lavender clouds of Forestica. The lavender clouds were beautiful against the sky blue background. Destin maneuvered the ship toward the house that his grandpa, Jerell, had built many years ago.

"Those ICE ships shouldn't be around this area for quite some time," Destin said.

"They won't be able to detect our ship, will they?" Arcacio asked.

"Not with the reflector shields enabled," Destin said.

They flew over the very tall pine trees of Forestica. It was a very beautiful view as they flew past mountains and waterfalls. Sky blue lakes reflected the lavender clouds from their smooth surfaces. A river could be seen, carved through the deep forest, its sky blue waters rapidly rushing by. Flying onward toward the hidden house, Destin made his way through the dense pine trees and down deep into the mountain forest. The house came into view. He landed the *Initial Voyage* next to the house and enabled the reflector shields. They stepped out onto the ground.

"Oh, this fresh air smells so good," Arcacio said.

"Oh, I know," Destin said. "And the scent of white pine trees is so awesome."

Cosmos took off and ran toward a stream of crystal clear, cold, flowing water. He rolled and jumped around in the fresh, cold water before drinking it. The stream flowed from the mountains above, past the house, and on down through the pine forest. Cosmos had never seen any other place besides the hot sands of Kas. Destin and Arcacio looked around. The house was surrounded by tall pine trees on the mountainside.

"It is so beautiful here," Arcacio said.

"It's the best place we'll probably ever see in our lives," Destin said.

"Yeah."

"Let's go see inside the house my grandpa built," Destin said.

They approached the brick stairs that led up to the front door. The house was made of large, grayish-blue stones and smooth logs taken from the mountainside. When they reached the front door, Destin pressed a button on the right side of the electronic door and it opened. They entered the house and were greeted by the living room's soft carpeting. An elegant stone fireplace sat on one side of the room. There were two levels in the living room. They passed the couch and table and went up a few stairs to the other level of the living room. From there, they entered the dining room. A cabinet of crystal glasses sat against one wall of the dining room. Passing through the dining room, they entered the kitchen. The kitchen had excellent food preparation facilities and an electronic door that opened up to a fenced-in back patio. The kitchen also led down to a small storage cellar. They went on into the family room. Off from the family room, there was a small bathroom. From the living room, a set a stairs led to the upper level of the beautiful house. Upstairs, there was a very large bedroom. The bedroom had an anti-gravitation controllable bed. There was an electronic door in the bedroom. On the other side, there was a deck that overlooked the front of the house. From there, the *Initial Voyage* and the flowing stream could be seen. In the other half of the upper level, there was a very large bathroom. It was all just as Destin had remembered it when he came there once with his grandpa.

"I like this house," Arcacio said.

"It's very nice," Destin said.

They gazed up at the large log joists at the peak of the ceiling.

"Maybe someday, when the governmental problems in this galaxy are taken care of, we can come back and live on this beautiful satellite," Destin said.

"That would be very nice," Arcacio said.

They headed back downstairs and outside. It was much brighter outside. They saw the lavender clouds blended in with the sky blue background.

"We're going to have to stay here for a few days to make sure those ICE ships are gone," Destin said.

"Hey, where's Cosmos?" Arcacio asked.

Destin looked toward the stream. Cosmos was not there. He looked around the parameter of the house. Cosmos was no where to be found.

"Well, he'll be back sooner or later," Destin said.

"I'm hungry," Arcacio said. "I think I'll go fix us something in the kitchen. I'll grab some food from the ship."

"Okay," Destin said.

Arcacio took some of their food supplies from the ship and went inside the house. Destin walked over to the stream and followed it uphill, as he explored around the area.

Later, they sat in the dining room and ate vegetable soup that she had made.

"The freezer had all kinds of freeze-dried vegetables. I thought vegetable soup would be good," Arcacio said. "Plus, we can save our supplies from the ship for later."

"Oh, it's delicious," Destin said as he ate the soup. "I haven't had a home-cooked meal in a very long time."

"Thank you," Arcacio said, looking at the reflection of herself in her soup.

There was a very long pause.

"Destin?"

"Yeah?"

After another long pause, she said, "I'm pregnant."

"You are? Oh, baby, that's wonderful. I love you so much," Destin said, hugging her tight. "I am so happy."

"I love you too," Arcacio said.

They continued to eat. After dinner they both retired for the evening.

Ten ICE ships entered the Xerica Star System. They headed toward the planet of Oceanic and its two satellites, Grandust and Grandust II. When they reached the planet, they turned on their scanners.

"I read that the atmosphere and water of the planet are both poisonous. And besides, there is no place to land anyway," the flight leader said.

"Neither satellite has an atmosphere," one of the pilots said.

"The scanners aren't detecting any ships here," another pilot said.

"Well, I guess we lost them. It's a shame we don't have lightspeed-plus capabilities. Well, let's pass the planet a couple more times and head back to Kas," the flight leader said.

The ICE ships circled Oceanic two times and flew back to Kas.

Destin and Arcacio were having sex in the anti-gravitation controllable bed. They were floating a meter above the bed. They were able to perform several new positions they never thought possible. Hours later they turned off the anti-gravitation and went to sleep, very satisfied.

Destin awoke in the early morning hours from a barking howl coming from outside the house. He stood up from the bed nude and went onto the deck that overlooked the front of the house. He saw Cosmos barking at the front door. He smiled to himself and went downstairs. He opened the front door and Cosmos ran in, wagging his tail.

"Hey, boy, where have you been?" Destin asked.

Cosmos howled at Destin. Arcacio came down the stairs.

"Hey, Cosmos," she said.

Cosmos ran over to her. She patted him on the head.

"So, do you think the ICE ships have passed through this star system yet?" Arcacio asked.

"I don't know. We'll stay a couple more days, just to be sure," Destin said.

They sat down on the couch.

"Last night was so incredible," she said.

Destin smiled and put his arm around her nude body.

"My grandparents must have been kinky to design a bed like that,"

Destin said.

"Not anymore than we are," she said.

"I guess not."

"Well, what are we going to do today?" Arcacio asked.

"Oh, I don't know. Maybe we can hike through the forest and explore," Destin said.

"Yeah. Well, do you want to get cleaned up now?" Arcacio asked.

"Yeah, let's do that," Destin said.

Destin and Arcacio went upstairs to the spacious bathroom and took a shower. Cosmos discovered the back patio where he lay down.

Destin, Arcacio, and Cosmos made their way through the tall pine trees of Forestica. They went uphill and deep into the thick forest. They crossed several streams on their way. Soon, they came to a small meadow of green grass. At the far edge of the meadow, there was a small ledge that dropped down to a lake of sky blue colored water. Surrounding the lake were large stones embedded in the ground. The three of them continued onward up the mountainside. They followed along the rocky terrain until they reached a hill that sloped downward. The hill was covered with small trees of various types and many large and small stones. They made their way down the hill. It led to another forest below. The forest was thick with trees. There were more streams of rapid flowing water running through it. They reached another lake, which had a small sandy beach. The beige sand was beautiful against the sky blue water. The water itself blended in with the sky. The lavender clouds set out against the gray mountainous background.

"This is so beautiful," Arcacio said.

"Just like you... Do you want to go swimming?" Destin asked, smiling.

"Sure," Arcacio said.

They took off their clothes and walked out into the lake. Cosmos jumped into the water as well.

"Do you think we can find our way back to the house?" Arcacio asked.

"I hope so," Destin said.

After some time at the small beach, they made their way back to the house.

"I thought it was this way," Destin said.

"Oh, great. *You thought?* Now what are we going to do?" Arcacio asked.

"I don't know," Destin said. "Don't be upset with me."

Cosmos started walking in a different direction and barked.

"Where's he going?" Arcacio asked.

"I don't know. Let's follow him. Maybe he knows where he's going," Destin said.

They followed the wolfdog through the forest. They started going downhill. Soon, they came out in the back of the house.

"Oh, Cosmos, you're such a good boy," Arcacio said as she petted his beautiful white and grayish-black coat.

"Well, that was quite a trip," Destin said.

A couple days later, they were ready to leave the satellite of Forestica.

"I think those ICE ships are gone by now," Destin said.

"I'll miss this place," Arcacio said.

"Yeah, me too. It *is* beautiful here. But who's to say that we will never be back to live here once the governmental problems in this galaxy are taken care of?" Destin said.

"*If* they can be taken care of. There are so many terrorist organizations throughout this galaxy, I don't think anyone knows the exact number of them. And then, there are our distant cousins in the Immortal Cantin Empire that are trying to kill us," Arcacio said.

"That is why we must go to Nytoorion. I must see to it that all of the Civil Resistance members throughout the galaxy are contacted. We'll need to use the code word in order to make contact. We must join together and put an end to this Reign of Terror campaign put forth by the Immortal Cantin Empire and the terrorist organizations throughout the BlueMar Galaxy.

"I'm glad that we had a place to hide out here on Forestica. I'm glad that my grandpa built it many years ago. Too bad he and my grandma had to perish in the Battle of Shoon," Destin said.

"I know. I pray that, in the end, it will all work out well," Arcacio said.

"Me too. Well, let's get going," Destin said.

They both took one more look at the house and surrounding area. Arcacio brought their food supplies with her and they climbed aboard the *Initial Voyage*. Destin engaged the engines and they lifted from the surface of Forestica, heading through the tall pine trees. They drifted upward through the lavender clouds and into space. Soon, they moved beyond the Xerica Star System and headed toward the planet of Nytoorion.

"I hope I can contact the rest of the Civil Resistance on Nytoorion. It was agreed that it would be our meeting place," Destin said.

"Where on Nytoorion?" Arcacio asked.

"In an intoxication joint, out in the middle of nowhere. It is supposed to be a big hangout for the galaxy's worst trash," Destin said.

"Oh, great," Arcacio said.

"Don't worry. I think we'll be pretty safe there. Cosmos is going to have to stay and guard the ship, though," Destin said.

"Yeah."

"Well, according to the computer, we should get there in five point two three lighthours," Destin said.

Arcacio looked through some of the things that she had brought from the kitchen back on Forestica. She took out a couple of blue colored carbonated beverages.

"Do you want a Sevela? These haven't expired yet," Arcacio said.

"Sure," Destin said. "My grandparents were there recently...before the Battle of Shoon. They must have stocked up. I'm sure going to miss them."

He took the Sevela, opened it up and took a long drink.

"Oh, that's good," he said.

Arcacio winked at him and opened her own Sevela, taking a long drink.

The wolfdog howled at them.

"No, Cosmos, you can't have any," she said.

CHAPTER SIX
DEFINITE ALLIES

THE *TIME EXPLORER* swiftly lowered to the rocky ground of the planet Nytoorion. Roedie and Tereena landed outside of an intoxication joint named Stone Shelf. The intoxication joint was a building with many sections located on a rocky outcrop area of Nytoorion. For kilometers around the intoxication joint, there was nothing but flat ground covered with small stones. Far into the distance, other rocky outcrop areas could be seen. Many millennia ago, the flat area with the many small stones was a sea of water. Parked outside the intoxication joint, there were many different types of spaceships. Roedie and Tereena landed the *Time Explorer* next to a black ship that looked like it had been setting there for years. The *Time Explorer* was the largest ship there. They secured the ship and stepped out onto the rocky ground. There was a stone trail that led up to the intoxication joint entrance. The trail twisted and wound its way up to the rocky outcrop. As they made their way up the trail, they could hear the faint noise of many conversations and music going on. Before they reached the entrance, they saw a creature of some sort to their left. It was lying on the ground, intoxicated.

As they reached the entrance, the double doors swiftly slid apart.

Inside, the noise of the many conversations was much louder. To one side of the room, there was a metal band playing a very fast song. The music could be heard throughout the room. The double-picking guitar sounds were very fast and heavy. The drums were thunderous and powerful. The band's name was Cosmic Metal, named after an old BlueMar Empire battleship. There were people and other beings sitting at tables throughout that section of the intoxication joint. Almost everyone in the place had a glass of ale in their hand. Smoke filled the large room. Some strange looking creatures stood at a table to the right with laser rifles slung over their shoulders. They were talking to some other creatures. Card games were going on at some tables.

Roedie and Tereena walked over to a counter on the far side of the room. Along the front of the counter, there were many stools. Roedie and Tereena sat down in front of the counter. A few stools over, there were a couple of people slumped over onto the counter. Apparently, they had too much to drink. The bartender asked Roedie and Tereena if they would like something to drink.

"Yes. We'll have a couple of ales," Roedie said.

The bartender left to get the drinks. He soon returned with two tall, slim glasses of ale. Frost drifted across the tops of the glasses. Roedie paid him and the bartender left. They slowly drank their ales. Roedie looked across the bar counter and noticed a *Nytoorion Chronicle* newspaper with a headline that read: "Zalho's World Brigade terrorists attack once again, killing 58 in the public square."

The *Initial Voyage* slowly landed on the rocky ground of Nytoorion. Destin and Arcacio landed the ship among the other ships. They stepped out of the ship and headed toward the entrance of the Stone Shelf, leaving Cosmos in the ship. They entered the intoxication joint and made their way to the back of the room. They sat on a couple of stools in front of the counter. The bartender asked them if they would like something to drink, sweat dripping from his bald head.

"I'll have an ale. What do you want, Arcacio?" Destin asked.

"I'll have a red Sevela," Arcacio said.

He left to get their drinks.

"I hope we can locate the Civil Resistance contact here," Destin said.

"So do I," Arcacio said.

The bartender returned with their drinks and Destin paid the man with some credits that he got in the house back on Forestica. They slowly drank their liquids. Destin looked at the couple next to them.

"How's it goin'?" Destin asked.

"Not too bad," Roedie said.

"Who's that?" Tereena whispered.

"How would I know?" Roedie whispered back.

Tereena gave Roedie a strange look.

"How's it going with you?" Roedie asked Destin.

"Pretty good. Destin Cantin's the name."

Roedie looked at Tereena with amazement. Destin and Arcacio saw they were shocked.

"We're not from the Immortal Cantin Empire," Destin said. "That part of our family is our distant cousins."

Roedie and Tereena still looked amazed.

"What's the matter?" Destin asked.

"Did you say that your last name is Cantin, but you're not from the Immortal Cantin Empire?" Roedie asked.

"Yes. They are our distant cousins. In fact, they are trying to kill us," Destin said.

"Have you ever heard of the ships that used to travel timespeed? They were in the time of the Claderane Government," Roedie said.

"Yes. One is still supposed to exist somewhere in the galaxy," Destin said.

"Tereena and I own that last timespeed ship. It's called the *Time Explorer*. Our last name is Cantin as well. We came to the future as a therapy of sorts. Our daughter is Phasheena Cantin," Roedie said.

"That was my great grandma," Destin said. "You mean, you two are my great great grandparents?" Destin asked.

"You could say that," Roedie said.

"Holy cosmic shit!" Destin exclaimed.

"What a coincidence," Tereena said.

"I'm Destin and this is my wife, Arcacio."

"My name's Roedie and this would be your great great grandmother, Tereena."

They all shook hands and then gave way to hugs.

"I'm here to find the contact to the rest of the Civil Resistance. I'm the leader of the Kas operation. We are trying to straighten out the galaxy. We are trying to get rid of the Immortal Cantin Empire and every terrorist organization that exists out there," Destin said.

"Yeah, the galaxy is kind of fucked up right now, isn't it?" Roedie said. "We'd like to help you out. So, where is this contact of yours?"

"I don't know. We've never been here before," Destin said.

"Neither have we," Roedie said.

As the bartender walked by, Arcacio got his attention.

"ICE Down," she whispered the code word.

The large, bald man looked around.

"You're from Kas?" he whispered.

"Yes," she said. "Would you happen to know where the Civil Resistance contact is?" Arcacio asked in a low voice.

"The bartender in the next section can tell you where the contact is. She knows," the man said.

Arcacio looked at the rest of them. They finished their drinks and headed for the next section of the intoxication joint. They walked further back into the room and through a dark passage that led to a narrow corridor. On the walls of the corridor, there was a liquid slime that reeked with odor. The floor had trash and other items scattered about. The corridor opened up to a dimly lit room that was smaller than the first one. Patrons sat at some of the tables; however, it was not as busy as the first section. Like the first section of the intoxication joint, the counter was located in the back of the room. Unlike the first section, the second section was much quieter and had a few doors to the left side of the room. Roedie, Tereena, Destin, and Arcacio sat down on the stools in front of the counter. The bartender walked over to them. She was a husky woman with a no-nonsense manner.

"Would any of you like some time with our Galactic Star Maidens?" the bartender asked.

"Galactic Star Maidens? What are they?" Roedie asked.

"They are an organized group of harlots. Where have you people been all your lives?" the bartender asked.

"No, we don't want time with any of the Galactic Star Maidens," Destin said, looking over to the three doors on the left of the room.

A beautiful blonde woman walked out from one of the three doors. She had no top on. Her revealing lace panties accented her elegant stockings. She was followed by another woman from the same door.

"Come again, now, you delicious hot thing," the topless blonde told the other woman who soon disappeared.

The blonde returned to the Galactic Star Maidens' sex palace. The bartender asked Roedie, Tereena, Destin, and Arcacio if they wanted something to drink.

"No. ICE Down... What we're here for is to locate the contact of the Civil Resistance," Destin said.

The woman looked at the four of them. She put down the glass that was in her hand.

"Follow me," she said.

They followed her through a curtain into a corridor that led from behind the counter. It was much like the other corridor. There were very old pieces of mechanical and metal junk against the walls. They came out into a room that was filled with more metal junk. They passed through that room and into another. This one was also filled with metal junk. In the room, there was a humanoid of some sort working on a robot. They passed through that room and entered another corridor, which reeked very badly. There were live as well as dead rodents throughout the long, dark corridor. The live ones were gnawing on various pieces of trash. It was very chilly in the passage. More wet slime covered the walls. They passed through the corridor and came out into a room that had several intoxicated creatures lying on the floor. A few rodents crawled in between them, searching for food. On the far side of the small room, there was an entrance to a stairway that led down beneath the surface of Nytoorion. They went down the stone steps. The stairs twisted and turned, opening up into a room where several masked figures stood.

"For security purposes, you must be blindfolded from this point," the bartender said as she gestured toward the masked figures.

Roedie, Tereena, Destin, and Arcacio looked at each other. The masked figures tied bandannas around each of their heads, blocking their vision. After they were all blindfolded, they were led through a passage. They could hear screeches, high pitched sounds, and faint screams echoing through the passages. Roedie hesitated and stopped.

"Don't worry. You'll be safe with us," one of the masked figures said.

As they went onward, sounds of creatures growling could be heard. They soon heard low pitched frequencies and the faint sound of machinery as they went through the passage. They came out into a warmer room. Someone shut the electronic door and it became quiet. The blindfolds were removed.

"Where are we?" Roedie asked one of the masked figures.

"You are far below the surface of the planet. There is a prison down here for the galaxy's worst trash," one of the masked figures said.

"I know the Immortal Cantin Empire didn't put these people in here, because they don't take prisoners. So then, who put these people in prison?" Destin asked.

"All of the people and other beings in the prison down here are terrorists. The Civil Resistance members brought them here," the man said.

"So, where is our contact?" Arcacio asked.

"He will meet you here in this room shortly. All of you wait here," the man said.

All of the masked figures left the room.

"Damn, it's nasty down here," Tereena said.

"I know," Roedie said.

"I had no idea the intoxication joint was this big—with a prison in its lower levels," Destin said.

The door opened and a man with short, brown hair walked in.

"Which one of you is Destin Cantin?" the man asked.

"I am," Destin said.

"You are the last of the Civil Resistance from the Kas operation?" he asked.

"Yes," Destin said.

"I'm sorry to hear about the carnage at the Battle of Shoon, but we must forge ahead," the man said.

"This is my wife, Arcacio. And these two are my great great grandparents, Roedie and Tereena," Destin said.

"What?" the man asked.

"They own the only ship left in the galaxy that has timespeed capabilities. They came from the past," Destin said.

"Is that true?" the man asked, looking at Roedie and Tereena.

"Yes, it is. We just met Destin and Arcacio upstairs in the first section of the intoxication joint. We were both surprised to see them. We would like to help you with the problems in the galaxy in any way we can," Roedie said.

"You are more than welcome to. I've heard of that last ship that travels the speed of time, but I never thought that I'd see it. Does it have a lot of weaponry on it?" the man asked.

"Have you ever heard of the *Galactic Explorer?*" Roedie asked.

"Ah, yeah. That was the ship that helped destroy the seat of the BlueMar Empire on the planet Andron in the old BlueMar War," the man said.

"Well, now it's called the *Time Explorer*. And that's our ship," Roedie said.

"Oh, wow!" the man said. "By the way, my name is Remyw Yortis. I've been the Civil Resistance contact here on Nytoorion for many years. I'm glad you reached this planet safely. Many Civil Resistance members are waiting for my reply. I have to inform them that you've reached Nytoorion safely and the fate of the Kas operation. We have worked out a plan. At a particular time in the near future, all of the Civil Resistance groups are going to attack every terrorist organization throughout the entire BlueMar Galaxy. But before we do that, the Immortal Cantin Empire has to be destroyed. We were hoping that most of that would have been done at the Battle of Shoon. Destin, is your ship large enough to handle an attack on the Immortal Cantin Empire?"

"No," Destin said.

"With the *Time Explorer,* we could probably handle it. But we will still have to use your ship, Destin. We will also have to use the Star Knight fighter ships inside the *Time Explorer,*" Roedie said.

"Okay. Do you think you guys can handle it?" Remyw Yortis asked.

"Hopefully," Arcacio said.

"As we've seen from the Battle of Shoon, ground troops don't work with these guys. Aerial and space battles will be the advantage," Destin said.

"Yes. I'm hoping you guys can pull this off. When your mission with the Immortal Cantin Empire is finished, I need you to contact me. Once you contact me, I will relay the message to other Civil Resistance operations across the galaxy. And the contacts at those posts will inform even more members of the counterterrorist organizations. Soon, the Civil Resistance throughout the BlueMar Galaxy will be prepared for their attacks on all the terrorist organizations. Since we lost the Battle of Shoon on Kas, this is another attempt at stage one of Operation Dark War," Remyw Yortis said.

"Okay. Is there anything else?" Roedie asked.

"Nothing," Remyw said. "Just be careful. God be with you."

"All right, we'll contact you as soon as we're finished," Destin said.

"We have to go make our plans," Roedie said.

"Okay, talk to you later. I'll have those masked figures bring you back to the point where they first blindfolded you. From there, you can find your way easily. The reason the blindfolds were necessary was to be sure you weren't terrorist agents or from the Immortal Cantin Empire. There is no need to put them on on your way out. See ya," Remyw Yortis said as he left the room.

Soon, the masked figures came in the room.

"Ready?" one of them asked.

"Yes. Why are you people wearing masks anyway?" Tereena asked.

"It is our custom," another of them said.

They all left the room and proceeded through the passages of the intoxication joint's lower levels. When they reached the point where they had originally been blindfolded, the masked figures left them. The four of them made their way to the stairs. When they reached the upper level, they made their way back to the first section of the intoxication joint. They all had one more drink before they left. Then they made their way to the entrance. An insect-like humanoid stepped in front of them as they tried to leave.

"Do you own that immense ship out there?" the creature asked in a reverberated tone.

"Why?" Roedie asked.

"'Cause I want it," the creature said as he grabbed the laser rifle that was slung over his shoulder.

He pointed it at the four of them.

"You didn't answer my inquiry," the creature said.

A bouncer shot the creature with a laser rifle of his own. A yellow liquid spurted out onto the wall and dripped to the floor next to the entrance, as the creature fell to the floor.

"Siinoid always bothered people," the bouncer said. "It was about time I killed the annoying piece of shit."

Everyone's attention in the room was focused on the entrance. The four of them left in a hurry. On their way down the rocky trail, they saw that same intoxicated creature still on the side of the trail.

Upon reaching the ships, they looked at each other.

"Where is your ship?" Roedie asked.

"The *Initial Voyage* is over there," Destin said, pointing toward his ship.

"Why don't we fly that ship into the docking bay of the *Time Explorer?*" Roedie said.

"Okay," Destin said.

They all entered the *Initial Voyage*. Cosmos ran up to them wagging his tail.

"Hey boy, how's it going?" Destin asked.

Cosmos barked.

"Oh, the dog is so adorable," Tereena said.

"Actually, it is a wolfdog," Destin said.

"Oh," Tereena said.

Roedie entered a security clearance code into his watch to disable the docking bay security field. Destin started the ship and flew it into the docking bay of the *Time Explorer*.

"Holy cosmos, this ship is big," Arcacio said.

Destin landed the *Initial Voyage* across from the Star Knights and an old ship named *Zoota 2001*. They stepped out of the ship and onto the metal floor of the docking bay. Destin and Arcacio followed Roedie and Tereena up the stairs, passed the observation deck, and all the way to the bridge.

"As soon as we're in space, we can make our plans for attack," Roedie said.

Roedie engaged the engines of the *Time Explorer* and it slowly rose from the rocky ground with a rumble. They flew through the grayish-white clouds of Nytoorion and proceeded into the darkness of space.

CHAPTER SEVEN
PLANS OF ACTION

THE *TIME EXPLORER* orbited the planet of Nytoorion. Roedie, Tereena, Destin, Arcacio, and Cosmos were all in the briefing room on the third level of the ship. They were planning the attack on the Immortal Cantin Empire. They had maps set up on the briefing room table, with several star systems circled in blue. Everything in the blue circle was inside the Immortal Cantin Empire's jurisdiction. The Kaskar Star System, the Tiosoon Star System, the Tuska Thaxe Star System, the Finitte Star System, the Andrexx Star System, the Althore Star System, and the Tri-Sintex Star System were all inside the blue circles. Roedie took a drink of red Sevela.

"This ship is huge. It must be difficult running the whole thing by yourselves," Destin said.

"Yes, it is. We have to take care of everything ourselves. It would be awesome to actually have a small crew," Tereena said.

"Well, at least we have the maps set up. Now, all we have to do is plan it out well," Roedie said.

"We're going to have to attack the Immortal Cantin Empire's royal domain first and then any of their armed forces they have in each of the systems that we've circled. But I don't want to attack cities with innocent people in them, if we can help it…even if there are information centers for the Immortal Cantin Empire in those cities. Without the empire itself, they cannot function. So, there is no reason to destroy them and kill innocent people. Enough innocent people will die as it is," Tereena said.

"Yeah, and those cities could be of use later," Arcacio said.

"Are you sure we can even destroy all of their armed forces with just this one ship?" Destin asked.

"I hope so. The *Time Explorer is* a powerful ship. I mean, they don't make them like this anymore. But we'll still need to use your ship, *Initial Voyage,* and my Star Knights, so that we'll have enough fire power to knock out all of their forces," Roedie said.

Roedie took another drink of his red Sevela. They all gazed over the maps of the Immortal Cantin Empire.

"Okay, I think when we knock out the empire's royal domain first, it should stop communications between them and the rest of their armed forces in the other systems. Once the empire's royal domain is taken out, it will take some time before the news reaches any of the cities on Kas, such as Krymoss, Antiqueech, and Kas Voya. During that time, we will be outbound for their armed forces in the other systems. We will not be able to destroy all of their armed forces before the remaining ones receive the information about the fate of the empire's royal domain. Once the information *does* reach the remaining forces, then we're going to have a fight on our hands. That's when things are going to get tough," Destin said.

"When it reaches that point, we'll have to use your ship and the Star Knights," Roedie said.

"Yeah," Destin said.

At that moment, the computer indicated that a ship flying from the surface of Nytoorion was on a collision course with the *Time Explorer.*

"Oh, shit! Just what we need—an intoxicated pilot," Arcacio said.

"I have to get the *Time Explorer* out of the way," Roedie said.

He ran for the bridge, while the others waited in the briefing room.

It was too late. The ship with the intoxicated pilot at its controls smashed into the side of the *Time Explorer.* The pilot died as his ship exploded into a storm of metal shrapnel. The explosion left a hole in the side of the *Time Explorer.* The resulting jolt knocked everyone in the briefing room to the floor. While Roedie was on his way to the bridge, he was knocked down a flight of stairs that led from the third level to the second level. He was hurt badly. Alarms started to sound on the ship.

Tereena got up from the floor of the briefing room. She helped the others up.

"Are you two okay?" Tereena asked.

"Yeah," Arcacio said.

"That ship must have hit," Destin said.

Arcacio looked at Cosmos. The wolfdog howled and hid under the briefing room table, frightened.

"Let's get to the bridge," Tereena said.

They all left for the bridge with haste. When they went down the stairs to the second level, they noticed Roedie lying on the floor.

"Oh, no," Tereena said.

She ran to him. He was unconscious.

"We have to get him to the medical center of the ship," she said.

They first checked to see if they were knocked out of orbit. They were not. They brought Roedie to the medical center on the second level. Tereena gave him a medical computer scan.

As she saw the results, she said, "He has a broken arm and a concussion."

Tereena hooked up a device that quickly mended his arm. She then placed another device over his head. Soon, the effects from the concussion were gone. He awoke.

"Tereena," He sat up on the bed and looked at the others. "I've got to get to the bridge to see how much damage there is," Roedie said.

"Okay, let's go. How do you feel?" Tereena asked.

"Like shit. Let's go."

They headed toward the bridge. The alarms continued to sound throughout the ship. When they reached the bridge, Roedie asked the computer how much damage there was.

"A large hole was blown in the hull of the ship and it was on fire. I took the appropriate action and sealed off that immediate area. The fire is now out. The sealed-off area is in vacuum and the doors have been locked. There is a problem, however. Where the hole is blown into the hull is also where a power cable runs through to one of the main engines. It is the positive power cable that connects to power cores two thousand forty-one through two thousand fifty. It is a five hundred kilovolt cable and must be repaired if the ship is to fly anywhere," the computer said.

"Leave it to the BlueMar Empire to design a ship with the power cables against the outer wall..." Roedie said.

"Oh, great! We have to repair a five hundred kilovolt cable?" Destin said.

"If we're going to attack the Immortal Cantin Empire, we have to," Roedie said. "So, let's get to it."

They all left the bridge—with the exception of Cosmos—and headed toward the lower levels to shut off the power to power cores 2241 through 2250. At the end of a maze of corridors, they came out to a corridor intersection not far from the docking bay's observation deck. They made a right turn and entered a room with a stairway that led to the lower levels of the ship.

The lower levels of the *Time Explorer* were made of metal stairways, catwalks, and ladders with illuminators fixed at specific points. Some areas of the lower levels were very cold, while others were hot. In most of the areas, a faint hum from the massive engines that still operated could be heard. Hissing sounds could also be heard from the cooling systems. Other areas were quiet, with the exception of dripping water caused from condensation. A faint musty odor lingered in the air.

They proceeded down a metal grate catwalk toward the power cores. Power cores were very small power source modules that emitted large amounts of power. They were much more effective than their ancient predecessors, such as batteries, generators, and nuclear reactors. The power cores were located near the main engines toward the back of the immense ship. Along the way, Roedie told his great great grandchildren the history of the ship.

"The *Time Explorer*—once known as the *Galactic Explorer*—was originally a BlueMar Empire ship. My brother, Baas, and I, along with our father, Olossky, took the *Galactic Explorer,* along with two other ships of the same size, and put them to use in the Claderane Resistance. The Claderane Resistance over-threw the BlueMar Empire in the BlueMar War, which took place in the year 230929 SA (Space Age). When our daughter, Phasheena—your great grandma—was of age and on her own, we started to travel time in this ship. We left in the year 230952 SA and have been doing this for approximately ten years. We are currently sixty-five years into the future from when we left. Now, the year is 231017 SA. This ship has been in two wars, to another galaxy, through time, and in an asteroid field. It is the first time something this bad happened to it. And it had to be from an intoxicated pilot," Roedie said.

"That's amazing," Destin said.

When they reached the power core room, Roedie shut off the power to the ten power cores.

"Now, we have to reconstruct the hull and repair that cable. Let's go to the tool room," Roedie said.

They headed for the first level. When they reached the tool room, Roedie and Destin took the required tools to accomplish their task. They put all the tools and also several large pieces of titanium hull-repair metal onto a cart.

"Arcacio, do you want to go to the recreation room with me while they work on the ship?" Tereena asked.

"Sure," Arcacio said. "That would be fine. Then we won't be in their way."

"We're going to the recreation room," Tereena said.

"Okay," Roedie said, "but you're not in our way. Have fun."

The two women left the tool room and headed for the second level. Roedie and Destin followed them out the door with the cart and headed for the destroyed portion of the ship.

At the corridor, just outside of the sealed-off vacuum section, Roedie and Destin put on spacesuits. Roedie then depressurized the corridor and slightly lowered the artificial gravitation in the area. The lower gravity would enable them to lift the heavy wall sections when completely welded. They opened the sealed door and entered the room where the hole was located in the hull. Debris from the impact lay scattered across the room. The room itself was not finished and wasn't used. Destin helped by setting up temporary illuminators. They placed the large, rectangular titanium pieces of hull-repair metal from the cart onto the floor. Roedie welded them together with a laser welder. When it was completed, the piece of metal was large enough to cover the hole in the wall. While the large piece of metal was still on the floor, they applied a liquid metal alloy onto the surface of it. The alloy soon covered the entire piece of metal. It did not take long for it to dry. As it dried, it hardened to become an extremely high temperature resistant metal for going through planet atmospheres. They placed the large, thick piece of metal against the wall where the hole was located. If Roedie had not turned down the artificial gravitation, they would not have been able to lift the heavy piece of metal. Roedie welded it to the metal hull. It sealed the outer hull. Roedie grabbed a device and checked the structure for pin holes and possible leaks. Fortunately, there were none. Next, they modified the power cable on either side of the repaired hull and attached connectors. Adding a new piece of cable, they attached it to the new connectors. The cable was then repaired. They filled the wall with another type of radiation-resistant, liquid metal alloy, covering the well-insulated cable. After welding more rectangular pieces of metal together, they moved it into place and welded it to the inner wall, completely sealing the destroyed portion of the ship. Roedie smoothed the wall surface with a laser sander. He then turned the artificial gravitation back to normal and slowly pressurized the room and adjacent corridor. They were also able to repair the illuminators in the room, which were much brighter than the temporary ones they had brought from the tool room. After cleaning up the debris in the room, they spray painted the repaired wall with a white paint to match the rest of the room. Since the empty storage room was not used, there was no concern about making it perfect.

They removed their spacesuits and returned all of the tools back to the tool room. From the tool room, they proceeded to the power core room. Roedie turned the ten power cores back on. They headed toward the bridge.

When the bridge's electronic door slid aside, Cosmos jumped out at them.

"Hey boy, how ya doin'?" Destin asked.

Roedie went over to the computer and asked it for the results.

"Structural damage is repaired. Cable is repaired. All engines are now operative," the computer said.

"Good. Well, Destin, shall we join the ladies in the recreation room?" Roedie asked.

"Sure," Destin said.

They left the bridge followed by Cosmos.

Tereena and Arcacio were talking and drinking blue Sevela when Roedie, Destin, and Cosmos joined them.

"Is it all repaired?" Arcacio asked.

"Yeah," Roedie said.

"That took all day," Tereena said.

"Well, shall we go back to the briefing room?" Destin asked.

"Yeah, that would be a good idea," Tereena said.

"Maybe I should move the ship someplace else this time..." Roedie said.

"That couldn't happen twice," Destin said.

Roedie looked at him for a long moment. "I'll meet you guys in the briefing room shortly. I'm moving the ship," he said, heading for the bridge.

The others proceeded toward the briefing room. When they reached the briefing room, they waited for Roedie. When he arrived, they all looked at the maps of the Immortal Cantin Empire.

"As we discussed earlier, we'll take the royal domain first. Then we can make our way to their other armed forces, starting from the forces nearest Kas and finishing with the ones farthest away," Roedie said.

"Well, we know everything that we've planned to do. So, let's do it," Destin said.

Tereena folded up the maps and put them in a drawer in the briefing room table.

"Let's go to the bridge," Roedie said.

On the bridge, Roedie turned the engines up to lightspeed. The *Time Explorer* left the Nytoorion Star System. They flew through the darkness of space toward the planet Kas.

Chapter Eight
Operation Dark War

The *Time Explorer* flew toward the Immortal Cantin Empire's territorial space boundary. They flew toward the Kaskar Star System. Roedie, Tereena, Destin, and Arcacio were all on the bridge of the ship.

"We'll be there in ten lightminutes," Roedie said.

"I sure hope this works," Tereena said.

"Yeah," Destin said.

Once the *Time Explorer* entered the Kaskar Star System, they flew directly toward the planet Kas. Roedie had the reflector shields on so they would not be detected. Destin gave Roedie the code to shut down the planet's deflector shield defenses. It was only turned off for a second as they entered the atmosphere of Kas. The sky blue color in the stratosphere set beautifully against the beige sand. Sand could be seen blowing around to form dust clouds. They flew onward to the empire's royal domain, located outside of what once was the town of Kanthas.

"This is strangely nostalgic," Roedie said.

A woman stood on a terrace, high above the grounds of the empire's royal domain. The woman leaned against the stone railing that surrounded the terrace, gazing far out into the desert sands at the horizon in the distance. Her name was Kathell Cantin—Blackie II Cantin's wife. She always went up to the terrace to think. It was so free and peaceful up there. Sometimes, she could just let all her worries slip away. This time, however, she thought about how cruel and evil the empire has been to innocent people over the years. She was getting tired of their tyrant rule and wanted out of it all. She was also pregnant with Blackie II's child. She put her head down onto her arms and closed her eyes.

What am I going to do? I don't want to be a part of this anymore... she thought.

She opened her eyes and gazed back out into the desert sands. In the distance, she saw a very large ship quickly approaching the empire's royal domain. She knew it was not one of their ships. It was much too large to be one of their ships. She had never seen a ship that large before.

I knew we would push it too far one of these days, she thought.

The ship came closer and closer. She ran.

The *Time Explorer* entered the empire's royal domain. Roedie hovered in front of the building for several seconds. He fired every laser cannon aboard the ship. They all hit the massive building. The intense lasers slammed into the concrete and metal of the building. Soon, the building was in ruins along with everyone inside. The remains of the massive building were covered by a cloud of smoke. Fires raged throughout the rubble.

Roedie saw a woman in the distance, running away from the burning ruins. She had exited the building just in time before the attack and was the only survivor. He lowered the *Time Explorer* to the sandy ground in front of the woman's path. Roedie went outside and ran toward the woman.

"Please, don't hurt me and my baby," she cried, backing away from Roedie.

Tears rolled down her face.

"I'm not going to hurt you. What baby?" Roedie asked.

"I'm pregnant," Kathell said.

"I'm not going to hurt you or your baby. But I must ask you to come aboard my ship. We need to have a discussion. Besides, it's a long walk to the nearest city from here," Roedie said.

With hesitation, she said, "Okay."

They both stepped aboard the *Time Explorer* and stood in a corridor.

"Okay, what we are doing is destroying this evil empire and all of the terrorist organizations throughout the galaxy. As soon as we're finished, a new favorable government will be set up throughout the BlueMar Galaxy. What's your name?" Roedie asked.

"Kathell Cantin, wife of Emperor Blackie II Cantin. Actually, widow of Blackie II Cantin. Who the hell are you?" she asked.

"I am Roedie Cantin. More will be explained to you on the bridge. Follow me," Roedie said, walking toward the bridge.

Kathell's jaw dropped. She was amazed to find out that he was also a Cantin.

He must be from the Civil Resistance, she thought.

She followed him to the bridge. When they reached the bridge, Roedie told Destin to explain to her who they were. He quietly asked Destin to decide whether she was dangerous or not. Destin started talking to her while Roedie flew the ship toward the Immortal Cantin Empire's armed forces in the Tiosoon Star System.

"What's your name?" Destin asked.

"Kathell Cantin," she said. "I am…was Blackie II's wife."

"I am Destin Cantin, your distant cousin-in-law. This is my wife, Arcacio. We are in the Civil Resistance. But Roedie and Tereena Cantin are not in the Civil Resistance…although they joined up with us to help out when we met them back on Nytoorion," Destin said.

"If you didn't know them before they joined up with you, then why do they have the same name as ours? Who are they? Where did you get this immense ship?" Kathell asked.

"They are from the past, before the Dark Years of terrorism and the Immortal Cantin Empire. They are from the time of the Old Claderane Government. This ship has the ability to travel timespeed. It is the only ship left in the galaxy that can travel the speed of time. Roedie is my great great grandfather. He is the uncle of the person who first developed the Immortal Cantin Empire—Reminall," Destin said.

Kathell could not find the words to say.

"What's the matter?" Destin asked.

"I contemplated leaving the empire. I've been tired of the evil rule and tyranny over innocent people," Kathell said.

"So has the whole Civil Resistance. That's why it's time to make some long overdue changes. Will you join the Civil Resistance in the fight?" Destin asked.

"Yes. Yes, I will," Kathell said.

"Good. I think you can be trusted around here," Destin said.

They proceeded toward the Tiosoon Star System that was a few days out. Although they alternated sleep periods during transit, Roedie could not seem to sleep well, as he was very anxious.

The *Time Explorer* entered the Tiosoon Star System. The Tiosoon System had two planets in it, both with outposts containing armed forces. It also had two space stations with armed forces as well.

Roedie decided to take the two planets first. He flew to the first planet, Montell Aillis. With a thundering sound, Roedie destroyed the outpost on Montell Aillis. He then proceeded to the second planet, Roiis Extt. There was another thundering explosion. The outpost on Roiis Extt was in flames. Roedie flew toward the two space stations. Both military targets didn't react in time and were easily destroyed.

"We did that faster than I expected," Destin said.

"Yeah. They weren't expecting it," Roedie said.

They proceeded toward the Andrexx Star System. When they reached the Andrexx System, the outpost on the system's single planet, Diamesh, was easily destroyed. They moved on to the Althore Star System and destroyed the space station there. From there, they reached the Tri-Sintex Star System.

The armed forces in the Tri-Sintex System were some of the Immortal Cantin Empire's most powerful. They were based on a spacecraft carrier space station. The spacecraft carrier had a long, flat deck with many fighter ships on its surface that could be seen from a distance in space. To the side of the flat deck was a towering building complex that stood five levels above it. The spacecraft carrier also had lower levels underneath the large deck. There was a magnetic field surrounding the entire deck with air on the inside. There was also a deflector shield on it, making it difficult for lasers to penetrate. The entire station had artificial gravitation. Not only could the fighter ships land and take off from the spacecraft carrier, but the entire carrier itself could fly through space.

The spacecraft carrier had already received information on the demise of the Immortal Cantin Empire's royal domain from the city of Antiqueech on Kas. They were prepared for an attack. They tried to contact all of the other armed forces throughout the entire Immortal Cantin Empire's territory. The only one they could reach was in the Tuska Thaxe Star System. That outpost was also prepared for an attack.

• • •

"Stop the ship!" Tereena said.

"What for?" Roedie asked.

"Just stop the ship!"

Roedie stopped the *Time Explorer.*

"Okay," Roedie said.

"I have a strange feeling about this. I have a feeling they're waiting for us," Tereena said.

Roedie looked at her for a moment.

"There are only two more armed forces left to destroy as we head further out from Kas. Both of them happen to be larger than all of the others that we have already destroyed. I'm glad you had that feeling, because they probably received the information about the empire's royal domain from Kas. We are still outside of their scanner range. I have an idea. We can travel a short time into the past at timespeed to a time before they received the information. And the coordinates of the *Time Explorer* can have us appear on the starboard side of the station. Then, the *Initial Voyage* can fly to the port side of the station. They won't know what hit them," Roedie said.

"Sounds good to me," Destin said. "Arcacio, you stay on this ship while I do that."

Destin headed for the docking bay to get aboard the *Initial Voyage.* Roedie started the tac-time engines. They flew a short distance into the past and toward the spacecraft carrier. When they came out of timespeed, Roedie told Destin to proceed. Destin left the *Time Explorer* and headed toward the port side of the spacecraft carrier.

"Here goes," Roedie said.

Roedie and Destin fired every laser they had toward the spacecraft carrier. All of their lasers could not penetrate the deflector shield.

"Oh, shit! Fire everything at the engines of the station," Roedie told Destin through the com.

Roedie flew the *Time Explorer* to the rear of the spacecraft carrier where Destin's ship already was. ICE fighter ships started flying from the surface of the deck. There were at least a hundred of them. All of the ICE fighter ships were equipped with devices that enabled them to pass through the deflector shield and the magnetic field that held air on the carrier. They flew toward the two assaulting ships, ready to defend their station.

Roedie and Destin fired all of their lasers at the rear engines of the spacecraft carrier. The engine area of the station was the only place where the deflector shield could not work at full capacity since the shield opened at the carrier's engine ports.

Just as the ICE fighter ships started firing their lasers at the attacking ships, the entire spacecraft carrier exploded into nothingness, taking all but a few of the ICE fighter ships with it. The *Time Explorer* and *Initial Voyage* moved out of the way just in time. They were able to easily pick off the remaining ICE fighter ships.

"We did it," Destin said.

"Yeah, we did," Roedie said.

Destin flew the *Initial Voyage* back into the docking bay of the *Time Explorer.* He went to the bridge.

"Are we prepared to take on the last armed forces of the Immortal Cantin Empire?" Roedie asked.

"I guess," Destin said.

Roedie smiled. He flew the ship toward the Tuska Thaxe Star System.

The *Time Explorer* entered the Tuska Thaxe Star System. They flew toward the planet Tuska.

"They're going to be waiting for us," Destin said.

"Yes, I know. Many, many years ago, I was on the planet Tuska with my brother when we were searching for our father. Other than one mountain, it was just a swamp planet back then. There were creatures called Tuskus on the planet at that time. But from what I'm getting from the scanners, there are a lot of cities on the planet now. There are still swampy areas, though. And also the Tuskus species are extinct. They must have killed them off when they took over the planet," Roedie said.

"Really?"

"Yes. Well, I have a plan for this one. The scanners show that this is the largest of all the Immortal Cantin Empire's armed forces," Roedie said.

"You guys better hurry up and figure out what you're gonna do before they spot us," Tereena said.

"Yeah. Well, there are five of us. Do you feel like flying?" Roedie asked Kathell.

"Sure, I'll fly," she said.

"Okay. The Star Knights are very easy to get used to. I'll fly the *Time Explorer* and Destin can fly the *Initial Voyage.* We will both attack the armed forces base. The scanners show that there is a power plant outside of a city named Futress. The plant runs the power to the armed forces base. Tereena, you can destroy that power plant in the *Zoota 2001.* The other two things that need to be destroyed are the weapons factory and the particle beam laser cannon that is pointed toward space from that mountaintop. Arcacio, you can take a Star Knight and destroy the laser cannon. Kathell, you can take another Star Knight and destroy the weapons factory," Roedie said. "To familiarize yourself with all the places that I mentioned, study the map on the screen. It should also display in your ships. Oh, how I wish I had some Kalaar robots right about now."

"Kalaar robots?" Destin gave Roedie a questioning look.

"They were robots that used to pilot the Star Knights during battle," Roedie said.

They all looked at the map.

"Okay. Here goes," Destin said.

They all went to the docking bay with the exception of Roedie and Cosmos. The *Initial Voyage,* the *Zoota 2001,* and two Star Knights left the docking bay of the *Time Explorer.* Roedie and Destin proceeded toward the armed forces base.

Tereena entered into the planet's atmosphere, piloting the *Zoota 2001.* She went on to the power plant in the city of Futress. On the way, she saw small areas of swamp through the observation window. There was a lot of green foliage in the swampy areas; however, there were also many dead trees lying halfway out of the murky water. Moss covered many of the remaining trees. Vines hung in the water from high above. The swamp slowly thinned out to the city of Futress. Streams of water rushed to a river in a valley just outside of the city. The swamp quickly gave way to concrete. Tereena flew to the power plant and fired her lasers at it. The explosion sent red flames rolling upward toward the sky. The bright, red flames contrasted against the dark green swamp in the background. The power went out at the armed forces base.

When the power went out at the armed forces base, Roedie and Destin attacked the complex. Just as ICE fighter ships lifted from the base's docking platform, the entire complex exploded. Roedie picked up some other ICE fighter ships on his scanners. Roedie and Destin took off to destroy them.

Arcacio flew her assigned Star Knight across a wide valley that was surrounded by a mountain. The valley was green with swamp and streams of water. She flew toward the laser cannon on the mountaintop. From her proximity, she could see the city of Futress in the background.

From her vantage point, the city looked a sea-green color with a mixture of silver from the metal pipes and towering buildings. Arcacio flew to the top of the mountain and fired her lasers at the particle beam laser cannon. It exploded, shaking the mountaintop.

Kathell flew the Star Knight assigned to her toward the weapons factory, deep inside the city of Futress. From her vantage point, many factories could be seen in the industrial area of the city. She destroyed the weapons factory. The explosion caused a storm of metal shrapnel that flew in all directions.

As Tereena flew away from the destroyed power plant, she was spotted by a group of ICE fighter ships that started shooting at her. She tried to outmaneuver them, but could not. Before long, they shot her down. The *Zoota 2001* crashed into the swamp, its nose buried into the murky water. Tereena was knocked to the ship floor. She picked herself up and found the *Zoota 2001* was damaged very badly. She quickly got an anti-gravitation transport out from the ship's compartment. She stepped into the Airglider and turned it on. It rose from the soft ground with a hiss. She flew away from the area, heading toward a long bridge that overlooked the valley below. There were streams that emptied into the river valley. The road led across the bridge and back to the city. The ICE fighter ships circled around and started shooting at her in the Airglider. She looked up, saw them, and kept going as fast as she could. Roedie and Destin came up behind the ICE fighter ships and picked them off, one by one. Tereena turned around and saw the *Time Explorer* and the *Initial Voyage* finish off the ICE fighters that were shooting at her. She was about three quarters of the way across the long bridge when she stopped the Airglider. The *Initial Voyage* was small enough to land on the bridge and pick her up.

After picking up Tereena, Destin flew back into the docking bay of the *Time Explorer*. Roedie flew the *Time Explorer* high above the city of Futress and waited for Arcacio and Kathell to return. After the two Star Knights flew into the docking bay of the *Time Explorer*, Roedie left Tuska and everyone met on the bridge.

"Well, we did it. The entire Immortal Cantin Empire no longer exists," Roedie said.

"Thanks for picking me up down there. I didn't know where to go," Tereena said.

"No problem, great great grandma," Destin said with a smile.

"Very funny…you're as old as you feel," she said and smiled back.

"Well, I guess it's time to return to Nytoorion and inform Remyw Yortis of our success," Arcacio said.

"Yes. Let's be on our way," Roedie said. "It's too bad we lost the *Zoota 2001,* but in the scheme of things, that is very minimal. I'm very happy that you are okay, Tereena."

Roedie flew the *Time Explorer* toward the Nytoorion Star System.

"Sorry about the *Zoota 2001,*" Tereena said.

"Don't worry about it, Tereena. It was an old ship anyway," Roedie said as he gave her a long hug. "I'm going to go lie down. I haven't slept well lately. You have the controls, babe."

Roedie left the bridge.

"Who is Remyw Yortis?" Kathell asked.

"That is our Civil Resistance contact. We'll explain it on the way to Nytoorion," Destin said.

Chapter Nine
Force of Militia

THE *TIME EXPLORER* landed on Nytoorion. Roedie, Tereena, Destin, Arcacio, and Kathell walked up the stone trail and into the intoxication joint. They made their way to the place where they met Remyw Yortis before. He was waiting for them when they arrived in the room.

"Well… I noticed your ship arrive outside," Remyw said.

"Well, we did it. The Immortal Cantin Empire no longer exists," Roedie said.

"So I've heard. The news has already reached me. Good. Congratulations on the victory. Now, we have to take care of all the terrorism throughout the galaxy. That will be much more difficult. Who is this?" Remyw pointed toward Kathell, his attraction evident.

"Her name is Kathell Cantin. She is from the Immortal Cantin Empire's royal domain. She's the only survivor. Before we even picked her up, she was planning to leave the empire," Roedie said.

"I am the emperor's widow. I was tired of the evil things that we did to people, the pain that we inflicted," Kathell said.

"She actually helped us destroy the last armed forces," Roedie said.

"People can only take so much," Remyw said.

"Yes, I know," she said.

"I think it would be best if you all stayed here on Nytoorion for a while. The other Civil Resistance operations throughout the galaxy will hopefully be able to destroy every terrorist organization that exists. If they need any help, they will contact me. Then, we can do what we have to in order to help. I'm going to go contact them right now. I will be back shortly. Down this corridor further, you will find a lounge, if you would like to sit down and relax," Remyw said.

"Okay," Tereena said.

Remyw left. They all went to the lounge to rest. They certainly needed it, since they have had a few long days.

Remyw Yortis started contacting Civil Resistance operation officials on many different planets. The ones he contacted would then contact other counterterrorist organizations closer to themselves in their resistance networks.

In the lounge, Roedie, Tereena, and Destin were talking about Destin's childhood and family, including his grandpa, Jerell, and great grandma, Phasheena. Roedie and Tereena really enjoyed hearing about their daughter as an older woman. They were drinking Sevela they had grabbed from a refrigerator in one corner of the lounge. Arcacio and Kathell were talking about having their babies. The time was getting closer.

In a distant part of the galaxy, a woman sat at a desk, her eyes fixed on the computer in front of her. Her name was Holly Emanns. She was in an office that sent and received data to and from different terrorist organizations for both information and logistics. The office was part of the Knights of Stygian terrorist organization, located in the Thisis Star System. The woman was part of the Civil Resistance and was working undercover. She received an encrypted message on the computer screen from Remyw Yortis. It was her cue to begin the second stage of Operation Dark War. She knew exactly what that meant and she began contacting other members of the Civil Resistance via computer encryption. She also contacted other counterterrorist organizations, such as Resistance Against Terrorism (RAT), Storm Defense, Metal Force, and the Galactic Counterterrorist Militia (GCM). After she contacted everyone that she could, she put in a program that would wipe out all communications between the terrorist organizations who used the information and logistics network. She then left the Thisis Star System without being noticed.

A group of workers were assembling electronic devices that were used in military ground vehicles and fighter ships in the war against terrorism. There were many different types of flexible, paper-thin, printed circuit boards, many wire-harnesses, and mechanical devices. They were all to go in the vehicles used in the Dark War against the terrorists. The secret factory was quite large. There were four divisions in the building: Electronics and Instrumentation, Wiring, Mechanical, and Vehicle Assembly. The woman in charge of the entire operation, Shellaa DeeArron, received a message on the com. It was from Remyw Yortis. He told her the second stage of Operation Dark War has begun. She would now have to increase production for the war.

A man stood in the darkened shadows of a very large, old room. He looked through a large observation window at the distant stars in space. His name was Baalin Moriish. He was in the lower levels of an old space freighter. Like an obsolete technology graveyard, the dark room was filled with metal junk and old equipment. The old space freighter was called the *E Liner*. It was a very large ship, owned by a group of terrorists called the Space Militia. The man that stood in the lower levels of the old space freighter was a member of the Civil Resistance. He had just received a signal from Remyw Yortis, which meant it was time to blow up the space freighter. As he stood looking at the distant stars, he thought about what he had to do. If he did not escape in time, he would die as well. He looked away from the observation window, started the timer on the explosives, and walked toward the docking bay. When he reached the docking bay, he entered a ship and left the space freighter. He reached a safe distance before the space freighter exploded into several large pieces of twisted metal that drifted onward in space. As Baalin Moriish flew away safely, he was thankful no one from the group on the freighter interrupted or delayed him from reaching the docking bay in time.

Months had gone by and the Civil Resistance and other counterterrorist organizations were making great progress in the war. It was not without losses; however, the losses were minimal. The major terrorist groups were defeated, but a few factions remained.

After Remyw Yortis finished contacting members of the Civil Resistance for a status update, he joined the others in the lounge on Nytoorion.

"Destin, since you are one of the main leaders of the Civil Resistance, I leave it up to you to decide whether you want to take it easy through the remainder of the Dark War—since you've already destroyed the Immortal Cantin Empire—or help destroy some terrorists," Remyw said.

"Well, I'm for destroying some terrorists. What about you, Roedie?" Destin asked.

"Sure. That's what I'm here for," Roedie said.

"From the members of the Civil Resistance that you've contacted, did you find out where there is a need for our service?" Destin asked.

"Yes. There is a ship owned by a terrorist faction that calls itself Dissension Harvest. They split off from one of the other organizations. They have been stealing water from many planets that have governments too small to fight back. Their ship is a very modern one. It has many large tanks filled with this water. We can't just destroy the ship, because the water has to be saved. It is estimated that there are approximately one hundred million liters on it," Remyw said.

"The water should be saved, but I don't know of a way to destroy the terrorists and not the water," Destin said.

"That is a tough one," Roedie said.

After giving it some thought, Destin said, "I have an idea. You can make a quick fly-by and eject me out of the ship with a spacesuit on. I'll get into the terrorist ship from a vacuum waste chute. Once I'm in, I'll try to take over the ship."

"It might work," Roedie said, "but it will be tough."

"You're crazy. I don't like it," Arcacio said.

The *Time Explorer* flew toward the ship that contained the stolen water. When they reached the terrorist ship, they made a quick fly-by and ejected Destin toward the ship, as planned.

The terrorist ship shot its lasers at the *Time Explorer* as it flew by. Some of the blue beams of energy missed the ship and others bounced off the reflector shields. The terrorist ship did not pursue the *Time Explorer* as it flew away.

Using a rocket pack, Destin made his way to a vacuum waste chute along the ship's hull. Frozen waste stained the hull around the opening. He reached it and tried to pry it open with his thick gloves, but it would not budge. He removed a tool from the side of his spacesuit and he pried the vacuum waste chute open. After climbing inside, Destin immediately felt the artificial gravitation of the ship. He climbed up the chute that led to a network of pipes. He was able to find a waste treatment area and removed plating that covered the pools. Destin was grateful that he was in the suit, because he could only imagine how bad the odor was. When he climbed out of the tanks, he found that he was in a waste water treatment room. He carefully removed his spacesuit and put it in a compartment that was next to the tanks. Holding his breath as much as he could, he got out his laser pistol and entered an empty corridor. He made his way through the ship to an area that had many large tanks in it. The tanks continued in the distance as far as he could see.

This must be the water, he thought.

He walked along the narrow passage between the water tanks. On the back wall of the large room, Destin could see a control panel with a display that read: 100,274,143.8 liters.

Holy cosmic shit! That's a lot of stolen water, he thought.

He walked out from between the water tanks and headed for the door. Leaving the water storage repository, Destin walked through a maze of corridors, until he reached a reinforced door that he suspected was the bridge.

A man came around the corner from another corridor. He had a surprised look on his face when he saw Destin. Destin shot him with his laser pistol before the man could respond. Destin looked around the corner where the man had come from. He did not see anyone else. He went around the corner and got a surprise of his own. Three men had exited the reinforced door. Lasers were fired. Two of the three terrorists fell to the ground. Destin was grazed in the leg by a laser beam from the third terrorist. He shot the man and then looked down at the small wound in his leg.

That was close, he thought.

Destin entered the room through the heavy door. As he suspected, it was the bridge. The two men on the bridge were so busy with the controls, they did not notice Destin enter. He shot them both and sealed off the bridge. His leg was hurting very badly. He sat down in one of the chairs on the bridge and rested for a moment. He saw a com on the control panel. He changed frequencies, reached the *Time Explorer,* and gave them his status.

The *Time Explorer* flew back toward the terrorist ship. After eliminating the rest of the terrorists onboard the ship, it was the end of Dissension Harvest. They flew the ship called *Black Fire* back to

Nytoorion. It was to be held at Nytoorion until after the Dark War was over. Then the water would be returned to the people that it belonged to.

Several months later, Roedie, Tereena, Destin, Arcacio, Kathell, Remyw, and Cosmos were all at the lounge in the lower levels of the intoxication joint on Nytoorion.

"I've just found out that the Civil Resistance and other counterterrorist organizations throughout the BlueMar Galaxy have finished destroying the remaining terrorist organizations in the Ipsinitorr, Rotooth Tanis-Sintex, Thisis, and Andron Star Systems. That means the Dark War is over. All of the terrorist organizations are gone. There can now be restoration of freedom in the galaxy. Now, we have to make preparations for the future," Remyw said.

"We still have a long road ahead of us," Destin said.

"Yeah," Roedie said.

"The sooner we get started, the better. Nytoorion can be a temporary government seat until an official government is set up. All of the terrorists in the prisons down here will either be sent to a new prison that will be built on another planet or they will be executed, depending upon the tribunal's decision," Remyw said.

"We also have to locate the owners of the water aboard the *Black Fire*," Tereena said.

"Arcacio and I will soon be having our babies, so we won't be of much help," Kathell said.

"Yeah," Arcacio said.

"You two have already been very helpful during the war. Now, it's time for you to focus on yourselves," Destin said as he gently rested his hand on Arcacio's abdomen.

They went to work.

Soon, a victory celebration was held at the Stone Shelf. All of the patrons joined in on the evening's festivities. The local heroes of the Dark War became familiar with the regular staff of the intoxication joint. Fun was had by all.

CHAPTER TEN
RESTORATION OF FREEDOM

WHEN TIA AND Saven received evidence that suggested Tereena was on the planet Nytoorion, they traveled there quickly. The *NTMO-191* landed on the surface of Nytoorion. They followed the trail up the rocky hill and into the intoxication joint called Stone Shelf. Tia scanned the room for possibilities. Saven discovered there was another section with a second intoxication joint. They made their way to the second section and sat at a couple stools, very alert of their surroundings. After ordering a couple drinks from the female bartender, they sat and sipped their drinks.

"I hope the information extracted from Nytoorion's telecommunications was correct," Saven said.

"Well, according to the report, she's here somewhere," Tia said.

Three very beautiful long-haired women walked by where Tia and Saven sat. Two of them were pregnant. One of the pregnant women was tall with long, black hair. The other was a blonde. The third woman was also blonde and a bit older, but equally as beautiful. When they reached the entrance of the room, they finished their conversation. The two pregnant women continued on toward the first section of the intoxication joint, while the older blonde woman walked back toward the counter and sat down next to Tia and Saven.

"I'll have a blue Sevela," she said as she sighed.

"Sure thing, Tereena," the bartender said.

Tia and Saven gasped.

"*Holy cosmos!* You're her! You're Tereena, the one the Monarchy of Obritess has been searching for for generations," Saven said.

Tereena looked at them strangely.

"What?"

"Our people started a campaign to search for you years ago. You are the queen of the Monarchy of Obritess," Tia explained. "Your parents were King Baman and Queen Shehlly. As a child, you ended up on the paradise planet of Siitap in the Velkonn Star System. For safety reasons, your parents left you there with a nanny robot until they returned from a dangerous mission. But when they returned, they were unable to find you, as the homing signal in Nanny had stopped working. They weren't sure if you were still on the planet or if the BlueMar Empire captured you. Before they died, your parents put the Monarchy of Obritess government in a state of interregnum while the people of Neo Terra searched for you through the years."

Tereena stared at them blankly for a long time, very stunned. It took her a while to accept this new reality. She started crying, filled with emotions.

As the bartender delivered Tereena's blue Sevela, she saw her crying.

"Is everything all right?" she asked, looking suspiciously at Tia and Saven.

"Yes. Everything is fine," Tereena said as she wiped the tears from her eyes.

As the bartender walked away, Tereena turned toward Tia and Saven.

"I used to think Siitap was called Ersent for some reason, before I was rescued. I don't even know why. I was on Siitap for my entire childhood, raised and educated by Nanny. Nanny stopped working when I was about fifteen years old, and I was so alone…until Roedie and Baas came there looking for their father a couple years later. They rescued me," Tereena said.

"Ersent was actually the planet where your parents went for their mission. It's interesting that you picked up on that name as a very young child. We're sorry that your childhood was lonely. Although it was before our time, we know your parents were heartbroken when they could not locate you. We have had specific history education and instructions for our mission to locate you. We knew you traveled time with your husband. With our complex telecommunications network sniffers and compiled information, we finally found you. We were close on another occasion when you left a comment at the Celestial Orchard restaurant in the city of Sparsburg on the planet Perytion," Saven said.

"We'd like to tell you everything about Neo Terra and the Monarchy of Obritess. We have so much to tell you about your parents as well," Tia said.

Tereena sat for a long time listening to all this new information. There were tears and more drinks. At the end of the conversation, Tereena stood up from the stool.

"I need to tell Roedie about this. I'll be back soon," Tereena said as she quickly left the room.

"You're shitting me," Roedie said.

"No," Tereena said.

"Remember when Baas and I found you there on Siitap? Wow, that was something," Roedie said.

"I don't know what to do now. Should I accept being a queen or should we still travel time after a new government is formed?" Tereena asked.

"You've said before that we should stop roaming through time and space and go home to Kaskoon. Personally, I am also tired of traveling time. But I don't want to go back to our normal time frame yet. There is too much work to be done here. So, if you are asking me, I would accept becoming queen," Roedie said.

"Okay. But I don't think I can rule from our normal time frame. I wish I could go back and meet my parents…but I can't! Going back and doing that would change Tia and Saven's search for me. It would mean that we would not have helped destroy the Immortal Cantin Empire. It would totally screw up the time continuum. I have to rule from the here and now," she said.

"That's true," Roedie said.

"If I do this, that means you'll have to stand by my side," she said with a smile.

"I wouldn't have it any other way. So, is that the only planet that you'll be reigning on?" Roedie asked.

"That is the only planet that is part of the Monarchy of Obritess," Tereena said.

"I see. Well, imagine that…Queen Tereena Cantin," he said, smiling at his beautiful blonde wife. "I have to talk with Destin and Remyw regarding another urgent matter. I'll be back in a while. Why don't you set Tia and Saven up with a suite to stay in?" Roedie asked as he left.

Roedie found Destin and Remyw in the lounge. He told them about the cloaked Neo Terra.

"Well, Roedie, from what I'm told, I'm going to be the new leader of the galaxy," Destin said.

"You've heard from the Civil Resistance members?" Roedie asked.

"Yes. They voted me as the new leader of the BlueMar Galaxy. But, I have been thinking about what us three talked about earlier. It would be much better to form two separate governments in the galaxy. If one goes bad, then the other one can overthrow it. And now that we've found out about the planet Neo Terra, it can be a part of this, if everyone is in agreement. Did Tereena make her decision?" Destin asked.

"Yes. She decided to become queen," Roedie said. "And that is a great idea to have the two separate governments."

"Thank you. Well, I'm excited for Tereena to become queen. That's awesome. Neo Terra will be under the control of Queen Tereena with her consort, Roedie," Destin said, patting his great great grandpa on the back. "So, since the Monarchy of Obritess has been cloaked in isolation, they may be apprehensive about joining one of the two new governments. I suggest, they don't actually join. Although, it is just one planet, it would really be a third stand-alone government of sorts, like it has been. It will just add to our safety balance. Since the Civil Resistance has chosen me for a leader, Arcacio and I will lead one of the two main governments of the galaxy. I have specific star systems in mind that we would like to include as part of the Civil Government."

"Destin, I am honored by your earlier suggestion for me to become the leader of the other major government. It is with great humility that I accept," Remyw said.

"Congratulations to you both," Roedie said. "I would think that since the people of Neo Terra have already been in isolation for so long, they would not have a problem with remaining a separate entity. This new era may also involve uncloaking the planet. They may be very hesitant."

"Well, talk it over with Tereena. It is really her decision," Remyw said.

"All right. I'll be back with an answer," Roedie said as he left the lounge.

After Roedie left, Remyw said, "We'll have two major governments that will both help the people of the galaxy with humanitarian needs. What a contrast from what it's been… I think that's great."

"Yeah," Destin said.

"Where will the new prison go?" Remyw asked.

"Oh, you didn't hear? There will be no prison. The tribunal's final decision was for execution. The terrorists will be transferred from Nytoorion to Rotoos Fyor for their execution," Destin said.

"I see."

"I wonder what ever happened to my mother," Destin said.

"Kathell and I had a lengthy conversation earlier. She said that your mother, Merisa, is somewhere on Kas," Remyw said. "Did I mention that I really like Kathell?"

Tereena helped Tia and Saven get settled into their suite for their short stay on Nytoorion.

"So, I would like to confirm my decision with you guys that I have accepted becoming queen of the Monarchy of Obritess," Tereena said.

"That's great…otherwise the search through the years will have been in vain," Saven said.

"Of course, had you decided not to accept, we would have totally honored your decision," Tia said. "Thank you for helping us get this place for our stay here."

"You're welcome," Tereena said.

Roedie showed up at the door to their suite. He introduced himself to Tia and Saven.

"Hey, guys. I just finished a meeting with Destin and Remyw. Decisions were made to have a balance of power with two separate governments, Destin as leader of one and Remyw as leader of the other. And with the discovery of Neo Terra and Tereena's decision, it could potentially be a third balance of power," Roedie said.

"The people of Neo Terra are grateful it has been cloaked from the outside galaxy. But when we return and they find that freedom has been restored in the galaxy, I'm sure they would enjoy their own new freedom to explore other planets without the fear of aggression," Saven said.

"All these decisions are really on you, Tereena," Tia said. "When we arrive on Neo Terra, there will be a lot for you to take care of at the beginning."

Tereena smiled and said, "I'm looking forward to it."

· · ·

They had just left the crowning ceremony. Tereena sat in the back of the most sleek Airglider that she'd ever been in. She wore an elegant gold and white gown. A sparkling crown sat atop her blond, braided hair. Roedie sat next to her.

"That diamond and white gold crown looks absolutely stunning on you," Roedie said.

"I wish I would have known my parents. I'm sure they would be proud of my coronation," Tereena said.

"You're crying," Roedie said as he wiped a tear from her eye.

Tereena turned to Roedie and said, "These are the happiest tears I've ever cried."

"The people absolutely adore you…but not as much as I adore you," Roedie said.

Holding her hand, Roedie gave Tereena a kiss.

The Monarchy of Obritess had the largest celebration in Neo Terra's history when Tereena was crowned queen. The Airglider was in the middle of a parade. They were both waving at the crowds of people cheering in the streets. She was 51 years old and as happy as she could be. The elegant crowning ceremony brought her so much joy. There were days of parades, music, dance, and food as the people expressed their absolute joy that she had been found. Tereena's first decision as queen was to uncloak the hidden planet. She also announced that Neo Terra would remain independent from the two new governments. With the advent of that decision, people were able to openly travel to and from Neo Terra. Tereena officially changed the Monarchy of Obritess to the Obritess Government. With the approval of the other new governments, Tereena claimed the planet Siitap as part of the Obritess Government and set it aside as a world park, not to be disturbed. She knew the paradise planet all too well and didn't want it developed…ever.

With the cooperation of the people, they were able to start implementing the two major governments. Destin, with the help and support of Arcacio, was the leader of the new Civil Government, chosen by the people of the Civil Resistance by popular vote. Its capital was Kas. Remyw was chosen by Destin to be the leader of the second, separate government called the Nytoorion Government. The people of the BlueMar Galaxy were satisfied with the two new governments and the safety balance that came with the dual systems. The star systems were evenly split. Travel to and from the two separate governments was not restricted, which satisfied the people of the galaxy.

Working with Destin and the Civil Government, Roedie saw to it that two new cities were built on the planet Kas. In addition to the cities of Krymoss, Antiqueech, Kas Voya, and the town of Keestoon, the cities of New Astossky and New Kanthas were developed.

Roedie also built a new robot. He named it KEN-104. It had all of the memories of KEN-102 and KEN-103 plus the memories of Tereena's Nanny robot. In addition, it had the memories of an old personal robot owned by Tereena's parents called RTSX-87, which had been referred to as Artie.

Officials from the Nytoorion Government and the Civil Government gathered together for a discussion to converge with the Regulominuss Galaxy. They came to the conclusion that it would be inefficient because of the nine month journey to the Regulominuss Galaxy from the BlueMar Galaxy at timespeed. Even then, they would need to negotiate with the governments in control of the Regulominuss Galaxy, not to mention negotiate with Roedie Cantin for use of his ship with the tac-time engine. And they had not been in contact with the Regulominuss Galaxy for approximately 85 years from their current time frame, not since the Claderane Government Explorers left there in 230932 SA. Perhaps someday they would consider reaching out beyond the BlueMar Galaxy once again, but it was not on their immediate agenda.

Arcacio and Kathell both had their babies. Arcacio named her son, Roedie II Cantin, after his great great great grandfather, Roedie. He was most likely the only person to ever meet his great great great grandfather. Kathell named her daughter, Arriel Cantin. Roedie II Cantin and Arriel Cantin were fifth cousins.

King Baman and Queen Shehlly stood together at the Monarchy of Obritess' annual ball. The large hall was filled with formally dressed guests. The king and queen were a beautiful couple, but there was a sadness in their eyes. One of the guests walked closer to them, her blond hair draped in front of her shoulders. She made her way closer and stood next to them. She looked at them closely. King Baman was a handsome man with gray hair and an average height. Queen Shehlly was such a beautiful lady. She was also blonde, with wrinkles around her eyes.

"What a beautiful dress you are wearing," the woman told the queen. "And your suit is very elegant," she said to the king.

They both looked at her and smiled.

"You look lovely yourself," the queen said.

"This message is for you," the woman said, handing the queen a note.

Queen Shehlly took the note and kept it in her hand while enjoying the ceremony. The blonde woman stealthily disappeared into the crowd. When Queen Shehlly turned back toward the woman, she was gone. The queen looked at the note in her hand and opened it.

> *Queen Shehlly, I just want you and King Baman to know that I see the sadness in your eyes. I also want you to know that there is hope. Please, keep them searching for Tereena. They will find her in the future. I love you, Mom.*

Lightyears II
Intragalactic Terrorism
Appendices

CANTIN FAMILY TREE
VERSION 2

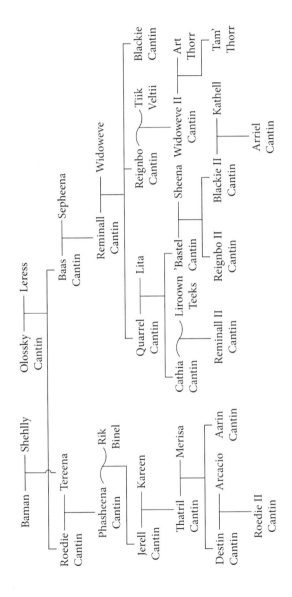

Lightyears II
Intragalactic Terrorism
Terminology Index

A

B

C

O

P

Q

R

S

C9   Storm Defense
C4   Sylikyt, Ikk

T

C4   Tabaannaann Plague
C2   tac-time engine
C3   Teeks, Liroown
C1   Thisis Militia
C1   Thisis Star System
C3   Thorr, Art
C3   Thorr, Tam'
C2   Tia
C4   *Time Explorer*
C2   timespeed (speed of time)
C1   Tiosoon Star System
C7   Tri-Sintex Star System
C8   Tuska
C1   Tuska Thaxe Star System
C8   Tuskus
C1   Tuviex Korr

V

C10 Velkonn Star System
C3   Veltii, Tiik

X

C5   Xerica Star System

Y

C6   Yortis, Remyw

Z

C6   Zalho's World Brigade
C4   *Zoota 2000*
C6   *Zoota 2001*

Lightyears III
Ominous Intervention

Lightyears III
Ominous Intervention
Contents

CHAPTER ONE
MARA-HARCHEIT

"ARE YOU ALL right?" Kortha asked as he ran to Mara-Harcheit's throne.

An old man with long, white hair and a matching white beard had stood from his throne, staggered a few steps and fell to the gray stone floor. He looked up at Kortha as he approached.

"No. I have sensed something very foreboding... Help me up. Bring me outside. I need some fresh air," Mara-Harcheit said.

Kortha brushed his own black and gray hair back and helped the old man up from the stone floor. He put his arm around Mara-Harcheit's red robe and assisted him to slowly exit the throne room. They walked together down a gray stone corridor. The passage opened up to an area at the top of a stairway where an odd looking skeleton could be seen on the floor, propped up against the wall. There was an old knife wedged in its ribs. They made their way down the set of stone steps to a dark atrium and exited the castle.

Outside, sunlight brightened the castle and surrounding field of golden grass. They walked toward the front pillars and Mara-Harcheit leaned up against one of them. Green vines wrapped up and around the stone pillars. He looked over to Kortha, a man with only one eye, as the other had been lost in an ancient battle. Only an empty socket remained.

"I haven't dreaded anything like this for over a millennia…" Mara-Harcheit said as he made his way to a stone bench.

They both sat down and looked down the hill and across the field toward the mountains.

"What did you sense?" Kortha asked.

"As you know, we Yithas live for many millennia. On rare occasion, some of us are born with the ability of telepathy, thought transfer, and clairvoyance…but most, like yourself, don't. Yet, I have never sensed anything like this, Kortha. You and I were exiled from the Nyctogluktoouss Galaxy almost one thousand one hundred years ago because we stood against the incredible evil there. I was different and they knew it. We were kicked out, sent through that awful wormhole and ended up here in the Regulominuss Galaxy. Shortly after we settled here on Yibon, we found they had sent their assassins to follow and kill us. They must have really thought I was a threat to them with my abilities. I'm so thankful that I was able to summon the Xyinna Wolves to help wipe out the assassins. I had you leave that skeleton up at the top of the stairs as a reminder of our persecution and exile. Thank you for standing by my side and being my good friend and aide.

"What I saw was like nothing I could have ever imagined before. This foreboding, ominous sense, this urgency…it overwhelms me. They are coming… Billions of the evil Yithas are coming this way. They are not after us this time. They are coming to invade both the Regulominuss Galaxy and also the BlueMar Galaxy. Their numbers seem endless. They're in battleships and fighter ships…all of them. In this vision, they haven't reached the Yitheria Wormhole yet.

"I have been aware of a very intelligent human inventor, named Sitell, for quite some time. For many centuries, the humans have come to me for advice, blessings, wisdom… I am a legend in their eyes. If they only knew that we were Yithas—probably the only two good Yithas in existence. I digress…" Mara-Harcheit said.

Kortha stood from the stone bench, his white robe fluttering in the wind. He looked up at the sky.

"So, this Sitell, what about him?" Kortha asked.

"Sitell has developed a couple of theories and is working on things that can bring the Regulominuss Galaxy and the BlueMar Galaxy together with a portal. I've always referred to both galaxies as Yiblos. We are close neighbors at 624,750 lightyears in distance. I must send a warning message to the leaders of the three Regulominuss Galaxy governments. Actually, Sitell is one of those leaders," Mara-Harcheit said.

"How much time do we have before the onslaught?" Kortha asked.

Mara-Harcheit shook his head. "I don't know...maybe several years. It's difficult to tell with a vision like that."

"I will aide you in any way I can with this urgency," Kortha said.

"Sir, we just received a strange message on the computer," a Yiseth Government official stated.

"Message?" Sitell asked.

"Yes. It is an urgent request for your presence on Yibon, directly from the Keeper himself, Mara-Harcheit. The coordinates are here as well," the woman said.

"The Keeper of the Regu, ominuss Galaxy... Wow! He is a legend. Somehow, he's been around for generations. Even my ancestor, Sintos, knew him. I wonder what he wants," Sitell said.

"There's more to the message. It says the leaders of the other two governments have also been contacted. He would like all of you to arrive together," she said.

Sitell put his finger to his mouth in thought, the illuminators reflecting from his shiny, bald head. As leader of the Yiseth Government, he felt that he should at least respond to the Keeper's request. He would have to contact both Queeab from the Ovlon Government and Jade Thane from the Rreen Government to coordinate this trip to Yibon in the Zasreen Star System.

"This is really going to cut into my time developing the Galactic Time Portal. I certainly hope it's important," Sitell said.

"Understood," the officer said, tipping her tan cap.

"Good day," Sitell said as he left the room.

CHAPTER TWO
THE GALACTIC TIME PORTAL

A SLEEK WHITE ship settled onto a docking platform at the Yiseth Government capital on the planet Yiseth. Two Syclone guards stepped out of the ship and stood on either side of the exit. Both men looked identical, bald and muscular. Soon, a third Syclone exited the ship. He also looked exactly like the two guards. He walked toward the greeting party.

"Hello, Queeab. Welcome to Yiseth," Sitell said, reaching out to shake the man's hand.

"Thank you."

"So, how are things in the Ovlon Government?" Sitell asked.

"Good. I've been busy lately at the capital on Olbah, but this message we received from the Keeper sounds urgent," Queeab said.

"Yes, it does," Sitell said. "It actually is interrupting the time I scheduled to work on the Galactic Time Portal."

"Are we still waiting on Jade?" Queeab asked.

Before Sitell could answer, another ship swooped around from overhead and settled onto the docking platform next to Queeab's ship. A tall woman, dressed in black leather stepped out of the ship and onto the docking platform. Her long, black hair flowed behind her as she made her way across the docking platform toward the greeting party.

"Sorry I'm late, gentlemen," she said.

"Hello, Jade. Welcome to Yiseth. You're looking lovely as usual," Sitell said.

"Hi, Jade," Queeab said. "I understand the Rreen Government is developing the R-89 Star System."

"Yes. I've been away from the capital on Rreen, dealing with those affairs for a few weeks now. So, what is your take on this message we received?" Jade asked.

"I have no idea. I have never been contacted by Mara-Harcheit before. So, I'm certain that it's urgent," Sitell said. "I figured it would be better coordinated if we just take one ship to Yibon to pay him a visit."

"Yes, thank you for the offer," she said.

"Well then, if you two will just follow my officials," Sitell said, gesturing toward four people dressed in tan uniforms. "My ship is on the other docking platform."

The four greeting party officials led the three leaders of the galactic governments toward the second docking platform where Sitell's ship, *Tributary*, was located.

Sitell flew the large ship through the atmosphere of Yibon. He slowed his speed as he passed over Verction's Canyon. An old, broken bridge that once crossed the canyon could be seen far below. A beautiful mountain set beyond the canyon. Passing over the mountain, they saw the Keeper's castle ahead, its ancient gray stones weathered with centuries of time. The ship settled at the edge of the field of tall, golden grass. Each of them stepped out of the ship and onto the ground of Yibon. Kortha was there to greet them.

"Greetings. Welcome to Yibon. My name is Kortha. I am the Keeper's aide. Thank you for responding so quickly. Mara-Harcheit is very grateful. If you will follow me, I will lead you to him," he said.

Kortha led them up a few mossy steps, past the pillars, and into the castle atrium. They followed him up the steps toward the corridor to the throne room. When they passed the strange skeleton, they all gave each other concerned looks. As they entered the throne room, Kortha gestured toward Mara-Harcheit, who sat on the throne.

"Thank you all for coming to Yibon so soon. Please be seated," Mara-Harcheit said, motioning toward the seats along the front of the room next to him.

They each sat down.

"I have a lot to tell you, some of which will come as a surprise. I know

I am in your legends, simply because I've been around for centuries. Those who are confident enough to seek me out, have received my wisdom and advice. Many years ago, a government from the BlueMar Galaxy, known as the Claderane Government, sent a fleet outbound to explore unknown regions of the BlueMar Galaxy. They soon discovered advanced humans in the Kameron Star System. One of the advanced people was Sintos, Sitell's ancestor. Upon agreement, they decided to explore the Regulominuss Galaxy. It was made possible with the advanced people's tac-time engines that were able to travel the speed of time, one million times faster than the speed of light. They sought my blessing to destroy the Rexxian Empire and set the Syclone slaves free—Queeab's ancestors—which I most certainly gave them. The fleet from the Claderane Government left the Regulominuss Galaxy and returned home to the BlueMar Galaxy, while Sintos and his crew remained in the Regulominuss Galaxy to explore the other eighty-five percent that had not yet been explored. I am thankful for the group that came from the BlueMar Galaxy. Because of them, we now have a peaceful Regulominuss Galaxy today with you three leaders. Although they have had many struggles over the years, I can tell you the BlueMar Galaxy is finally at peace with its governments," Mara-Harcheit said.

"How do you know this stuff?" Sitell asked as he shifted slightly in his seat.

"I have...abilities that are not normal. The reason why Kortha and I have lived so long is because we are not human. We are Yithas. We actually came from the Nyctogluktoouss Galaxy over one thousand years ago. We are not immortal, but we do live for a few millennia. In fact, I'm just past middle-age. You may recall walking past the skeleton at the top of the stairs as you were led to the throne room. As you may have seen, that is not a human skeleton with the knife wedged in the rib cage. That was a Yitha. That is what we are.

"You see, I was exiled from the Nyctogluktoouss Galaxy over a millennia ago and ended up here in the Regulominuss Galaxy on Yibon. Kortha was good enough to have my back during those trying times. They sent us through the Yitheria Wormhole that connects the Nyctogluktoouss Galaxy and the Regulominuss Galaxy. They then sent a group of assassins to kill us, but failed. That is one of them at the top of the stairs. It stays there as a reminder," Mara-Harcheit said.

Queeab turned a bit pale in his seat. Jade looked at Mara-Harcheit suspiciously.

"Why were you exiled from the Nyctogluktoouss Galaxy?" Sitell asked.

"I also am not like most Yithas, as I have gifts that very few have in our species. Even Kortha does not have these gifts. I see the future, I have telepathy, I have an abundance of wisdom. I use it for good, for the well being of my new galaxy and ultimately for the BlueMar Galaxy as well. Most Yithas that control the entire Nyctogluktoouss Galaxy are extremely evil. I am one of the rare good ones that see things differently, as is Kortha. That's what happens to good Yithas, they get exiled," he said.

"Why do you look human and not like that skeleton?" Jade asked.

Mara-Harcheit stood from the throne and suddenly altered his appearance in a surreal moment. He changed from an old man with long, white hair to a frightening creature that resembled the skeleton they saw earlier. The three guests gasped and moved back in their seats. Queeab got up and ran toward the door. Kortha stood in his way.

"Please, Queeab, just return to your seat. We seriously need your help here," Kortha said.

Queeab stopped and looked at him. He turned toward Mara-Harcheit. The being that stood there was brown and leathery with very little hair. He morphed back to the familiar man with long, white hair and sat back on his throne. Hesitantly, Queeab returned to his seat.

"I'm sorry to have frightened you. You see, we also have the ability to transform ourselves. Kortha and I are not the enemy. In fact, we are just the opposite. We are here to protect. I have recently had a very ominous vision of a future event that will take place. Both the Regulominuss Galaxy and the BlueMar Galaxy will be attacked with an onslaught of billions of Yithas from the Nyctogluktoouss Galaxy. They will be invading to conquer and exterminate all humans from both galaxies. The thought sickens me, literally. That is why I have summoned you three leaders. We need the Yiseth Government, the Ovlon Government, and the Rreen Government to work together to accomplish this goal, if we are to save Yiblos," Mara-Harcheit said.

"Yiblos?" Jade looked at him questioningly.

"Yiblos is the name given to the Regulominuss Galaxy and the BlueMar Galaxy as a whole," Mara-Harcheit said.

"And where does the Keeper come into all this?" Queeab asked.

"I am considered the Keeper of the Regulominuss Galaxy. I sit on this throne as such. I've watched over this galaxy for centuries. But the advent of this new information has made me desperate for your help. I am aware from my foresight, that Sitell is working on the Galactic Time Portal to bridge the gap between the Regulominuss Galaxy and the

BlueMar Galaxy. This Galactic Time Portal is made possible from your Second Sitell Theory and will take a nine month journey at timespeed and make it into an instantaneous journey at lightspeed, thus bridging the gap. Sitell, you come from a long line of advanced thinkers…all the way back to Sintos and beyond. Your ancestors developed the tac-time engine, porting, and much more. Although those two things are no longer used for security and safety reasons, you still discover concepts that amaze even me," Mara-Harcheit said.

"Well, I've been implementing the Second Sitell Theory and the Galactic Time Portal construction is complete. I gave the Galactic Time Portal its name because it does replace timespeed. We just need to do programming and placement. I like it even better than the First Sitell Theory I came up with, where a forcefield can be stretched across lightyears of space and can obstruct anything that consists of matter. The Sitell Field has yet to be implemented for anything," Sitell said.

"Both of those concepts are exactly what we need to stop this alien onslaught from the Nyctogluktoouss Galaxy. I urge you to complete the Galactic Time Portal and then implement the Sitell Field to enclose Yiblos from this impending doom that will approach from the Nyctogluktoouss Galaxy at some point in the near future," Mara-Harcheit said.

"We will do our best to achieve the goals you mention. It also means working with the governments of the BlueMar Galaxy once we've bridged the gap," Sitell said.

"Yes. There is one bit of advice that I must give you to make this really happen. You've never been through a wormhole. It's not a pleasant experience. The approaching threat must go through one to arrive here. They may lose ten percent of their numbers in the Yitheria Wormhole. There is a reason humans appeared in the Regulominuss Galaxy in the first place. Some of the Mazits or "migrating people" discovered a different wormhole that connects the BlueMar Galaxy to the Regulominuss Galaxy. After passing through, there was no one else from the BlueMar Galaxy that knew where the Kalistorr Wormhole's location was. Nevertheless, the tac-time engines worked to get people here later on. As you are aware, the Kalerson Star System drifts farther away from the Regulominuss Galaxy each year. No one alive today knows this, but the Kalerson Star System is drifting toward a black hole called Janthia's Abyss. It was named after one of the early Mazits named Wells Janthia. He was studying the black hole but miscalculated the location of the event horizon. He was never seen again. By placing and activating the Galactic Time Portal near the Kalerson Star System, you risk it being affected by Janthia's Abyss. I suggest you change your planned location and put it at the forgotten Kalistorr Wormhole. You will harness the power of the wormhole and actually control it. It is similar to our Galactic Channels that bridge between systems within our galaxy, but on a universal scale," Mara-Harcheit said.

"How did you know that I planned on locating the Galactic Time Portal near the Kalerson Star System? Oh…never mind, it's you… This new information is absolutely fascinating," Sitell said.

"It sounds like you will need some fairly large ships to haul the Galactic Time Portal into position. I can have a fleet of my work ships from the R-89 Star System help with that," Jade said.

"I can certainly provide the labor you need to get the job done as well," Queeab said.

"Wonderful. Time is not on our side, so stay on this, for all of us," Mara-Harcheit said.

The three government leaders stood and said their farewells. Kortha led them back down to their ship.

Sitell finished programming the Galactic Time Portal with the complex calculations specified in his Second Sitell Theory. Studying the archived logs of Sintos's old ship *Keen Saber* and the history of the tac-time engine was helpful in the programming. Each galaxy had moved forward in history about 105 years since Sintos first arrived in the new galaxy. So, theoretically, Sitell would meet the sixth or seventh generation from the explorers that came to the Regulominuss Galaxy with his ancestor, Sintos.

With the help of the Rreen Government and the Ovlon Government, Sitell and his own Yiseth Government officials were able to transport the Galactic Time Portal to the newly rediscovered Kalistorr Wormhole. Thanks to Mara-Harcheit's knowledge, they were able to harness the power of the wormhole.

The Galactic Time Portal was developed from an immense, circular, metal framework in space. Illuminators were evenly spaced around the circle, allowing for easy visibility. Small engines were mounted on the Galactic Time Portal to keep it in position so it would not be swayed by the wormhole just beyond.

People watched on news feeds as Sitell's ship, *Tributary,* began its maiden flight through the Galactic Time Portal at lightspeed and disappeared from the Regulominuss Galaxy.

CHAPTER THREE
DESTINATION NYTOORION

"That's absolutely incredible, Destin. Holy cosmic shit!" Arcacio said, breathing heavily.

Destin looked up at her and smiled, as he continued to perform cunnilingus. Her beautiful, blond hair partially covered her left breast. Soon, he slipped into her as they kissed, their tongues blending together. He kissed and sucked along her neck. After some time, they both exploded with simultaneous orgasms. Exhausted, they lay with their legs interlaced for what seemed like an eternity. Suddenly, Arcacio sat straight up on the bed.

"Oh shit, we're gonna be late!" she said as she got up and ran to the bathroom.

"Oh well, that was worth it," Destin said as he joined her to get cleaned up.

"We still have to pick up your mother and our Roedie," she said.

They quickly dressed and looked at each other.

"We'll have to do some more of that later," Arcacio said with a smile.

"It's too bad you don't care for the anti-gravitational mode on the bed," Destin said.

She straightened his light brown hair that was out of place. They went down a set of wooden stairs and into their spacious two-level living room. A beautiful stone fireplace was on one side of the room.

"It still amazes me…the beautiful work that my grandpa, Jerell, put into this house. I'm so glad we chose to live here on Forestica," Destin said.

"Yes, it's been perfect for these last twenty years," Arcacio said, grabbing a few things for the trip.

"Raising our Roedie here was very rewarding," Destin said.

"Well, I don't think anyone expected us to live at the capital of the Civil Government on Kas, just because you're the leader," Arcacio said.

"No, but it is like a second home to us," he said. "Ready?"

"Yes. Oh, let me grab a couple of Sevelas from the refrigerator," she said.

She took the carbonated beverages from the refrigerator while Destin waited in the living room. He stared at the large picture of his grandparents, Jerell and Kareen, that hung on the mantel. When Arcacio entered the room, they left the house. Walking down the brick steps to the *Initial Voyage*, they passed a gravestone on the left of the steps that read: Here lies Cosmos, the greatest wolfdog the galaxy has ever known… Below the text, there was an engraved picture of Cosmos and a paw print. The wolfdog's blue eyes in the graphic set beautifully against the gray stone. Destin paused at the gravestone. All was quiet, except the nearby stream of rushing water. Destin took a deep breath, smelling the scent of pine that filled the air.

"I miss you, buddy," he said and then continued toward the ship.

"Cosmos was a great wolfdog," Arcacio said.

They stepped into the ship and Destin engaged the engines. From the observation window, the beautiful stone and log house could be seen, surrounded by pine trees. They lifted from the surface of Forestica, the surrounding pine forest and mountainside coming into full view. Soon, they were in space. Destin set a course for Kas.

The *Initial Voyage* landed in the city of Antiqueech on the planet Kas.

"You're behind schedule," Merisa said as she stepped into the ship from the docking area next to her house. She was an older brunette woman.

"Yes…something came up," Destin said, looking at Arcacio with a smile.

"I'll bet," she said, looking at the couple with a grin.

"We still have time to make the seminar on Nytoorion, Mom," Destin said.

"Yes, but I told Roedie that we would be picking him up too," Arcacio said.

"Seriously? I forgot about that. Okay, I'll head over to the Civil Government building," Destin said.

The ship lifted from Antiqueech and moved along the endless sands toward New Kanthas. They slowly passed by the beige dunes and tan outcrops, as they made their way across the bright, hot desert landscape.

"It's about time," Roedie II said, brushing his fingers through his brown hair as he entered the ship. "At least you gave me time to finish all of my office work for the day."

"Well, good. It will be less work for me," Destin said. "Preparing you to become the next leader of the Civil Government makes me feel proud, son. For being twenty and in your position, I just want you to know you've done a fine job with everything."

"Thanks, Dad," Roedie II said. "So, how are you, Grandma?"

"I'm fine. …A bit lonely, but fine, nonetheless," Merisa said. "I'm waiting to find a good man to change my name from Merisa Cantin-Istraxx to something more respectable."

"You can change your name back to just Cantin, you know," Destin said.

"Nah… Why bother? I'll tell you, being married to a terrorist was not one of my better ideas," she said.

"I certainly didn't understand it. But hey…that was a long time ago. I'm just happy that Kathell searched for you here on Kas at my request and found you. It's still ironic that you ended up living in the Caverns of the Sandkeens where our Civil Resistance operation was located," Destin said.

"It was a couple years of hell, but I survived. Thanks again for Kathell's search party. And I'm sorry I left you and the Civil Resistance," Merisa said.

"So, Mom, how are you doing?" Roedie II asked as he turned toward his mother.

"Very good. We—"

"Is that a hickey on your neck?" Roedie II cut her off.

Arcacio looked at Destin.

"You better not have!"

Tereena made her way down the long marble corridor toward the palace atheneum where Roedie was working on a book. She passed through the great room, with its large fireplace and luxurious burgundy furniture. Pictures of her parents hung on the wall, framed in gold. A side door on the right led to the elegant atheneum. Roedie was busy typing on the computer. He sat at a large desk with his left side toward the door. The desk was adjacent to a staircase. The room was surrounded with book shelves, filled with a wide variety of books, with the exception of one wall, where there was a window that overlooked the palace courtyard below. King Baman and Queen Shehlly were buried in that courtyard, surrounded by a lovely garden of greenery. A small indoor tree sat next to the window that overlooked the courtyard, its green leaves soaking up the sunlight. The room was decorated with a beautiful patterned rug. On the right of the atheneum entrance, next to the desk, a wooden staircase curved upward to a second level mezzanine. Several more book shelves were located against the upper wall. The wooden railing along the mezzanine reflected light from its glossy finish.

"Hi," Tereena said as she walked around the desk and behind him. She put her arms around him where he sat.

Her once blond hair had become mostly gray and wrinkles were visible on her face. Roedie looked up at her warm smile and leaned against her loving touch. He removed his glasses and set them on the desk. He too showed signs of his age, his blond hair had turned all gray. They were both 71 years old and not as active as they once were.

In the twenty years that she had been queen of the Obritess Government, she and Roedie had had a good life. In that time, Roedie took it upon himself to destroy the last tac-time engine for security reasons. Years before, someone tried to steal their ship and murder them, but Tereena killed the man before he succeeded. Roedie renamed his ship from *Time Explorer* to simply *Explorer*.

"I'm just putting the finishing touches on my book, *The Adventures of Baas and Roedie*," he said.

"I really like our chapter that you read to me, 'The Essence of Tereena.' I love you, Roedie," she said, kissing him.

"Can you do me a favor? I left chapter one on the dresser. Can you get that for me?" Roedie asked.

"Sure, but we need to leave soon, if we are going to make it to the seminar on Nytoorion in a timely manner. I'll be right back," Tereena said.

Tereena made her way through the palace to the upper levels where their bedroom chamber was located. She saw the printed chapter setting on the dresser next to their wedding picture. The picture showed them at their double wedding, along with Roedie's brother, Baas, and his wife, Sepheena. As she picked up Roedie's chapter, two pages fell behind the dresser.

"Shit!" she exclaimed.

She tried to move the dresser, but it would not budge. She was not as strong as she once was. She summoned for a couple of palace workers to help her slide the dresser aside. When she reached for the two pages, she noticed something else. There was a small note setting behind the dresser as well. After the workers returned the dresser to its proper position and left the bedroom chamber, she opened the note. She realized this was the note that she had given to her mother when she went into a past time frame so that she could actually see her parents with her own eyes. It read:

> *Queen Shehlly, I just want you and King Baman to know that I see the sadness in your eyes. I also want you to know that there is hope. Please, keep them searching for Tereena. They will find her in the future. I love you, Mom.*

But there was an additional note below the first one. The additional note read:

> *Dearest Tereena, thank you for the note. Thank you for coming to see your father and I. You turned out to be a beautiful woman. And you will be a lovely queen. We are so very sorry that we could not locate you when you were a child. I now know that our searchers will find you in the future. We're thankful that you were able to travel back in time to see us. I can't pretend to know all the consequences of changing time events that could affect the future, but I could imagine it would be disastrous. So, I understand what you must do. I leave this note for you in the hope that you will find it one day when you are queen. We love you and we will see you again one day on the other side. Mom and Dad...*

Tereena's eyes filled with tears. She returned to the atheneum to show Roedie the note and bring him the pages he requested. She read him the note.

"Oh, honey, that is precious," Roedie said as he gave her a long hug.

"I wish I would have found that years ago," Tereena said.

"Well, I'm glad you did find it. We need to frame that and mount it on the wall. So, are you about ready to go see our great great great grandson, Roedie II? From what I understand, he will be at the seminar as well," Roedie said.

"I am," she said.

KEN-104 popped his head in the door of the atheneum.

"If you two don't get going, you'll be late," he said.

"We were just leaving, KEN-104. But thank you for the reminder," Roedie said.

Queen Tereena Cantin and her consort, Roedie, left the Obritess Government palace on Neo Terra and flew the *Explorer* to Nytoorion.

Kathell and Remyw sat at a small round table in a secluded section of the Celestial Orchard restaurant. It was located in the city of Sparsburg on the planet Perytion. They were just finishing their lavish meal.

"Thank you for the surprise anniversary dinner, my love," Kathell said.

Remyw held her hand, her gold and diamond wedding ring sparkling in the light.

"You are most welcome, my dear," Remyw said.

It was Kathell and Remyw's 15th wedding anniversary. They married several years after the Dark War. Remyw recalled being very attracted to Kathell from the moment when they first met. She was a tall, beautiful woman with long, black hair. Remyw was a handsome man with short, brown hair.

Before they met, he had been a lonely man and the fit seemed to work well. Remyw Yortis helped raise Kathell's daughter from her previous relationship with Emperor Blackie II Cantin of the Immortal Cantin Empire. During the several years as a widow, Kathell had reflected on how Blackie II had treated her very well. It was how he treated others that actually hurt her. Although Kathell was happy to flee the Immortal Cantin Empire before it fell and Blackie II perished, she did keep her name as Kathell Cantin-Yortis. She didn't want to raise a child alone and Remyw didn't mind stepping in and raising her like his own. Her child, Arriel Cantin, was a wonderful girl and she had grown up too quickly. Now 20, she was being prepared for the leadership of the Nytoorion Government, which was still led by Remyw.

"May I interest you in another drink?" the waiter asked as he stopped at their table.

"No. I think we're good. But if we could get the bill, that would be great. We need to be going, as we have a seminar to attend shortly," Remyw said.

"Of course. I'll return with the bill shortly," the waiter said.

"This seminar should be interesting," Kathell said.

"Yes, from what I understand, there's never been anything quite like this before," Remyw said.

Chapter Four
Project Thraxion

THE NYTOORION GOVERNMENT charter established that a new leader be assigned every 20 years by the seated leader. As a power balance, the seated leader could be removed by a majority of the citizens at any time, if a special vote was called. The Civil Government had a similar charter. Arriel Cantin was selected to replace her step-father, Remyw Yortis, as leader of the Nytoorion Government in the next few months. Likewise, Roedie II Cantin was selected by his father, Destin Cantin, to become the new Civil Government leader. Arriel Cantin and Roedie II Cantin were fifth cousins and both would be 20 years old that year. For the most part, they had grown up together and were very close.

Arriel Cantin was in her government office on Nytoorion. She had been learning the everyday government business tasks for several months. She had just finished resolving a dispute in one of their star systems. All of her work was complete for the day. She stood up from her chair and stretched, her brown hair shifting to one side. She grabbed an anniversary card and a small gift from her desk that she had picked up from a gift shop earlier in the day. Arriel left her office and headed for the parking garage. She stepped into her Airglider and left the capital city of Mosstone, headed for the big seminar that was being held in City Ommawee. The anti-gravitational transport flew about one meter from the stone laden ground. Most Airgliders were exposed to the outside elements, unless they had a shield. Her particular Airglider was isolated from the outside with a covered top. The Airglider had been having issues running smoothly in the past several days.

Arriel looked forward to seeing all of her family at the seminar. She knew they would all be there. Arriel was just entering City Ommawee when her Airglider started running hot and the indicator lights came on. Suddenly, it started to smoke. She quickly exited the main highway, separating from the busy traffic that moved toward downtown City Ommawee. The exit that she turned onto went beneath the city. She flew into the tunnel and underground. The daylight disappeared into darkness as her Airglider slowly descended down the incline. The only visible light was the dim illuminators along the tunnel walls. She did not know exactly what to do about her Airglider. She did not know exactly where she was. She had never been underneath the city before. She did not even know that the place existed. There was no other traffic down there. She pulled the Airglider over until it slowed to a stop, smoke pouring out from the engine. She sat there for a moment, staring in disbelief.

This cannot be happening right now. I'm going to be late! she thought.

The tunnel road looked dark and eerie. Dim light from the illuminators revealed a green slime on the walls and ceiling of the tunnel. The Airglider com was dead, so she had no way of contacting anyone for help. Arriel stepped out of the Airglider with her card and gift and started walking down a walkway that ran along the left side of the tunnel road. The air was very damp and musty. A railing ran along the right of the walkway, next to the road, while the tunnel wall was on the left. Soon, she came to a section where the tunnel wall became recessed. Railings were on both sides of the walkway from that point forward. Below the new railing on her left side, a connection of drainage systems purged into a dark waterway that looked very deep. Water also flowed from a small drain near the bottom of the wall. Pipes ran along the ceiling above the waterway. One of the pipes had a crack in it and a liquid was seeping along the wall and down into the water below. Arriel did not know where she was going, but kept walking, hoping to find someone to help her.

Ahead of her, she saw the tunnel road end at another tunnel road that ran perpendicular to the one she was on. When she reached that point, she looked to her right. It looked too dark that way…almost pitch black. She turned to her left and started down the road that was better lit. The waterway that was on the left side went underneath a bridge and behind a wall. The pipes that ran along the tunnel ceiling crossed above the bridge and disappeared behind the wall as well. Arriel saw a door across the road on the right wall of the tunnel. Crossing the road to the walkway on the right, she opened the door, a loud squeak echoing through the tunnels.

Upon entering, she noticed there was an old, metal stairway inside that led upward. The black and yellow paint was worn and chipped away. She went up the stairs. The faint hum of some type of machinery could be heard. She reached the top of the stairs and saw a large number of pipes running in all different directions. The entire floor was a metal grate. She looked down through the metal grate and saw a connection of drainage system waterways beneath it. Arriel saw another stairway that went up further. She walked across the floor grating and started up the second stairway that led to a long corridor. When she reached the end of the corridor, she noticed an open, gray, metal door. It was a maintenance room with large control panels located throughout. A short man with thin, gray hair sat with his back to the door. He was working on some type of control board as she came up behind him.

"Excuse me…" Arriel said.

The man was so startled that he jumped off his stool and fell backwards to the concrete floor.

"Holy cosmic shit!" he exclaimed.

"I'm sorry. Are you all right?" she asked. "I didn't mean to startle you."

The man stood up and rubbed his leg.

"Yes, I'll be fine. Who are you? This is a restricted area," he said.

"My name is Arriel Cantin from the Nytoorion Government."

"*The* Arriel Cantin?" he asked with surprise.

"Yes. My Airglider broke down, so I pulled off into the tunnel. Can you help me?" she asked.

"Well, of course," he said. "Jepner's the name…Jepner Meads. It's nice to meet you."

"Thank you. I need to get to the Project Thraxion seminar as soon as possible. I'm already running late. I'll deal with the Airglider later," Arriel said.

"Okay. Let me contact a couple people and get you to City Ommawee's surface. We're not far from the seminar," Jepner said.

• • •

A low rumble of many people talking filled the hall. The vast majority of seats were filled and the Project Thraxion seminar was about to begin. The speaker held off starting his presentation as several people were still arriving. The leaders of the governments—Destin Cantin of the Civil Government and Remyw Yortis of the Nytoorion Government—along with Queen Tereena Cantin of the smaller Obritess Government, were all invited to attend the seminar by 'Tallic Iver, CEO of the Axehaven Myriad Construction Corporation.

Destin, Arcacio, Merisa, and Roedie II arrived and made their way to the special government official section of the hall. They sat down and noticed the empty seats next to theirs.

"Where is everyone else?" Arcacio asked as she tried to pull her collar higher on her neck.

"And I thought we were going to be late..." Destin said.

They looked around the large hall and then up to the stage. At that moment, Queen Tereena and Roedie arrived and found their seats next to the others.

"Hi," Roedie said.

"Sorry we're late. Where is Remyw and the others?" Tereena asked.

"Good question. So, how are you two?" Destin asked.

"We're doing fine," Roedie said.

"You may want to adjust your collar, there, Arcacio," Tereena said. Arcacio quickly tugged on the collar.

Roedie got up and gave Roedie II a hug. "How's my great great great grandson?" he asked.

"I'm doing well, Grandpa. I'm learning all the ropes for my new upcoming leadership position," Roedie II said.

"That's great," Roedie said.

"He's doing a remarkable job," Destin said.

"We've been meaning to talk to you about some important things," Tereena told Destin. "Perhaps after the seminar, we can discuss them."

"Okay," Destin said.

Destin was curious as to what it was regarding. The BlueMar Galaxy's governments have had open communications and open borders with no conflicts for 20 years, since their inception in 231017 SA (Space Age). He hoped there wasn't a problem.

Remyw and Kathell entered the hall with a quick stride. They walked over to the government official section and made their way to the seats next to the rest of the group.

"Sorry we're late…we just got back from our anniversary dinner on Perytion," Remyw said.

"The Celestial Orchard? Great place… Happy anniversary," Destin said.

"Congratulations!" Arcacio said.

"Well, congrats! What is this, fifteen years?" Tereena asked.

"It is," Remyw said.

"Nice," Roedie said. "We're on our, like, one hundred and seventh anniversary. Traveling to the future really screwed that up. No…it's actually about our fifty-second. But who's counting anymore?" Roedie said.

They all laughed.

"Happy anniversary, you two. I hope I am able to find a decent man before I'm too old," Merisa said.

"I'm proud of you two," Roedie II said.

"Well, thank you all. It's been a great fifteen years," Kathell said.

A tall and thin man, dressed in a formal blue outfit, walked across the stage toward the podium at the center. A large screen was lowered down in front of the burgundy curtains. After setting some papers down, he adjusted the microphone.

"Good afternoon and welcome to City Ommawee. My name is 'Tallic Iver and I am CEO of the Axehaven Myriad Construction Corporation. We are the largest construction corporation in the galaxy. Our remarkably large headquarters is a space station located in the Kameron Star System. Thank you all for attending the Project Thraxion seminar. I want to give special tribute to the Civil Government, the Nytoorion Government, and the Obritess Government leaders and their dignitaries. Without them, none of this would be possible," he said.

There was a round of applause from the crowd. A side door opened to reveal Arriel Cantin quickly making her way to the government officials section, near the front, right side of the stage. The speaker paused while she made her way to her seat.

"Sorry I'm late," she whispered loudly.

"What is Project Thraxion?" the speaker continued. "Project Thraxion is a construction project for the largest spaceship ever to be built in history. It will be one hundred kilometers in length, fifty kilometers in width, and ten kilometers high at its tallest point. It definitely has to be built in space. Even ships that are eighty-five percent smaller would be too large to be built on a planet or other massive gravitational force. The ship will be constructed in space a short distance from our corporate headquarters. It will be easy access for all the different types of equipment that will be needed to accomplish the task. The name of this immense ship is *Thraxion*."

'Tallic Iver stood at the podium and paused for a moment as he took a drink of water. Everyone's attention was focused on him. Arriel took the opportunity to hand the anniversary card and small gift to her mother.

"Thanks," Kathell whispered.

"I'll explain what happened after the seminar," Arriel said.

'Tallic continued, "I know a lot of you are concerned about the uses of the ship *Thraxion*. The people of this galaxy—people from all three governments—and the businesses in those jurisdictions have funded this project. No, it's not cheap to build. In fact, it is very, very expensive. The Axehaven Myriad Construction Corporation takes pride in building great products, not products with cheap shortcuts. Take City Ommawee here for instance… We built this entire city here on Nytoorion. It is a companion city to Mosstone, the capital city of the Nytoorion Government. City Ommawee was built quite a few years ago. I'm sure you've all visited this city from time to time. If you haven't taken advantage of all the amenities this city has to offer, you are certainly missing out on the adventure. This is just one example of the Axehaven Myriad Construction Corporation's work. So, you can be sure that *Thraxion* will be well built.

"To let you all know that the credits funding Project Thraxion are well spent, I will list both the private and public purposes the ship will be used for. There will be the galaxy's largest shopping mall that includes many stores, condominiums, apartments, restaurants, many businesses and business offices, public dispute offices for those with the same home jurisdiction, galactic dispute offices for those from different home jurisdictions, telecommunication services, adventure parks, a very large garden, a fresh water supply, there will be a lake in the ship, beaches, simulated rain in the garden and the lake areas, the galaxy's largest zoo, with many different types of animals from planets all over the galaxy, a large museum with interesting things from history around the galaxy, clubs, intoxication joints, and many other things. There will be Airglider transportation throughout the ship. There will be docking bays located at key points along the ship for public, private, and business use. Excellent high-tech security has been incorporated into the design and highly trained officers will handle all misconduct and disputes. For those who commit crimes, they will be sent off-ship to their own government for prosecution. There will be a large section in *Thraxion's* lower levels for maintenance throughout the ship. The pilots and navigators and other employees of the ship will have a very large section in the seven-hundredth level of the ship for their use. This will also include the captain's quarters and ship control room, engine rooms, and the like. There will also be hospitals, doctors, and fire departments throughout the ship. One entire level of the ship will be left unconstructed on the inside for future use. The front portion of the top level will be an observation deck to see the stars and planets of the galaxy. The ship's engines were designed to make as little noise as possible. It will be able to travel at lightspeed. It will never be able to land on any planet, of course. It will contain the largest artificial gravitational force ever developed.

"The ship's flight schedule will be determined by the two main governments of the galaxy. There will be many employment opportunities created for people. There will be over one million people constructing it on three different shifts. It will take three years to complete. As I mentioned, it will be constructed near the Axehaven Myriad Construction Corporation's headquarters. So, that's where the large amount of credits is going. On the display behind me, you will see the ship design and labeled sections for the many establishments," 'Tallic Iver said as he enable the display behind him. "Does anyone have any questions?"

"Where do the people register for the apartments, condominiums, and employment opportunities?" a man in the crowd asked.

"People can register at the capital of their own government."

A pause followed.

"What about air quality and circulation?" a woman asked.

"We will have many filtering systems throughout the ship. There will also be fresh air exchanged on occasion from a supply ship," 'Tallic said.

"Where will it travel to?" another man from the audience asked.

"The schedules will be coordinated from the governments, but the plan is to rotate through all of the star systems of the BlueMar Galaxy," 'Tallic said.

"When is the project scheduled to begin?" another person asked.

"The operation is beginning as we speak," 'Tallic said.

There was a long pause.

"Well, if there are no further questions… At this time, I would like to introduce my colleague, Unell Sarptious. He will explain the details of each section of the *Thraxion* ship shown up on the screen. There are printed layouts of the ship located along each of your seats as well. You are free to keep those copies," 'Tallic Iver said.

With that, he made room for the second speaker who walked across the stage and shook his hand.

"Hello. My name is Unell Sarptious. I've had the privilege to work with 'Tallic Iver for many years. I can assure you, he knows his stuff when it comes to coordinating design, logistics, and purpose. I will be going over the details of each section."

Unell Sarptious continued as he methodically described the details of each section of the ship.

"Well, I think this project will be well developed," Roedie II said in a low voice, looking at the others in his group.

"Yeah, it sounds like it," Arriel said, "...Just like that broken pipe under City Ommawee. That's well developed too."

"Is that sarcasm? What are you talking about?" Roedie II asked.

"I just had the worst experience ever. My Airglider broke down in the tunnels under the city. I had to walk in the dark, creepy tunnels to find help. And the Airglider is still there," Arriel said, her frustration very visible.

"Calm down. We'll get the Airglider picked up. And as far as a leaky pipe…the Axehaven Myriad Construction Corporation may have built this city long ago, but they are not responsible for maintaining it. We are! And now that you've pointed that out, I want you to have a team repair it," Remyw said.

"They may want to clean the green slime while they're at it," Arriel said. "Happy anniversary, by the way."

"Thanks for the gift," Kathell said as she opened the small package.

Opening the gift, Kathell smiled. It was a bottle of Grenagaihn export white wine from 230929 SA. It was a BlueMar War victory celebration special edition. Remyw read the card.

"Wow! That's nice. It reminds me of the time when my grandpa, Serenitol, opened a similar bottle to celebrate his true identity from within the Claderane Resistance," Roedie said.

"I remember that," Tereena said. "I believe that is when I first met your grandfather."

"We should probably pay attention to the seminar," Merisa interjected.

They all looked at Merisa and realized they had stopped listening to the speaker. From that point, they listened attentively. Unell Sarptious was near the front of the ship diagram at that point. Soon, he finished the presentation.

"That concludes the Project Thraxion seminar. We appreciate all of you coming to City Ommawee. Please enjoy the refreshments along the back of the hall. If there are any further questions that you may have, please contact either the Axehaven Myriad Construction Corporation public relations or you can contact your own government as well. Have a great day," he said.

The audience remained in the hall while they looked at the printed diagrams and helped themselves to the refreshments against the back wall.

Roedie II walked over to Arriel and gave her a hug. "I'm sorry you had a frustrating day."

"Thanks, Roedie," Arriel said.

Suddenly, there was an interruption from one of the Nytoorion Government dignitaries, Shandia Merell, who ran over to them through the crowd.

"Remyw, we have a major situation. An emergency communique has been received. I'll discuss it on the way. We must hurry," the woman said.

Their group followed the dignitary from the seminar hall at a quick pace.

CHAPTER FIVE
ONSLAUGHT FROM NYCTOGLUKTOOUSS

SITELL ENTERED THE BlueMar Galaxy from the Kalistorr Wormhole and stopped the ship. For the most part, it was a quick, smooth flight. He checked the ship for any issues and found none. After entering the BlueMar Galaxy near the Kameron Star System, he scanned public communications and learned about the governmental demographics and other information relating to jurisdiction. He chose to fly to the capital of the Civil Government on Kas. He could visit the other ones on Nytoorion and Neo Terra later. Setting a course for Kas, he put the ship back to lightspeed. He sent an emergency communique to the Civil Government, but had yet to receive a response.

After quickly leaving the Project Thraxion seminar, the Nytoorion Government dignitary found a secure, private location to discuss the matter.

"The Civil Government just relayed a message to our Nytoorion Government they themselves had just received. It was an emergency communique from someone named Sitell, who claims to be from the Regulominuss Galaxy and needs to have an urgent meeting with all the government leaders," Shandia said.

There was a long pause as the group exchanged glances.

"Perhaps Tereena and I can be of assistance with this. We have actually been to the Regulominuss Galaxy and are familiar with things there as they were back in 230932 SA," Roedie said.

"That was, like, one hundred and five years ago. A lot could have changed," Roedie II said.

"Well, it sounds urgent. I guess we'll find out," Remyw said.

"He is en route to Kas as we speak," Shandia said.

"Okay, shall we all go to New Kanthas?" Destin asked.

"Let's go," Remyw said. He turned to the dignitary. "Thank you for informing us, Shandia."

"Can you have a team pick up one of our Airgliders in the tunnels under City Ommawee?" Arriel asked.

"I'll get right on it," Shandia said.

They left Nytoorion and traveled to Kas at lightspeed.

The *Tributary* settled onto the sandy docking area outside of the Civil Government building in New Kanthas. Sitell stepped out onto the ground and stared at the surrounding landscape. The sand seemed endless. He hadn't seen anything like it before. The beige sand against the blue sky was beautiful. He made his way to the entrance of the building. Destin and the others had arrived shortly before he did.

The receptionist contacted Destin's office over the com.

"Sitell is here to see you, Destin," she said.

"Please bring him to the conference room," Destin said.

"Yes, sir," she said.

There was a knock at the conference room door. The group looked with anticipation toward the door.

"Come in," Destin said.

Sitell walked in as the electronic door swiftly slid aside. They saw that he was a middle-aged man.

"We received your message," Destin said.

"Yes. My name is Sitell. I just arrived from the Regulominuss Galaxy. I am a descendant of the famous Sintos who was from the Kameron System. I developed the Galactic Time Portal that makes it possible to fly from the Regulominuss Galaxy to the BlueMar Galaxy instantaneously at lightspeed. There is no more need for tac-time engines. There is no more need to go timespeed," Sitell said.

"Holy cosmic shit!" Roedie II managed.

"We want to learn as much as possible about the current state of the BlueMar Galaxy. But since I'm the one showing up on your doorstep, let me briefly tell you about the current state of the Regulominuss Galaxy. The entire galaxy has been explored. There are three governments, all with open borders. We're all friends, basically. We have the Yiseth Government, which I am the leader of, we have the Ovlon Government, which Queeab is the leader of, and we have the Rreen Government, which Jade Thane is the leader of," Sitell said.

"Hi Sitell. I am Destin Cantin, leader of the Civil Government. This is my wife, Arcacio, and our son Roedie II. And this is my mother, Merisa. Roedie II will soon be succeeding me as the new leader of the Civil Government," Destin said.

"Nice to meet you," Sitell said.

Merisa smiled at Sitell, admiring the bald man. Sitell smiled back at Merisa.

"My name is Remyw Yortis. I'm the leader of the Nytoorion Government. This is my wife, Kathell, and our daughter Arriel. Likewise, Arriel will soon be replacing me as the leader of the Nytoorion Government," Remyw said.

"Roedie II, you must be named after the commander, Roedie Cantin, that is in our history books, the one that journeyed to the Regulominuss Galaxy with my ancestor, Sintos, and the Claderane Government Explorers. He helped defeat the Rexxian Empire," Sitell said.

"I am named after him. He is my great great great grandfather. And best of all, he's right here," Roedie II said, gesturing toward Roedie.

Roedie stood up and shook Sitell's hand.

"Seriously? What an unexpected surprise," Sitell said.

"Roedie Cantin...and this is my wife, Queen Tereena. She is queen of the Obritess Government. Like your galaxy, all of our governments are friends as well. It is so very nice to meet a descendant of Sintos. Wow, I have so many stories I could share. But we'll get to those later. So, you've built a Galactic Time Portal that is similar to a wormhole and makes the use of tac-time engines obsolete?" Roedie said.

"Yes. I'm a bit of a physicist and I have personally developed the complex theories behind both the Galactic Time Portal, which is from my Second Sitell Theory, and the Sitell Field, which is from my First Sitell Theory. I was also able to harness the power of the Kalistorr Wormhole. It would have worked without the wormhole, but it really enhanced the experience," Sitell said.

"We no longer have tac-time engines because of the dangers and security risks involved with them," Roedie said. "In fact, Tereena and I were the last ones to have one and we traveled to the future to live. That's why I'm still around," Roedie said.

"That makes sense now," Sitell said.

"Roedie and Tereena helped destroy the BlueMar Empire, the Rexxian Empire, the Immortal Cantin Empire, and a bunch of terrorist organizations. Roedie also helped destroy the Xalgoma Stride that was going to wipe out the entire BlueMar Galaxy," Remyw said.

"Well now's your chance to save the galaxy again. You see, there is a really pressing matter that I must discuss with all of you. All the leaders of the Regulominuss Galaxy were contacted by the Keeper, Mara-Harcheit, regarding an imminent threat that is approaching both of our galaxies. Approximately one billion battleships and fighter ships are coming to invade, conquer, and exterminate the humans in both of our galaxies. They are aliens called Yithas. They come from the Nyctogluktoouss Galaxy, which is full of them. And with few exceptions, they are all evil. I was urged by Mara-Harcheit to complete the Galactic Time Portal, make contact with the BlueMar Galaxy and implement the Sitell Field. We must unite our galaxies. We must unite Yiblos. Yiblos is the name given to both the BlueMar Galaxy and the Regulominuss Galaxy together as one," Sitell said.

"I know of Mara-Harcheit. He was the most mysterious person I've ever met in my life. He just seemed to know things and do things that could not be explained. We went to him seeking approval to destroy the Rexxian Empire because the Syclones said that would be the right thing to do," Roedie said.

"You've met Mara-Harcheit?" Sitell asked.

"Yes. It was an interesting visit. There was a strange skeleton in the castle—"

"It's still there! And there is something else…Mara-Harcheit and his aide, Kortha, are also those same creatures, like the skeleton. Those are the aliens that are coming from the Nyctogluktoouss Galaxy. Mara-Harcheit, along with Kortha, was exiled millennia ago for being different. They sent assassins after them to kill them afterward, but failed. Now they want us all dead. Mara-Harcheit knew of my discoveries, inventions, and theories. You might say, I am on a mission to save both of our galaxies and I can't do it without your help," Sitell said.

"Wow! So, Mara-Harcheit is an alien? That explains a lot," Roedie said.

"He is not like the others of his species. Even Kortha cannot do what he does with his telepathy, clairvoyance, and such. That is one of the reasons why he was exiled. Kortha stood by his side as a friend and aide," Sitell said.

"We have wanted to unite with the Regulominuss Galaxy for years, but we didn't know how it would be possible or practical," Remyw said.

"So, what must we do to help stop this invasion?" Destin asked.

"Before we do too much, we have to build a Galactic Time Portal on this side of the Kalistorr Wormhole and program it correctly to get back to the Regulominuss Galaxy. I'm going to need help with that," Sitell said.

"We can set you up with the Axehaven Myriad Construction Corporation. They are just starting a new massive project. But under the circumstances, this is an intergalactic emergency. We can have them build it and put it into position for you. All you have to do is program it to do what it is supposed to do," Destin said.

"That would be great," Sitell said.

"And once we are united, how do we deal with the Yithas?" Roedie II asked.

"I designed the Sitell Field, based on my First Sitell Theory," Sitell said. "It is a field that will block the invading aliens and protect us from the onslaught and certain doom. It is able to stretch across lightyears of space. I will need help to set the origination points up as well. The difficult part is going to be incorporating it into the Galactic Time Portal. I'm still working on that."

"Well, let me contact 'Tallic Iver of the Axehaven Myriad Construction Corporation and get this ball rolling. I will have him meet with you to get all the details," Remyw said.

'Tallic Iver met with the group over lunch to discuss the urgent project. Project Thraxion was suspended until the immediate situation was resolved. The Axehaven Myriad Construction Corporation built the Galactic Time Portal according to Sitell's descriptive plans. It was completed in just a month. During the construction phase, Sitell and Merisa had dated a few times.

When they moved the Galactic Time Portal into position near the rediscovered Kalistorr Wormhole, they spotted some mysterious equipment with old BlueMar Empire markings drifting in space nearby. Upon learning of this discovery, Roedie realized it was this wormhole that his father Olossky had learned about years before and was subsequently taken prisoner.

Sitell performed all of the complex programming. After testing the Galactic Time Portal from the BlueMar Galaxy side, Sitell flew the *Tributary* to his Yiseth Government and gave them an update of the Galactic Time Portal and BlueMar Galaxy contact situation. He gave instructions to pass the message along to the Ovlon Government and the Rreen Government. He then returned to the BlueMar Galaxy to implement the Sitell Field.

Sitell landed the *Tributary* on Kas and stepped out onto the sandy ground. To his surprise, Merisa was there to greet him.

"Hello, Sitell. I'm so glad to see you," Merisa said.

"You look absolutely stunning, Merisa. I'm glad to see you as well," Sitell said.

He walked with her in silence toward the building entrance. They both felt a bit awkward.

"Would you like to go to dinner again sometime?" Sitell asked.

She looked up at him, her brown hair shifting in the wind. She had the biggest smile.

"I would absolutely love to. I know you have urgent matters to attend to. I will be around here, so when you are finished with saving the galaxies, come and find me," Merisa said.

"That, I will do," he said opening the entrance door.

"I will see you later, then," she said.

Sitell made his way to Destin's office. He found Roedie II sitting in the chair.

"Oh, hi, Roedie. Is your father around?" Sitell asked.

"He won't be returning until this evening," Roedie II said.

"Okay. I'm ready to proceed with the Sitell Field. I believe I've worked out a way to incorporate the field into the Galactic Time Portal," Sitell said.

"That's wonderful. The protection will be nice, as is the new portal. The people from the two galaxies can now transit through the Galactic Time Portal. All of our governments from both galaxies should have a meeting to introduce each other. Yiblos will have a new dawn of peace and prosperity," Roedie II said.

"Yes, I'm looking forward to it. Well, since your father isn't returning until later, I have time for a lunch date with your grandmother," Sitell said as he left the office.

Roedie II just looked at him with a blank expression as he left the office.

• • •

Merisa showed Sitell a fabulous restaurant in New Astossky called The Outcrop. As the waitress brought their orders, the aroma of the food tantalized their senses.

"This is very nice," Merisa said.

"Yes, it is. You look stunning. I don't know what it is about you, but I am so attracted to you, Merisa. You just…"

"…arouse you?" she asked.

"Yes! Like no one else…ever. Sure I've been in relationships, but with you, everything seems to just come naturally. Is it love at first sight? I don't know. You are very attractive," Sitell said.

"Those are my exact thoughts! Sitell, honestly, you make me wet just looking at you," Merisa said.

She leaned over the table and kissed him. His tongue felt warm against hers.

"I can't wait until we get back to your ship," she said.

Sitell found himself breathing heavily and adjusted his chair.

"That would be really nice," he said.

"Yes, it would," Merisa said as she started eating her meal.

It had been so long since Merisa had sex, she was beyond aroused. After entering the *Tributary*, Sitell flew to a remote area of Kas where the view was spectacular from the observation window. After removing their footwear, Merisa slowly undressed, removing her shirt first and then her pants. She wore sexy red panties that matched her bra. Sitell removed his shirt and pants as well. She removed her bra, revealing her breasts. They bounced slightly as she removed her socks. They could both feel their sexual tension and excitement. He reached down and slowly removed her red panties. In turn, she reached down and removed Sitell's briefs. Sitell took her hand and led her to a couch in a small lounge near the back of the ship. She lay on the soft cushions. He knelt down as they began a lengthy, exciting oral foreplay. Soon, Sitell grabbed a package from a cabinet and turned around to face her. She took the condom from his hand and opened it. She slid it onto him and lay on the couch. The sensation was incredible as they moved through the natural motions. Soon, he turned her over on hands and knees.

This position still reminds me of when I was raped in the desert years ago. Damn, I thought I was over that feeling, Merisa thought.

"I can't reach an orgasm in this position. Do you mind if we switch back?" she asked.

"No problem. Communication is always number one," he said as Merisa turned around and lay on her back again.

She didn't feel it was the appropriate time to explain what happened all those years ago.

"Oh, I've needed this for so long," Merisa said.

She soon reached an epic orgasm, her toes pointed outward and tingling. He followed as he groaned loudly.

"You're amazing," Sitell said as he sighed deeply.

Destin had returned from his earlier affairs and Arcacio was in his office with him. They both looked up as Sitell and Merisa entered the room.

"Well, hi, Mom. Hey, Sitell. I understand you stopped by earlier today. I'm sorry I missed you. Roedie said you are ready to proceed with the Sitell Field," Destin said.

"Yes. If I could get help with the Sitell Field, we need to set up the projection or origination points at key locations around the BlueMar Galaxy. Then I will need to do the same thing in the Regulominuss Galaxy," Sitell said.

Arcacio lifted her head and turned it sideways as she looked at Merisa.

"After the meeting, can I...talk to you outside?" Arcacio asked her.

"Sure," Merisa said.

"Actually, Sitell and I just need to go over some details. If you ladies want to take off, it's fine by me," Destin said.

"Okay. We'll be back," Arcacio said.

The two ladies left the office and walked to a secluded area of the outer corridor.

"What's wrong?" Merisa asked.

"I noticed a faint scent of pussy when you two walked into the office. Did you two...?"

After a brief silence, Merisa said, "Yes. And it was the best sex I've had in years."

"Mom...really?"

"Don't start with me, Ms. Hickey!" Merisa said.

"Destin might feel weird about it. He has to work with Sitell," Arcacio said.

"I'm a grown woman. You need to get out of my business," Merisa said.

"Fine...but you still smell like sex," Arcacio said as one of the office personnel walked by.

He looked back at the two women and kept walking.

"That's too damn bad," Merisa said.

"Okay. Forget that I mentioned it," Arcacio said. "I'm sorry."

"I will," Merisa said.

They returned to an empty office. The receptionist stopped them by the door.

"Destin wanted me to give you a message that he went to the Axehaven Myriad Construction Corporation with Sitell," she said.

"Well, how about a drink?" Arcacio asked.

"That would be nice. It's not very often my daughter-in-law invites me to drink," Merisa said.

They left the government building and walked down the street toward an intoxication joint in New Kanthas called The Oasis.

The team at the Axehaven Myriad Construction Corporation had been extremely helpful to Sitell. While Destin flew back to Kas for governmental affairs, Sitell and the team flew to the specific projection points across the BlueMar Galaxy to drop the Sitell Field emanator modules into position. It took the team several months to complete the task. Sitell worked diligently to incorporate the Sitell Field into the Galactic Time Portal by adding collector modules around the parameter of the circular metal framework. Following the completion of the Sitell Field work within the BlueMar Galaxy, the Axehaven Myriad Construction Corporation focused all of their efforts back on Project Thraxion. When the time came to implement the Sitell Field in the BlueMar Galaxy, Sitell traveled to Kas with the remote management system. They installed the equipment in a secure location within the Civil Government building on Kas. Both the Nytoorion Government and the Obritess Government had access to the remote management system.

The leaders and their dignitaries gathered around the remote system with anticipation. A 3D projection with an exploded view of the BlueMar Galaxy was displayed in the room.

"This is the epic moment," Sitell said.

He flicked a series of switches, enabling the power to each emanator module. Once all were powered, the 3D display showed a blueish field start to slowly expand across the BlueMar Galaxy. It rippled with energy as the blue field continued connecting to all of the projection points. As it completed its encompassing spread, the energy converged at the Galactic Time Portal.

"It's a success!" Sitell shouted with excitement.

The rest of the group cheered.

"This is wonderful protection against the threat that we face," Destin said.

"Yes. But we're not entirely safe yet. I still have to implement the Sitell Field in the Regulominuss Galaxy. That will take several more months. But we are half way there. Before I return to the Regulominuss Galaxy, I plan to visit my distant relatives in the Kameron Star System. There are many stories of Sintos that I would love to share with them," Sitell said.

"Well, you have safe travels. Do you have a team that will help you set up the Sitell Field there?" Remyw asked.

"Yes, I do. Once it is operational, I will return to discuss everything with you all," he said.

Sitell walked over to Merisa and kissed her passionately. The others looked on in surprise.

"May I take you to another galaxy?" he asked her.

Merisa smiled and took his hand.

"Yes, you may," she said. "Destin, watch over my house in Antiqueech."

"Yes, Mother," Destin said as they walked out the door.

Sitell traveled to the Kameron Star System with Merisa. It was somewhat awkward, but he found his distant relatives and they were able to share stories together. Their stay was short, as he had important work to complete.

Sitell flew the *Tributary* through the Galactic Time Portal and entered into the Regulominuss Galaxy, a journey that once took nine months at timespeed. Merisa was in awe at the many different stars and planets. Their first destination was Yiseth.

Upon landing, Sitell called for a meeting with the other two government leaders. As the other leaders arrived, Sitell introduced Merisa to Queeab and Jade Thane, as well as to his own close government dignitaries.

Over the next few months, Merisa made herself familiar with things on Yiseth as Sitell was busy implementing the Sitell Field around the Regulominuss Galaxy. As with the Sitell Field that had been set up in the BlueMar Galaxy, he installed the remote management system in a secure location on Yiseth, giving access to the Ovlon Government and the Rreen Government.

Sitell, Merisa, Queeab, Jade, and some of their dignitaries stood around the 3D display, watching as the Sitell Field enclosed around the Regulominuss Galaxy. Like it had done in the BlueMar Galaxy, it converged around the collector modules on the Galactic Time Portal, completing its enclosure. They all cheered.

"Now, Yiblos is entirely secure from the coming threat of the Yithas," Sitell said.

"You are a genius, Sitell," Merisa said.

"Well, thank you. I'm happy to serve," he said.

"I have arranged for a celebration this evening," Jade said.

Jade Thane's long, black hair was elegantly braided along the back and its tail rested against the left front breast of her leather outfit.

"So, you had confidence that it would work and you planned a party?" Sitell asked.

"I did," she said, smiling.

"Well, I am certainly ready for a celebration," Queeab said.

"Well, after the festivities, we need to get together and plan a trip to meet with the governments of the BlueMar Galaxy. There is much to discuss," Sitell said.

"I look forward to it," Jade said.

"Yes, it will be nice to form strong bonds with our new neighbors," Queeab said.

"I'm confident that strong bonds will happen. My son is the leader of the Civil Government over there," Merisa said.

"There is so much to learn about each other," Queeab said.

"After we meet with the governments of the BlueMar Galaxy, we will return to Yibon and give the Keeper an update on the status of things," Sitell said.

"Like he needs one," Jade said sarcastically.

"Well, I like to keep things formal," Sitell said.

The day after the large celebration on Rreen, the four of them traveled together in the *Tributary* through the Galactic Time Portal to the BlueMar Galaxy. Sitell sent a communique ahead to let Destin know he would arrive soon along with the other leaders of the Regulominuss Galaxy. Destin contacted the other government officials to arrange a meeting on Kas.

• • •

Soon, several ships landed at the Civil Government docking area in New Kanthas. As they arrived, they each made their way into the building. It was announced that the meeting would take place in the conference room. One by one, the officials entered the room and made themselves comfortable in the soft, cushioned chairs.

"Thank you all for coming. This is a special government meeting. We have representatives from every government in Yiblos. I would like to have each of you introduce yourself before we discuss our current situation," Destin said. "I will start first. My name is Destin Cantin. I am the current leader of the Civil Government. My son is scheduled to take my place when I leave office."

"My name is Remyw Yortis. I've been the leader of the Nytoorion Government for twenty years and my daughter will soon take my place."

"Hello. I am Queen Tereena Cantin of the Obritess Government. We are a small government with two star systems in our jurisdiction."

"I am Roedie II Cantin and I will be taking over the Civil Government this year."

"I am Roedie Cantin, the consort of Queen Tereena."

"My name is Arriel Cantin. I am the daughter of Kathell and Remyw. I will be succeeding Remyw in the leadership of the Nytoorion Government."

"I am Arcacio Cantin, wife of Destin."

"My name is Kathell Cantin-Yortis. I am the wife of Remyw."

"As you all already know, I'm Merisa Cantin-Istraxx. I'm the mother of Destin."

"Likewise, you've all met me, but I am Sitell, leader of the Yiseth Government."

"Thank you all for the introductions. My name is Jade Thane. I am the leader of the Rreen Government."

"I am Queeab, leader of the Ovlon Government."

"So, I noticed that almost all of you have the Cantin name. Are you all related?" Jade asked.

"You could say that. It's a long story. Roedie and Tereena came here from the past. They are my great great grandparents," Destin said. "My mom, Merisa, was widowed to their great grandson Thatril. Kathell was widowed to my fourth cousin, Blackie II. Arriel and Roedie II are fifth cousins."

"Wow! So, you are the Roedie in our history books, the one that came to the Regulominuss Galaxy with Sintos?" Jade asked.

"That would be me. But Tereena was there also," Roedie said.

"Can I, like, hug you guys?" Jade asked.

"Of course," Tereena said.

Jade stood up, her leather outfit squeaking slightly. She walked over and gave them both a hug.

"This is so incredible. Thank you for your service and involvement in the Rexxian War," Jade said.

"Thank you for setting my ancestors free. The Syclones would probably still be slaves if it wasn't for you," Queeab said in a sudden emotional moment.

He too walked over and hugged them both before returning to his seat.

"I've noticed, Queeab, that you are no longer using a letter and number combination as a suffix to the Syclone names," Roedie said.

"Yes! That ended with the Rexxian Empire," Queeab said.

"So, did Quee-A3/B6 ever become president of the Ovlon Government?" Roedie asked.

"He did. And I am named after him!" Queeab said.

"Well, we can all thank Sitell for saving both of our galaxies," Remyw said.

"You know...I may be advanced in my comprehension and so forth, but we would not have known about this impending invasion if it wasn't for Mara-Harcheit. It is to him that we should give thanks for saving us all. In fact, I propose that all of the leaders of the governments travel to Yibon and personally thank him," Sitell said.

"I agree. I was on Yibon to see Mara-Harcheit when I was about twenty-one years old. I would love to see him again, now that I'm seventy-one," Roedie said.

"Well, I will make it happen," Sitell said. "Now that we have all introduced ourselves, I want you all to know the Sitell Field is enabled and surrounds both galaxies. It is the Regulominuss Galaxy in which we will initially see the invasion since that is where the Yitheria Wormhole opens from the Nyctogluktoouss Galaxy. But you can be assured that the Sitell Field that surrounds Yiblos will keep them out."

"I would like to propose that we set up a communications and transportation system through the Galactic Time Portal that can bring our two galaxies together in new ways," Queeab said.

"I agree. We all have open borders. It will be nice to travel freely between galaxies as well," Destin said.

"We should draft a bi-galactic treaty that will define our mission and discuss the communications, transportation, logistics, powers, enforcement, justice, citizens, and such," Remyw said.

"Yes, that would be a good thing," Queeab said.

"I also propose that we adopt the BlueMar Galaxy's Space Age system of time for the Regulominuss Galaxy, when we draft this treaty," Sitell said.

"Well, Destin, I've tried on several occasions over the last several months to explain some important information to you. But it seems we always are interrupted," Tereena said. "So, now would be a good time."

"Yes, you first mentioned it at the Project Thraxion seminar. I'm sorry things have been so hectic," Destin said. "What is it that you would like to discuss?"

"Roedie and I are getting old and I need to set a plan in motion for the Obritess Government for when I pass on. You see, I am the heir to the throne and normally it would be succeeded by our daughter, Phasheena. Unfortunately, we traveled into the future when she was twenty and, as you know, she is no longer with us, nor is her son, Jerell, or his son Thatril. Since Roedie II is going to be the new leader of the Civil Government and you will be available, the throne rightly belongs to you when I die. King Destin Cantin… That doesn't mean you have to feel obligated to take the position. But at least think about it. If it is something that you do not want to do, then I have a plan B," Tereena said.

"Oh, Grandma. I love you. I would—"

"Just hear me out, Destin. If you choose not to accept the throne, I will have the Obritess Government annex with the Civil Government so that my heir, Roedie II can still rule it, even if it is in a different way," Tereena said. "Just think about it, Destin. I don't want an answer right now. Also, it is our wishes to be buried on the paradise planet, Siitap, when we die. That is where we first met. Do you have all that?"

"Yes, ma'am," Destin said, a tear rolling down his right cheek.

The galactic leaders worked diligently for a few days drafting a treaty. They soon had a final draft they could all agree upon. It was the Yiblos Treaty.

Soon after the Yiblos Treaty was ratified, the group traveled to Yibon to pay Mara-Harcheit a visit. He was happy to see them all. They gave him great thanks for the ominous intervention that he provided by warning them about the imminent attack. Without him, there would be no bi-galactic peace in Yiblos.

. . .

Three years later, the Axehaven Myriad Construction Corporation finished covering the last few metal beams of the *Thraxion* with hull plating. The ship was finally ready for its maiden voyage. The travel schedules had been set with the governments of both galaxies.

Roedie II had become the leader of the Civil Government. He really enjoyed the position. Arriel also found the leadership of the Nytoorion Government to be exciting. Destin had decided to accept Tereena's offer to become king of the Obritess Government at some point in the future, which he hoped would not be anytime soon.

Sitell had traveled to the BlueMar Galaxy on business. He stopped in to see Roedie II.

"Well, hello," Roedie II said. "What brings you all this way?"

"I have set up a vacation package for the entire Cantin family on the *Thraxion's* maiden voyage to the Regulominuss Galaxy. And it is a gift from me. You see, I'm getting married to your grandma onboard the *Thraxion*. And I want you all to be there," Sitell said.

"I wouldn't miss it for anything," Roedie II said. "When do we leave?"

"Tomorrow."

"Shit!"

Roedie, Tereena, Destin, Arcacio, Roedie II, Remyw, Kathell, Arriel, Merisa, and Sitell were all aboard the *Tributary*, approaching one of *Thraxion's* many docking bays.

"I also invited Queeab and Jade Thane. They should be here someplace," Sitell said.

One of Sitell's officials contacted him over the *Tributary's* com. He was informed that there was a Yiblos emergency.

"It has been reported that an extremely large number of spaceships from the Nyctogluktoouss Galaxy have been spotted on long-range scanners. The hostile alien creatures are certainly on the war path to conquer Yiblos. I am thankful that we have implemented the Sitell Field around Yiblos," Sitell said.

The others agreed.

Soon, the *Tributary* settled onto the docking bay and they each made their way out and onto the metal floor. They were greeted by a host who showed them to the suites they would be staying in while on their *Thraxion* cruise.

The luxurious suites were perfect. They had every amenity they needed. They each took the time to explore all that *Thraxion* had to offer. By the end of the day, they were exhausted. The ship had already left its port near the Axehaven Myriad Construction Corporation's galactic headquarters.

"We need to get some sleep. The wedding is tomorrow," Destin said.

"That won't be difficult. I'm exhausted," Arcacio said as she lay on the bed of their suite.

"So, what did you think of that theme park and all those shops?" Destin asked.

There was no answer. Destin turned to find Arcacio fast asleep with her clothes on, lying diagonally across the bed.

"Someone's tired..."

Sitell and Merisa stood in a ceremonial hall aboard the *Thraxion*. One of the observation windows was above them, displaying the beautiful stars. Sitell wore a handsome gray tuxedo and Merisa wore an elegant white dress, its revealing lace patterns strategically located. They had a fairly large wedding party. Sitell's best man was Queeab. The groomsmen were Destin, Roedie, Roedie II, and Remyw. Merisa's matron of honor was Arcacio. The bride's maids were Arriel, Jade, Tereena, and Kathell.

As they repeated the words of the wedding officiant in front of them, they noticed the *Thraxion* begin to pass through the Galactic Time Portal. They both said "I do" as they passed through to the Regulominuss Galaxy. Sitell and Merisa kissed passionately before turning to the crowd that had gathered. There was an applause and cheering. Since generations of Sitell's family had never used last names, Merisa was simply stripped of a last name. After Sitell and Merisa's wedding ceremony, they had a beautiful reception on the same observation deck.

In the days to follow, they all enjoyed their unexpected vacation aboard the *Thraxion* cruise ship. Many stories were shared between them. They especially enjoyed the observation deck and the beauty that it offered from the celestial bodies of the Regulominuss Galaxy. That's where they found themselves when the onslaught took place.

Suddenly, out in space, everyone on the observation deck could see flashing lights and explosions, visible on the starboard side of the ship.

The aliens had arrived. Laser fire concentrated on the Sitell Field. It did no good as the ships slammed into the surface of the energy field. One after another, the battleships and fighter ships continued to slam into the invisible wall. Silent explosions brightened the darkness of space. The onslaught continued on, the ships continuing to explode.

Even when the wedding party departed the *Thraxion* a week after the ceremony, the aliens were still continuing to slam into the field, again and again. The Yithas' ships disintegrated when they hit the Sitell Field. After months of constant attacks the hostile aliens disappeared. The fear was over.

Lightyears III
Ominous Intervention
Appendix

LIGHTYEARS III
OMINOUS INTERVENTION
TERMINOLOGY INDEX

A

C4   Airglider
C3   Antiqueech
C4   Axehaven Myriad Construction Corporation

B

C1   BlueMar Galaxy
C4   BlueMar War

C

C3   Cantin, Arcacio
C3   Cantin, Arriel
C3   Cantin, Baas
C3   Cantin, Blackie II
C3   Cantin, Destin *See also* King Destin Cantin
C3   Cantin, Jerell
C3   Cantin, Kareen
C5   Cantin, Olossky
C3   Cantin, Roedie
C3   Cantin, Roedie II
C3   Cantin, Sepheena
C4   Cantin, Serenitol
C3   Cantin, Tereena *See also* Queen Tereena Cantin
C5   Cantin, Thatril
C3   Cantin-Istraxx, Merisa
C3   Cantin-Yortis, Kathell

P

Q

R

S

T

Lightyears Trilogy
Appendices

Lightyears Trilogy
Timespeed Information

Lightspeed = 9,460,730,472,580.8 km/year (1 lightyear)
Lightspeed x 1,000,000 = Timespeed
Timespeed = 9,460,730,472,580,800,000 km/year

Space Travel between BlueMar Galaxy and Regulominuss Galaxy at timespeed
Distance: 624,750 Lightyears (5,910,591,362,744,854,800 km)
Speed: Tac-time engine at 83.3% max safe speed =
7,880,788,483,659,806,400 km/y
Time: .75 year (9 months)

Time Travel (Future or Past)
1 month at timespeed = 212 years

Lightyears Trilogy
Timeline

0 BSA	Humans mysteriously appeared on Kylon
224050 SA	Humans fled to Kelson I, Kelson II, and Kelson III
225452 SA	Humans fled to Kelsar I, Kelsar II, and Kelsar III
229167 SA	Humans migrated to Kelsar I
229770 SA	Mazits "migrating people" dispersed across the galaxy
229776 SA	BlueMar Empire founded
223326 SA	Kelson War radiation reached Kelsar I
230332 SA	Tarr Kingdom founded
230532 SA	Xalgoma Stride launched / Xalgoma Stride destroyed
230655 SA	BlueMar Empire seized control of Tarr Kingdom
230736 SA	Claderane Resistance founded
230929 SA	BlueMar War / Claderane Government founded
230930 SA	Roedie Cantin and Tereena married and Baas Cantin and Sepheena married at double wedding
230931 SA	Roedie, Tereena, and Sepheena turned 20 / Baas turned 19 / Claderane Government Explorers launched / Reminall Cantin born
230932 SA	Rexxian War (Regulominuss Galaxy) / Phasheena Cantin born
230933 SA	Claderane Government Explorers returned / Final mission date
230934 SA	Olossky Cantin died
230935 SA	Serenitol Cantin died
230952 SA	Phasheena Cantin turned 20 / Roedie and Tereena began time travel for 10 years before settling 65 years into the future
231017 SA	Dark War / Civil Government founded / Nytoorion Government founded / Tereena crowned queen of the Monarchy of Obritess / Roedie II Cantin born / Arriel Cantin born

231022 SA Remyw Yortis and Kathell Cantin married
231037 SA Roedie II Cantin and Arriel Cantin turned 20 / Galactic Time Portal and Sitell Field implemented / *Thraxion* maiden voyage / Sitell and Merisa Cantin-Istraxx married
231145 SA Xalgoma Stride detonation date (avoided)

Novelist Bio

Troy D. Wymer started writing in 1984 when he was 15. He enjoys reading and writing science fiction novels. He also enjoys graphic and web design, drumming, trains, and listening to various subgenres of metal music. After a long hiatus in writing, he continues to capture the imagination of readers with new science fiction stories.